MW01716110

Book I of The Chosen

WATCHER

Book I of The Chosen

WATCHER

ROH MORGON

dark dreams publishing

WATCHER: BOOK I OF THE CHOSEN

Published by Dark Dreams Publishing
Cover design by Deranged Doctor Design
Interior design by Roh Morgon

PUBLISHER'S NOTE

This book is a work of fiction. Any references to historical events, real people, or real locales are used fictitiously. Other names, characters, places, or incidents are the product of the author's imagination, and any resemblance to actual events, locales, or persons, living or dead, are purely coincidental.

DARK DREAMS PUBLISHING
darkdreamspublishing.com

ISBN-13: 978-0-9981581-2-9 - ISBN-10: 0-9981581-2-9

Second paperback edition October 2017

Printed in the United States of America

Dedicated to

all of the outsiders

struggling to find their place

in the world

and to

my one love

PROLOGUE

I watch my daughter, the sunlight dancing across her long dark hair, cradle her swollen belly as she kneels to place the flowers on my empty grave. Pink carnations this time . . . last year was red roses; the year before, golden mums.

Her shoulders quake with her sobs and, swallowing, I fight to stifle my own. Her lips move as she whispers to the flower-strewn ground, but I'm too far away to hear her precious words. Throat tight, I struggle to remain still, hidden by the large eucalyptus at the other end of the cemetery.

She caresses my name etched into the grey granite, tracing the letters one by one before wiping the tears from her cheeks. Her fingers touch her lips, then the top of the cold, hard stone.

My own fingers clamp against my mouth and smother the impulse to cry out to her.

She looks so much like me—the me I used to be. Tall, willowy, she's become a woman since I disappeared five years ago and soon, to my surprise, will become a mother. The inferno of emotions ignited by her pregnancy threatens to devour me and I do not think I can remain quiet much longer. For once, I hope she will end her visit soon and leave.

She stands and turns toward her car. A breath of summer wind lifts a few dark strands of her hair and they float for a moment, waving goodbye.

Her scent reaches out to me and triggers memories of our brief life together. Seventeen years was not enough—not enough time to share with her, to hold her and teach her and tell her how much I love her. In a flash of anger, I curse the evil creature that stole me away, leaving my daughter to finish growing up alone, and leaving me . . . leaving me no longer human.

My chest heaving, I watch her drive away, then step between the markers and cross the lawn to my grave. Once again, I read the inscription on my headstone:

Sunshine Collins
Beloved Mother and Best Friend
October 10, 1969 –

Trembling, I rest my fingers where hers last touched, press them softly against my lips, and whisper, "I love you, Andrea."

PART I

CALIFORNIA

SUNDAY

CHAPTER 1

"Happy birthday to you, happy birthday to you . . ."

Wincing, I try to block out the song from the back room of the bar and reach down into the cooler for three bottles of Bud. I twist them open, set the beer on Sally's tray, and collect the money from her.

"Thanks, Sunny!" Sally grins, her blond curls bouncing as she turns and walks away. My thoughts drift while I wait for Lenny to finish with the cash register.

Birthdays.

I hate them. My daughter's twenty-second was yesterday, and I couldn't be there to share it with her, any more than she can share mine with me.

It's pretty hard to celebrate birthdays with a dead person.

A filthy comment and raucous laughter rise above the club din and my pity party evaporates. I look up in time to see which foul mouth is spewing obscenities and realize its target once again is Sally.

Oh, hell no. Apparently their earlier warning wasn't strong enough.

The buzz of voices and clink of ice in glasses fade as I move out from behind the bar and step to the table where Sally is standing, her mouth and eyes wide.

I glare down at the jerks sitting at the table.

"You need to leave." I wait, but they make no movement. "*Now.*"

The spike-haired punk, pale eyes shining with an unnatural glint, tips back his chair and makes a show of drinking his beer. His two buddies glance at him and guzzle the last of theirs.

An empty bottle slams down on the table.

Conversations die and a shroud of silence descends over the room. The chair legs thud against the wooden floor as the punk rocks forward. He wipes his mouth with a tattooed hand, then springs to his feet, knocking the chair over. Pierced lip curled into a sneer, he steps toward me and tenses as though he's going to swing.

I lean forward, nails ready and low at my side, and stare him directly in the eye. As the pink haze drops over my vision, a growl slips out, just loud enough that only he can hear.

His blue eyes widen as he looks into the faint red of mine and, blanching, he freezes and slowly lowers his fists. He drops his gaze, shifts back, and lets out his breath. As he glances around at the watching crowd, he scowls and curses, then shoots me an ugly look. But he avoids meeting my eyes. One look at the beast peering out of them must have been enough.

Lenny trips and swears as he comes out from behind his end of the counter. The punk straightens his jacket as he stares past me at the approaching bartender.

"Let's bounce. This dump is killin' my buzz." He leans sideways and spits on the floor.

Chairs scraping, his buddies stand, then follow him as he saunters out the door.

A collective sigh weaves through the room once the doors swing shut. I close my eyes and try to breathe calmness back into my body as the crazed beast within me rages in frustration.

"Sunny girl, I thought he was gonna hit ya," says Lenny, a few feet behind me.

"It's a good thing he didn't." Relief crawls in as I raise my eyes to cleared vision.

Because if he had tried, it would have been all over. Everything I've built here. The stable life, the friendships—all gone in an explosion of red violence.

Shaken, I head back to the bar. Sally stops me as I step behind the counter.

"Thanks, Sunny. I'd had enough of those creeps." The perky little waitress smiles up at me, her soft brown eyes bright with unshed tears. Her first week here hasn't been easy.

"You're welcome. You don't need to put up with that crap." I glance at her, flash a quick smile, and force the beast to quiet down and myself to relax. Apparently Sally, who was closest to the table, hadn't noticed the scarlet that briefly flamed in my eyes, so hopefully neither did anyone else.

Except, of course, the spike-haired punk. A chuckle escapes my lips.

"All right, folks. Show's over," Lenny announces from his end of the bar.

The nightclub resumes its normal clamor as people talk and laugh about the little standoff. Someone feeds the jukebox and Queen's "We Are the Champions" floats through the air.

"Good job handling those a-holes, Sunny." Walking past me, Lenny grabs a bottle from the back shelf.

"No problem." It could've been, though. A big one.

"But *I* shoulda handled it. You might've been hurt." He stops. I can feel his gaze on me.

"I can take care of myself. You don't need to worry about me." Emptying the red slush of a strawberry daiquiri into a wide-mouthed glass, I grit my teeth and shake my head.

The only thing he should worry about is me losing it and tearing up his bar.

The fresh, sea-laced air is a welcome relief from the stale smell of alcohol and humans. I take another deep breath as the bar door closes and step into the night. Glancing around at the Santa Cruz fog settling in, I head for the little black BMW at the far end of the parking lot.

Though the rest of the evening was quiet, I haven't been able to shake the tension that began vibrating through me the moment those jerks walked into the bar, nor completely calm the beast they triggered with their abuse of Sally. It's still restless, and is now joined by its partner, the cold hunter. Together they prowl inside me, anxious for the hunt.

The rasp of an ignition echoes through the fog.

My body flinches and I take a sharp breath, then laugh and shake my head.

Damn, I'm jittery tonight.

From the other end of the near-empty parking lot an engine rumbles, accompanied by the crunch of tires on asphalt. A casual look over my shoulder reveals a green Ford pickup cruising in my direction. With three guys in the cab.

The three guys I threw out of the bar.

Uh-oh.

The agitated beast growls. I shove it down and walk faster. The hunter snaps to attention.

The truck races past me and screeches to a halt behind my car, blocking it in.

Oh crap. This can't be happening.

Struggling to maintain control, I stop and look out to the deserted street. I could run, but they'd probably trash my car. I can't let that happen—my survival depends on that car.

So that leaves only one other option.

Damn it. Damn them. I don't want to do this.

As the driver's door opens, my anger blossoms and both the beast and hunter strain against their bonds. Control over them begins to fail and I focus on the demented beast, trying to tighten its leash. The calculating hunter slips free.

The spike-haired punk steps out of the open door. Walking to the rear of the truck, he leans against the side and takes a cigarette from his jacket pocket. The other two join him at the tailgate, passing a half-empty bottle of whiskey between them. The bald one with the three-pronged goatee is pretty good sized, but even through his faded army coat it's obvious his muscle has gone mostly to fat. The other guy peers out at me from beneath a six-inch green mohawk as he zips his black leather jacket. His slight build might lend itself to some degree of agility, but I dismiss him along with his buddy and look back at Spike.

He smiles. It doesn't reach his eyes, though, which do their best to avoid looking at mine. I go still and wait for one of the punks to make the first move.

Tension ripples through the damp air as the fog swirls around us.

A nervous cough from the tailgate tells me they were expecting me to do something else, like cry or plead or run. Spike takes a hit from his cigarette, his gaze darting to the street.

"Well, c'mon, dude. Thought you said we're gonna teach her a lesson, teach her some respect. What're ya waitin' for?" The guy with the goatee looks at Spike, then takes a step away from the truck toward me.

The beast screams in rage and slams itself around in my head. My hold on it weakens.

"Here, gimme that. She's just a stupid whore." Mohawk pushes off from the truck, grabs the bottle from Goatee and downs several swallows, then shoves the bottle back at him.

"Call them off," I growl. "Before someone gets hurt."

I stare at Spike through a red veil.

Spike shifts and looks away. He glances at his buddies, then back at me. A sadistic gleam brightens his eyes and he smiles and looks at the other two again.

"Go for it. Show that bitch she don't call the shots around here."

The two at the tailgate snicker and pass the bottle back and forth again.

"Oh yeah. Wonder what she'd look like without that pretty dark hair. Think she'd be as beautiful as me?" Goatee laughs, rubbing his shaved head.

"We're gonna go for a little ride, bitch. And then when we get somewhere quiet—" Mohawk snickers. "We're gonna make you scream." He wipes his mouth, cracks his knuckles, and steps in my direction.

"You *don't* want to do this," I rumble through gritted teeth, dropping my bag.

The beast and the hunter take over and I feel myself lower into a crouch. A guttural snarl rips from my throat in a final warning, but the fools are too drunk and arrogant to understand.

Mohawk sneers and advances, while Goatee sets down the bottle and starts after him, chuckling. As I focus on the green-haired one in the lead, Goatee stumbles.

The sudden movement triggers the beast. With a roar I launch and, landing inches from Mohawk, grab him by the front of the jacket. I pick him up, yank him to me, and stare into his terror-filled eyes through the red tinting of mine.

"Uhh-uhh-uhh!" His feet hammer my shins. His impotent attempts to loosen my grip only excite the killers inside me.

No!

I heave him at the back of the truck. He hits the tailgate and collapses into a heap.

Goatee's still coming at me, a knife in his hand. I move in and slash him across the chest with my nails. The fabric of his jacket splits and blood soaks the front of him. He looks down and shrieks.

The beast flies into a frenzy at the sight of the flowering red. I wrench my eyes away from the blood to see Spike picking up the whiskey bottle.

He cracks it against the bumper and amber liquid splashes as the glass shatters. Half crouched, holding the jagged bottleneck, he backs slowly along the side of the pickup.

I snarl and his eyes widen and he runs for the door. But the hunter is faster. Spike's face smashes into the window as I slam him against the truck. He screams. The scent of his blood just inches away fills me, draws me in. Overpowers me.

My eyes fix on his neck. My hand grabs him by the hair, pulls his head back. Exposes his throat. *His throat.*

An image of my daughter flares to life, a visual barrier to the insanity consuming me. It brings me enough awareness to realize what I'm doing—what I'm about to do. With a cry I throw myself off him, landing hard on my ass. I watch as the punk sags, then slumps to the asphalt.

Oh crap. What have I done?

Looking at the three guys lying on the ground, I focus on breathing through my mouth—to keep from smelling the blood—and try to regain rational thought. The psychotic beast and the ferocious hunter whirl around in my head, threatening to tear control away from me yet again.

I've got to get out of here.

With a last deep breath through my teeth, I leap up, run and grab my bag, then dash back to the truck. As I step over Spike's groaning body and reach for the door handle, an alarm goes off in my head.

Fingerprints.

I fish my gloves out of the bag and slip them on, yank open the door and climb into the truck. It coughs, starts, and I pull forward enough to clear the way for my car, then exit through the passenger door. The BMW purrs to life and I back out. Mohawk, green hair askew, climbs to his feet and staggers over to Goatee who's holding his chest as he tries to get up.

Good. Didn't kill any of them.

But oh, so close. Too close.

Fear and guilt war with the anger coursing through my veins. Gritting my teeth, I hit the gas and screech out of the parking lot.

Way too close.

CHAPTER 2

Deep into the Santa Cruz Mountains, I park on a dirt road amidst fog-enshrouded oaks and get out of the car, still consumed by waves of fury, my vision still painted in crimson.

The hunger claws through my belly and into my veins, triggered by the rage and the red-laced violence. My mind keeps spinning back to how close I was to sinking my teeth into his throat, and how sweet the fire of his blood would've been.

God, I hate it when I get like this.

Heading into the forest, I drink in the fresh, living smells that cling to the damp air. The one that catches my attention is the musky scent of a deer, a mature buck. The scent is strong, so he's not far. Silently stalking through the brush, I pause to check his position. He hasn't moved—maybe he's bedded down.

Closer . . .

He explodes from the ground not ten feet ahead of me. I slam into him on his second leap and we tumble to the dirt. His legs flailing, he slings his head up, fighting to free himself of my weight.

I grab his nose and yank it upward, slash open his throat with my nails, and sink my teeth into the gaping red wound.

His hot blood bursts into my mouth and I swallow, swallow, and the beast in me sings in triumph. The heat of his blood fills my belly and begins spreading its welcome warmth throughout my veins. I continue to drink even as the deer kicks and thrashes. My body embraces his and slowly begins crushing him to stillness, and I rejoice in my strength. And I continue to drink.

The warm blood haze enveloping me, I point my car toward home. But as the events in the parking lot begin to replay in my head, worms of paranoia wriggle their way into my nerves. Three bodies sprawled on the asphalt, a broken and bleeding face, a ragged red chest—the images flash through my mind and the wheels of thought spin into gear.

Crap. At least one of them needed to go to the hospital. Not that I really care. I shudder to think what they would've done to a human woman. The hospital staff might care, though, since there was obviously a fight. And that could mean a police report.

Don't know if they have enough balls to admit a woman kicked their asses. Not just any woman. The bartender. The bartender from Lenny's. The one who turned into a monster.

All my senses are on high alert as I park and walk to my apartment. No foreign scents linger about my door. I ease it open, listening, and taste the air.

Seems clean.

I relax somewhat, step in and lock the door, then glance around at my little home.

Damn it. I don't want to pack again.

Six months. I made it six months this time, the longest yet. My coworkers are comfortable around me now and seem to actually like me. Even better, I like them. Yet that makes little difference. It's the same thing over and over. Every time I think I'm settled, something happens, threatening to expose me for what I am, and I have to move on.

But what I need right now is a hot shower. I strip and dump my bloody clothes into the washing machine with enzyme cleaner.

Steaming water pours over me while I mull over the things that need to be done in case I have to leave. I won't have time to do any of it tonight, though. The sun will be up soon. Hopefully my precautions and my various IDs will keep me safe until tomorrow.

I lean my face into the spray and try to wash away my prickling anxiety, hoping tonight wasn't as bad as I remember. Guess I'll find out if the cops start snooping around the club.

The outer warmth of the hot water and the inner warmth of the stag's blood help me unwind and I stay in as long as I dare. Feeling more in control, I turn off the faucet, towel myself dry, and get out.

~

The reflection approaching the mirrored closet door grabs my attention and I stop a few feet from the glass to examine it.

Mirrors never cease to amaze me. The woman looking back at me is . . . not me. Not the me I once was. She looks like me, yet she's different, scary. I don't know if I'll ever get used to her.

Always tall, she's now lean and well-muscled instead of willowy and soft. Her curves are still the right fullness and in the right places, but this body is the wiry one of a huntress. The perpetual tan her skin once wore has given way to a pale translucence, like the color of skim milk. Childhood scars and blemishes have vanished. Her thick hair is about the only thing that's the same and is still a dark, rich brown, almost black, as it waves gently past her shoulders.

The teeth, surprisingly, haven't changed either. But the jaw is much stronger now.

It's the other changes in her face that are the most disturbing. Though in her early thirties, she seems ageless now, with no lines of worry, nor those of laughter. The soft roundness of her cheeks and easy-going expression are gone, replaced by sharp angles and a predator's intensity that intimidates even me.

And the eyes . . . the eyes are no longer mine. When the hunger is sated, as now, they are an impossibly brilliant pale blue. I get a bit lost in them, as do most people upon meeting me.

As the hunger grows, they gradually darken and lose a little of their brilliance, becoming a more somber, deeper blue, like the ocean. Then people tend to drown in them, unwilling to try to swim to the surface. I guess that's what these eyes are for—to entrap my prey with nothing more than a stare. Just like any good predator.

And there's another color that they possess, but it's not a pleasant one. It starts within the pupil, then expands out into the iris. The assholes from this evening got a good look at it because they only turn this color when I'm angry or hunting—or both. It's the color of violence, of mortality, and my victims can't help but note the striking resemblance between my eyes . . . and their blood.

~

Grabbing the furry black teddy bear from the pile of stuffed animals on my bed, I climb in between the flannel sheets. The soft bed, warmed by an electric blanket, feels wonderful as I curl up around the bear and snuggle beneath the covers. The sun's coming up and it's forcing me into a dreamless state like it does every morning. I relax and willingly give myself over to the inner darkness.

But as it swallows me down, I see a shadowy image in the blackness of my mind—a tall, pale figure standing in the distance. He's strange, unearthly.

And he . . . he's watching me.

MONDAY

CHAPTER 3

I wake, instantly alert, and glance at the clock—1:08 PM, a little late for me. But I feel refreshed and last night's problem seems far away for the moment. Climbing out of bed, I pull on jeans and a long-sleeved top. My plan had been to check out new hunting areas online, but I'm not in the mood to sit at my desk. It's supposed to be cloudy today, so I should be able to run errands without worrying about the sun.

That's another interesting change I've undergone. I used to tan easily and spent hours on the beach drinking in the warmth of the sun. Now I'm so fair that I burn instantly. Any direct ray turns my bare skin bright pink and I fear I'm about to burst into flames. I haven't yet, and the burn fades once I'm out of the sun, but it does make me a bit nervous.

I fix a cup of hot tea, grateful to have something from my old life that I can still enjoy. Food is another story—apparently my digestive system is designed only for liquids. Well, one liquid specifically, but my stomach can handle others in small quantities. It's kind of helpful for keeping up human appearances.

My cell phone rings, startling me.

Lenny's number. Tentacles of anxiety writhe up my spine.

"Hello?"

"Hey, Sunny. How you doin' today?" Lenny's voice lacks its usual gaiety.

"Okay. What's up?" I try to sound nonchalant.

"Well, I just got a call from Karen at the club. The police came in asking for you."

The police.

Fear explodes throughout my body and both the beast and the hunter go berserk. I stare at the wall through a red haze and fight to keep from running out the door.

My last encounter with police almost ended with me in a cage. I barely escaped.

"Sunny? Are you still there?"

Lenny's voice is a lifeline to sanity.

"Yeah, Lenny. I . . . I'm still here."

"They wouldn't tell her why, other than they wanted to ask you some questions."

"Okay."

"Are you? Okay, I mean? You sound funny. Are you in some kinda trouble? Is there anything I can do to help?"

Yeah, sweet Lenny, just keep talking while I try to regain some control.

"No, no, everything's fine."

"Well, okay. I just thought I'd let you know." The concern in his voice is endearing and it saddens me that I have to leave without saying goodbye.

"Thanks. I appreciate it."

"No problem. They left a number for you to call. Do you want it?"

"Sure." I don't bother writing it down as he rattles it off.

"Well, let me know if you need anything. See ya tonight?" Doubt colors his voice.

"Uh, yeah. I'll be there."

"All right then. Later."

"Yeah. And Lenny? Thanks again."

"No problem."

The phone goes silent and I take a deep breath. Over my initial shock, I quiet the beast and use the hunter's focus to begin working on my list of things to do.

I'm not worried about the cops showing up here, at least for a little while. The club has a PO box for my address and the apartment is rented under a different name. My driver's license and registration are under yet another name. It'll take some time to connect the dots, if they bother to do so with a minor assault case. Either way, I'll be long gone by then.

It's tempting to stay and tough it out. I don't want to leave my job, or Lenny and Sally—but I don't dare talk to the police, let alone walk into a police station. There's no way I can keep the beast from panicking over the idea of being locked up, regardless of how remote the possibility or how innocent I might be. And when the beast panics, things usually get very bloody.

Crap. I head into the bedroom to start packing.

Suitcases by the door, I retrieve one last item secured under the carpet and floorboards beneath my bed. The small travel bag is one of several emergency kits I've stashed up and down the West Coast and contains enough cash and identifications to start over somewhere else.

Glancing around the apartment, I shake my head at the things I'm leaving behind. They're just books and stupid little knick-knacks that won't fit into my over-packed car. But they made this place feel . . . like home.

The apartment lease and the rental furniture are paid up through next month. I shove letters terminating both agreements into my bag to mail on my way out.

I take one last look around and, biting my lip, grab the suitcases and head to the car.

CHAPTER 4

The BMW hums as I leave Santa Cruz and head south to Santa Barbara. The anxiety I've felt since Lenny's phone call is fading, replaced with an emptiness inside that bleeds out into everything around me. The asphalt disappearing beneath the hood, the dull grey of streetlights and railing, the palette of painted steel machines that I pass—all of it blurs into nothingness.

My chest tightens as I think about the life I just left behind. It was the closest I've felt to fitting in, to *belonging*. Lenny and the others accepted me and my moodiness, along with my need to stay apart from them. I didn't talk much, but they didn't pry and were always just *there*, laughing and kidding around. Watching them as we worked together made me feel not so alone—which is as close to friendship as I'm capable of now.

When I first returned to civilization three years ago, I wasn't sure I could make it living among people. But after several years of near-mindless life in the wild, I could no longer bear the isolation. And as memories of my daughter, Andrea, began to resurface and dominate all other thoughts, including those of blood, I started finding myself again. And I knew I had to try.

It was tougher in the beginning, when the hunger was more demanding and I had almost no control over the explosive beast. In those days, I was lucky to last a week in the same place.

But Andrea saved me. Memories of her gave me the self-control necessary to live among people and resist the urge to kill them. There were some close calls at first, but like a guardian angel, Andrea's face would break through the red haze and freeze me in my tracks. She gave me the strength to stop the beast, because I was—I still am—unable to do to someone else what had been done to me. Unwilling to rip them from their family and leave their loved ones with a gaping hole.

A chill runs through me and I shrink from the blurred images of that horrific nightmare and the one who took me.

Forcing my thoughts away from the dark place that threatens to swallow my soul whenever I think about that night, I focus on the California landscape framing Highway 101, its rolling green hills sprinkled with majestic oaks and vineyards. I lower the windows and breathe in the scents of spring grasses and trees and those who live among them. March wildflowers remind me of Andrea and the flowers she leaves on my grave.

Andrea. I was only seventeen when she was born, and she was my whole life until it ended.

It took a long time to find her after I came in from the wild. I searched for months, surviving one day at a time, fighting the frustration and doubt that I would ever see her again.

I'll never forget the day I saw her name online in an article about the Santa Barbara City College soccer team. I sat frozen, my eyes locked to her picture in the midst of her teammates, terrified that if I looked away, she would vanish.

I didn't go to work that night. I didn't hunt. I didn't leave my chair. The only thing that moved was my hand on the mouse every so often to keep the screensaver from activating.

The first time I actually saw her was on campus. Padding filled my baggy shirt and pants. I still have the red wig I wore. A cap and sunglasses protected my face from the sun—and from her eyes. I followed her throughout the day, watching her in her new life. Day after day I watched her, always disguised, sometimes as faculty, sometimes as a boy.

It wasn't long before I noticed her looking over her shoulder, peering in my direction. I'd quickly turn away from those questioning blue eyes and step behind a corner or melt into the surrounding students—all the while fighting the impulse to run to her and take her in my arms and tell her I loved her.

The heartache of watching without being a part of her life began to take its toll. That, and the fear she'd finally recognize me, gave me the strength to back off. She looked happy and seemed to be doing well, and that was all that really mattered. Reluctantly I moved north, putting distance and hours between us to help me resist the temptation to watch her just one more day, one more minute.

But every few weeks, I'd slip down the highway, anxious and hoping that she was still okay, still where I left her.

Until Andrea disappeared over summer break.

My days became frantic with searching. My nights in the oak-covered hills northeast of Santa Barbara became . . . bloody. Those were the longest nine weeks of my life, waiting for fall semester, hoping that she re-enrolled.

When I finally saw her on the soccer field, relief nearly dropped me to my knees. Watching her go to classes throughout the day, I realized that her life had changed again. Because now there was a boy, a sweet blond boy who looked at her as adoringly as she did him.

And so I've watched. I watched as they fell in love, watched as they married. And I watched as together they waited for their new baby.

But that is all I can do. Watch.

Because I would rather she believe me dead than know what I really am.

A toddler's face, cushioned by the bright blue padding of a car seat, flickers in and out of my vision as I pass a white SUV. I press the accelerator and scream south down the 101.

My granddaughter. She's almost seven months old now. I wonder if she's crawling yet. Another stage I'll miss. It's not like I can peek in their window to watch her scoot across the carpet. Hopefully I'll get to see her if Andrea takes her out. I'll just have to park down the street and watch for her to get in the car. Maybe she'll take her to the beach to see the waves roll in and seagulls fly by, screeching in their seagull language.

I don't even know what she looks like. All I've ever seen is a bundle of pink blankets.

My throat tightens. Crying doesn't do any good. Ever since I changed, I've been unable to shed tears. I don't know why. Maybe it has something to do with my ever-shifting eye color, or the increase in visual sharpness. Or maybe it's because I am what I am. I just know that I can't cry like I used to. All I get are sick gasping sounds pretending to be sobs and my eyes feeling like they're going to burst from the pressure, and this misery bottled up inside with no way to let it out.

Except to run something down, rip out its throat, and drain away every drop of its life.

The motel bed isn't nearly as comfortable as the one at my old apartment, but in a few moments it won't matter. At least I'm warm and comfy on the inside. Though I hunted last night, negative feelings always fuel the hunger, so the beast was in quite a state by the time I checked into the motel on the outskirts of Santa Barbara.

Lucky for the desk clerk I maintain such a strict diet.

Lucky for me the hills north of Santa Barbara are full of deer.

I clutch the teddy bear to my chest as the lassitude of the stag's blood and the rising sun start to take me down. As I fade, I sense something, or someone. I struggle to open my eyes, but realize he's in my head, yet far away. Tall, powerful. Familiar, but I don't know why. The last thing I see as I slip into the blackness is a pair of emerald eyes, watching me.

TUESDAY

CHAPTER 5

It's 11:16 a.m. Crap. I spring out of bed and quickly get dressed. I wish I could set an alarm to wake me up. But they don't make an alarm loud enough to wake the dead.

Sure enough, her driveway's empty as I cruise by. Great.

I don't know if she's already left or if her car is still in the garage. I hate trying to figure out her schedule so that I can catch more than just a glimpse. It was a lot easier when she was in school and I could pretend to be a student.

Parking down the street, I yank a magazine from the stack I bought at the bookstore yesterday, but can't make myself open it. I sit staring at the house, trying to regain some measure of calm.

I'm still staring when the garage door opens and her car backs out. When she's nearly at the stop sign, I pull out and follow her, noting the time—12:24.

After getting off the freeway, Andrea drives into a residential area. The short streets make it difficult to keep her in sight without getting too close. She pulls over in front of a tan house and I drive past, turning onto the next street. I make a U-turn and park so I can see her car across the postage-stamp lawns.

She gets out and opens the rear door. Andrea appears to have slimmed down more since I last saw her, but it's difficult to tell underneath her red wool coat. Her face is somewhat hidden beneath the slightly cocked brim of her matching hat. She leans into the car and comes back up holding my granddaughter.

But I can't see the baby's face. Not because of the distance, which is no problem for my hunter's eyes, but because she's wearing a puffy pink jacket with an oversized hood drawn around her face. A pale yellow blanket is sandwiched between the baby's waist and my daughter's arm. A pink shoe kicks back and forth as my daughter bends again to retrieve a yellow diaper bag.

She walks to the front door, knocks, and disappears inside.

That's it. That's all I'll get to see of my granddaughter today. I'm sure this evening will only be a repeat performance, pink jacket and all. I won't get to see her hair, or the color of her eyes, or whether she resembles her father or her mother.

I don't even know her name.

I glare at the dark grey sky that is threatening rain. Usually I welcome these low-hanging storm clouds, heavy with their burden of water, because it means I don't have to worry about being fried by the sun.

But today, I curse them.

Her car is nearly at the stop sign when I pull out. Andrea retraces her route to the freeway, getting off at the second downtown exit. She might be headed to her old job, the one she had before the baby. My suspicions are confirmed when she turns into the driveway. I cruise past and get all the way to the intersection, only to find that U-turns aren't allowed and I have to go around the block. By the time I get back, she's inside.

Damn it. I just wanted to see her one more time.

I park and slouch against the door, frustrated. I could go to the motel and my laptop to look for a new place to live, but I need to know what time she gets off work. If it's late enough, I might be able to make a run to Los Angeles tomorrow afternoon and get back before she heads home.

Watching Andrea means waiting—a lot. Resigned to a long afternoon, I grab the new Yarbro book from the bookstore bag and settle in.

About four-thirty, people start to trickle out the doors. The stream increases, and a few minutes after five, they pour out of the building. Her red hat and coat catch my eye as she hurries to her car and gets in. I hang back a moment—at least I know where she's going this time.

Just as I thought, I only get glimpses of chubby cheeks and hands as my daughter hustles the baby into the car and takes off. I follow, hoping she has errands to run, that I might have a chance to get closer. But she heads straight home and pulls into the garage and the door closes.

It takes everything in me to keep from slamming my fist into the dash of my car.

~

After allowing the young buck to lead me on a merry chase halfway around the lake, I decide I'm being overly cruel and bring him tumbling down. His tangy hot blood pumps out furiously from the running, and, too soon, there is no more. There never seems to be enough. I'm not really that hungry, having fed the past two nights. But the onslaught of emotions keeps provoking the beast. Blood is the only thing that pacifies it.

I got over the Bambi complex long ago. It's not that I don't regret killing. I do. I feel remorse every time I take a life. But I need to feed in order to survive, like every other living thing. Only my food doesn't come wrapped in cellophane and marked Grade A.

It starts to sprinkle as I run along the shoreline of Lake Cachuma. I don't care. Being wet doesn't bother me and neither does the cold. I feel it, but it doesn't cause me discomfort and can even be invigorating. Warmth, on the other hand, is quite pleasurable, especially on the inside after a hot meal. Warm days are great, too, if I can protect my skin from the direct sun, which isn't easy. People look at you funny when you're wearing a long-sleeved turtleneck and gloves and it's ninety degrees outside.

The weather forecast predicted rain until tomorrow evening. That means I'll probably see even less of my daughter and the baby tomorrow. Instead of dealing with my inevitable frustration, I think I'll head directly to Los Angeles in the morning to take care of my banking.

Jogging back to the BMW, I catch the scent of wild pig and veer off to follow it. Pigs are tough to kill because they are so low to the ground and their barrel-shaped bodies are difficult to grip. Their necks are short and stout—breaking them is not very feasible. And they have tusks, right near my target area. I did kill one once, though—a young adult—and I greatly enjoyed his buttery-sweet blood.

Scent trails are easier to follow when the weather's damp. Detecting several, I slow as the scents become stronger. I weave through the bushes and freeze. Three adult female pigs and six babies are foraging along a marshy area. I watch for a moment, then melt back into the brush.

That is one thing I will not do. I will not kill mothers or babies.

Retracing my steps, I pick up my trail again and continue on to the car. Between the deer and my twenty-mile run, I'm finally relaxed, and I smile from the sheer joy of being in the woods. The sprinkles have become rain, and I stop and lift my face to the sky. I rejoice as the cool drops hit and trail down my cheeks, and open my mouth to see if I can feel them on the inside as well. A few tap dance on my tongue and I laugh.

Rain leaps across the leaves and rocks in a liquid ballet, and each drop makes its own music, creating a soft woodland symphony. Laughing again, I shake my head, flinging water off my hair to add to the performance, and take off running once more.

WEDNESDAY

CHAPTER 6

Ugh. I hate driving in L.A. just as much as I do the Bay Area. Too many cars driven by too many people who don't really know how to drive. Especially in the rain.

I leave the BMW in an underground garage off Hollywood Boulevard and walk several blocks. The bar I'm headed to is tucked away on a side street and I locate it by the faint numbers painted on its door. It has no name or sign.

Shaking off my umbrella, I step inside. Besides the bartender and two men sitting at the far end of the bar, the place is empty.

"Hey, Joe." I walk up to the bar and slide onto a stool.

"Sunny! Long time no see! I've been wondering how you were doing." Joe finishes drying a glass, throws the towel on his shoulder, and rests one hand on the top of the bar.

The other has slipped beneath the countertop. I can visualize the .45 caliber that is stashed within its reach. Joe's a pretty careful guy, and we haven't seen one another for a while. Glancing in the direction of his hidden hand, I smile and shake my head. He chuckles and, shrugging, brings his hand out empty and runs it through his non-existent hair.

"How've you been? How's L.A. working out for you?" I ask, surveying the dimly lit room, and look again at the guys nursing their beers.

He used to have a bar in Oakland, which was where I met him.

"Just fine. Same thing, different location. You know how it is." He laughs, and his belly laughs with him. Reaching back around his broad girth, he unties his wet apron.

Joe's bar was the third place I worked when I decided to try and live among people again. I was a lot more tightly wound back then, and my first couple jobs had only lasted a few days. I remember walking in and asking if he needed a bartender, and telling him that I needed to be paid in cash. He was agreeable to that, and turned out to be pretty agreeable to work for, too.

I suppress a smile as I think about why. He's some sort of former CIA or black ops or something, and seems to think that I am as well. He'd said my edgy awareness and the way I move had tipped him off. I'm perfectly happy to go along with that. Guess he was never able to dig anything up on my background, at least that I know of.

"Come on, let's go in the back and talk. Hey, Mike, watch the bar, will ya?" Joe glances at his customers, and one of them raises his mug and nods. The man's dark eyes are sharp as he peers at me from beneath his baseball cap, and he wears a tense stillness that I've noticed with Joe's regulars. They're either spooks or former spooks, which means they're all still spooks. Kinda like the mob. They never really retire.

Following Joe, I think again about how well he treated me during our brief association. As he had explained, these guys always take care of their own. Joe had sensed I was in some sort of trouble and wanted to help me get back on my feet.

And he was right, although he had no idea what kind of trouble I was really in. But after a few months and a couple of tense incidents, he started asking more questions, and I reluctantly told him it was time for me to move on.

"Have a seat." Stepping around behind the desk, he indicates the chair across from him and sits in his own.

"You look well. You look more . . . relaxed. That's good." Joe leans back in his chair, his brown eyes thoughtful.

"Thanks. I've been working on it." I'm sure he hasn't forgotten the time I leapt over the bar top and slammed a belligerent customer up against the wall. I'd come a little too close that day to revealing my true nature and left shortly afterward.

"It's been, what, three years? You managing all right?" He leans forward with genuine concern in his eyes.

"Yeah, I'm okay. I've got my own place and have been at the same job for a while now."

Or did until yesterday, but he doesn't need to know that.

"Your own place? Good." He nods. "Still have the BMW?"

"Yeah. I love that car. You have no idea how much I've appreciated it."

"I was short on parking then, and you needed transportation. Glad it's worked out."

I never quite trusted his motives for giving it to me. The ex-spy car was practically brand new. But just to humor him, I left the GPS and tracking devices I found on it—until the day I left.

Joe purses his lips and I wait for his next question. He's never been good at hiding his interrogation background, but he also knows not to press me.

"How much do you need?" He ends our little chitchat and gets straight to the point.

Fake IDs are expensive. Otherwise, I wouldn't be here talking to him. I take a breath.

"Fifteen. Just as a loan, though. I'm doing better now and will be able to pay you back."

"Bullshit. I told you the day you walked into my bar that we're family around here. Just because you're the weird cousin with freaky eyes doesn't mean you're not part of us."

A stab of fear tightens my gut and I remember why I left. He's just too damn observant.

Joe looks down, opens a drawer in his desk, and presses a keypad.

"So how's the weather out there? Rain still coming down?" he asks as he looks back up.

The electronic hum from the desk is beyond human hearing, but not mine. I bite back a smile, wondering which word he'd used to trigger the voice recognition lock. Probably *weather*, which would work in any situation. He opens another drawer.

"Yeah, it was still raining just before I walked in. Traffic's a mess." I shake my head.

"Always is. It's always bad, and then sometimes it's worse." He rummages around in the drawer and I study the wall behind him.

Hung in the center is a large framed reprint of the poker-playing dogs. I imagine the picture's on hinges and swings out to reveal a wall safe that likely has nothing in it. Glancing at the fedora hanging from a hook next to his long overcoat, I smile. Joe fancies himself to be a modern espionage version of Humphrey Bogart or Edward G. Robinson. He's always been enamored with the twenties and thirties gangster era, yet usually has the latest in high-tech gadgets. I chuckle quietly to myself as I recall what an eccentric he is.

"What are you grinning about?" He glances over his shoulder at the wall behind him, his expression puzzled. He looks back at me, eyebrows raised, as he sets several half-inch stacks of bills on the desk in front of him.

"Nothing. I just hadn't realized how much I've missed you." I smile again and note the surprise that crosses his face.

"I can always use a good courier or a bartender with keen eyes and ears and a closed mouth. You did both jobs pretty well, as I recall." A wry smile tugs his lips. "Except for the little . . . temper problem."

"Yeeahh, there is that. I've gotten better, but every once in a while—" I glance to the side and shrug.

"Regardless, you're still welcome here anytime. I mean that." He wraps rubber bands around the money, stuffs it into a manila envelope, and fastens it.

I nod. His expression shifts, becoming more serious.

"You're not in any trouble now, are you?" he asks.

"I'm . . . not real sure yet. I'll find out when I get back home."

He smiles, shaking his head. "Whatever it was, I'd have given my left arm to see it."

"No, wouldn't have been worth it. It wasn't as bad as it could've been." I chuckle.

"But I'm sure he or they deserved it."

"They did. Let's just say I left them with a lasting impression."

He snorts. "I'm surprised I got that much out of you."

"Don't get used to it." I smile, but my voice and eyes carry a hint of warning.

He laughs. "Yep, there's the Sunny I remember. Keep 'em at arm's distance. That's the key to survival."

I can't help but laugh out loud and he laughs again with me.

He has no idea the survival he's referring to pertains to those at the *other* end of my arm as well as my own. Or maybe he does.

He grows serious again and sets the envelope in front of me. "Here's twenty grand. If you need more, I have work for someone with your unique talents."

"I, uh . . . I can't take that much." I sit back, shocked. I don't even know what to say.

"Bullshit. No option. How're the ID contacts holding up?"

"Fine, as far as I know. I haven't needed to use them for a while, but I may soon."

"Here's a couple more in case you run into dead ends." He scribbles on a piece of paper and hands it to me, along with his business card.

Both of the names listed on the paper are men's clothing companies, which makes me chuckle again. Getting a new ID is sometimes referred to as changing clothes. In this case I'd be buying a suit, wearing a new label, and giving myself a new look. Funny shit.

"Thank you." I stand, pick up the envelope, and put it in my bag. "And thanks again for this. I'll pay you back."

"Well, I won't accept it—at least not in cash. But it's not free. I'm serious about needing your help. Just let me know when you're available." Joe gets up and walks around the desk.

He puts out his left hand. His non-weapon hand. I hesitate, then take it, and we shake.

Something flickers in his eyes at the touch of my cool skin and I quickly let go.

He smiles. "Now that's progress. Three years to get a handshake. We'll work on a hug next time."

I snort.

"Don't hold your breath." I head to the door. But before opening it, I turn back around.

"Joe, I just want to thank you for everything you've done for me. If it wasn't for you, I don't know if I could have made it." My chest tightens with emotion, as he's the closest I've had to a true friend since I came into this . . . life, or whatever it is.

"Well, don't be such a stranger. You can visit more often than every couple years, you know. My cell is on the card—call me when you get things straightened out. At least let me know you're still alive."

Alive. Right.

"Okay, I will." I slip out the door, regretting that I can't stick around. But he's too sharp, and it won't take him much longer to figure out that I'm not human.

If he hasn't already.

The rain has tapered to a drizzle, but the roads are still slick and the traffic still lousy. The trip back to Santa Barbara takes a little longer than the trip down this morning, but I make it back in time to swing by my daughter's work. Her car isn't in the lot. Fighting a twinge of worry, I head to her house and cruise by the empty driveway. I didn't really expect anything different, but the disappointment surfaces nonetheless.

It's still drizzling. I'm not in the mood to get muddy tonight, so I stop at Starbucks for a hot tea. Soaking in a steamy bath and drinking tea sounds like a nice warm way to spend the evening before curling up in bed with my book.

As I get my bath ready, I think back on my visit with Joe and how comfortable I felt with him today—at least most of the time. I guess it's because we know that we each have secrets that must be protected. But I can't fight the paranoia that arises when I think of him knowing exactly what my secret is. As friendly and helpful as he seems to be, I have no doubt that his loyalties to his own self-interest far outweigh any he would have toward me. No matter how lonely I get, it's just not worth the risk.

I shudder at the thought of what the military or other agency might do to someone like me.

As for working for him again? Not likely. Once I get stable with a job and a place to live, the only payment he's getting from me will be a wire transfer of cash.

Anger boils up at the thought of the isolation I can't seem to escape. Snarling, I slip under the hot water. I'm such a freak that I can't even drown myself.

THURSDAY

CHAPTER 7

My eyes fly open and I look at the clock—10:08 AM. A peek out the window reveals the storm has passed. Pale grey clouds drift eastward, separated from one another by freshly washed sky, its brilliant blue almost painful to my eyes.

I dress for a day in the sun, hoping that the outside temperatures are still cool enough that a long-sleeved blouse and gloves won't stand out. From my small collection of wigs, I choose the red one, its hair long and straight, and tug it on, shoving the dark ends of my ponytail underneath. A wide-brimmed straw hat and flower-framed sunglasses top off the semi-hippie look, and I chuckle at how cliché and dorky the woman in the mirror appears to be. As long as she keeps on those goofy glasses, that is.

Andrea's turning onto the main road just as I approach her street. Crap. I whip around and try to catch up without appearing obvious. After several blocks, she pulls into a small shopping center. I park a few dozen spaces away as she hurries around to the passenger side and takes out a large plastic bag. She carries it into the dry cleaner, and a minute later she walks out empty-handed and gets back in the car. Her next stop is a florist down the street.

Great. Looks like I get to chase her around the city this morning.

Suppressing a growl, I stay two to three cars behind her. She turns again and I crowd the bumper of the car ahead of me to keep her in sight.

Electricity runs through me as she parks in front of the grocery store. She gets out, opens the rear door, and retrieves my granddaughter. A stray breeze flips back the hood on the baby's lavender jacket. Short dark curls dance across her tiny head.

My throat tightens. Dark hair, like her mother's. Like mine.

They head into the store, the baby balanced on Andrea's hip. I get out and take a breath, trying to quell the spasms in my chest, and follow them.

On my left is a minivan. I hear its side door open and young girls in soccer uniforms burst out onto the pavement, chattering and laughing and being girls. They must be on Easter break—typically tournament season. The van has soccer stickers on the rear windows, and a young woman gets out of the driver's door and walks around to the other side, trying to calm the giggling girls.

Soccer mom. I was one once. I took her to all her practices, all her games. I cheered when she scored and consoled when they lost.

But now I'm something else.

Stalker mom. It would be funny if it wasn't so goddamn painful.

Because that's all I can do now with my daughter. Stalk her and watch her and try to catch whatever tiny glimpses of her life that I can.

Clenching my fists, I speed up, hoping that today I might get a little more.

As I hurry through the door, I see Andrea already in the checkout line, a package of disposable diapers tucked under her arm. I turn away, but can still see the baby's face.

And I can see her eyes.

Blue. Bright, startling blue. Just like her mother's. Just like mine used to be.

I nearly choke trying to maintain control. Head down, I grab a box of something from a shelf and get into the checkout line that is to my daughter's back.

"Oh, she's darling. Look at those eyes and those black curls. What a cutie pie!" The checker reaches out and gently wiggles a tiny lavender shoe.

My granddaughter shyly lays her head on Andrea's shoulder, then turns her face away.

Toward me.

And our eyes meet. And she smiles.

And part of me dies as I realize I will never get to know this beautiful child.

"What's her name?" The checker asks.

"Rhianna. Rhianna Sunshine."

Oh God.

Insides churning, I set down the box and flee the store.

My chest heaves in dry, wracking sobs. I feel like everything in me is going to explode, that I will end up a bloody splatter all over the inside of my car.

I open my eyes in time to see her toss the diapers into the back of the car, fasten the baby into the car seat, and get in.

Biting my lip, I start the BMW and follow her. After a few blocks, it's apparent she's heading to the babysitter and I hang back, hoping she's been in too big of a hurry to notice the black car tailing her all morning. Fortunately, there are a lot of black BMWs on the road these days, and I take a gamble and follow her onto the babysitter's street.

From a driveway several doors away, I watch as she hoists my granddaughter onto her hip, grabs the diaper bag and diapers, and disappears around the corner of the garage. Several minutes pass before she reappears, hurrying back to the car. She makes a U-turn and speeds past me down the street.

But I can't follow her. I can't do this anymore, at least not for now.

It was difficult enough when I was just watching *her*. My heart would ache at all the moments I was unable to share with her, and I could only bear to visit every few months.

But everything changed today with those black curls and bright blue eyes and that little smile. That little smile that said *I know you.*

Because I don't think I can watch any longer and not be a part of their lives, of *her* life as she grows up.

Frustration finally breaks through my anguish, and a growl slips out in place of the sobs that were clawing out of my throat.

Screw this. I can't take it anymore.

With a last look at the house that swallowed those blue eyes, I start the BMW and head down the street.

I don't know when I'll be back.

The highway beckons me eastward, away from the setting sun and into the night. I'm numb as I let the BMW follow the dark path to another beginning and another new life. A life far from the memories that haunt me, the memories that hold me, the memories of my old one—one stolen from me in a night of pain and terror and blood.

One I can *never* have again.

PART II

COLORADO

MONDAY

CHAPTER 8

Walking into the little house I've rented, I feel pretty satisfied with my day. I found a bartending job at a decent club in downtown Colorado Springs, about a half hour away. Getting work isn't usually a problem, as most clubs are constantly on the lookout for a competent and attractive female bartender.

Keeping the job is always another story.

They want me to start tomorrow night. Tuesdays are typically slow in the nightclub world, but I have to prove that I can do the job before they give me a weekend shift. My visits to the club on Friday and Saturday nights revealed that there weren't many repeat customers, which suits me just fine. Regulars eventually get a little too talkative and a little too curious.

One of the reasons I've chosen Colorado Springs is because it has everything I need. A medium-sized city, it offers plenty of work options. A big part of its population is military, with Air Force, Army, and even Navy personnel rotating through on their tours of duty. And that means a wide variety of busy nightclubs.

The other thing this city offers is a little harder to find. The entire area west of the Springs is mountainous, with forests, reservoirs, and grazing meadows—perfect habitat for deer and elk, and those who feed upon them.

I dress for hunting, impatience prickling my skin, and wait for evening to arrive. Though it's been less than a week since I fed outside of Cortez, I'm anxious to try something besides mule deer. The muleys here taste a little different from those on the West Coast, but still, I'm tired of deer. What I'm really looking forward to is my first encounter with an elk. The size of a small horse, an elk will present a challenging fight, and the hunter in me vibrates with anticipation. And the blood . . . gallons and gallons of it. The beast will be ecstatic.

My new home, nestled at the base of a mountain, is in the tiny town of Cascade, west of Colorado Springs. It's bordered on all sides by the Pike National Forest. No more "eating out"—I can enjoy my meals right in my own backyard. It couldn't be more perfect.

The sun slides beneath the western horizon and I open the back door and head up the mountain. The early April air is cold and patches of snow hug the ground. I walk slowly, savoring the exotic scents of my new home. The tapestry of fragrances, dominated by pines, firs, and unfamiliar shrubs, is unlike that of California mountains, and the variety of animal smells is rich and tantalizing.

Deepening darkness cloaks me as pine needles crunch beneath my feet, and I smile at the sounds of small mammals scurrying for cover from the predator moving in their midst. The hunter whines, but makes no attempt to give chase.

Moving up the slope, I'm struck by the magnificence of the night. The moon is full and its light reflects off the snow-covered mountainsides, the soaring peaks shimmering as they reach for the stars. The trees sparkle in their frosty blankets and the air is crisp and refreshing. I drink in my surroundings and experience a rare moment of feeling that I am exactly where I'm supposed to be.

An unusual scent catches my attention, and following it, I discover a huge porcupine lumbering across a clearing. It peers at me, snarling, and rattles its quills. As fascinated as I am by the creature and how it might taste, I heed its warning. Perhaps another time. Tonight I'm after something bigger and less prickly.

I skirt the clearing and work my way through the trees, heading uphill. Scenting a herd of deer across the slope I hesitate, the beast growling in impatience. But I want to keep my edge, and since the evening is young, I continue up the slope.

Above the tree line now, I become aware of *something* in the sky behind me and turn around. I stop and stare in amazement at Pikes Peak looming, godlike, over its dominion, its snowy flanks glowing in the full moon.

According to my research, the Peak towers more than seven thousand feet above its base, with a total elevation of over fourteen thousand feet.

It stands alone, dwarfing the surrounding mountains and landscape. I stand in awe, feeling humbled in its presence. I reflect over my life, and what brought me here, and somehow feel like I've been summoned. By what, I do not know.

A breeze picks up, bringing the scent of something like a deer, but not. My body tenses. I zero in on the direction and drop into a hunting crouch. The scent is coming from below and across the slope. I quietly start working my way back through the trees to its source.

The smells of water and grass tell me I'm approaching a small mountain lake and surrounding meadow. As I move to the edge of the trees, I spot them. They are huge and magnificent, their rich blood coursing through thick muscles and veins. My jaw tingles and my mouth waters, and my whole body electrifies.

The small herd of elk appears to be all bulls. They've shed last year's antlers and wear only the velvet-covered nubs of spring. Part of the meadow has cast off its snowy coat and it's in this open area that they are grazing. Several are lying down, chewing their cud, like cows. But there is nothing else cowlike about them. All are alert, their ears constantly swiveling, frequently raising their heads to look around as they graze and chew.

Quietly moving deeper into the trees, I begin to circle around to their end of the meadow. I've done a little research on elk, reading up on their habitat and behavior. But seven hundred pounds of bone and muscle sure looks a lot bigger than I imagined.

The hunter understands the need to watch and wait, but I'm barely able to keep the beast restrained. Finally one of the smaller bulls on the edge of the herd drifts a bit toward the trees.

I tense, wait until he's broadside to me, then explode from the forest and slam myself hard into his front legs. He grunts as his bones crack. I sweep his legs out from under him, his shoulder smashes into the ground, and the earth resonates with the impact of his heavy rump.

Spinning, I leap onto his head as he rolls to his belly, struggling to get his broken legs under him. He tries to throw me off and I slip to the back of his neck and straddle him. He lunges under me, and I grip him *hard* at the base of the skull, my sharp nails penetrating his flesh, and reach around and grab his muzzle. As he tries to sling his head, I yank his nose sharply up and to the side. The vertebrae in his neck crunch and he collapses beneath me.

Still gripping him by the back of his neck, I release his nose and slice open his throat. His heart is still pumping, pumping, and I drink and drink. I succumb to the ecstasy that is his hot rich blood, and lose myself as I gorge.

Awareness comes back to me slowly. Bloated with excess blood, I sluggishly peel myself from the lifeless body and stand to contemplate the red river that is still draining from his torn throat. I shake my head at the waste. Hell, there's enough there for two or three meals, but I literally can't take in another drop. I stretch and look around me.

I feel a part of this natural world, because in a way I'm helping to feed it. The carcass will become dinner for others and nothing will go to waste. Some of those others are nearby, their scents drifting in the breeze as they await their turn. I detect a coyote and a skunk, and I've read there are bear here. I shudder. *That* would be a different ballgame. A scary one, I think.

Stepping back, I look again at the elk whose existence I'd just snuffed out. Part of me feels sad for him, as he was young and beautiful and just beginning his life. But the predator in me feels satisfied, and for once the hunger seems tamed.

I walk down to the water and wash off. No sense in bear-baiting tonight.

TUESDAY

CHAPTER 9

The sun is radiating through my bedroom curtains and alarm rips through me as I wake up. I'm not burning, but this will absolutely not do. Squinting, I roll over and look at the clock—9:27 AM. Way too early for me. I roll back and yank the quilt over my head. My irritation fades as the memories of last night surface.

I stayed on the mountain until nearly dawn, learning my new territory and becoming more enamored with the area. The forests and meadows were vibrantly alive with creatures great and small, and I made a mental list of all the intriguing flavors to sample. I smile, recalling how exhilarating it was to run the pine-covered mountainside top to bottom. I'm going to love it here.

Throwing off the covers, I get up and dress for the sun, since that is what's persistently leaking through the curtains at the moment. But the weather in this part of the country is known to be fickle. The locals have a saying: "If you don't like the weather, wait a minute—it'll change."

And it seems to be true. It switches back and forth between sunshine, clouds, and rain several times within a single day. The mountain storms have moods as well, and can be gentle showers or raging thunder and lightning. I set my hat and sunglasses and the umbrella next to the door.

My plan for the day is to do a little shopping before work, so I add heavy drapes to the list and quickly measure my windows.

I moved into the partially furnished house on Friday. I tend to live like a Spartan, with few possessions. But I do like a few comforts here and there, and make note of other things to pick up while out.

On the way to the car, I stop a moment to look up the mountain. *My* mountain. Guess I'll have to find out its name since it appears that we are going to be close friends.

I step out of the downtown boutique feeling quite satisfied with my shopping adventure. In addition to heavy curtains, I've found a few interesting odds and ends to add some décor to the house. I pause to look up at the clouds that have gathered overhead, grateful for their cover.

And then I feel it.

Something, or someone, is watching me. My gut clenches and an electric charge shoots through me, making my skin crawl as every hair on my body stands up. Alarmed, I step to the curb and study the people and cars nearby, trying to find the source of the eerie attention.

And then I see *him*.

He is standing directly across the street, focusing intently on *me*.

As I peer back at the tall figure in the long, tailored coat, at his striking looks, his stillness, his pale skin, everything in me slams to a stop.

He is like me. He is . . . just . . . like . . . me.

I freeze, unsure of what to do. Since I was reborn to this life, I have always been alone. I've never encountered one of my kind—except the one who brutally ripped away my humanity and left me for dead.

One of my kind. The thought chills me as I fight the rising panic. And while my mind races, he gives me a small smile, a slight nod, and is gone. Just vanishes, too fast for even my eyes.

My insides churn and I stand locked to the sidewalk, unable to move, my gaze pinned to the spot in which he'd stood. People flow around me, like water in a river, until I get bumped. I snarl and nearly lash out, but catch myself, and with a final anxious look across the street, head to my car.

CHAPTER 10

I walk into the house and set my bags on the couch. My new job starts in a couple of hours, and I feel so unsettled that I debate whether or not to show up. I think about going up the mountain and just staying there. I could do it, I could survive up there with little problem.

But the one thing in this life that I crave, almost more than blood, is companionship. The isolation I endure tortures my very soul, and I just can't stay away from people for long. I *need* to be around them, even if being with them requires absolute secrecy and unrelenting control.

I head to the shower. I need some time to think.

~

His image remains frozen in my mind. There's something vaguely familiar about it, almost like a dream.

But I don't dream. At least I don't think I do.

Tall, with a medium-to-slender build, his dark hair in sharp contrast to his pale skin. And those eyes . . . those green eyes penetrating mine even from across the street, watching me, questioning me. "*Who are you?*" they appeared to ask. They seem so familiar.

I study the woman in the mirror as she gets dressed, wondering what he saw. He knew I was like him, but what did he think of me? He looked so confident, so strong, and I felt so unsure, so vulnerable. Did he see me as friend, or kin, or did he see an interloper, a trespasser?

And the next question—are there others?

I decide to go to work, to keep trying to make it here in my new home, to not give in to my paranoia and run—again. I grab my bag and walk out.

The evening is purple and the mountain smiles down at me. I take a deep, cold breath, inhaling the rich aromas of the forest life. The hunter in me growls in satisfaction. I *can* do this.

Heading down the highway to the Springs, traffic is light, as most of the evening commuters are coming up the pass to their homes in the scattered mountain towns. I park in a nearby garage and walk the block or so to the club.

Jerry, the craggy-faced manager who hired me, grunts and introduces me to the other bartender, Shauna. She's older, a bit rough around the edges, but seems friendly enough. She shows me the bar setup and storage areas. All pretty simple, all pretty much the same. Which is good, because I'm having trouble concentrating on work.

I can't stop thinking about *him.*

The evening gets off to a slow start. Thankfully, Shauna does not seem to be one for mindless talk, at least with me. Jerry sticks around but stays in the back much of the night. Tina, the streaky-haired waitress, is a babbler and talks about nothing but guys, the ones she's dated and the ones she wants to.

The customers tonight are mostly military, although they try to look otherwise. They come in groups of two or three, have a couple of drinks, then leave. A few try to engage me in conversation. I stay polite but reserved. Fortunately, they get the message and no one hassles me. Closing time finally arrives and Shauna shows me the cleanup and setup duties. I didn't do too well in tips tonight, but no one else did either. Jerry counts out the till and asks me to come in early tomorrow so he can show me how to set up the cash.

I tell everyone goodnight and head out the door. The clouds are hanging heavy in the cold air—maybe it'll snow. I walk up the street toward the parking garage.

Then, out of nowhere—there he is. He's standing on the sidewalk about thirty feet ahead, watching me.

Something extremely powerful radiates from him. Energy, aura, I don't know what to call it, but I can feel it in every cell of my body, and it's very disturbing.

I hesitate, then take a breath and keep walking. He waits, and I slow as I draw near, and finally stop.

He studies me a moment while fear races through my veins.

"Would you like to get something to drink?" he asks.

My mind shies away from what he might mean by *drink* and I hesitate before answering.

"A cup of hot tea would be nice."

"Tea. That sounds perfect. There is an all-night coffee shop around the corner. Would you care to walk with me?" His voice is cultured, with a hint of European, but I can't place the accent.

I pause, then join him as he proceeds up the street. My body and mind are both numb. I didn't expect to see him again so soon. But apparently he expected to see me.

We arrive at the coffee shop. He holds the door open, and I walk through and wait as he comes in. Nodding to me, he heads to a booth in the back and I admire his physique as he passes. He's about six-three, trim, but there are definitely muscles beneath his expensive, tailored suit.

I'm stirred from my trance as he graciously waves his hand to one of the seats. I make my way to the booth and he waits until I'm seated before sitting across from me.

The waitress comes to the table and offers us menus.

"We will have two cups of hot tea," he says without looking at her. She nods, staring, then walks away.

She was staring, as I am, because he has the most beautiful and mesmerizing face I've ever seen. His features are noble, refined, elegant, his nose straight and his jaw strong. His age is hard to decipher. Physically, thirtyish. But bearing? Ageless. Ancient.

"So. You are new to the city. How long have you been in Colorado Springs?" His hair is raven black, and his eyes, light emerald green, flicker with intensity.

"About a week," I reply, hoping the trembling in my body isn't leaking into my voice.

"Tell me, then—where are you from? What brought you here?" His tone, though friendly, seems to carry an undercurrent of warning. I choose my answer carefully.

"I'm from the West Coast. I decided to try somewhere new, and this area looked like it had a lot to offer."

He smiles and nods as the waitress sets cups and stainless steel teapots on the table. We prepare our tea in heavy silence.

Picking up a spoon, he stirs his and asks, "Are you here with anyone else?"

I hesitate, unwilling to reveal how defenseless I might be. But then the beast in me sits up and reminds me I'm not.

"No, I'm alone."

"Hmm." His green eyes reveal nothing.

We sip our tea.

He sets down his cup, his intense gaze fixed on me, and, leaning forward, breathes in deeply through his nose.

"You have a most unusual scent. I cannot quite place it," he says as he sits back.

A bit shocked, I stare at him. No one has ever *smelled* me before, at least not like that.

Perhaps this is a custom among our kind? Unsure, I discreetly take in *his* scent.

It's quite different from any I've ever encountered, yet there's also something familiar about it. The blood in his veins has an exotic, rich fragrance that's very alluring. But there's another aroma woven in, one I finally recognize. It's the coppery-sweet smell of human blood.

And it's carried on his breath.

I was afraid of that.

"If you do not mind me asking, where is it that you obtain your . . . sustenance?" He takes another sip of tea. His eyes never leave mine.

"The . . . the mountains near my home."

"The mountains? West of the city?" He looks puzzled.

"Yes. Is that someone else's territory?"

He laughs.

"Someone *else's* territory? No. My concern, though, is that the population up there is a bit sparse, and too many disappearances could draw unwanted attention."

I swallow as scenes from horror movies, of human throats and fangs, flash through my head.

"That . . . that won't be a problem."

"Indeed. Then perhaps next time I may accompany you?"

"Uh, sure." Though I doubt his diet includes anything on four legs.

His answering smile is warm and appears genuine. I can't tell if he's aware of the turmoil he's sparking within me.

"Good. However, I would like to see you again before then. Do you enjoy the theater?" He watches me over the brim of his cup as he finishes his tea.

My mind spinning, I fumble for an excuse to turn him down. And fail.

"I haven't been to the theater in a long time."

"Then you must come with me." His tone indicates he is not accustomed to being denied.

"I . . . I'll think about it."

"Nonsense. Are you available Friday night? I have season tickets."

"I work until two-thirty that night."

"Work?" He frowns.

"Yes, I tend bar at the club you saw me leave. I just started there tonight."

"This is something you do often?"

"The last three years. At clubs on the coast." I'm puzzled by his reaction.

"Hmm. I find that interesting. In fact, I find *you* interesting, very interesting. I look forward to getting to know you." He smiles that genuine smile again, his eyes warm and friendly.

But I don't trust him. Part of me is terrified of him, and yet, the other part of me—the part that is tired of being alone—is becoming captivated by him. I quell my thoughts as the waitress brings us the check.

He picks it up and, with a tip of his head to me, asks, "Shall we?"

Nodding, I stand and he follows me to the register. I can feel his energy emanating behind me, like a powerful electric force field. It's unnerving, yet enticing.

He pays and we head out the door. He walks me to my car, which makes me even more nervous, because now he knows my license plate. However, I suspect he already knew. He certainly seemed to know where my car was parked.

"Perhaps we can meet when you are not working. Would you like me to show you around the city? We have several museums and galleries specializing in the history of the area that you may find fascinating."

"I'd like that." I'm fascinated already, and not in museums and galleries.

"How is Friday? We can meet at the coffee shop if you like. Say . . . noon?"

"One o'clock would be better for me." Hopefully I'll be awake in time.

"Then one it is. I am looking forward to it. And now, I must say good-night." He returns my smile and bows slightly and, with a brief ruffling of the cold air, is no longer there.

I didn't even get his name.

ΛꟿϽᚼᛖᚺϽᛏ ϽᛩΛϽᛏᛏϽ

IIV⋇

április 3., kedd

Today, upon my return from Denver, I felt an uninvited and foreign presence in my city. My initial reaction was to hunt it down and destroy it for the sheer audacity of entering without permission. But my investigation revealed it to be a female, alone, and there was something quite strange, yet familiar, about her. Almost haunting, as if I have met her before. I know not yet what new threat this may be, but I will find out. She lives, for now.

The Elders knew nothing of her. When I returned from making my inquiries, she had disappeared from the city. I hunted for several hours, but was unable to locate her. Then, tonight after leaving Club Vér, I felt her again. I traced her to a downtown bar and waited.

She nearly ran when she saw me. She feigns innocence, but I am not sure it is an act. I have the distinct impression she has no knowledge of who I am.

Our conversation in the café gave me the opportunity to observe her a little more closely. Her scent is unknown to me, yet it carries a familiarity I cannot explain. As earlier, I almost feel as though I have seen her before, perhaps in a dream. But dreams are for those who sleep.

What caught my attention, though, was her complete lack of any human blood scent. She did not appear to be suffering from hunger, as her eyes were a pale, glacial blue—they were quite enchanting, I might add. I can only surmise that perhaps she does not feed on humans, which is highly unusual among The Chosen.

I was pleased when she agreed to meet with me again, which gives me time to verify her story.

I tracked her as she left the city and headed west into the mountains. At one point she abandoned her car and vanished into the forest on foot. I was called away shortly afterward and do not know if she returned. I have no choice now but to wait for our meeting. In the meantime, I will be watching for her.

And as I write this, it occurs to me that I do not even know her name.

THURSDAY

CHAPTER 11

It's Thursday night, and my shift is almost over. I glance again at the clock. My new coworkers must not think much of me at this point. Since I began this job, I've been distracted and detached. The detachment is not new, but I usually maintain it with a little more grace. The distraction, though, is a bit unusual for me.

I just can't seem to get him out of my head. My thoughts continually revolve around him and the world he may represent. He was well-dressed and well-mannered and undeniably good looking. His self-assurance and sophistication could only belong to someone who is at the top of society. The question is—whose society?

I'm shaken out of my mental ramblings as I realize that he is not just in my head. He is *here*. In the bar. Right now.

He walks to a table near the door, gives me a smile and nod, then, unbuttoning his jacket, sits down.

Tina heads to his table to take his order. His low, cultured voice asks for a glass of merlot, and I hear her stammer something unintelligible in reply. She hurries back to the bar.

"Oh my God! Did you see what just walked in? He's gorgeous! He has the most beautiful green eyes I've ever seen! I felt like I could just fall right into them!" Tina, blushing bright red, fans herself.

I haven't agreed with Tina on anything, but on this, I do.

However, all I say is, "What did he order?"

She glances back at him, blushes again, and says, "Wine. Um, merlot. A glass of merlot."

I hand her the glass I already poured and look up at him as she sets it on her tray. His expression of disdain is fierce, almost feral, but he quickly smoothes his features before she turns around and heads back to his table. She shakily sets the glass down, almost spilling it. He thanks her and hands her a bill, telling her to keep the change. She blushes and mumbles a thank you and comes back to the bar, eyes wide.

"He gave me a twenty and told me to keep the change! Oh my God, I think I'm in love!"

Tina's always falling in love, and in this case it might be warranted. However, judging from his expression, perhaps pretty dangerous, too.

Shauna strolls over to me, nodding. "Now that's something you don't see every day. He looks like some fancy guy from an old movie or something. That's class."

I glance over at him. He smiles, takes a sip of his wine, and stands to leave. He moves like a dancer. Or a big cat. More the latter, I think.

"Oh, he's leaving already," whines Tina.

Shauna shakes her head. "Too bad. Sure is nice on the eyes."

He walks out the door without looking back. I start cleaning up and Shauna mutters something about it being a little early to do that, but I ignore her.

As the last customer leaves at two o'clock, I finish drying the remaining glasses. I check to be sure everything is in order, then ask Shauna if there is anything else she'd like me to do.

She frowns and says, "Naw, I guess you can take off. We'll see you tomorrow night."

I grab my bag from the back and head out the door. He's waiting on the sidewalk for me.

"Hello again," he says, his voice deep, rich.

"Hello."

"I thought I would drop by to see if your plans might have changed."

I think he means if my mind has changed. He undoubtedly can sense my insecurity.

"No, I'm still planning on meeting you tomorrow. One o'clock, right?"

"Yes, if that is convenient for you. I have several places I thought we could visit, and we should have plenty of time before you need to report to work." He smiles, a hint of amusement on his refined features.

"But," he says, "I am remiss and must apologize for my lack of manners. Let me introduce myself. My name is Nicolas Ambrus."

Nicolas Ambrus. If I could blush, I would. Even his name is tantalizing.

"I'm Sunshine. Sunshine Martin. But most people just call me Sunny." It's not the first time I've felt embarrassed by my name, but somehow I am even more so at this moment.

"Sunny! How delightful!" He chuckles, definitely amused now. "Well, then, Sunny, I will see you tomorrow." He smiles warmly and dips his head. "I bid you goodnight."

And he disappears—again.

How does he DO that? I wonder if he'll teach me.

április 5., csütörtök

I visited her workplace tonight and all seems to be as she claimed. I am quite puzzled—I do not see what attracts her. The bar was filthy with the stink of unwashed lower-class humans. The waitress practically begged me to take her, but she was clearly below my normal standards.

The female has a most unusual name for one of our dark nature. Sunshine, of all things! With any other Chosen, I would assume she adopted it out of arrogance and perhaps as an enticement. However, with this one I am not so sure. She does seem quite fearful of me, and I will need to handle her carefully so I can learn why she is really here and who might have sent her.

I must admit, I do find her very intriguing.

FRIDAY

CHAPTER 12

After trying on nearly everything decent I own, I settle on a light blue angora sweater with a dark blue tailored jacket and matching slacks, wishing I'd had time to shop for something new to wear. I add a wide-brimmed hat and gloves—the weather here is too unpredictable to count on this morning's cloud cover remaining throughout the day. Frustrated and nervous, I grab my purse, get into the car, and head down the pass to the Springs.

A date. A real date—my first in over five years—and with someone from whom I don't have to guard my secret, or worry about accidentally killing. Someone who, despite my attraction to him, scares the hell out of me.

It's a little before 1:00 PM when I get to the coffee shop. My nerves are so jacked up, I'm sure everyone can see me shaking.

Just as I sit down at the booth in the back, Nicolas comes in the door and smiles in greeting. He's dressed more casually than in our previous encounters, wearing black slacks and a dark grey cashmere sweater that reveals the sculpted muscles previously hidden beneath his suit. I stand as he approaches the booth.

"You look very nice today. Please, sit for a moment." He sits across from me. "How are you? You look well rested."

He has that amused smile again.

I suspect he means well fed. My eyes are palest blue today, and I notice that his are very pale green. Seems like we both prepared for a day of close contact with people.

"Yes, I am. Thank you." I return his smile.

"Well then, shall we?" He stands and offers me his hand.

His hand. I hesitate, then reach out. As his fingers touch mine, a warm vibration pulsates up my arm and throughout my entire body. My breath catches and I look up to see him staring at me, wonder etched across his face. Standing, I quickly release his hand, shift my gaze ahead of me, and walk to the front of the café.

His cool skin had warmed an instant after we touched, as had mine, and I marvel over the sensation that raced through me. His reaction leads me to believe that not only did he feel it, too, but that this is something that doesn't usually happen.

I can't wait for him to touch me again.

As we reach the door, I barely remember to put on my hat and sunglasses. He laughs lightly, touching my hat. "Very fetching."

I grin in embarrassment as he puts on his own sunglasses and we step outside under the awning. The sun is peeking through the clouds. I pull my jacket around me and tug on my gloves, and notice him giving me a puzzled glance.

I also notice *he* isn't wearing a hat, jacket, or gloves.

And he isn't burning.

Huh.

We walk a half-dozen blocks or so to the Colorado Springs Fine Arts Center, where they have a museum and several galleries. Nicolas takes me through many of the exhibits, explaining this bit of history or that artist.

He's right—I do find it all quite fascinating. But not as fascinating as I'm finding him. I'm enthralled by him. I listen as he talks, absorbing the cadence of his speech, the grace of his movements, the flash of his smiles.

As we're leaving, I laugh at something he says and we walk outside.

The sun is now high overhead. The hat and the gloves are in my bag.

My exposed skin feels as though flames are racing across it. I look down to see my hands turning bright pink and can feel my face doing the same.

I freeze outside the door as panic takes over all thoughts. Nicolas peers down at me, frowning.

"Sunny?"

"Nicolas, I have to get back inside." I try to keep the alarm from my voice. He steps ahead and opens the door, holding my elbow to usher me in. We quickly make our way to the restrooms and he stops me before I go in, worry lines creasing his face.

"Are you all right? Is there anything I can do?"

"Yes, no. I . . . I'll be fine. The burn will fade soon. I just need to get some cool water on my hands and face." I squeeze his arm, walk into the restroom, and look in the mirror.

The burn doesn't look as bad as it feels. Bending over the sink, I splash water on my face several times. The pink starts to fade and the burning sensation lessens to a tingle.

I wait a few more moments, take a deep breath, and go back out into the lobby area. Nicolas is right outside the door. He gently grasps my shoulders as he examines my face, then sliding his hands down, takes my wrists to look at the back of my hands.

"This has happened before?" he asks.

"Yes. Anytime my skin is exposed to the direct sun." I look at him, wondering why he doesn't seem to be affected in the same way.

"I see. Well, Sunny, I must say that you have a most ironic name." His amused smile is softer than usual, with a trace of sympathy.

"I've frequently thought so myself." I get the hat and gloves out of my bag, and as I put them on, ask, "Why is it you don't burn?"

His answering smile is serious now. "I assume you have many questions, as do I." He glances at the scattered tourists wandering past us. "But we will save that discussion for another time."

I nod in agreement, wondering when—and where—that discussion might happen.

We walk back to the front door. Nicolas looks me over, tugging my hat down a little on one side, and touches my now pale cheek.

"We do not want to damage that beautiful porcelain skin." Smiling, he pushes open the door and holds it for me.

If I could blush, it would definitely be turning pink again.

We walk back down the street in the direction of the parking garage and stop in several small galleries and shops along the way, laughing and making idle conversation. The rest of the day passes quickly and, too soon, we are at my car.

"My dear, I have had a delightful afternoon with you. We should do this another time. But I think we will wait for a cloudier day." His expression is sober, but the amusement is dancing in his green eyes.

"Well, I'm usually more careful about being covered when the sun is out. I guess I was a little distracted when we walked outside." I shrug, embarrassed by my stupidity.

"Then I must apologize." His mouth quirks. "I will make an effort to avoid distracting you in the future."

That's impossible. His very existence is distracting me.

"And speaking of the future, when can we get together again?" he asks.

A little dazed by his continued interest, I try not to stutter my answer. "I have both Sunday and Monday nights off."

"Indeed." He purses his lips. "Do you like the opera? There is a small theater here that has a performance Sunday evening."

"I . . . I would love to go. I've never been to an opera."

"Wonderful! The performance starts at seven. Shall we meet at our little coffee shop at, say, six? We can have a cup of tea and then drive over in my car, if you would like."

Our little coffee shop?

"Uh, that would be fine. I'll meet you there at six on Sunday." I smile, feeling even more off balance.

"Then it is settled. And now, my dear, I must let you go or you will be late for your work," he says warmly.

"Oh, you're right." I glance at my watch. "Thank you for giving me such a wonderful tour of the city. I really enjoyed this afternoon, in spite of the sun. I can't recall when I've had such a nice time."

"And I, as well. I hope your work is satisfying tonight. I look forward to seeing you on Sunday." He nods as he turns from me.

And then he just walks away. No disappearing act this time.

Good, cuz it kinda spooks me.

I drive home after my shift, thinking about this afternoon. What an unbelievable day. I haven't been able to be so relaxed with someone since this whole nightmare of a life started. To be able to be myself and not have to worry about my secret and what I am. I think of his charm, his humor, his kindness, and how easy it is to be with him, and I realize I might be in trouble. I feel so drawn to him that it scares me. *He* scares me. There is something powerful lurking beneath that polished surface, and I'm not sure I want to know what it is.

But I think I'm going find out.

április 6., péntek

I spent the day with the Sun, in the form of an innocent Chosen who is not all she appears to be.

Her reaction to the sunlight when we stepped outside of the museum was not that of a mature Chosen who can move about during the day. Rather, her skin burned like that of a newborn, and she appeared to be in some distress and pain from it.

I truly do not know what to make of this.

And when we touched, the instant heat that flared in my blood caught me by complete surprise. I am inexplicably drawn to her in a way I have not felt in a very long time, and am greatly puzzled by the sense of familiarity I feel when with her.

I am now most curious about her and wait impatiently for our next rendezvous.

SUNDAY

CHAPTER 13

When I arrive at the coffee shop, he's already there, waiting for me at the back booth. He stands as I approach, saying, "My, but you do look lovely this evening. How are you?"

"Thank you. I'm well," I lie.

The past couple of days have been beyond difficult as I have thought of nothing but Nicolas. I've spent the last two nights running the mountain until dawn, staying out as late as I dare. The days have been worse. I'm not sleeping as long, so I've ended up driving throughout half the state, looking for new hunting areas and trying to keep myself occupied.

Nicolas orders tea from the waitress and tells me a little of what to expect at the opera. I listen, drinking in his words, while part of me wonders what this power is that he seems to have over me. I watch his face, the way his eyes light up, the curve of his lip, strong and soft at the same time.

"Sunny?"

"What?"

"I asked if you were ready to go." He looks at me, eyebrows arched.

"Oh, yes. Sorry." Embarrassment tugs at my face before I can hide it.

The corners of his mouth twitch and Nicolas stands, his green eyes laughing. He offers his hand and I rise, and once again my skin tingles at his touch. He studies me, looking thoughtful as he drapes my long coat over my shoulders. Thankfully it's late enough in the evening that I don't need my hat or gloves.

We walk to the parking level where I normally park. A few rows over from my BMW is a handsome black Jaguar sedan, fairly new. I smile at the emblem of the leaping cat. Yeah, that looks like what he would drive.

Nicolas helps me into his car, its interior masculine and immaculate, like him. I breathe in the smell of him, complemented by the scent of rich leather, and another part of me crumbles.

He tells me a little about the part of downtown that we are passing through. There is so much history in this area, and I pay close attention, determined not to be caught daydreaming again.

The opera is like nothing I've ever experienced. For a little while I'm able to focus more on it and less on Nicolas, although I never lose the awareness I have of him by my side. He seems to enjoy my absorption in the performance as much as he does the opera itself.

"Well," he says as we are pulling out of the parking lot. "What did you think of it?"

"It was amazing. I never realized what beautiful instruments human voices could be."

"Humans do have many fine talents." But there is an odd tone to his voice, and I'm not sure what it means.

We park next to my car and he helps me out of the Jag.

"I must say, I do enjoy spending time with you, Sunny. I had a very pleasant evening, and I hope you did as well." He smiles and continues to hold my hand as he walks me to my car.

"Oh, I did. Thank you for introducing me to the opera, and to this city. I'm afraid I would have missed out on an important part of the area without your company." I doubt I would have been interested without it.

"Ah, well, there is much more that I would like to show you." His look is, as usual, a little amused, but a little mysterious as well.

"Actually, I think it's my turn to show *you*. You were curious about where I 'obtain my sustenance' when we first met. Are you still?" Though I've been planning to ask him along on a hunt, I instantly regret my decision to do so now.

Too late to take it back. But it's best to make it clear what I feed on, before we get in any deeper. It would certainly be exhilarating to hunt with another of my kind—if he'll participate, that is.

"Yes. Yes, I am. Very much so," he replies. His expression shifts, becoming more intense.

"I could even give you a little tour of the mountain area. How does tomorrow evening sound?" I ask, part of me hoping he will say no.

"That would be perfect. Where would you like to meet?" He listens as I give him directions to one of the lakes north of Cascade.

"I thank you, Sunny, for spending the evening with me. I am looking forward to our meeting tomorrow." He smiles, but his eyes still shine with intensity.

"Well, thank *you* again for the opera. And, uh, tomorrow? Wear your running shoes." I give him a slightly wicked smile.

He raises his eyebrows. "Running shoes. Hmm. All right, I will."

As I'm driving home, I reflect on the evening and how it ended. I'm so stupid sometimes.

I'm more than a little concerned that I invited him to go hunting with me so soon. I don't know why I did that. We've only spent a short time together and I should have waited until I knew him better. I'm pretty sure venison, or anything like it, is not on his menu. I haven't detected any blood but that of human on his breath. And part of me is petrified of that.

But the other part of me worries what he thinks about the blood on my breath. Does he know it's not human? He said he couldn't place my scent.

Crap. Even worse—what if he thinks I'm an animal because that's what I hunt? I have trouble imagining him, with his cultured sophistication, bringing down a deer or an elk and feeding on it. What's he going to think of me, my face smeared with animal blood?

If he *does* hunt, what will it be like to hunt with another of my kind? If we even *are* the same kind. I'm beginning to suspect we are not as alike as I had first imagined.

My thoughts jumbled, I realize I'm way out of my element. I have no idea what proper protocol might be when hunting with another. I don't know if there are rules, or consequences for breaking them, but I'm sure he does.

At least I had the presence of mind to choose a hunting area well away from my home and my mountain. The lake we're meeting at is one of several I scouted the first couple of days here, and there shouldn't be any trouble finding game. Who knows, maybe he'll like it. Or not.

I spin my tires up the driveway, yank the key from the ignition, and stalk into the house. The jittery agitation building in me feels like the worst-imaginable caffeine overload. I start to open my laptop, then slam the lid down. A hot shower doesn't even sound good. To hell with it, even though I just fed last night, there's only one thing that will calm me down. I quickly change my clothes and head up the mountain.

április 8., vasámap

I am quite taken with this blue-eyed beauty. Her shy innocence and charm are so fresh, so humanlike, that I have trouble remembering she is a Chosen. I do not believe I have ever encountered anyone, of either species, who is so enchanting.

And the touch of her skin, the warmth it brings—is extraordinary.

She has invited me to accompany her tomorrow, and I am most curious as to what I will witness. My initial suspicion that she does not feed on humans seems to be substantiated by the fact that I have not yet detected any trace of human blood beneath her exotic aroma.

She asked me to wear running shoes, of all things. Tomorrow we shall see what manner of Chosen this creature truly is.

MONDAY

CHAPTER 14

About a mile up the dirt road that leads to the lake, I pull into a turnout. He is not here yet, and I wait, anxious, wondering if he decided not to show, or if my directions were bad, or if he's just not here yet. My mind has been a whirlwind these last few days, with thoughts of Nicolas and all my conflicting emotions spinning relentlessly through my head.

Car lights approach from behind me and I hold my breath, waiting. The Jaguar pulls off the road and parks. I breathe a small sigh of relief and get out.

He is dressed as I am, sweater and jeans in dark colors, and is wearing black running shoes. I smile in greeting and teasingly comment, "Well, you do own a pair of running shoes. Or did you have to buy them especially for tonight?"

He chuckles and looks down at them, appearing somewhat embarrassed. "I suppose they do look brand new. We will just have to break them in."

My quiet laugh triggers one from him, then he takes my hand and asks, "And how have you been since I last saw you?"

"Busy," I reply. Busy going crazy over him. "And you?"

"Ah, I have been a bit . . . preoccupied." He doesn't elaborate, but he looks at me intensely.

Hmm, thinking about me? I can only hope. Or not. He still scares the hell out of me.

"Well, then, are you ready?" I ask. He nods, and together we set out up the road, bathed in shadow from the towering pines.

The moon is half full tonight and its light shines through a break in the trees up ahead. We step into the bright patch on the road, and I glance at Nicolas and stop in amazement. His pale, perfect face and hands are almost glowing in the moonlight, like the snow that still dots the landscape. I look down at my own hands. I guess they do as well.

"The moonlight does you great honor. You really are quite beautiful. Perhaps you should change your name from Sunny to Luna," he says quietly, smiling.

I laugh and beckon him on. As we step into the shadows, I veer off the road and into the trees.

Laughing again, I break into a run. I can feel him racing along behind, leaping over the fallen branches and rocks that dot the forest floor. I jump onto a boulder and look back, smiling as he clears a downed tree, then launch myself across a small stream. Running and ducking tree limbs, we burst through a small opening in the forest, and laughing wildly, I come to an abrupt stop.

"So, how're those new shoes working out?" I ask, grinning as I turn to look at him.

Nicolas doesn't answer. His eyes are feral, tinged with red, his expression intense and savage. He looks at me strangely, then seems to come back to himself. He takes a breath.

"Well enough. So far they are holding up, but I am not sure they were designed for this." He's still serious, though. His normal amusement seems to be buried beneath that something else that lies within him.

Perhaps we better get down to the business of hunting.

I start off across the meadow at a walk, shifting my attention to the surrounding forest. He follows quietly, but I can feel him watching me as I start casting about the air for scent.

We climb up a small slope, and I pause at the top, inhaling the breezes that are swirling around it. I catch a faint hint, glance at Nicolas, and head off down the hill. We slip through the trees, my silent partner and I, and the scent grows stronger.

Moonlight is breaking through the pines up ahead. We slow, creeping along without a sound. As we approach the small clearing, I see three bull elk grazing by a beaver pond. Like the elk from last week, their antlers have just started growing. Soft and covered in velvet, they are only four to five inches long and shouldn't get in the way.

I melt back into the trees, Nicolas following.

"I'm going to work my way around to the other side of the clearing," I whisper. "When you sense me near the big log, walk straight out toward them. If they start angling to the left of the pond, you need to move quickly in that direction. That will force them to veer around to my side."

He nods, eyes blazing. We steal back to the edge of the trees, and I point out where he should move and where I will be. I leave him and circle the meadow, gliding quietly through the woods, then stop at a point about three yards behind the log and crouch, waiting for him to make his move.

I can see the elk, still near their original positions.

And then I see Nicolas. He once again reminds me of a big cat, a panther perhaps. I catch my breath in admiration as he saunters out from the trees with steely grace. The elk startle, and with steaming breath and heads held high, begin trotting toward the pond. They drift to the left, and Nicolas sprints forward, cutting them off. They then swerve, their hooves pounding the ground as they gallop in my direction. He stops and they slow back to a trot, heads turned to watch him.

As they start to pass me, I spring onto the log and launch high at the right side of the nearest one, wrapping my arms around the base of his neck as I slam onto him. He grunts loudly and staggers. I hook my heel into his left flank and dig my hand deep into the flesh in front of his shoulder. Reaching up with my right, I grab his throat just below the jaw, and *squeeze*. His thick flesh and coat give way to my sharp grasp and his windpipe begins to collapse.

Bucking and lunging, he wheezes as he tries to dislodge me. I grip tighter, crushing his airway in a spray of blood, then sharply yank his neck to the right. He crashes to the earth, gasping in vain, and I scramble to the safety of his back as his deadly hooves start raking the ground. I pull his neck around even farther, and reaching over with my other hand, grab his muzzle and jerk hard toward my shoulder. His neck breaks with an audible snap and he goes limp.

Shifting, I sink my teeth into his ragged throat and begin taking his blood as it pumps out from his still beating heart, my mind quickly lost in its hot embrace.

Awareness of Nicolas standing next to me breaks through my feeding fog. In a moment of coherence, I force myself to break away and invite him in. He slowly shakes his head and gestures for me to continue. I'm too immersed in the song of the blood to insist. Returning to the glistening red maw that was once a throat, I drink until the last spark of life flares out.

I stay there a moment, trying to regain my senses, and finally release the elk. I start to stand, and Nicolas reaches down to help me to my feet. His eyes a crimson blaze, he pulls me to him and takes my shoulders. He stares down into my own red-veiled eyes and kisses me, long and deep.

His lips keep their promise of soft yet firm, and my knees nearly buckle at the warm, tingling sensation his kiss sends throughout my body.

My blood reignites, though I have just fed. But it is singing a new song, one I have never heard.

Before I can respond, Nicolas slowly breaks away and, still holding my shoulders, says huskily, "Yes. A most unique taste."

I don't know if he means the elk, or me.

He releases me and steps back, his eyes wild and hungry.

"You are an exquisite creature, standing here in the moonlight, wearing the blood of your prey. I do believe you are the most beautiful and deadly huntress I have ever seen."

I'm spellbound, by the blood and by him. I look at Nicolas, his perfect features, his lithe and agile body, his gentle but fierce manner. And I feel my soul falling into an abyss . . . one from which it may not be able—or want—to escape.

The yip of a fox breaks the spell. I look around, sensing the other hunters and scavengers awaiting their turns.

"We need to leave." I look at Nicolas and indicate the dead elk. "This now belongs to the forest."

He scents the air, looking around as well, but says nothing. I walk down to the pond to clean up and he follows, waiting until I am done washing. He takes my hand and we walk across the little meadow. As we step into the trees on the other side, I look back and point.

"See?"

Nicolas turns and watches as a fox and her two kits tear into the carcass. A huge raccoon shambles along the edge of the trees toward the feast, hoping to get its share.

"Ah," he says, smiling for the first time in a while. "It seems you hunt for more than yourself."

"Well, it sorta works out that way. I feel as though it's a payment for the life I take."

He looks at me oddly, gives a small laugh, and tousles my hair. "You are quite the enigma. How did you get to be this way?"

I shake my head. "I don't know. But I do know of a place where we can sit and have one of those conversations you promised."

He smiles and nods.

"But first, um, well, would *you* like to hunt? I mean, if you weren't hungry before, you must be now." Even though his eyes at this moment have faded back to green, they are dark. I know how blood can ignite the hunger, no matter how well fed one might be.

Soberly, he reaches out and gently brushes my lips with his fingertips. "No. I've had what I want tonight. I wish to savor it for a while."

I don't think he means the elk.

CHAPTER 15

We walk through the trees in the direction of the large reservoir. Nicolas seems to be as deep in thought as I am. He has a quiet and steady presence, and it feels so right to have him here by my side.

We finally come to the edge of the forest overlooking the lake. I point down to a rock outcrop that juts out high above the water and we make our way down the slope to its base. There is a flat boulder near the top, a perfect bench. We scale the natural tower of stones, Nicolas helping me climb the rocks.

I chuckle quietly to myself. He is ever the gentleman. I could make it to the top in about two jumps, and I'm sure he knows that.

We sit down on the boulder and gaze out across the partially thawed lake. The moon's reflection, muted and soft on the ice, creates sparkles on the surface of the water like tiny stars. I look up and see the real stars scattered across the night sky. Pikes Peak towers to the south, standing majestic and proud, its slopes glistening with snow.

I look at Nicolas, and can't help but compare him to the Peak as his face reflects the moonlight.

"Well, what do you think of my tour so far?" I ask quietly.

He pauses a moment before answering.

"Sunny, I do not believe I have ever heard an opera whose songs are as rich as the music of this forest." He looks out over the lake. "And I must admit that the artworks I have shown you pale in comparison."

He gestures slowly at the scenery around us. "Nor have I seen a portrait or a landscape that can come close to this."

Nicolas turns his gaze on me and gently cups my cheek. "And I have never seen a sculpture that surpasses this."

I look down, not knowing what to say.

"And so I must ask you . . . How did you come to be this way?" he gently demands, repeating his earlier question.

"I'm not sure I understand what you mean." I look up at him, searching his face.

"Who was your Maker? Who brought you into this life?"

"I . . . I don't really know."

"You do not know? Did he not give you his name as he schooled you to our ways?" His surprise is colored with a hint of outrage.

I pause a moment before I reply.

"I wasn't schooled in anything. The last thing I clearly remember of my old life was being dragged out of my broken car window and some monster tearing at my throat. He took me somewhere, and I have hazy memories of him biting and feeding from me again and again. I don't know how many days it went on, but eventually I woke up in a dark room, alone."

He looks shocked, then grows thoughtful.

"Please, continue," he says gravely.

"Well, I screamed and pounded on the door, but no one came. There were no windows, no furniture, no food or water. I remember being so hungry and thirsty, and half out of my mind. I finally got so desperate that I began tearing at the door, and to my surprise, it started to come apart. I ripped a hole in it large enough to climb through and made my escape.

"The room I'd been in was inside an abandoned warehouse. I was so afraid he was going to hear me and come to kill me or lock me up again. I made my way to a door, and it opened, so I left as quickly and quietly as I could." I stop and he squeezes my hand. I begin again.

"He had taken me to a rundown area near a harbor, but I had no idea which harbor. I started walking, and as I looked around I realized that I felt different somehow. It was night, and there was no moon and no streetlights, yet I could see everything as though it were daytime. I could hear sounds from a long distance, and the scurry of something small, maybe rodents, nearby.

"Smells started to overwhelm me, and then . . . then this *hunger* grabbed hold. I felt like my stomach was going to eat itself, and I was so thirsty, and then it got worse. It was torture, like being on fire all through my insides, and my stomach and throat felt as though flames were raging within them."

I break off, feeling a sense of horror as I vividly remember the hellish burning.

Nicolas reaches over and, stroking my cheek, says, "Go on."

"I stumbled down the street, holding my stomach, and could think of nothing else but the hunger and the pain. And then I became aware of a smell. It was rich and wonderful, and I forgot all about my stomach and followed the scent. I traced it to a fenced area behind an abandoned building. The gate was open and I went inside.

"The smell seemed to lead directly to a pair of stray dogs that were digging around near a trash bin. They didn't seem to hear me as I came through the gate. I stopped, and the hunger started raging again, and all I could see were these dogs. Then they saw me and tried to run past, but without even thinking, I tackled one of them. He started yelping and biting, and I grabbed his muzzle to shut him up, and then . . ."

I glance up at Nicolas as he waits patiently, a mixture of sympathy and disbelief in his expression. I lower my face in shame and softly continue.

"Then I, uh, I bit into his throat and his blood started pouring out and I started drinking it and I couldn't stop."

I can't go on. My gut twists at the surging memories of agony and confusion and horror. This is something I have deliberately blocked out, too painful to acknowledge even to myself.

Nicolas puts his arm around me and draws me against his side. He strokes my hair and my face and says nothing.

We sit there a while, looking out over the lake as the ice sparkles and the water shimmers. The wind picks up a bit, and the pines sing a song of comfort, their smell rich and reassuring.

I have to finish this. I've never talked about it, and now I have someone to tell, someone who might understand.

"When he didn't move anymore, when I couldn't get any more blood, I stopped. The hunger was gone, the pain was gone, and my body felt warm and peaceful from the inside out. And then I looked down at the body in my arms and realized what I'd done. I started crying, even though no tears would come, which made me cry more.

"I cried over what I'd done to the poor dog. I cried over what had been done to me. And I cried when I realized what I must have become. Something out of a horror movie, something that kills, something that drinks . . . blood."

My last words are barely above a whisper. The reawakening emotions from that night, raw and oozing, are ripping me apart. With a shuddering breath, I force myself to continue.

"But the worst part wasn't when I realized I'd lost my humanity. The worst part was when I realized I'd lost my family. That I could never . . . go home."

I close my eyes, the pain flooding through my veins as though this all happened just yesterday.

Nicolas takes a deep breath and presses me tighter against his side. He holds me for a while, but I can sense his tension building, and with another breath, he eases me away.

"Come." He stands, his face dark with anger. "We should walk."

He grasps my hand and helps me to my feet, and we step down the face of the rocks. We work our way slowly to the lakeshore where he stops, looking out over the water. I am still in the grip of the past and cannot speak.

"This . . . what happened to you . . . this is not our way. Whoever did this to you should be destroyed. You are right, he was a monster, and we cannot allow such as him to exist. It threatens our very survival as a species." The fury in his voice and on his face startles me.

"We call ourselves The Chosen. Those who are brought into our way of life are carefully selected and are fully aware of what we are offering.

"When we bring a Chosen one over, there is a specific sequence of processes. The new ones are attended and reassured at each step, and come into this life with the knowledge that they will have guidance throughout every stage."

I think about this, about the world it hints at, and as he speaks, the pain and sadness start to ease a bit, drifting away with the forest breezes.

"If you do not mind me asking, how long ago was your change?" He looks at me intently.

"Almost five years ago," I whisper.

"Five years? Only five years?" He appears shocked. "That you survived at all is remarkable. That you have thrived as well as you have, without any support and in such a short amount of time, is unheard of."

He gazes at me speculatively, then continues.

"There is so much more I wish to know about you, but I think we have talked enough for one night." He reaches out and takes my hand, and we start walking back in the direction of the cars.

When we get to the road, Nicolas looks at me and, raising my hand to his lips, kisses it softly. We continue on to the cars and he leads me to the Jag. He opens the door, leans in, and reaches into the center console. As he straightens, he gently places a cell phone into my palm.

"This is for you. You are to call me any time of day or night that you feel the need, no matter how trivial you may think it is."

I nod, saying nothing.

"I do not want you to feel alone ever again. I will be here for you, whenever you need."

He pulls me close and wraps his arms tightly around me. My soul melts as I hold on to him. No one has embraced me in over five years. I had given up ever having this again.

He gently releases me and, softly brushing my lips with his, steps back. We stand a moment, looking at each other in the fading moonlight. Dawn is near, and glancing at the eastern sky, Nicolas takes my hand and walks me over to my car.

"My number is programmed into the phone," he explains. "All you have to do is push ONE and hit SEND."

"Okay." I nod again.

"Your keys?" He raises his eyebrows, amusement flitting across his face as he reaches out to stroke my cheek.

"Oh. Yeah." I fish them out of my pocket and push the unlock button. He opens my door and waits as I get in.

Leaning over me, he touches the side of my face with his fingertips and breathes, "Good night."

He closes my door and walks back to his car. I start mine and slowly turn around, and he follows me back to the highway. Once on the paved road, he quickly passes me and is gone.

Damn, he even does it in his car.

április 9., hétfö

I am undone. This shy, unassuming creature, so sweet, so innocent, is one of the most ruthless and efficient killers I have ever encountered. As I watched her take down a bull elk and completely give herself to the blood, I was overwhelmed with a rush of emotion such as I have never experienced before.

I felt my whole existence suddenly anchor itself to her in a way that surpasses even bonding. I now cannot contemplate my future without her in it.

Her story of her Change, of her rape into our way of life, enraged me to the point that I could scarcely maintain my composure. That she was treated so viciously, with no offer of the Choice, is unforgiveable.

And I know how she suffered, for her story parallels my own.

I will find who did this to her, and he will pay—for eternity.

TUESDAY

CHAPTER 16

I wake up a little later than usual, feeling a bit lethargic from the glut of blood I've been overindulging in all week. To add to it, the last several days have been a hurricane of emotions, and I still feel a little wind-whipped by last night's confession.

Dragging myself out of bed, I peek through the curtains. Clouds have moved in and are hunkering down low, hiding even the bottom slopes of the mountains. I open the back door, feeling the heavy promise of snow, and take in a lungful of the cold mountain air. The energy of the forest is quiet and mute, as it and all its creatures prepare for the coming storm.

I head back inside and quickly dress, anxious to get on the mountain. My first snowstorm. I've been hoping we would have one before summer. The storm has perfect timing, as if called by my own internal tempest.

As I'm leaving, I glance at Nicolas's cell phone on the table and wonder if he'll call while I'm gone. It rings.

Weird. I pick it up.

"Hello?"

"Hello, Sunny." His rich, deep voice floods through me. "I called to see how you are this morning. I have been concerned, as I believe last night may have been a little . . . difficult for you."

"I'm doing better. In fact, right now, I'm getting ready to head up the mountain. It's starting to snow, and I want to be there as it falls and changes everything."

"Ah, you wish to witness nature create a new canvas. I wish I could be there to watch it with you."

"You're welcome to join me," I say hopefully.

"Unfortunately, I have business to which I must attend. I will have to take a rain check, or should I say a snow check." I can hear the silent laughter in his voice.

"Okay, I'll hold you to that."

"Indeed. But for now, I do not wish to keep you from your mountain. I just called to ensure that you are well. I will phone you later when we both have more time."

"That sounds good."

"Goodbye until then. Enjoy the snow."

"Thank you."

The phone goes silent. I set it down, my mood considerably brighter. He actually called me to see how I was. Elated, I step outside and take a breath of the cold, crisp air, and head up the mountain.

The snowflakes are huge, drifting down like miniature parachutes. Everything is silent and very still, except for the falling snow. It's already starting to accumulate, and any bare patches are rapidly donning their white carpet. The trees look like they are reaching out, trying to catch their share.

I reach out and catch my own little white puffs. When I examine them closer, I can see the individual crystals forming snow lace—they're amazing. I look up to the sky and open my mouth and can feel each one as it lands on my tongue. To my surprise, they don't melt. I collect them and form a tiny snowball in my mouth. Laughing, I spit it out and throw it into the air to join its brethren.

Hiking past the trees to the rocky top of the mountain, I turn around to look at Pikes Peak. But the falling snow forms a curtain, wrapping me in gossamer white, and I can see nothing beyond it. The mountain is silent, yet I can still hear the soft patter of the flakes as they land.

I walk back down into the forest, which is thickly covered now, and wander among the pines and firs. They are starting to look like Christmas trees, proudly wearing their flocking in anticipation of that special day. The logs and rocks are disappearing under their snow blankets as the forest floor transforms into a big, fluffy white bed.

The scene is surreal, and I agree with Nicolas. It's like watching the creation of a painting, only it is being unpainted, with the forest colors slowly becoming the white of the canvas.

I wander for the rest of the afternoon, eventually making my way to a small meadow. It looks like a giant down pillow. I can't resist, and I throw myself backward, sinking into its cold, soft embrace. I try to make a snow angel, but the snow is too deep and keeps caving in on me. I jump up, laughing wildly, and run across the white powder, sinking to my knees with each step.

My affection for the mountain deepens. It seems like somehow it brought this storm for me. I feel cleansed, strong, and more like my old self than I have in a while. As thoughts of Nicolas begin to resurface, I shove them down, determined not to dwell on him. A rabbit saves me, bolting from its shelter, and I give it merry chase. We zigzag through the snow in the eternal race of prey and predator, and I thrill to the hunt. But I finally stop and let him go, reluctant to see the pure white snow sullied by the red stain of his death.

The snow is still falling when I get back and, in fact, is coming down even thicker than before. Brushing it from my clothes and stomping my feet, I walk into the house feeling refreshed and alive. I look at the clock and register the time in alarm. I'm definitely going to be late for work, if I can even get there. I turn on the radio and scan the channels for information about the storm.

". . . Ute Pass is closed. Stay tuned . . ."

Well, that takes care of me being late. Guess being snowed in is a good excuse to miss work.

But now what am I going to do for the rest of the evening?

I pick up the cell phone to see if there are any messages, and it rings. Is Nicolas psychic on top of everything else?

"Hello!" I announce cheerfully.

"Well, that answers my question as to how your day was. I assume by your response you enjoyed yourself in the snow?" His voice is warm and inviting.

"It was amazing! I haven't been in snow since before . . . well, anyway, in a very long time. My perspective's a little different now, and snow is much more fascinating than it used to be. I had fun."

"I am glad you enjoyed yourself. I only wish I had been there to enjoy it with you."

"Me, too. I think you would've appreciated its beauty and watching the forest change. But it's probably a good thing you didn't come. The pass has closed and you would've been snowed in here."

On second thought, that might've been pretty interesting. And somehow, scary as all hell.

"Now I regret not coming up even more."

His disappointment-laced words send a shiver down my spine.

"So," he continues, "I take it you are not going to work tonight. Have you given any consideration as to what you might do instead?"

"No, not yet. I just finished listening to the road conditions when you called. To be honest, I'm not sure what I'm going to do. I guess I'll have to start building a library to keep me busy on snow days."

"You do not have any books? I find that quite surprising. You strike me as someone who is rather well-read." His cultured voice reflects his astonishment.

"I . . . left my books behind when I moved here."

"We will have to remedy that situation. I am sure I have some titles of interest you can borrow until you replace them with your own."

"Thank you. That would be very nice." I wonder what kind of collection he has. They're probably all first editions.

"Well, now I regret even more not being able to rescue you from an evening of boredom. I will make it up to you, I promise."

And I'm regretting not being able to be rescued.

"I'll be fine. I have some stuff I need to get done on the computer that I've been putting off. This will be the perfect time to do it," I reassure him.

"Good. Then perhaps I will see you tomorrow evening after work?"

"Uh, yeah, that would be great. I'm off after two."

"I will be there. Good night."

"Good night."

április 10., kedd

The snowstorm kept me from seeing her today. All I could do was think of her. I imagined her in the forest with the snow caressing her skin as it fell, wishing it was me touching her instead. I could see her running through the white landscape, and longed to be by her side, matching her stride for stride, as lovers instinctively do.

But I can sense her fear of me, and I need to go slowly or I will frighten her off like the wild creature that she is.

And so I must wait until tomorrow, while images of her in the snow torture me—mind, body, and soul.

WEDNESDAY

CHAPTER 17

The world is silent outside my walls when I wake. I look out the window—the snow is nearly even with the window sill, and it's still coming down. Like yesterday, there's no wind, and the snow falls like white rain, heavier and less delicate than before.

Turning on the radio confirms my suspicions. The pass is still closed, and I'm still snowed in. Great.

I glance at the laptop but was on it most of the night working with the photos I took on my cross-country trip to Colorado. When I tired of that, it was the internet the rest of the night. I don't think I can stand to look at that screen today. So now I'm faced with the boredom that Nicolas warned me of. And of course, that leads me to thoughts of him, thoughts I had successfully buried in snow and web surfing.

Even though I deliberately try not to look at the cell phone, it rings anyway.

I'm beginning to think he somehow implanted a chip in my head that makes me think of nothing but him, and tells him whenever I do.

Waiting a moment, I try to still the excitement that is fluttering through my veins in anticipation of his voice. I finally give in and answer.

"Hello?"

"Hello." The warmth in it washes over me. "How are you today?"

"Fine." I doubt I sound it, though.

"I believe I sense a damsel in distress. I assume you are once again snowbound?"

"Yeah. I was just trying to figure out what I'm going to do today."

"I am sorry I cannot be there. Perhaps one of the coffee shops in the surrounding community is open. You could hike there for hot tea and companionship, if that is what you are missing."

Actually, what I'm missing is *him*, but I hesitate to tell him that.

"That's a good idea. I'll look in the phone book and see what I can come up with. I was thinking about heading back out into the snow anyway, so this will just give me a destination." I try to sound lighthearted.

"I, for one, am greatly disappointed I will not see you this evening."

"Me, too," I quietly admit.

He is silent for a moment.

"Yes, well, I suggest you take your walk and enjoy the snow while you can. This may possibly be our last significant storm. I would not want you to regret missing any of it by staying cooped up in the house."

"Okay."

"Then I will say goodbye for now. Go for a walk. I know you will feel better."

"All right. Goodbye." The cell goes dead, but I hold it for a moment, wishing he was still on the other end. Sure doesn't seem to be one to chitchat on the phone.

With a big sigh, I set it on the table and grab the phone book.

None of the local coffee shops answer their phones, so I decide to do a little more research online. But it ends up being pointless, and I sit looking at the computer screen feeling frustrated. So far I have found *nothing* on Nicolas Ambrus.

I laugh, recalling one thing. *Ambrus* is Hungarian for immortal.

He's either very arrogant or has a wry sense of humor. Or both.

Whatever his background, he's stayed under the radar. That means he's very careful, and has the money to be very careful.

I finally give up and close the laptop. It's late in the afternoon and the snow is *still* falling. It seems to have lessened, though, so maybe the storm is coming to an end. I think about Nicolas's advice and decide to go up the mountain to see how much has fallen since yesterday.

But first I flip on the radio—just in time to hear that the pass is still closed. I call the club, but no one answers. The city must be snowed in as well. I leave a voicemail and head into the bedroom to dress for a night in the snow.

It's eerie up here on the mountain. The stillness is heavy, like the snow that shrouds the entire forest. The darkness is heavy, too, weighed down by the clouds still shedding their frosty burden, though much slower than before.

The snow is as deep as I am tall in some places, but I discover that if I walk lightly and quickly, I can stay on the surface and not sink. Pretty amazing.

All of the forest creatures are bedded down, hidden, waiting for storm's end. In utter solitude, I make my way up and across the slopes, my only companion the mountain itself.

The cell rings as I walk in the door. I shake my head and answer it.

"You have perfect timing. I just got back from the mountain."

He laughs. "And how was it?"

"Quiet. It's still snowing a little, but it feels like it might stop soon."

"Yes, the weather reports indicate that the storm is finally moving out over the plains to the east. I anticipate the roads will be cleared in time for you to go to your work tomorrow." His confidence is reassuring.

"I hope so. I don't know if I can handle being stuck here much longer." And not being able to see him.

"So did you find a coffee shop today?"

"No, they were all closed. I ended up on the computer most of the day. I didn't get up the mountain until this evening."

"I see. And did you . . . hunt tonight?" he quietly asks.

"No, I . . . don't really need to yet. Besides, all the game has taken shelter. Nothing is stirring up there." It feels awkward to talk about my eating habits.

"Ahh. I had not given thought to what influence the weather might have on your diet." His tone is careful, and now I'm embarrassed.

My diet? My insecurities resurface, and I wonder again how he really feels about my choice of food.

"Well, it hasn't been much of a problem in the past. I usually go a week or so between hunts, but can go longer if necessary."

"Really. That is unusual. But then, there is much about you that is."

I want to ask what the "usual" is, but I'm not sure I'm ready for the answer to that, or any related questions. I fumble for what to say next, but Nicolas beats me to it.

"I must go now. I just called to hear how you are, and I am glad you have found ways to occupy your time." He sounds distant, as though his attention is suddenly elsewhere.

"Well, I'm doing okay, but I'm looking forward to getting out of here, even if it's just to go to work."

"And I am looking forward to seeing you. I trust that I can do so tomorrow evening?"

"I'm finished after two."

"Then I wish you good night. I wish we could talk longer, but I really must go."

"Okay. Good night."

The phone is silent a moment before the call ends.

I wonder what might have called him away.

április 11., szerda

I have developed a strong dislike for snow, because that is what is keeping me from her. Another long day and night, and all I have is the memory of the sweet fire of her lips bathed in the pungent musk of elk's blood.

This evening Corey caused another problem at the club. I told his sponsor that he has one more chance, and then he is done. I will not tolerate his recent behavior any longer.

The storm is to clear by morning and I am looking forward to delivering her presents. Gathering them for her has been the only thing keeping me remotely sane these last few days. I cannot wait to see her tomorrow.

THURSDAY

CHAPTER 18

I wake to the sound of birds chirping. A quick peek behind the draperies reveals a bright sun reflecting off sparkling snow. Scattered clouds still hang in the sky, but they're slowly drifting eastward, the last remnants of the storm. Weird. Blizzard one day, bright sunshine the next.

The clock reads 11:16. I walk into the kitchen to make some tea, and the cell phone rings.

How the hell does he do that?

"Hello," I answer, excitement racing through my veins.

"Good morning! You sound much better today. I assume you are no longer a prisoner of the storm?" His voice contains a curious mixture of anticipation and relief.

"I just woke up to birds singing and blue sky. That seems really strange after several days of constant snow."

"Our weather is known for its abrupt changes." The phone is silent a moment. "Did you say you just woke up?" He sounds puzzled.

"Yeah."

"You sleep."

"Yes. Don't you?"

"No, I do not."

Okay, now that's weird.

"Sunny, how many hours do you normally sleep?"

"Maybe four to five, sometimes more, sometimes less."

"And you fall asleep with the dawn."

"I don't have a choice. The sun rises and I go down."

"I see."

Well I don't. He doesn't sleep? At all?

"Do not worry. Sleep is normal in one who is still relatively new to our life. It becomes unnecessary with age."

"Oh." I wonder just how old he really is.

"So have you made your plans for today?"

"I haven't yet, other than going to work this evening if the pass is clear. And looking outside at the sun, I would guess the snowplows are out there right now."

"Excellent. You will be home this afternoon?" The anticipation in his voice is back.

"Yeeaahh, until I leave for work at five o'clock or so."

"Good. I have a gift to be delivered to you. But first I need your address. You do not mind, do you?"

My paranoia momentarily flares. As obsessed as I am with Nicolas, I don't really know anything about him, and I'm still a little wary of him and the world he represents.

"Well . . . I don't think anyone can get up my driveway just yet."

"I do not think it will be a problem."

"Uh, well, okay." I give him the address and directions. Damn.

"You may expect the delivery around one-thirty. I think you will be pleased."

The smugness in his voice is unmistakable.

"Well, I'll be here," I reply, as my curiosity wars with my concern.

"Do not worry," he laughs. "I believe you will like it. Until then." The phone goes quiet.

Until then? Is he delivering it personally? He's coming here?

Frowning, I look around at my barely furnished and decorated house and move into high gear straightening and rearranging. Great. I never have visitors, other than furniture delivery guys. No doubt Nicolas is accustomed to much fancier surroundings. Embarrassment creeps over me at the thought of his visit.

I finish cleaning, then dress for the sun and head outside to shovel the sidewalks and pavement around the garage. Clearing the snow from the entire length of the driveway will take some time, though, even for someone like me.

I'm about a quarter of the way down to the highway when I hear the roar of a large truck coming up my hill. As it appears around the slight bend, I'm stunned. A snowplow? Plowing my driveway? It barely fits between the trees as it comes up the road, and I jog back to the garage to get out of its way. The truck reaches the house and manages to turn around, the operator waving as he heads back down my freshly plowed driveway.

Huh. Guess getting up my hill won't be much of a problem after all.

I put the shovel away and head back into the house to wait for my mystery gift.

About a half hour later, another truck comes up the driveway and I step out the front door as a delivery van turns around and parks. Two guys get out, and one of them raises the rear door while the other walks over to me.

"Afternoon, ma'am. Where would you like us to put this?" He points to a tall, rectangular box being lowered on a hydraulic lift.

"What is it?" The ludicrous image of a double-wide coffin pops into my head and becomes even more vivid as I recall our conversation about my sleep habits.

"Says here it's a bookcase. Mr. Ambrus ordered it to be delivered to this address. This is the right place, isn't it?" He shows me the shipping papers.

A bookcase? I breathe a sigh of relief and laugh.

"Yes, this is the right address. Come inside and we'll find a place for it." I take him in and, with a little rearranging, make space for it in the living room.

He goes back outside, and a few minutes later the two of them wheel the box into the house on a heavy-duty dolly. They cut the box open and move the bookcase into place.

I can barely take my eyes from it while signing the papers. The delivery guys leave, and I close the door and turn to examine the dark red wood polished to a glass finish.

It's about seven feet tall and five feet wide, and the beautiful antique wood is covered in ornate carvings. It must be worth thousands of dollars. While I'm digesting this, a car purrs up the hill, its tires crunching the gravel and snow. I step outside in time to see the black Jaguar park and Nicolas get out. The trunk opens, and he walks back and pulls a large box from it.

"Good afternoon, Miss Sunshine!" He's smiling over the top of the box as he nears.

"Hello. Come in." I move back as he enters and, watching him, close the door.

Nicolas sets the box down, turns to me and, touching my face, quietly says, "I am . . . glad to see you. You have no idea how I have missed you."

Something dark stirs in the depths of those smoky green eyes.

Caught off guard, I'm speechless, and can barely nod, returning his look.

He reaches out with one hand, then the other, and takes hold of me around the waist. Pulling me to him, he kisses me fiercely, then slowly softens. My knees go weak and my whole body ignites in flame. He gently pulls his mouth away, then touches my forehead with his lips and wraps his arms tightly around me. I'm shocked and helpless and surrender completely. He holds me for several moments, then gradually releases me, brushing my face with his fingertips as he steps back.

His eyes are tinged with red, and I look back at him through a pink veil of my own. He takes a breath and his fists clench, as though he's trying to regain control. I'm not sure I want him to, but the world as I know it has just tilted. I'm not ready for anything more.

"I must apologize. I did not intend to be so presumptuous. Please forgive me." His eyes are slowly regaining their emerald color, but they still hold a fire that now burns in my soul.

"There's nothing to forgive. I missed you as well," I whisper.

He tilts his head and smiles.

"Well, then, shall we have a look at your present?" He gently takes my hand and leads me over to the bookcase.

"It's beautiful. I've never seen anything like it." I'm awed by both the bookcase and him.

"It is eighteenth century cherrywood." He runs his fingers along a carved leaf, smiling down at me. "I am delighted it pleases you.

"But," he continues, "it is missing something."

Releasing my hand, he walks over to the box and brings it back, setting it on the floor in front of the bookcase. He kneels and, with a slice of his fingernail, cuts the tape and opens the flaps. The box is filled with books.

"These are from my personal library. I selected a variety of authors you might enjoy. You may have read some of them, but they are always worth reading again."

He takes one out, stands, and hands it to me. It's *Jane Eyre* by Charlotte Brontë. I open it, and just as I expected, it's a first edition and likely priceless. I carefully turn its delicate pages, then look up at Nicolas.

"It's lovely," I murmur, gently closing it.

"Come, come, it is just a book. I expect you to read it as well as the others. Here, look them over while I get something else from the car." He indicates the box, then walks out the front door. I kneel and look at the books that are visible, hesitating to even touch them.

Nicolas returns with two more boxes and joins me on the floor. He opens one and pulls out a beautiful set of bookends made from black onyx, carved with great detail into the shape of ravens.

"These are a family symbol. I thought they would go well with the cherrywood." He holds up one of the ravens, its polished ebony reflecting the ambient light in the room.

"And these remind me of someone I know." Opening the second box, he takes out another set of bookends made of sparkling blue crystal. They appear to be women from ancient times, perhaps goddesses, and are exquisitely detailed as well.

He holds one up to the light and smiles at me, and I glance down in embarrassment, grateful yet again that I cannot blush.

Nicolas helps me take out all the books and together we set them on the shelves, nestling them between the stunning sets of bookends. We talk and laugh quietly as he tells me how he acquired each of the works.

"There. This will give you something to read while you work on filling the rest of the shelves with volumes of your choosing." He looks down at me, his eyes bright, and continues.

"We cannot have you sitting here bored the next time you get snowed in. You might go for a mountain trek and never come back. And where will that leave me? Calling uselessly on an unanswered cell phone?" He grins and strokes my hair.

My mind goes blank, unable to put words together.

"Come, show me this spectacular mountain of which you speak. I am anxious to meet my competition." He smiles again and takes my hand.

Bemused, I grab my hat and gloves, putting them on before I lead him out the back door. I'd cleared the snow away from the house earlier and created a pathway leading up the hill, and it's at the edge of the pathway that he stops. He stands under the shade of a pine, looking up, his gaze sweeping the mountainside cloaked in trees and snow.

"It is magnificent. It seems to have a protective presence, as though it is watching over you. I appreciate that." He cups my chin for a moment before shifting his attention back to the mountain, staring upward.

"If we hike a little ways up the trail, we can see Pikes Peak over the treetops."

He looks down at his polished shoes and dress slacks, his expression regretful. "Ah . . . I do not believe I am properly dressed for hiking in the snow. And unfortunately, I have other business to which I must attend and need to get back. So it seems I am once again in the position of having to take a 'snow check.'"

He gives me a sad-eyed look and I instantly burst out laughing. Nicolas has such constant control over himself and his surroundings, I can't imagine him having to be sad-eyed over anything.

"All right. I'll hold you to this one, too. But my patience is starting to wear a little thin, and Mr. Mountain is still a serious contender for my affections." I stick my nose in the air, feigning indignity.

Lightning-quick, he turns, slides an arm around me and, lifting my chin, gives me a long and passionate kiss.

Everything condenses to the feel of his mouth upon mine, his body pressing against me.

He slowly stops, and his lips brush my jaw and move to my throat, lingering. And then he releases me. His eyes are crimson and full of fire.

"Can Mr. Mountain do that?" he murmurs, his voice deep with emotion.

My voice won't work. Nothing works. All I can do is look at him wide-eyed.

He softly laughs.

"I think not." He smiles and, raising my gloved hand to his lips, gently kisses it, his green eyes never leaving mine. "Shall we?" He gestures toward the house.

I'm numb as he walks beside me to the door. Once inside, he slowly lets go of my hand, then steps over to the bookcase and begins collecting the empty boxes. "Do you have a place to store these?"

Nodding, I manage to choke out, "We . . . we can put them in the garage."

I grab a box and head out the back door, Nicolas following with the remaining boxes. We stack them in a corner of the garage, and when we come back out, he strolls to his car.

"Regretfully, I must cut my visit short. I need to get back to the city. And you need time to look at your books before you leave for work."

I nod and look past him, trying to mask my disappointment. The sight of the plowed driveway jars my memory of a question I have for him.

"The snowplow. Did you . . . arrange that?"

The corners of his mouth quirk upward, and his eyes laugh at me.

"Oh. Well, thank you. It sure was a lot faster than using a shovel." I shake my head.

Nicolas laughs aloud.

"Yes, I can just picture you out here shoveling the snow at whirlwind speed. You must have looked like your own miniature blizzard." He reaches out and touches my hair.

I drop my gaze and bite back a smile, embarrassed, as he is probably right.

Looking back up into those emerald depths, my thoughts suddenly jumble again.

"I . . . I also want to thank you for the beautiful bookcase and the loan of all those incredible books. You really didn't need to do that. I'll take good care of them and will return them as soon as I can."

"Nonsense, it is my pleasure. I enjoy seeing you smile, and do not wish to think of you bored and lonely. As for the books, keep them as long as you like. I suspect you may have more time to read them than I do as I am constantly being called away on business." He smiles and reaches out, gently squeezing my arm.

"And now, I really must go. Thank you for such a pleasant afternoon. Enjoy your reading."

His eyes bright, he gets into the Jag and starts it. I step back and watch him turn around and head down the drive. His engine roars as he accelerates onto the highway. I listen until it fades into the distance, then walk back to the house.

My mind is a bedlam of emotion as I enter the living room and look at the bookcase sheltering the rare and expensive volumes. I walk over to read the spines—Austen, D. H. Lawrence, T. S. Eliot, Hemingway, Byron, Whitman, Longfellow, Milton, Nietzsche. The list is as long as it is eclectic. I pull out Poe and open the cover, and the pages follow of their own accord, stopping on "The Raven." I read the poem and think of Nicolas, and wonder why he favors this work, if it's because of the family connection, or something deeper.

Closing the book, I glance at the clock and realize it's time to get ready for work. I put it back on the shelf and take a deep breath, strangely reluctant now to re-enter the outer world.

CHAPTER 19

Work has been difficult tonight. I glance at the clock again, anxious for my shift to be over. Shauna gives me a sidelong look and shakes her head. She doesn't seem too pleased with my mood, and I can't blame her. I really don't want to be here, and she knows it.

It's not *where* that's the problem. It's *with whom.* And it certainly isn't with these people.

This has been my first shift with Jackie, the other waitress, and I don't like her. At all. Whereas Tina is just annoying, Jackie's a downright bitch, and I find myself constantly struggling to keep from biting her head off—literally.

"Ya know, they never fail me. Isn't that right, Shauna?" Jackie plunks her empty tray onto the counter. "I just got a twenty dollar tip from that table of G.I. jerkoffs over there. All for leaning over a bit so they could get a real good look at these babies." She adjusts her blouse to better expose her generous cleavage.

I curl my lip in disgust and focus on washing the blender.

The door opens, and *he* is here. I look up as he walks in, and I smile, instantly forgetting my frustrations.

"Well, look who just came in the door," Shauna says under her breath.

Jackie turns and her eyes widen as she watches him weave past the tables and chairs.

"Holy shit," she says.

Nicolas continues up to the bar, his gaze fastened on mine and a slight smile tugging at his lips.

"You *know* him?" Shauna sets a glass into the sink next to me.

I ignore her and Nicolas stops across from me, a demanding fire filling his eyes. Jackie sidles up to him.

"Hey handsome, what can I getcha?" Her hand glides up to rest on his arm.

The growls that slip out of both our throats are barely audible. Nicolas turns his head and glares at Jackie with disdain. The hunter in me leaps up, snarling, ready to tear her apart.

Get your slimy hand off him, you *skank*.

She pales as she sees his face and jerks her hand away, then looks at *my* face and goes even paler. She slowly steps back.

"What the—?" Shauna moves away from me as well.

Still staring at Jackie through a pink haze, I take off my apron and set it on the counter. I glance at Shauna.

"I'm done. Tell Jerry I'll be in tomorrow to get my paycheck." I retrieve my bag from the office and join Nicolas at the door. With his hand on the small of my back, he escorts me outside. I catch a glimpse of their faces as we exit and feel a sense of satisfaction at their obvious fear.

"Well, *that* was interesting." I take a deep breath once we're on the sidewalk.

Nicolas looks at me. "They are nothing. I fail to see your attraction to spending time with such as them."

"Well, to be honest, that wasn't the best club I've ever tended bar for. I usually work with a better caliber of coworkers. And clientele."

"Then my rescue was timely. It appears I have managed to save you from yet another evening of tedium and boredom, yes?" His dark green eyes glint with humor.

"I suppose. But now I'll need to go out and find another job. Hopefully the next place will be a little classier."

"If you do not mind me asking, why do you work in nightclubs in such close proximity to humans? Is there not something else you could do that is more . . . rewarding?" His hand strokes my back as we walk to the parking garage.

"Well, honestly? I don't *mind* being around people. Most of the time." But my loneliness is not something I want to discuss and I scramble for a better reason.

"Bartending also gives me something to do with my evenings, which would otherwise be 'tedious and boring,' as you put it. And of course, the money helps."

"I see."

But I can see that he really doesn't.

We walk the rest of the way to the car in silence. His Jag is parked next to my BMW, and the two black cars make a handsome couple.

"The evening is still quite young. Would you like to come to my home for something warm to drink, some tea perhaps?" He looks down at me with an intensity that sends a thrill through my body, a thrill laced with alarm. I sense we're reaching a point from which there may be no turning back.

Or maybe we've already passed it.

"Uh, sure. That would be . . . nice."

"Ah. Not to fear. I will endeavor to behave like a proper gentleman." His smile is slightly wicked.

I can't respond, as part of me hopes he doesn't.

"I think it will be best if you follow me in your car. Are you ready?"

I am . . . and I'm not.

CHAPTER 20

I follow the Jag through the exclusive streets of the Broadmoor area. At the end of a long, winding road, near the top of a hill, we finally pull up to a pair of black wrought-iron gates. They swing inward, and as we pass through, I notice in the middle of each gate is a crest embracing a pair of ravens.

The tree-lined drive winds a little farther up the hill, then curves to the right, and the house comes into view. It's a large Tudor-style, just what I would expect someone like Nicolas to have. The sweeping front lawn, its several acres buried in snow, is dotted with strange shapes, some reaching nearly nine feet high. As we get closer, I realize that they are topiary in the shape of life-sized animals and mythical creatures. We pass a prancing unicorn, its horn thrusting skyward, and I wonder why they don't have any snow on them.

The circular driveway curves back to the left as it nears the house and Nicolas stops at the stone steps that lead up to the front door. I park behind him. He gets out and a man appears from the side of the house. He bows to Nicolas, gets in the car, and takes it onto a side road that leads to a large multi-door garage set off a little distance from the house.

Nicolas appears at my door and, opening it, extends his hand to help me from the car.

"Thank you."

"You are quite welcome."

My gaze settles on the fantastic topiary across the driveway.

"Those are so beautiful! But why don't they have any snow on them?"

He smiles. "They are covered with burlap prior to storms to protect them from the weight of the snow. When it stops snowing, the burlap is removed, leaving them snow-free."

"I'd love to see them up close."

"Perhaps we will come visit them later. They form quite a remarkable collection, and I enjoy showing them." He turns toward the front door and takes my arm. "Shall we?"

I nod, and we walk up the dark steps to the intricately carved double doors, each emblazoned with the raven crest. One opens as we reach the top, and a slender young woman in a simple blue dress, her blond hair gathered in a bun, bows her head to us as we walk in.

"Good evening, sir," she says in a heavy French accent.

She's human, as was the man who parked the Jag, and I look sidelong at Nicolas in question. He smiles.

"We'll be comfortable in the library. Marie, would you please bring us some hot tea? Darjeeling?" He looks at me, his eyebrows raised.

"Yes, that's fine."

He nods at Marie, who disappears down the hallway. I look around the huge foyer, and at the other end, elegant staircases on either wall curve upward to the next floor. There's a large gold chandelier directly overhead, and the walls are adorned with pieces of magnificently framed art. Polished mahogany trim stands in stark contrast to the soft yellow walls, which are covered in a richly textured fabric.

Everything is so surreal—the topiary, the house, the servants. I feel like I've stepped into a movie, and I don't know how to react.

"Shall we go into the library?" Nicolas's eyes hold their familiar amusement.

"Sure."

But I'm not. Not sure at all. I think of my mountain and wish for a little of the serenity it brings me.

We enter the first door on the right, and this room is overwhelming as well. It's a classic library, straight out of a gothic novel, with floor-to-ceiling bookshelves lining the entire back wall to our left. A fire is gently burning at the far end of the room, and as we walk in, I notice a view of the topiary garden out a room-length window to the right. Two over-stuffed chairs bracket the fireplace and it's to these that Nicolas heads.

"Come, sit down and enjoy the fire. Marie will be here in a moment with our tea." He stands next to one of the chairs and I uneasily take a seat in it, then he sits in the other.

I can feel Nicolas studying me as I stare into the fire. After several long moments, a knock sounds at the library door.

"Come in, Marie." Nicolas continues to watch me and I resist squirming in my seat.

Marie walks in carrying a silver tray with an ornate porcelain teapot and two matching cups and saucers. She sets the tray on the small table next to Nicolas's chair, pours the tea, and puts one of the cups on the table next to me.

"Can I get you anything else, sir?" She folds her hands, her blue eyes downcast.

"No, that will be all for this evening. Thank you, Marie."

"You are welcome, sir. Good night." She bows her head first to Nicolas, then to me.

I feel like a character in a script or stage play or something. This is just too weird.

As she closes the door, I look at Nicolas questioningly. "She's human. They both are."

"Ah, yes, my staff is well-trained and well-paid, enough to not notice anything, shall we say, out of the ordinary. They also live here on the grounds and rarely go into town, so there is little opportunity for outside gossip." He smiles, the master of his house, and takes a sip of tea.

I'm way out of my league here. I realized when we first spoke that Nicolas, with his sophistication and manner of dress, was likely wealthy. But I tend to forget due to his easygoing nature and underlying sense of humor. However, now that we are in *his* environment, his domain, I'm acutely aware of our differences and wonder what he sees in *me*. I think back to earlier in the day, with Nicolas in my small and austere home, and feel embarrassed again.

"You are deep in thought, my dear, and look rather uncomfortable. Is there anything wrong?" Concern colors his voice.

"Uh, no. Well, maybe." I take a deep breath. "Do you mind if I ask you a question?"

"Please, feel free. You have shared much about yourself, and I have shared very little."

"Well, to use your words, how did *you* come to be this way?" I look at him half expectantly, half afraid, worried that this might be too personal a question.

He stares intensely at me for a moment, then takes a deep breath.

"Ah . . . well, that is a rather long story, so I will attempt to keep it brief." His normal light tone becomes serious. I start to regret asking.

"I was born Rusa Nicolao, or, as you would say, Nicolao Rusa, in what was then Hungary—Magyarország, as we call it. My mother was in the service of a local lord when the new king, Matthias Corvinus, stayed at the manor for several days. He was quite young, seventeen, and she was a pretty young girl of sixteen. I was born the requisite nine months later. That was in 1461." He takes a sip of his tea.

In 1461? That makes him nearly five hundred and fifty years old! As I do the mental math, I look up and realize he's looking at me with his amused smile.

"Yes, I have lived for over half a millennium. Do not be too disturbed. I felt a similar sense of disbelief when you told me you had been in this life a mere five years." He raises his eyebrows, light dancing in his deep green eyes. Then his expression grows somber once again, and Nicolas continues.

"I was twenty-seven when a former associate of the king came to visit. I was working in the stables at the time as an apprentice to the horse-master. I heard that the visitor was asking about my mother, who had died when I was but three years old." Nicolas stands and begins slowly pacing the library as he speaks.

"He learned of me, and came to the stables late one night while I was tending an injured horse. The animal started to spook, and I turned to see a man standing at the stall entrance. He just stood there looking at me, and then said, 'I can definitely see him in you. It is remarkable that you have escaped notice all these years.'

"I knew to whom he was referring, as I had heard the whispers growing up that I was a king's bastard. But as far as I was concerned, they were just rumors and of no interest to me.

"My horse continued to shy, and with good reason, as my visitor emanated evil in its purest form. I tried to calm the beast, and when I turned back to the doorway, it was empty.

"The next day the horsemaster, who had been like a father to me, told me that my services now belonged to someone else and to pack my things. I was shocked, as it had been a given that I would follow in his footsteps and eventually assume his position." Nicolas takes a deep breath, and the look in his dark emerald eyes is far away.

"I packed my meager belongings, and waited, for what I did not know. Finally, a little after nightfall, a coach pulled up to the stable. The door opened and I was told to get in. My visitor from the evening before was inside, veiled by the darkness, and regretfully, I complied." He stops and slowly shakes his head, then continues.

"Little did I know that was to be my last evening in my human life. We traveled hard and fast all night, but I recall being more concerned about the poor horses than I was for myself.

"We arrived near dawn at a run-down castle somewhere in the outer reaches of Wallachia. He got out and told me to follow him. He led me inside to a room with a bed and a small table, bid me good night, and closed and locked the door.

"So you see, I understand about rooms with no windows and locks on the door." His quick smile is bleak, and I feel a wave of sympathy for the young innocent man he had been.

"I had no way to mark time, but I imagine it was the next night when he came to me. I have no wish to go into details, but some weeks later I finally emerged from that room, no longer human."

Nicolas goes silent, and stays very still for several moments as he leans against the mantel and stares into the fire, seemingly lost in his memories. His story resonates with me—I can sense the loneliness and despair he felt, even five hundred years ago, as it mirrors my own.

"I have not told this story to anyone in a very long time, so please bear with me." He looks up at me with a vulnerability that he has so far kept hidden.

I rise to stand next to him, then wrap my arms around his waist and just hold him. He turns to hold me, and I grieve for the lives and families we both had stolen from us.

At length, he loosens his arms and gently shifts back. Looking down at me, his eyes crimson, he touches my face and steps away.

"I promised to remain a gentleman tonight, though it is with great regret." He smiles and tilts his head, his breathing faster than before.

As is mine.

"Come, let me show you my garden." He reaches out and I take his hand.

We walk down the steps and across the drive to an opening in the low hedge that borders the lawn. He introduces me to each living statue, calling them by name and giving me their real-life histories. Many of them are horses, bearing names like Bucephalus, the horse of Alexander the Great, or Man O' War, the famous racehorse, his image captured in a full racing stride. Mythical horses are represented as well—a prancing unicorn, and Pegasus, his wings stretching six feet to either side. Cheiron the Centaur, half-man and half-horse, stands firing an arrow at the Minotaur, half-man and half-bull.

Even in the waning moon, the life-sized figures stand out in sharp relief, every detail carefully sculpted in leaf and vine. They tremble and whisper in response to a gentle breeze.

"These are unbelievable. Your gardener is amazing." I shake my head in wonder.

Nicolas laughs.

"Thank you. I accept your compliment."

"Did *you* do these? This is *your* work?" I try to imagine him out here, clippers and shears in hand, and fail.

"You pass your time with insignificant humans. I care for my various collections." He smiles, a mischievous look in his eyes.

I laugh, then shake my head again. I've never been in any one place long enough to build a collection of anything.

"So, what happened after you were . . . changed. How did you end up here?" I feel braver asking him questions now, hoping his earlier willingness to answer remains.

"Ah, well, I do not wish to dwell on the ensuing unpleasantness. But suffice it to say, my Maker had delusions of placing me on the throne as the son of the king, and under his complete control. However, he had not taken into account the rabid thirst that descends upon the newly changed, nor their other limitations, as I was evidently his first.

"And apparently his memories of his own early years were dim, as the bloodletting he now engaged in was little different from his human life. When he realized I would not be able to maintain a human façade long enough to make usurping the throne possible, he tried to kill me." His eyes hold a distant fire.

"I managed to escape. I can only surmise that he did not understand the relationship between Maker and newly made, or I would be truly dead.

"And five hundred years later, here I am, holding this unusual conversation with someone who hasn't been on this earth fifty." He smiles down at me teasingly, and kisses the top of my head.

I mull over his story, the next question forming in my head.

"So, what about being chosen and having a choice, like you said the other night?"

I'm a bit stunned to realize it was only three nights ago. Strange, it seems like a lifetime.

"My Maker was eventually eliminated. It was determined at that time that the process, including selection, needed to have more stringent controls to safeguard against unwanted exposure.

"But come, enough of this talk. I have other things I would like to show you." He smiles down at me, and taking me gently by the arm, leads me back to the house.

We walk into the foyer and Nicolas opens the door to a room opposite that of the library. It's a music room, full of classical instruments. He ushers me in and I stop in the center and slowly take in the instruments lining the walls. Most of them are stringed, though I do see a few exotic flutelike instruments that must be from other times and cultures.

"Do you play?" Eyebrows raised, he gestures around the room.

"No. No, I don't. I . . . never had the opportunity to learn." My lack of culture embarrasses me once again.

"Well, then, I must teach you. But not tonight. Tonight I will play for you. Please, sit." Nicolas waves toward a sofa against the wall. He walks over to the other end of the room, opens a glass cabinet, and takes out a violin and a bow.

"This was made for me by Stradivari in the early 1700s. It is my favorite instrument."

He then puts the violin up to his chin, and the most beautiful sounds I have ever heard slip softly from its strings. I sit entranced, all thoughts gone from my head as his music slowly surrounds and embraces me.

His eyes are closed, his carefully controlled face for once relaxed and serene, and he seems as lost in the song as me. The soft notes eventually fade away to a whisper, and he stops. His eyes open, and they hold a gentle fire as he looks at me.

Neither one of us speaks as he crosses the room and replaces the violin in the cabinet. When he returns, he reaches out to take my hand.

"Come," he says.

We leave the music room and head up the stairs. My body feels like it's vibrating, like the strings of the violin, and I walk carefully as my control begins to slip. We get to the top of the stairs and walk down a short hallway to a closed door. Nicolas turns to me and, like his music, embraces and holds me for a long moment. He then leans back, brushing the hair from my face, and gives me a gentle kiss, his lips burning like a cold fire against mine. I start to crush myself against him and his breath catches. He pulls away and eases me back.

"I promised, and that is not something I do lightly." His eyes are deep, smoky green, and hold a hint of their fiery red.

Nicolas steps back and opens the door. The bedroom is luxurious, complete with its own bathroom, sitting area, dressing table, and a bed piled high in fluffy white, like the snow on my mountain. He motions me inside, but as I walk in, he stops at the doorframe.

"It is near dawn. I had Marie prepare the room and you should find everything you need. Tomorrow I have a surprise for you. I look forward to seeing you when you arise." His voice is warm, but strained. His eyes fix on mine a moment, his expression unreadable.

"Good night," he says, tipping his head, and he closes the door. His footsteps fade away.

And I'm left staring at the closed bedroom door.

No.

Keeping his promise to remain a gentleman may be a sign of his honor, but at the moment I wish he were not so honorable. He's awakened emotions and feelings within me I thought were long dead. All I can see are those green eyes staring down into my soul, and for once the hunger in my body is not for blood.

I shake my head, trying to clear it. I've been so immersed in him I hadn't even realized the sun would soon be creeping over the horizon and drowning me to sleep. The helpless lethargy begins to tug at me, and I peek out the window to see the pale eastern sky and the tip of that glowing orb.

My arms get heavier and slower as I struggle out of my clothes. My knees weaken and I barely make it to the bed in time. I crawl beneath the mountain of silky-lined softness, and snuggle into the most comfortable bed I've ever been in. Nicolas floats through my mind, and I fight to keep him there as I'm pulled down into a pool of darkness.

április 12., csütörtök

I am free to exist another day. I could not help myself—I kissed her before I was barely through her door, and felt her give to me, ever so slightly, like a young filly accepting her first touch.

When I kissed her again in the shadow of her mountain, there was no resistance at all.

She left her job tonight and I am quite pleased. She is far too superior to be wasting her time with marha. *She did catch me by surprise, however. I thought she might actually tear apart that filthy waitress for touching me.*

When she agreed to accompany me home, I felt such a profound sense of relief and hope that I nearly wept. I do not know what spell this is that she has cast over me, but I cannot bear the thought of us being apart.

She has awakened something deep within my soul, something I had long forgotten. I see it reflected in her eyes, and I want to be for her what it is she sees.

I can only hope to keep the other part of me hidden, the part that has ruled my life these many years. I can tell that she senses it, and I must be vigilant and resolute in my efforts to prevent its escape.

I was quite unprepared for her questions regarding my origins. Her childlike curiosity, bearing no trace of covert purpose, completely disarmed me, and I found myself spilling the tale of my Change to her as though she was my confessor.

But there is nothing childlike in the passion I can sense running beneath her skin.

This evening, when I kissed her again in spite of my vow to remain a gentleman, there was a willingness in her response that very nearly pushed me over the edge.

She is asleep in the guest room now. It is taking everything I have not to go in there.

FRIDAY

CHAPTER 21

I wake to a light footfall outside the door, followed by a quiet knock.

"Mademoiselle? Are you awake?" Marie softly asks.

How odd. I haven't been woken by anyone since . . .

Blinking, I answer, "Yes, I'm awake."

"Mr. Ambrus is waiting for you downstairs."

"Okay. Tell him I'll be down in a few minutes."

"Yes, mademoiselle."

I stretch, delighting in the soft cocoon of the down mattress and comforter, and the whispering caress of the silk sheets. This is something I could get used to.

I have no idea what time it is and regret not asking Marie. Coming out of the bathroom after a quick shower, I find a pale blue cashmere turtleneck, a light blue jacket, and black wool slacks laid out on the bed, which has been neatly made. Wow—she's good. Quickly dressing, I comb out my hair, then open the door and head downstairs.

Nicolas is standing in the foyer, watching me as I come down. He smiles warmly and says, "Good morning, Sunshine. You look quite lovely. How did you sleep?"

"Very well. That's a wonderful bed."

"Consider it yours. Come, let me look at you this morning." Nicolas takes my hand as I step onto the floor, his pale green eyes searching mine. He brushes my brow with his thumb and his forehead creases momentarily, and now all I want to do is look in the mirror.

"Do you need anything?" His tone and pensive expression are puzzling. But then I get it. It's been four nights since I hunted, and the blue in my eyes is probably darker than he's seen.

I suppress a smile and shake my head.

"No, but who do I thank for the loan of the clothing?"

"They are yours. I asked Marie to run into the city this morning. She selected your outfit. She has excellent taste."

"Oh. Well, thank you." His thoughtfulness surprises me yet again.

"Are you ready for your surprise?" he asks, almost smirking.

"I . . . guess . . ."

"Good. It will require a bit of a drive, if you do not mind." His smirk grows even more mysterious.

"No, I don't. I'm ready." His buoyant mood lifts mine even higher.

"Marie?" He looks back over his shoulder.

Marie approaches carrying a pale blue wide-brimmed hat, light blue gloves, and sunglasses. She offers them to me. "Mademoiselle?"

"Thank you." I give a sidelong smile to Nicolas. His mouth quirks and he nods in return. I put on the hat and gloves, and he reaches out to tug the hat a little more securely in place.

"And Marie?" I look over at her standing by the door. "Thank you for your shopping expertise. Everything is beautiful and fits perfectly."

"You are welcome, mademoiselle," she says demurely.

"Shall we?" asks Nicolas. I nod and he leads me out the front door, Marie closing it behind us.

There's a black Mercedes limousine parked in front of my car. I look at Nicolas questioningly and he waves his hand toward it. The stocky dark-haired man I'd seen last night is standing next to the rear door, and opens it as we approach. I get in, unsure of which seat to take, and Nicolas indicates the one facing backward. He climbs in, takes the rear seat across from me, and the driver shuts the door.

"Can I ask where we're going?"

Nicolas laughs. "You may ask, but I am not answering. I told you, it is a surprise."

I frown, and watch out the windows as we head down the driveway and through the streets. We pass a variety of luxury homes, a golf course, and a large resort hotel with signs proclaiming it as The Broadmoor, then get on the freeway heading north. Nicolas points out various landmarks and explains their history, and once again I'm entranced by my tour guide. Signs in the opposite lane recede into the distance, indicating exits for the Air Force Academy and Black Forest, which sounds intriguing. After about an hour, we pass through communities on the outskirts of Denver and soon catch another freeway heading west.

Nicolas continues to fill me in on Colorado history, and I listen with rapt attention. I realize his stories are not necessarily from books, but from his own experiences. It must be amazing to have lived through so many historical periods. I can't really fathom it.

After heading west for an hour or so, we get off the freeway onto a smaller, winding highway. I watch miles of snow-covered scenery pass by, then notice Nicolas watching me.

"What?" I ask.

He laughs. "I just enjoy looking at you."

I frown and shake my head, though I can easily say the same thing about looking at him.

We turn onto a smaller road, and I start seeing signs for Keystone Ski Resort, ski shops, parking lots . . .

Ski resort?

Wide-eyed, I look back at Nicolas, and now he's grinning.

"Skiing? We're going skiing?"

"It seems I owe you several 'snow checks.' I am hoping this might be an acceptable method to make good on them." He smiles, and humor dances in his pale eyes.

"I've never skied before."

"I do not believe that will be a problem. I have made arrangements with the local ski school for instruction. I am sure they will find you to be the most apt student they have ever had."

I laugh. Yeah, he's probably right.

We stop in front of a ski shop, and the driver gets out and opens the back door.

I peer at the sun barely visible through the clouds and put on my hat and sunglasses anyway. The gloves I shove in my pockets. The sun is muted enough that I shouldn't burn, but who knows how bright it might be later.

We get out and Nicolas looks at the driver. "Thank you, Alfonso. Will you see about getting ski racks installed on the car? I will call you when we are ready to be picked up."

"Yes, sir," Alfonso replies, his accent thick, but I can't place it. He gets back in the car and drives away.

Placing his hand on my arm, Nicolas says, "Shall we do a little shopping first? This store should have ski clothing as well as equipment."

"Do we really need the clothing? I mean, the cold is irrelevant, so it seems like a waste of . . . money." My words fade as I realize that the cost of ski clothing would be less than pocket change to Nicolas.

"No, but we are skiing with humans. We will be less noticeable if we are dressed in their manner."

I chuckle. "You and I tend to be noticeable no matter what we wear. But you're right. We should at least appear to be as bundled up as they are."

Nicolas smiles, opens the door of the ski shop, and follows me in. The store is crowded—Fridays are the lead-in for the weekend, and everyone is anxious to get out on the slopes. We spend the next hour or so picking out clothing and ski equipment. When the technician is almost finished mounting the bindings on our skis, Nicolas calls Alfonso and tells him we're ready.

Less than a minute later, Alfonso walks into the shop, gathers our packages, and heads back out the door. He returns almost immediately and collects the skis and poles, then follows us out to the waiting car and opens the back door. We climb in while he snaps the equipment into the roof-mounted ski rack.

"Thank you, Alfonso," Nicolas says as the man shuts the door.

We head down the street and follow the signs to another area of the resort, finally stopping in front of the main entrance. I check for the sun once again. It has now disappeared in a sky that is solid clouds. Nicolas smiles at me.

Hell, he probably ordered the sky to be cloudy this afternoon.

We'd purchased our ski clothing without changing back into our street clothes. All we need to do now is put on our ski boots, which we do while Alfonso gets the skis from the rack.

"Alfonso, you are free to enjoy the resort after you have parked the car. We plan on being here for quite some time. But please be available by phone should we need to leave sooner than anticipated."

"Yes, sir. Thank you, sir." Alfonso replies. I finally place the accent. Italian, I think.

Nicolas takes my free hand, and we walk up the steps carrying the skis and poles against our shoulders. We weave our way through the crowds and I catch a trace of tightness in his jaw, something I noticed in him when we were in the shop that was packed with people. I'm usually okay with crowds, except for physical contact—that I don't like. It also helps if I'm not hungry.

We get in line for the ticket window, keeping a little distance from the people ahead of us. Nicolas stands facing me and says, "Have I told you how attractive you are in your pretty new ski outfit?" He'd insisted on the powder blue one.

"Yes, you have, several times. Thank you. You can say it as much as you like. And I think you look quite dashing in your new attire as well." The dark grey goes well with his black hair and pale green eyes.

He laughs, but then his smile fades and he stiffens, staring behind me. At about the same time I realize whoever is behind me is now very close. I look over my shoulder at two college-age guys standing barely a foot away.

"Excuse me," I turn partially toward them, my hand pressing against Nicolas's chest. "Would you mind giving us a little space? There's no need to crowd."

"Uh, sure, ma'am. Sorry." They grin and step back a couple feet. Fortunately, they are still staring at me, and haven't noticed the venomous glare Nicolas is directing at them.

"They're fine," I whisper to Nicolas. The chest muscles under my hand begin to relax.

This is odd. I don't recall him reacting this way when we visited the museums and the opera. He'd basically ignored the people around us, and his interactions with them, though few, had been polite.

I study his face, which has returned to its civilized mask, but I can still sense some residual tension.

"Are you okay?" I ask.

"Perfectly." He steps to my side, and puts his arm around my waist, pulling me close, and keeps me there the rest of the time we are in line.

Possessiveness? Jealousy? I'm a little puzzled. It's a bit uncharacteristic for someone who seems so confident and in control of the world.

We finally get to the window and I wait a little off to the side while Nicolas speaks to the cashier. I notice that he's fine now, talking pleasantly to her and even smiling.

Huh.

Leaving the window, we make our way to the ski school area. I glance again at Nicolas and admire the sure and expert way he negotiates the terrain in his ski boots. He moves in sharp contrast to the throngs around us, like he does this every day.

"How long has it been since you last skied?"

"Ah, well, let me think. Several decades, I believe." He looks down at me, smiling. "Why do you ask?"

"You just look like you ski all the time, like you belong here."

"Well, perhaps not here. But I have spent time on ski slopes in the past." His smile has a hint of mystery to it. I decide not to pursue the topic further—at least in public.

We arrive at the instruction area. Nicolas has reserved a private lesson for me, and I wait while he informs the instructor that I'm ready. He walks back toward me, his gracefulness unaffected by snow or ski boots.

"So, what are you going to do while I have my lesson?"

"Watch, of course."

"Well, why don't you just teach me yourself?" I ask, frowning.

"I will, my dear, once you have been shown the basics." He glances up the slope.

His impatient tone surprises me. Maybe it's a good thing he's not the one teaching me the beginner stuff.

A bleached blond with a skier's sunburn walks over, smiling, and introduces himself as John. Nicolas frowns and walks a short distance away, then stands, arms folded as he watches us. Though I'm focused on John's instructions, I can't completely ignore the intensity radiating across the snow from Nicolas.

He follows us as we ski over to the lift for my first trip down the slope. John explains how to get safely into and out of the lift chair and, since each chair holds only two people, suggests that Nicolas either ride in the one behind us or wait at the bottom of the slope. From John's tone, I'm guessing he prefers the latter, as Nicolas seems to be making him nervous. Hell, he's making *me* nervous.

Nicolas's expression darkens in response to John's comment, and he elects to ride in the chair behind ours.

We shuffle up through the instructor's entrance, followed closely by Nicolas. As the chair comes around, we step into position and it scoops us up. I giggle and slowly wave my skis in the air. John laughs and waves his too, though I'm sure he does this dozens of times in a single weekend. He starts making little jokes that rapidly give way to full-on flirting, and I realize Nicolas has been cramping this guy's style. That might explain Nicolas's behavior. He sensed what I hadn't during my lesson. I grow quiet, all playfulness gone, but John doesn't notice.

I wait a moment, then say, "Look John, I'm here strictly for a lesson. Let's stick to business, okay?"

"Oh yeah, no problem. Sorry if I offended you." He seems taken aback, but I don't care.

Dumb ski bum. Offending me could get you hurt. Offending me in Nicolas's moody presence will likely get you killed.

We're almost to the end of the lift, and John reminds me how to exit safely. As the chair nears the ground, I touch down and smoothly glide to a flat area and stop. John says something about an awesome dismount, not like a beginner at all, but I ignore him and wait for Nicolas.

Nicolas gracefully skis up behind me and, taking me by the shoulders, kisses me on the side of the neck. He then looks up at John, and I can pretty much guess that his expression is gloating. *This is mine*, his body language says. I lean into him, give a small laugh, and reach back to touch his face, smiling as his lips caress my palm.

John looks down, embarrassed, and asks if I'm ready to ski down the hill. We walk over to the launching point, where he reviews the basics yet again. He tells me to follow him and to try to stay in his tracks as best as I can, turning where he does, and that we'll stop halfway down to see how I'm doing. I nod and tell him I'm ready.

I look at Nicolas and he smiles, and then I take off after John. Nicolas trails a little off to the side.

Easily following John's tracks back and forth across the slope, I discover that my speed increases if I angle my skis more downhill. I start shortening the turns, then abandon John's trail altogether. My turns become smaller and smaller S's, and I go faster and faster. Nicolas catches up and passes me, and I start following him as he leans into his skis one way and then the other. He then drops into a crouch and flies straight down the mountain. I mimic him, laughing as the cold wind rushes past my face. He reaches the bottom, makes a gentle arc, and comes to a halt. I do the same and wonder why all the nonsense about snowplowing to stop.

John arrives a minute or so later, a mixture of confusion and anger on his face. "I thought you said you'd never skied before."

"She hasn't. Her newfound skill must be due to her excellent instructor." Nicolas gives me a sidelong glance and smiles. He isn't talking about John.

I laugh. "Thank you, John, for a wonderful lesson, but I think we're done now. Nicolas?"

He takes my outstretched hand, and we leave John standing there, shaking his head.

We spend the rest of the short afternoon exploring the various runs. I have little problem keeping up with Nicolas, although certainly not in quite the same style. *Poetry in motion*, as cliché as it sounds, is one thought that comes to mind as I watch him. He embodies all the grace and artistry of a figure skater as he weaves his way down the slopes. I marvel at what a magnificent being he is.

Late in the day, we reach a ski run that is quite steep and obviously constructed for speed. Nicolas shoots me a look, challenge in his eyes, and takes off. I launch after him and try vainly to catch him. But he is a rocket and I am quickly left in his exhaust. I drink in the wind as it whips past me, crouching low and straight, trying for more speed, but don't catch up to him until reaching the bottom. He's standing there, nonchalantly waiting for me, Cheshire-cat smirk on his face. He's probably been holding back all day.

Laughing, I bend down and scoop up a handful of snow to throw at him, but he's no longer there. I look around and he's halfway across the slope. I throw it anyway, but it only hits empty air. Oh yeah, I forgot how fast he can move. Silly me.

Thwack! The snowball explodes against my back. I groan and collapse as though injured, and he's bending over me before I hit the ground. I plant a fistful of snow in his hair in revenge.

Chuckling, he grabs me, pulls me to my skis, and kisses me, hard. I go still, then start to respond, and he gently shifts back.

"Ah, you see? I still know the best way to win." He laughs again and then rubs snow in *my* hair.

I brush it out and suggestively answer, "You're right, I give up. To the victor goes the spoils . . . do with me as you will."

At that his eyes grow intense, and the crimson starts to creep in. He roughly pulls me to him and kisses me again, longer this time. He breaks away, holding me by the shoulders, question in his eyes.

"You see, two can play that game." I stare mockingly back at him and shift out of his grasp. He looks at me a moment, then relaxes and tips his head, holding out his hand in concession. I take it, and we ski over to the edge of the paved area and step out of our skis.

It's about four o'clock, and most of the outlying runs and lifts are shutting down for the day. But the main runs and lifts stay open for night-skiing, and Nicolas suggests we find a place to have some tea and wait for the crowds to thin out.

CHAPTER 22

We walk into yet another restaurant-bar. Like the previous two, it's packed with people both sitting and milling around. Nicolas's jaw tightens, and without stopping, we turn and walk out.

He reaches into his jacket's inside pocket and takes out his cell phone. As he's talking to Alfonso, we head back to the entrance.

"Are we leaving? What about the skis?" I ask. They're locked in a rack back at the first place we'd stopped.

"No, not yet. We will wait in the car for nightfall."

"Okay." Again, I'm puzzled by his sudden intolerance toward people.

The limousine is double-parked out front and Alfonso is standing next to it with the rear door open. I get in and take my earlier seat, while Nicolas resumes his. Alfonso closes the door, then heads into the restaurant area.

Nicolas stares out the window, faint lines creasing his brow.

I gather my courage and touch his arm.

"Nicolas? Is something wrong?"

"No, my dear. Everything is fine." He glances at me, and his eyes, distinctly darker than earlier, carry a hint of a warning.

Fine? Doesn't look that way to me.

My lips pressing into a tight line, I slowly remove my hand.

He frowns, reaches out, and gently squeezes my arm.

"Please forgive me. Excuse me for a moment."

Nicolas opens the door and gets out of the car. He crosses the parking lot, his cell phone against his ear. When he reaches its edge, he begins pacing back and forth, reminding me of a caged panther.

A cough outside the window on the other side of the car startles me. Alfonso's holding a tray with a chrome teapot and two cups, and I bite back a laugh at the picture he makes. He's just not the butler type. He's more like a bodyguard, or perhaps an Italian mobster, and would look more comfortable holding either an Uzi or an old-fashioned Tommy gun.

I open the door for him, then turn and watch Nicolas as he returns to the car, still talking on the phone. Why would *he* need a bodyguard? His physical abilities far outweigh that of any human. But five hundred years is enough time to make a few enemies—of any origin.

Nicolas slows as he nears us, nods several times, then tucks the phone back inside his jacket before opening the door and climbing in. He seems calmer now, but his smile is still tight.

His gaze meets mine, flickers away, then returns, filled with the sparkle of amusement. His mouth quirks and he tips his head.

"Sunny? Your tea?"

Alfonso's leaning into the car, holding a steaming teacup in my direction. He's probably been holding that cup the whole time I was watching Nicolas.

"Oh. Sorry." I duck my head. "Thank you, Alfonso."

Some alert hunter I am.

Nicolas is smiling as he takes his cup from the swarthy driver. Alfonso shuts the door and gets into the driver's seat, and we slowly cruise to the back part of the parking lot. Nicolas, his expression sober again, sips his tea and watches me speculatively. I resist squirming in my seat.

"So," he says, "how did you like your first time skiing? Are my snow debts paid?"

"Yes, I'll consider your 'snow debts' paid, several times over. I really enjoyed it. Thank you for bringing me."

"Good. And you are welcome. It has been my pleasure.

"But," he continues, "the best is yet to come. Night skiing has a particular appeal, especially to our kind."

I take a breath, debating whether to ask him a question I've had since I first saw him standing across the street from me. I look over my shoulder at the closed partition between the driver's section and ours, then back to Nicolas.

"Do not worry. The partition, as well as this entire compartment, is soundproof. He cannot hear anything we say." He looks at me curiously and waits.

"You've . . . mentioned 'our kind' several times. Are there many others here in Colorado like you? I mean, like us?"

"Sunny, I have been wondering why you have avoided asking this question. I assume it is but one of many unasked inquiries you have. I do not understand your hesitation, but please rest assured you may ask me anything about The Chosen that you would like to know." Nicolas reaches out to brush a strand of hair away from my face, then continues.

"The answer to this one is . . . yes. There are other Chosen here, mostly in Denver and the Springs. And since your curiosity has finally overcome your apprehension, I believe you might be ready to meet some of them." He looks at me, head tilted, gauging my reaction.

Which isn't real great. I knew there had to be others and was somewhat prepared for his answer. But the thought of coming face-to-face with them sends icy panic through my veins and I'm sure he can sense it.

Unwilling to admit my terror aloud to him, I stammer, "Oh. Okay." I take a deep breath. "When?"

"Soon, I think. The sooner you confront your fear, the better. I believe you will find the company of The Chosen preferable to that of the humans with whom you have been forced to associate."

He may believe that, but I'm not sure. I take a sip of my now-cold tea, my mind spinning dangerously out of control. The beast and the hunter, both curiously quiet for days, waken.

"If you do not mind me asking, Sunny, why does the idea of meeting others of our kind disturb you so?"

"I don't know."

But I do. The only one of *my kind* I've met, besides Nicolas, turned my life into a nightmare. The pain and violence and horror associated with that experience is embedded in my very soul. However, that's not my only concern.

"You say I'm different. What if I'm *too* different? What if they don't accept me? What if they're stronger than me?"

This last is important, because I instinctively sense that strength and speed are crucial for survival in their world. For all of Nicolas's sophistication and culture, I feel that whatever it is that lies within him is quite deadly.

Nicolas reaches out and raises my chin.

"Ah, well, I think they will find you fascinating, as have I, and will appreciate your differences. And as to your last concern?" He laughs. "I do not know any who have the skills necessary to wrestle a full-grown bull elk to the ground and kill it. Most of them would be afraid to soil their clothing or muss their hair.

"No, you are more than a match for them, in spite of the short time you have spent in this life." His eyes spark dangerously. "Besides, if any of them threaten you in any way, I will simply eliminate them."

I swallow. Is that how they usually resolve their arguments? By eliminating one another?

"But come, it will be dark soon, and we have ski slopes to conquer. We can talk more about this later, if you wish. Yes?" His question is more like a command, and in my anxious state, I nod, eager to end this particular conversation.

He presses a button on the armrest and seconds later Alfonso opens the rear door. Nicolas gets out and turns to assist me. I take his hand, along with a deep breath of the cold mountain air, and feel some of my fears begin to dissipate.

Nicolas seems to be in no hurry as we stroll back to the slopes and the storage rack holding our skis and poles. He unlocks them, hands me mine, and shoulders his own. When we get to the staging area, he drops his skis and steps into the bindings. I do the same, then we make our way to the chairlift that will take us to the top of the night-skiing area and wait in line. The lights of the ski runs wrap around the mountain, like Christmas bulbs strung around a tree, and excitement fills the crisp air.

But just as we near the front of the line, the lift stops. We wait a few minutes, then a guy walks down the line and tells us the lift is temporarily out of order and that we'll need to take the gondola to the top.

Nicolas frowns and I realize that so far we've avoided the crowded gondolas—or sharing a lift chair with anyone, for that matter.

"Perhaps we should wait until they complete the repairs," he says as we leave the line and wander to an open area away from the other skiers.

"Why?"

"Sunny, it is not unusual for human crowds to place great anxiety upon a young Chosen. To be in such close quarters that contact with them is unavoidable can trigger impulses that are not easily restrained. I do not wish you to endure such stress."

What?

"But Nicolas, we've been to museums and the opera, and everything was fine. I don't understand what's changed."

He reaches out to brush the hair back from my face.

"If I had known then how new you are to this life, I would never have placed you in such circumstances."

"Do you forget that just earlier today we were in the ski shop, and in the restaurants? Those were both crowded."

"What I do tend to forget is even though you can move about during the day, other aspects of your physical and emotional development are less mature. The gondola will be very tight. There will be no way to avoid contact."

Less mature?

Indignation begins to fester within me.

"Nicolas, I can handle myself just fine. And you forget, they are not my prey, nor have they ever been. So you don't need to worry about someone touching me and 'triggering' any impulses. I'm not going to freak out and attack anyone, if that's what you're worried about."

"Please do not be offended. I did not intend any insult." He takes me by the shoulders. "No, my only concern was for your well-being. Nothing more. And you *have* spent much time in close association with humans, so of course you have greater control than other Chosen of your age." He draws me close and kisses my forehead. "Please forgive me."

As suddenly as it flared, my anger melts away.

I squeeze his arm and he looks down at me.

"It'll be fine. It's not that long of a ride," I tell him. He nods, and we walk over to get in the other line.

After waiting several minutes, we climb into a packed gondola, make our way to the side, and face the window. Nicolas stands behind me, hands pressed to the glass on either side of my head, as though he were sheltering me from the crush of humanity. I look back up at his face, but he's staring out at the scenery, eyes dark and jaw tense.

I nestle against his chest in reassurance, and he looks down and gives me a tight smile. We do seem to share a common aversion to being touched by people, but I suspect the causes of that are not quite the same. Mine stems mostly from the need to protect my secret. I'd rather not think about his reasons.

The long ride comes to an end, and we gather our skis and poles and step out. We both take a deep breath once we are out and away from the mass of people, then work our way over to the edge of the hilltop.

Unfortunately, the runs appear to be nearly as crowded as the gondola, and Nicolas scowls at the swarming slopes. Rather than let his mood get anymore foul, I shout, "Race ya!"

With a powerful push of the ski poles, I hurtle myself down the slope. I crouch low, my poles tucked under my arms, and weave at top speed through the forest of skiers with Nicolas hot on my heels.

He pulls alongside, but rather than pass me, he waves his pole in front of me. I start to slow down, cutting across the slope in several sweeping arcs, and he matches me, then slips in front, all the time slowing. Puzzled, I follow.

As I work back across the slope, someone slams into me from behind.

Knocked flying, I twist around, barely getting my skis untangled in time to land on them, but then one of them catches on something, and I can't right myself. I tumble and lose one ski and then the other, but now I'm sliding down the mountain even faster. As I wrench around trying to stop, Nicolas appears, skiing right beside me in a deep crouch. He reaches out and grabs my jacket while veering back uphill, slinging me along with him until he jams us to a stop.

I lie on my back looking up at him, and his face is rigid, his eyes full of fear.

"Get up. We have to move before another fool hits us."

I scramble to my feet and we quickly work our way to the edge of the run. He steps out of his skis and grabs me, pulling me tightly to him. He then steps back and starts checking me over, looking for injuries.

"Are you all right?" he asks, his voice shadowing the fear in his eyes as he moves first my head and then my arms.

"Yeah, I think so." Nothing seems to be broken. But I do feel a little shell-shocked and shake my head trying to clear it.

He unzips my jacket, apparently still looking for damage.

"I'm okay, really. Just a bit shook up. I'm fine." I lean back, a little annoyed at his relentless examination.

He stops and looks at me, the fear in his face giving way to anger.

"Have you ever been seriously injured, since your change?" he demands, his eyes full of fire.

"No, just cuts and scrapes I get when hunting. They heal almost immediately, so I don't worry too much about getting hurt."

"'When hunting.' In other words, when you feed. Yes, the blood heals us almost instantly. Have you ever been injured and not fed shortly thereafter?" His eyes narrow, and I shift back, not sure what he's getting at.

"No, not that I can recall."

"Ah . . ." He rolls his eyes and shakes his head. "Well, let me explain to you what happens to one of our kind if we get injured and there is no blood readily available."

My eyes widen as I begin to grasp his implication.

"If it is a break, there will be some pain accompanying the injury itself. The real pain sets in when it starts to heal on its own without the benefit of fresh blood, and the pain will continue to increase until it drives one mad. In addition, the natural response our bodies have to injury of any sort is instant hunger, and the more severe the injury, the more intense and uncontrollable the hunger." He looks grim, as though he speaks from personal experience.

"If bleeding is involved, the need for blood is tenfold. The more blood we lose, the more insane we become, until we will attack anything or anyone. As you can imagine, this is a highly dangerous state to be in, and one to be avoided at all costs.

"Had you been seriously injured, do you have any idea what I would have been forced to do? Elk are not readily available. There is only one source of blood here. I do not think you are ready to make that Choice." He looks at me, his eyes asking the question as well.

I swallow. No, that's not a choice I'm willing to make. I've been avoiding it for the last five years.

"And I do not want to have to make it *for* you. It is your Choice, and one you will make if and when you are ready. But make no mistake, should you suffer injury, I will gladly take the first human that comes along, no matter who or when or where. And that puts us *both* in danger."

I look at him a moment, then down at my feet, alarmed as the truth of what he's saying sinks in. He steps forward, opens his arms and gently embraces me.

We stand, motionless, until finally Nicolas relaxes his hold. He lifts my chin and brushes my lips with his thumb.

"Wait here while I go find your skis."

I nod, watching as he hikes up the slope carrying his skis and remaining pole. When he gets part way up the hill, he steps into the bindings, and then checking uphill for oncoming skiers, he zips across the slope to where I'd been hit. I see no sign of the person who crashed into me and guess that he or she is probably all right. Nicolas retrieves my gear, stops once more to pick up the pole he'd dropped when he grabbed me, and returns to where I'm waiting.

"As I was hoping to explain before you took off, the slopes are only open to the public until nine p.m. When I saw how crowded it was, I decided we would take our time, get safely to the bottom, and wait until everyone leaves."

"I'm sorry. I didn't—"

"The final part of your surprise is that I have reserved the slopes for us for two hours after closing. They are ours and ours alone until eleven."

He steps forward and cups my cheek.

"It is nearly nine, and most of the people are taking their last run. Are you ready to try it again? If you would rather not, I will call Alfonso and we will go home." He looks at me expectantly.

"The slopes are ours? No one else will be on them?"

He nods, smiling.

"Great! I'm ready to tear up some snow. I'll even beat you—"

"No. We stay only on one condition."

I raise my eyebrows.

"No racing," he says sternly.

"No racing? But we did earlier today, before our tea break."

"Yes, well, that was rather impulsive of me and I instantly regretted my actions once I recalled the ramifications of an accident. I am sorry to have put you at risk."

"Oh, don't say that. It was too fun, and I enjoyed every speeding second. But all right. I agree not to race anymore. At least for tonight."

"Good. Then shall we?" He hands me my poles and I grin, then step into my skis.

We take off together and, carefully crisscrossing the slope, make our way to the bottom.

I lean against Nicolas, my back against his chest, his arm around my waist. The streetlights of the freeway zip past as the Mercedes speeds us home. Neither of us speaks, seemingly lost in our thoughts and memories of the night.

The rest of the evening on the mountain was spectacular. We made repeated runs, matching our turns, swaying like dancers as we skied down the slopes. I practiced my form and technique and saw the approval in Nicolas's eyes whenever he looked over at me.

Our final run was the most amazing of all. Nicolas had tipped the lift operator quite generously to turn out the slope lights. The cloud cover blotted out the stars, as well as the waning moon, and we had come down the hill in absolute darkness. Being true creatures of the night, we could see better without the lights, and the details of the snow and the surrounding forest jumped out, crisp and clear and absolutely beautiful.

Nicolas had stopped us partway down the hill, planted his poles, and stepped out of his skis. I did the same, and he moved to stand behind me, wrapping his arms tightly around my waist. We stood there, looking out over the mountain, and drank in the night, and I could feel a soft humming in his chest. At one point he started to say something, but apparently thought better of it and stayed silent. After a while, he said it was time to go and, with a final tightening of his arms, released me. We skied to the bottom holding hands in the dark.

I nestle deeper against him, recalling our time on the mountain, and reflect at how quickly everything has happened. It's been only ten days since I first saw Nicolas, but it feels like we've been together ten thousand years.

CHAPTER 23

We arrive back at the estate a little after one in the morning. I get out, Nicolas behind me, and together we walk up the steps. The door opens and Marie welcomes us.

"Good evening, sir. Good evening, mademoiselle."

"Good evening, Marie," Nicolas responds, and I smile and nod to her.

We walk in and Nicolas, his hand on the small of my back, heads to the library door. Opening it, he says, "I will return momentarily. Make yourself comfortable. I will have Marie bring in a pot of tea."

I nod and go in, and he closes the door. His footsteps echo down the hall.

Drifting over to the bookshelves, I start reading the titles. Many are in other languages. I recognize French and German, but I don't have any idea what the rest are. I guess if you're five hundred years old and don't need sleep, you would have plenty of time to learn all sorts of things.

Marie's step outside the door precedes her soft knock.

"Mademoiselle?"

"Come in, Marie."

She walks in with a serving tray and sets the teapot and cups on one of the tables by the fireplace.

"Will there be anything else, mademoiselle?" she asks.

"No, that's fine. Thank you."

"You are welcome." She walks to the door.

"Wait, Marie. Can you please tell me something?"

She stops and faces me, waiting.

"How long have you worked for Mr. Ambrus?"

She hesitates. "A while, mademoiselle."

Nicolas walks in carrying a stack of books, looking pointedly at Marie. She blushes, bows her head, and leaves.

That was kinda weird. Like he doesn't want her talking to me, or vice versa. Or maybe it's just a servant thing. I too easily forget what a different world it is that Nicolas comes from.

He moves over to the round table near the window and sets down the books.

"I thought perhaps you might be interested in a little of our history. Here are several volumes that focus on our European experiences. Look them over. They may help answer some of those questions you have so far opted not to ask." He smiles and holds his arm out, inviting me to the table.

I walk over and pick up one of the books. It's thick, heavy, and bound in rich, dark leather. Embossed in the center of the cover is Nicolas's crest with the two ravens. I look up at him and he gives me a brief smile.

"I have business to which I must attend. Please, sit by the fireplace, have some tea, and enjoy." His dark eyes are somewhat distant. I wonder again what it is that calls him away.

He nods to me and leaves the room, closing the door behind him. I pick up the other books, walk over to the fireplace, and set them all on the empty table. After pouring a cup of tea, I settle into one of the chairs and again pick up the book with the crest on it.

After examining its beautiful leather cover, I carefully leaf through it. It's not a diary, as I first thought, but rather a history of Europe from a different perspective—that of what Nicolas calls The Chosen. Fascinated, I read about the various ways The Chosen have tried to blend with human society, some successful, many not. Humans seem to have a problem with being a food source, and as a consequence, only Chosen who are very smart and have excellent self-control are able to survive for any length of time.

Oddly, a number of Chosen worked as healers in villages and cities all across Europe. Their particular talent was diagnosing disease. Chosen senses, distinctly tuned to the smell of blood, could detect any taint or abnormalities. Their diagnostic abilities and treatment skills were passed down from their Makers, and many had significant status as disease specialists in their communities.

I chuckle, noticing the book doesn't mention the fate of patients who came in bleeding.

The door opens, and Nicolas strides across the room wearing a black three-piece suit.

"That was fast. I've barely started the first book." I smile up at him, but he doesn't return it. The earlier distant look has now become troubled.

"Ah. Unfortunately, I am being called away. I will not be back until morning. But you are welcome to stay and read. Marie has your room made up for you. She will take good care of you until I return." He looks at me, but his thoughts are clearly elsewhere.

"Well, actually, I need to go home for a while. I have some business of my own to attend to on the mountain." I stand and set the book on the table with the others.

He looks at me, his eyes dark and intense.

"Please be careful. I worry about you hunting up there alone."

I laugh. "Nicolas, I've been hunting alone since day one of this life. I'll be fine."

As I start to walk past him, he reaches out and, catching my arm, pulls me to him. He pushes my hair back, stroking my temple with his thumb, and takes a deep breath.

"You have become . . . extremely important to me. I cannot bear the thought of something happening to you." The look in his eyes, shaded in faint red, sends an electric pulse through me.

I reach up and touch his cheek, and wrap my arms tightly around him. He hugs me in return, then slowly releases me.

As I start to move away, he grabs my waist and pulls me to him again, rougher this time, and kisses me fiercely. His lips move to my jaw, and then to my throat, and his sharp teeth are against my skin. He stands there, my throat in his teeth, and growls, low and deep. And I wait, fire running through my veins, for what I don't know, except that I know I want it.

We stand frozen for several moments, neither daring to move, until he slowly relaxes his jaw, then kisses my neck in parting. He gently lets me go and, with a long, searching look in his blazing scarlet eyes, steps away.

I swallow and take a deep breath. I'm not sure what just happened, but it's significant.

Nicolas starts to say something, but seems unable to speak. He then closes his eyes and, shaking his head, walks to the door. I follow him and he holds the door open for me.

As I head upstairs to fetch my things from the bedroom, I hear him pause at the bottom of the staircase. He's still waiting there when I return a moment later, and he walks me to the front door, hand on my back.

"I'm sorry I cannot accompany you. Please call me when you return from your hunt so that I know you are safe," he says huskily.

"I will. And thank you for a wonderful day. I, uh . . ."

The thought of leaving him suddenly tightens my throat and a feeling of panic races through me.

I don't want to go.

But it's too late now, and I swallow back my anxiety and reluctantly allow Nicolas to usher me outside and down the stairs. His Jag is parked behind my car, and he walks me around it to my door.

"Thank you again for . . . everything." I bravely smile at him as I get in.

"You are welcome. Good night. And please be careful." He closes my door.

I start the engine and slowly move down the driveway. Nicolas follows me, the Jag parking lights glowing in my mirror. I speed up, as I realize he must be in a hurry. We pass through the gates, then he zips around me and is gone.

Driving home, I slowly become aware of the fact that I'm ravenous. I hunted both Sunday and Monday—this is only Friday, so I'm a bit puzzled. Maybe I burned through my stores of energy with all the physical activity of skiing, although that seems a little unlikely. I suspect it has more to do with all the emotional activity and the strain I feel sometimes when I'm with Nicolas. As much as I love to be with him, I think I also need some downtime to be by myself. Guess I've kind of gotten used to that over the years.

When I enter the house, my gaze is drawn to the bookcase that now dominates the living room. He certainly made sure I'd be aware of his presence, even if he physically can't be with me. I shake my head and walk into the bedroom to change into hunting clothes.

~

The hot shower pummels me as I try in vain to wash off some of the edginess that accompanies my unsatisfied hunger. The small muley buck didn't completely quell my cravings, but the eastern sky was beginning to lighten, and there was no time to hunt for another. I may have spoiled myself with elk.

After leaving a voice mail for Nicolas—he doesn't answer when I call as promised—I slip into bed and lie there a while, thinking about how my life has changed. And it has, forever, because what part of me feared would happen—has happened.

I have fallen in love with Nicolas.

Desperately, hopelessly in love.

And I will never be the same again.

Wonder and joy that this could happen to me—to *me*—race through my body, sending shivers along every vein. But they're quickly followed by fear—fear of losing my independence, of having to consider the needs of another, of changes I can't anticipate.

Worse, I don't even know if he loves *me*. I believe he cares for me, maybe even deeply, but for how long?

And what will he think of my need to visit California now and again, to check on my daughter and her family? Nicolas hasn't been human for centuries. He likely won't understand my need to keep in touch with my former human life, even if all I can do is watch.

My gut suddenly twists, and an icy chill runs up my spine. I can't tell him about my family and their hold over me—not ever. He must never learn of their existence. I have no explanation, other than every instinct in me screaming in deadly warning.

Andrea . . .

As the rising sun drags me down into the black depths of unconsciousness, my chest aches with the knowledge that I must put her out of my mind once and for all, and that yet again my love for someone is tarnished by the burden of secrecy.

április 13., péntek

I took her skiing today. It was her first time, and she was stunning as she mastered the slopes. And she did so with grace and humor and a joy for life that I have not experienced for a very long time. But through her, I was able to do so, and I cannot wait to share more adventures with her.

Yet what I had hoped would be a pleasant day nearly ended in a nightmare. When I saw that accursed skier hit her, it felt as though my chest had ripped open. Her accident made me keenly aware of her vulnerability to injury, as she has yet to develop the damage-resistant physique of a mature Chosen. I realized just how easily I could lose her, and how limited I am in trying to keep her safe.

Now she has gone hunting on the mountain by herself. I should have gone with her. All I think of is how easily she could be speared with an antler, or have her head crushed by a hoof. But that fool Corey created another unacceptable problem at the club and had to be dealt with. He will not cause any more. It was unfortunate for him that he chose this night to lose control, when I was beside myself with worry for my love.

SATURDAY

CHAPTER 24

I roll out of bed, feeling emotionally drained and, unfortunately, hungry.

What's the matter with me? Last night's deer should've satisfied the damn hunger, but it doesn't seem to have even put a dent in it.

And whatever sleep I had doesn't feel like it was restful. Just what I need—a case of the grouchies. Hope Nicolas doesn't return my call and find out what I'm like when I have a bad day. But then I'll probably have a total breakdown if he doesn't call at all.

Feeling crankier by the minute, I shuffle into the kitchen, turn on the burner to heat some water for tea, and start the laptop. I stare dejectedly at the club list I'd made when I first came to town. I'm definitely not in the mood to go job hunting today, but I can at least figure out what places to hit on Monday.

Didn't pick up my paycheck yesterday like I'd planned. Maybe today would be a good day to do it. Bet they wouldn't give me any crap. Of course, if they do, I just might find I like something better than elk. Hah. Not funny.

Picking up the cell phone from the table, I check it for missed calls and voice mails. Nothing. I pour my tea and glance at the clock—1:08 and no word from Nicolas. Great.

I wander over to the bookcase and read the titles and authors once again. I don't dare take any books out. In my current mood I'd probably tear one in half just pulling it off the shelf.

The phone finally rings.

Thank God. I was getting more than a little annoyed at him.

"Hello," I answer, trying to keep the irritation out of my voice.

"Hello," he says quietly. "How are you today?"

"Fine." The lie leaks through.

"I see." He pauses. "Is there anything I can do to help?"

"No, yes . . . I don't know." My throat tightens as I choke off an unbidden sob.

"Ah, Sunny. Unfortunately I cannot come up there right now, but would you like to come down here?"

And see you? And hold you? And never let you go?

"Yes," I whisper. "I . . . I just need a moment to change clothes."

"Good. I should be at the house by the time you arrive. I will see you there." His quiet reassurance sends relief surging through me. I feel like I'm taking my first breath of the day.

"Okay, see you soon."

The phone goes silent. I look at it, thinking.

Is he just now getting back from wherever he rushed off to last night? Where has he been? Was he with someone else? *Is* there someone else?

Oh, girl. Get real. You don't own him. You hardly know him.

Feeling even more unsettled than before, I pour out my tea and go into the bedroom to get dressed.

I pull up to the black gates, but before I can push the call button, they open. I follow the driveway around and park behind the Jag in front of the stairs. I get out and look at the house, and a small part of me feels the fear again—the fear of the life that accompanies this house, the fear of its master, and the dark secrets they both hold.

But it's too late to run. I can't bear to be apart from him, and I sense that he feels the same about me. With a deep breath, I walk up the steps.

"Good afternoon, mademoiselle," Marie says as she opens the door. "Mr. Ambrus asked if you could wait in the library."

"Thank you, Marie." I walk past her across the foyer and into the library. She closes the door behind me.

Arms crossed, I stroll over to the window and look out at the lawn and its topiary forest. Much of the snow from the big storm has melted, leaving patches of brown grass peeking out here and there.

The door opens and I turn as Nicolas walks in. His black hair still appears damp from his shower; his crisply pressed shirt, open at the collar with the sleeves rolled back, is neatly tucked into his slacks.

But it's his strained expression that I notice the most, and my own problems fade into sudden concern for him.

Yet as he approaches, relief replaces the tension. His sea-green gaze locked onto me, he places his hands on my shoulders for a moment, then pulls me to him and takes me into his arms.

His evening and morning must have been much worse than mine. I hold him tighter, wanting to comfort him and tell him everything will be all right.

He slowly lets me go, touches my face, and takes a deep breath.

"Thank you for coming down. I, ah . . ." His voice fades.

I touch his lips with my fingers. "It's okay. I'm here."

He hugs me again, then releases me and steps away. He walks across the room, his hands clenched behind his back. He stops and turns to look at me.

"My life is very . . . complicated. I have many responsibilities that simply cannot be ignored until a more convenient time." He takes a breath and starts pacing the room again.

"When I first felt the presence of a stranger in my city, without my permission, I was quite concerned. That this presence was able to move about during the day caused me even greater alarm. You see, only the older and more powerful among us are able to do this. But I did not sense an Elder. In fact, I did not sense anything I recognized." His brow furrows.

"I located this uninvited visitor, and waited across the street, and then *you* stepped out of the shop. You. You with your pale skin, unearthly beauty, and bearing that could only belong to one of The Chosen. Yet there was something about you that was different, and I could not pin down what it was.

"I could tell from your reaction you were surprised to see me. I could only assume then that you were here covertly, hoping not to be discovered. I was determined to find out who you were, with whom you were aligned, and what business you had in my city."

His city. I recall that day vividly—the shock I felt, the fear that I would be seen as an intruder. And I had been right.

"I made some calls, but none of my associates knew anything. I was quite frustrated, as I could tell you were no longer in the Springs and I was not sure how to track you down. But that evening, you came back and I traced your presence to a nightclub. You stayed inside the club, surrounded by humans, for what seemed to be an interminably long time. I searched and found your car and decided to wait." He stops his pacing and stands just a few feet from me.

"Then you stepped out of the club and I watched you hesitate as you saw me. I expected you to run, which would have done you little good." His head tilts and I swallow.

"But you did not run. You walked directly up to me, and I realized you had no idea who I was. Any Chosen would know me instantly, but you were clueless."

I still am. Who *are* you, Nicolas?

"When we were sitting in the restaurant, I found your scent to be completely unreadable. I could not identify what lineage you were, and your blood had an unusual fragrance that puzzled me." He slowly shakes his head. "You bore absolutely no trace of human blood. You did not feed on humans. I was intrigued as to what you did feed on, and imagined perhaps rabbits or other small game."

He quickly suppresses a grimace, but not quickly enough.

I frown. My choice of diet *does* disgust him.

"Then I saw you in the forest, agile and swift and so totally alive. I watched you hunt, as a true predator does, seeking out and stalking your prey. But you came into your full glory when you magnificently took down that huge elk. I have never seen anything so impressive, so efficient, so beautiful." His eyes, dark and smoky, are blossoming red. He reaches out and touches my cheek.

"It was when you went in for the kill, and the way you gave yourself over so completely to the embrace that marks our kind, that I realized I was in danger of falling in love with you," he says quietly, his crimson eyes blazing. "And since then, I have."

Everything in me stops.

"I will never forget that first kiss, the taste of you, thick with the blood of your prey."

He steps closer, and carefully gathers me in his arms, and kisses me, deeply and slowly. He moves from my lips and begins kissing each part of my face, lingering on my jaw, then moving down to my throat. I tip my head back, and he holds me tighter, and his mouth begins tracing along my jugular. I feel his lips part, and his teeth brush my skin. He gently takes hold of my throat, and groans. His teeth are sharp, like needles, and I realize that what I feel are . . . fangs.

Part of me panics and wants to run, but the other part of me leans into him. He freezes and pulls back slightly, and I don't understand, but I freeze as well. We stand there, barely breathing, until his grip softens, and he gently releases my throat. He moves his mouth to my hair, nuzzling it, and I feel such a wave of emotion I start to shake and cry my tearless cry.

He holds me tighter, stroking my hair and softly whispering reassurances. I finally regain control and grow still, as does he, and I lose all sense of time as we stand wrapped around one another.

He holds my hand as we walk among the forest of creatures standing guard over the estate. The day is overcast, the sun safely hidden behind grey clouds.

We haven't said anything since we were in the library, since he told me he loved me.

"One of my greatest concerns for you is about the Choice that you did not have. I want you to know that you will always have a Choice here, but it is difficult for you to choose when you do not understand what it is that is being offered.

"I have reached a point where I can no longer shelter you from the complexities that make up The Chosen society. I have been neglectful of my duties to the others as of late, though I have most enjoyed the reason." He raises my hand to his lips, his emerald eyes shining.

"I am hosting a small gathering tomorrow night, and I would like you to be there." He looks at me expectantly.

I knew this was coming. He warned me. But I still have to fight down the rising anxiety.

"All right," I whisper.

"To help you prepare, I have a close associate who will advise you as to our protocols. She will teach you how to properly interact with the others. It is important to listen carefully and do exactly as she says. Our communications have many nuances, and you need to understand the meanings behind the questions you may be asked."

My anxiety blossoms into full-blown panic. I stop, frozen in place, the urge to run hammering up my spine.

"Ah . . . I've frightened you. Forgive me. You are so like the prey that you hunt, ever-vigilant and ready to flee." Nicolas takes me into his arms and gently rests his chin on my head. "And it triggers the hunter in me, making me want to pursue you even more."

"But," he says, as he slowly lets me go, "you need to conquer your fears, the way you conquer the beasts in the forest. You are much stronger than you realize. You have abilities typically seen only in our Elders, and are unusual enough in your ways that the others will respect you."

His words make sense, but it's difficult to calm myself. I've been on the run too long.

But maybe I'm ready to stop.

"All right. I'll try." But my attempt to sound confident fails, even to my own ears.

"Well, that is a start. But I want you to know that if it becomes too difficult, too much of a strain, you are welcome to excuse yourself. And remember, you will not be alone. I will be there." He strokes my hair, then taking my arm, turns, and we resume our walk through the garden.

And all I can think about is that tomorrow I'm meeting others like him. Like me. Or maybe not so like me.

Nicolas glances down at me and smiles.

"How would you like to take a little shopping trip? I have something special in mind. I believe you will like it." His green eyes dance with that amusement I love so much.

"Okay." I look up at him, shaking my head. He sure likes his surprises.

CHAPTER 25

We walk into the garage, Nicolas flips on the light switch, and I stop in disbelief. This isn't a garage—it's a showroom. Before me is a row of polished exotic cars in all colors, their deep lacquer and chrome reflecting the light beaming from strategically placed fixtures.

"Which one should we take today? Choose." His eyes sparkle like the shiny toys lining the room.

"I don't know. There are so many." I walk slowly along the row. Ferrari, Bughatti, Lamborghini, Pantera, even a DeLorean, and more that I don't know. Then I see the one I want to ride in. The two-seater convertible is a gleaming bright yellow with classic black racing stripes down the hood.

"That one." I point to the 427 Cobra.

"Ah, you have most excellent taste. One of my favorites," he says, grinning.

"I will have Alfonso bring the car around to the front. We should return to the house and see if Marie has a scarf you can borrow, or I am afraid you will never be able to untangle your hair."

We are flying down the highway in the jet engine that masquerades as a car. Its deep growl reminds me of Nicolas, and I reach over and stroke his jaw and throat. He looks over at me, eyes suddenly flaring red, and touches my throat in response.

Nicolas wanted to take the car out and let it stretch its legs, as he called it, and we blasted onto I-25 heading south toward Pueblo. But apparently he feels we've gone far enough and takes the next off-ramp, then gets back on the highway heading north. He punches the accelerator and the Cobra leaps forward with a roar, pinning me back in the seat.

I laugh wildly, and he glances at me and grins.

Quickly reaching the downtown off-ramps, Nicolas takes one, reining in this beast of a car. Slowly cruising through the city streets, the Cobra thunder echoes off the buildings as we pass. I'm now in love with this car as well as its owner.

We park on the street in front of a string of boutiques. Nicolas gets out, feeds the meter, and opens my door.

"Aren't you afraid to leave it here?"

"Do not worry. No one will touch her."

People pass by on the sidewalk, stopping to admire the flashy yellow car, and seem to instinctively stay back to do so.

Nicolas, his hand softly resting on my back, guides me into a formal-wear dress shop.

"I thought you might like to wear something new tomorrow evening. Unless you already have a dress that is suitable?" His eyebrows raise in question.

"Yes, no, I mean I don't have anything really . . ." At least nothing to wear to a party at an upper-class estate.

"Good." He then turns to the anxiously waiting saleswoman and says something about gowns on hold. She disappears into the back of the store.

I start looking at the dresses hanging on a rack, mesmerized by the styles and colors. The saleswoman walks out carrying a couple more.

Nicolas gestures to the dresses she's holding and says, "Perhaps you could start with these? I selected several I thought you might like."

I blink in surprise. He picked them out? When did he have time to do that? Maybe this morning?

"Oh . . . how nice. Thank you." I start to take them from the saleswoman, but she motions to the rear of the store.

"Would you like me to put them in a dressing room for you?" she asks.

"Yes, that would be fine." I follow her down a short hall and into the rather elegant room, then close the door when she leaves.

All three are long gowns and finely made. I try the lavender one first. It's quite lovely and fits perfectly, and goes surprisingly well with my pale skin and dark hair. As I model it in the mirror, Nicolas's voice echoes down the hallway.

"Would you mind coming out to show me how they look?"

I suddenly feel embarrassed. I've never worn anything particularly sexy for him, and these three gowns are decidedly so. Feeling a bit like a dress-up doll, I open the door and shyly step out from the hall.

"Ah, even better than I imagined. Now, turn around, slowly."

If I could blush, I would. I do as he asks, feeling his avid gaze as it travels over me.

"Hmm. Very nice. Now go try the blue one."

Yessir . . .

This one has an even more revealing bustline. The soft satin glides over my hips, its color the deep cobalt of an evening sky. It goes well with my eyes, which are quite dark today.

I take a breath and walk out. Nicolas catches his, and I feel a bit of satisfaction in that.

Smiling, feeling more confident, I seductively drift past him, lingering a little as I pivot around, then walk back. I stop in front of him, head tilted.

His eyes are faintly glowing red and I slowly smile in return. He tenses. I leave to go back to the dressing room before anything more can happen.

Wow, guess I better be more careful. I'm still getting used to how easily I can make Mr. Control lose it—it's probably not too smart to do it in public.

Taking off the blue dress, I hang it up and slip into the black one. It's much more refined and elegant, and I feel almost regal in it. The bustline is more modest than the blue one and is trimmed in black rhinestones that give off glimmers of light without standing out. An ebony waterfall of silk cascades to the floor, shimmering as it moves through the air.

I walk out, more stately this time, and behave myself as I pass Nicolas. The silk floats ahead of me with each step, and ripples in shiny black waves as it trails behind.

Watching Nicolas as I turn around, he reminds me of the cat that ate the canary. His approving gaze slowly sweeps over me from head to toe. He smiles and nods with satisfaction.

I smile in return. "You like this one, then?"

"Yes. I think it will be perfect for tomorrow evening. You will make a magnificent first impression."

I nod and go back into the dressing room to change into my street clothes. As I start to zip my jeans, a soft knock on the door stops me.

"Miss Martin?"

"Yes?"

"I have one more dress that Mr. Ambrus thought you might like to try on."

"Oh. Okay." I open the door and the saleswoman hands me another long gown, this one in bright red.

"Thank you," I tell her as I take it, frowning.

Red? Not a color I normally wear—at least in clothing form. Maybe that's why Nicolas picked it out.

With a sigh, I strip again and look closer at the dress. Like the black one, this dress is made of shimmery silk. When I slip it over my head, the crimson flows over my hips as though it was truly liquid. A one-shouldered affair, its bold statement is a stark contrast to the quiet dignity of the black dress. The daring design and blood red silk literally scream, "Look at me," which is certainly not the impression I want to give Nicolas's guests.

It's undeniably stunning, though. I turn sideways and admire the way the fabric drapes over my shoulder to curve across my back. But this dress is too much for me.

"Miss Martin?"

I take a deep breath.

"Yes?"

"Mr. Ambrus asked if you've tried on the red dress yet. He'd like to see it if you have."

Taking another deep breath, I shake my head and open the door.

"Oh my, Miss Martin!" she exclaims. "That dress is just absolutely breathtaking!"

She steps back as I murmur a thank you and resignedly leave the sanctuary of the dressing room.

Nicolas is staring out the store window, his hands in his pockets, when I walk into the room. He turns, slowly withdrawing his hands as his eyes flash the color of my dress, and stands for a moment, the muscles in his jaw flexing.

"Yes" is all he says in a guttural whisper.

He says nothing more, instead motioning for me to turn around. I do so, slowly, and when I face him the look of raw desire on his face takes my breath away.

At a loss for words as much as he seems to be, I give him a brief smile and head back to the dressing room, the silk caressing my hips as I walk.

When I finish changing back into my clothes and open the door, the saleswoman is waiting.

"I'll take the black one," I tell her. It's much more my style. There's no way I'm wearing that red one, in spite of how much Nicolas likes it.

If Chosen society is anything like human society, I'm not willing to risk either unwanted attention from the male guests or jealousy and criticism from the females by wearing something so provocative.

"Mr. Ambrus has already taken care of it, miss," she responds as she gathers the dresses and walks out.

Nicolas stands as I rejoin him.

"Well, that was fun. Thank you."

"I certainly enjoyed it," he replies, his emerald eyes bright. "But we are not quite done. I believe you will need shoes, yes?"

"Uh, yes, I do. I don't have anything suitable for that dress."

"There is a shop several doors down. They will hold our purchase here, and we will pick it up on our way back." He smiles again, amusement flickering in his eyes.

Now what does he have up his sleeve?

We walk down to the shoe store, and I quickly find a pair of black Italian strap sandals with a tall heel that should be the right height for the black dress. But as I start to put my shoes back on, Nicolas walks up with a pair of blue ones—and a pair of red ones.

"Try these on," he says, smirking.

"You didn't."

"Did you think we would leave that store without the red dress? Or the blue one? The black one is for you to wear for our guests tomorrow, if you prefer, but the others are for you to wear for me."

"Oh."

I take the shoes and try them on. Like everything else he's picked out for me, both pair are just the right shades and fit perfectly.

"We have one more stop across the street. Shall we?" Nicolas asks as we leave the shoe store. The corner of his mouth twitches as he holds out his arm. Shaking my head, I grasp the inside of his elbow and we step off the curb and cross the road.

We pass several shops, then he stops at a jewelry store and opens the door. I glance up at him and he smiles that Cheshire cat grin again.

Nicolas really has fun with these little games.

He walks up to the counter and talks to the jeweler while I look at the display cases.

"Sunny?"

I join him at the counter. On a black velvet display cloth is a necklace with a large blue sapphire as the centerpiece. The stone is round and perches alone in its white gold mounting, which is suspended in a chain of small diamonds.

I don't know a lot about fine jewelry, but I suspect this piece may be worth as much as one of Nicolas's cars.

"Come, turn around," Nicolas says, a tad impatiently.

I dutifully do so, and he lifts the necklace over my head and fastens it. Fortunately, the black sweater I'm wearing has a scoop neckline, and the necklace rests perfectly against my bare skin.

Nicolas gently turns me around by the shoulders and steps back. He tilts his head and smiles, then hands me a mirror.

The necklace is stunning, the sapphire clear and cut beautifully. It's an intense medium blue, and its rich color is a nice contrast to my darker eyes. But I suspect it would complement them no matter what shade they were.

"I think this will do, yes?" He looks at me in the mirror, eyebrows raised, and I nod.

"It's beautiful," I whisper, staring at the jewel in my reflection. I then look at his reflection, and again see something stirring in the depths of his emerald eyes.

I feel like a princess who's met her Prince Charming, though perhaps one a bit more dangerous than the fairy tale version.

But then, I'm not anything that's stepped out of a normal fairy tale either.

I smile at his image and he returns it.

"Good. I am glad you like it." He reaches up and brushes the side of my neck with his fingertips, and I catch a flash of red in his eyes as he moves to unfasten the catch on the necklace.

I'm looking forward to meeting this associate of his, and am relieved she's female. Hopefully some of her etiquette instructions will include tips on Chosen courtship. I have a feeling there's a lot more to it than human dating.

While Nicolas takes care of the bill, I wait by the door. I don't want to know what the necklace cost, because then I'll be afraid to wear it. I'm going to have enough trouble with the shoes, which were hundreds of dollars, and the dresses, totaling several thousand. I shake my head in disbelief. Yeah, I'm in a fairy tale, all right . . . one that's written in blood.

We get back to the estate just before dark. I'm anxious now to get home, as the hunger is starting to make itself known. I've been pleasantly distracted all day, and was only faintly aware of it hovering in the background a few times.

And I need a break from Nicolas, though the thought of our separation bothers me more than I want to admit. But he's been especially smothering today, and I feel the need for some space.

As we get out of the Cobra, Marie comes down the steps and collects the packages. Nicolas tells her to take them up to my room and starts to walk up the steps to the house. I stay next to the car and he turns to look at me in question.

"Nicolas, I . . . I just want to thank you for a wonderful afternoon, and for the beautiful gifts. I don't want to seem ungrateful, but I really must go home for now."

His eyes narrow slightly, and he takes a breath. He starts to say something, then doesn't.

He walks back down the steps to me and reaches up to caress the side of my face.

"Please be careful tonight." He obviously understands why I need to leave.

"I will." No more flippant remarks about how I've been doing this a while. I can see the thought of me out there wrestling elk worries him greatly, and I don't want to belittle his fears.

He kisses my forehead, then steps back and watches me as I walk to my car. His eyes are dark and unfathomable.

That's a bit odd. He usually opens my door for me.

I get in, start my car, and head down the driveway.

április 14., szombat

I bared my soul to her today, as I can no longer hide how I feel. I doubt she grasps the depth of my feelings, and I have no way to begin to express them. I think she may feel something for me, but she seems unsure. I hope I have not made a mistake by telling her too soon. To make it worse, I nearly lost control with her. I had her exquisite throat in my teeth and could almost taste her fiery blood running beneath her soft skin. I was so close, but I could feel her fear, and I realized she would not understand.

I took her shopping this afternoon. She stole my breath away each time she walked out in one of the dresses I had selected for her. The red one, and the sapphire jewel that pales next to the brilliance of her eyes, will be perfect for tomorrow's Council meeting. They will be completely awed by her, yet baffled, which should disrupt their plotting, at least for the time being.

To my immense disappointment, she went home to her mountain this evening after our trip, no doubt to hunt. I had hoped to speak with her about tomorrow night.

And I am greatly unsettled when she is not at my side. I fear for her safety and will be plagued with worry until she returns.

I am starting to hate the very thing that made me fall in love with her .

SUNDAY

CHAPTER 26

I wake up and look at the clock—10:17, a little early for me. But there's nothing I can do about it now, so I get up.

Last night's hunt was a bit like the previous night. I'd taken the first thing I came across, a small mule deer buck, and hopefully he was enough to hold me for a couple of days. I'll get serious about finding an elk after Nicolas's party, which I'm really not looking forward to.

Of course, wearing the black dress and the necklace will make the whole affair a bit more bearable. I smile as I think how impressive the ensemble will look once I have it all on. At least I won't be embarrassed by something from my own modest wardrobe.

I don't know what time to go down there, as Nicolas didn't say when his "associate" would be available. He didn't even tell me her name. I wonder about her, and what the other females will be like. And I think about how many Nicolas might have loved in his five hundred years. That's a bit disturbing, but realistic. He's extremely passionate. I can't imagine him being alone for any length of time.

The cell phone rings. Yeah, I'm pretty sure he can tell when I'm dwelling on him. That phone never fails to ring whenever I am.

"Hi. I was just thinking about you."

"Apparently I was thinking of you as well." His laughter drifts through the phone.

Smart ass.

"What time would you like for me to come down?" I ask.

"Whenever you are ready. Éva has arrived and is looking forward to meeting you."

Éva. Sounds European. I wonder how long he's known her.

"Well, I need to gather a few things for tonight's party first."

"Excellent. We shall be waiting. Until then." Silence.

It's funny. Face-to-face, it seems like he's always talking. But on the phone, it's short and to the point.

I set down the cell and go into the bedroom to dress and pack. Since the sun appears to be out at the moment, I slip on a black turtleneck. The mirror catches my attention, and I realize the cornflower blue of my eyes today will go well with the sapphire necklace, better than if they were pale. Maybe it's a good thing I didn't gorge on elk last night.

With a last look through my closet and toiletries to make sure I have everything, I head outside to the car.

I pull up in front of the stairway, take a deep breath to calm myself, and, switching off the ignition, get out. As I start to walk toward the steps, Alfonso appears from around the corner.

"Good morning, miss," he says. I think it's the first time he's ever spoken directly to me. "Mr. Ambrus asked if you would mind me parking your car in the back. He's expecting guests this evening, and he didn't want your car to get blocked in."

"How thoughtful. Yes, that would be fine." I reluctantly hand him my keys. I appreciate Nicolas ensuring I can make an easy escape, but I don't like not having them.

"You can just leave the keys in the ignition. I doubt anyone will steal it." I smile, and he gives a quick nod as he climbs into the BMW.

"Yes, miss."

Watching as he drives it around the corner, I hope that, if needed, I can find it quickly.

My jaw tightens in frustration. I've got to stop thinking like a runner. I can handle this.

After several deep breaths, I slowly walk up the steps. The door opens, and Marie greets me with her lovely French accent. "Good morning, mademoiselle."

"Good morning, Marie." I smile warmly. She's sweet. I really like her.

"Mr. Ambrus is waiting in the library for you." She walks over and knocks on the door.

"Yes, Marie. Please, have her come in." Excitement ripples through me at the sound of his voice. It's amazing how much of an effect he has on me.

Nicolas is standing next to the round table looking over a stack of papers as I walk in. He straightens, and his eyes light up when he sees me. He walks over and takes me by the shoulders, then brushes the hair back from my eyes and embraces me.

"I missed you," he says, holding me tight.

"I missed you, too."

He relaxes his arms and leans back, looking at me.

"You did not feed well again last night. How are you feeling?" Concern wrinkles his brow.

"All right. It was enough to get me through the next few days."

I hope. Tonight may prove enough of a strain that I could quickly exhaust my reserves.

"I see." He's clearly not too happy with the situation. He releases me and walks back to the table.

"Really, I'm fine. I've mentioned that I usually go a week or so, and I *have* fed the last two nights." I try to sound convincing. But things have changed lately and my hunger seems to have become unpredictable.

"Yes, I recall. But what you seem to have forgotten is the impact that emotions have on our hunger. And I am not talking just about anger and anxiety, but any strong emotions . . ." He stares out the window.

"Like love?" I quietly ask. I haven't been able to say it, though he has.

His back stiffens as he stops breathing.

"Like love, and everything associated with it."

I walk up behind him and put my arms around his waist, and hold him tightly. He presses his arms against mine, gently stroking my fingers.

We stand there a moment, then he takes a breath and says, "Éva is waiting to meet you, impatiently I would guess."

He pats my hand and I release him, then he turns and kisses me softly on the lips before walking out of the room.

Thinking about what Nicolas said about our emotions, I realize that he's right. It all makes sense now. No wonder I've been so hungry lately.

The door opens. I turn and prepare to meet another of my kind.

CHAPTER 27

A tall, slender female comes in, followed by Nicolas. Wearing a cream blouse tucked into khaki slacks, her light brown hair gathered into an elegant updo, she is stunning—a tawny lioness to Nicolas's black panther. Seeing them together is . . . unsettling.

Her hazel eyes appraise me as she walks gracefully across the room, and she smiles and stops a few feet from me, Nicolas by her side.

"Éva," he says. "May I present Miss Martin."

"Hello." She nods once. "I am Éva Basarab. I am pleased to meet you." Her expression, though a bit guarded, seems friendly as she clasps her hands in front of her.

Apparently it's not the custom to shake hands. Good.

"Hello. I'm Sunny. Sunny Martin." I nod once.

"I have been looking forward to this ever since Nicolas told me about you," Éva says.

Her accent is similar to his. Perhaps she is also Hungarian?

"Yes, I have as well, although I just learned about you yesterday." I smile and glance at Nicolas as he walks by on his way to the table.

"I am afraid I have some work to do," he says as he gathers his papers. "So I will leave the two of you to get acquainted. In a little while, I will have Marie come in with hot tea, and if you need anything else, please feel free to ask her."

He stops and kisses me on the cheek as he leaves the room, closing the door behind him.

Abandoning me.

"Shall we sit?" Éva waves toward the chairs that face the window. I settle into one, then move it back a little from the beam of sunlight that's coming through the glass. I notice her raise an eyebrow as she sits in the other chair.

She tilts her head, curiosity apparent in her golden eyes, and takes in my scent, then frowns, obviously puzzled.

But the examination is twofold. Her scent is very similar to that of Nicolas's, and woven thickly with human blood, but still a little different. She seems to give off a similar sense of power, though nowhere near as strong. Perhaps she's one of the Elders that Nicolas mentioned.

Alarm and fascination blend into a sense of unease that I hope I'm able to hide.

Éva, watching me, leans forward and holds her bare arm in the sunbeam. Nothing happens. Like Nicolas, she is not sensitive to the sun. So she *is* an Elder. I debate a moment, then take a gamble. I push up my sleeve and put my arm in the beam as well. My skin starts to turn pink and the fiery pain begins, but I hold it there. The skin gets pinker, then red. I resist giving in to the agony for a moment longer, then slowly pull it back. My arm feels like flames are racing up and down it, but I refuse to even wince.

Éva takes a slow breath and says, "That was stupid. *Do not ever* reveal your weaknesses to one of us."

She glances down at my arm as it slowly loses the redness. "You are fortunate that Nicolas asked me to be your tutor. You need to pay attention to what I say if you are to survive.

"The Chosen thrive on the manipulation of others, constantly seeking to improve their status within our society. You must be very careful in whom you confide, as anything you say or do will be noted for its value in the Game."

I stay silent, but not with the fear I'd expected. Rather, I feel my blood tingle at the prospect of the challenge that is opening up before me. The hunter rouses, fully alert now.

"Good. Nicolas was concerned about your reactions, but it seems he may have underestimated you."

"What is the 'game'?" I ask.

"The Game is one of domination and power. We have an instinctive need to control our surroundings and everyone in them. It stems from self-preservation. Those who are best at it are the most likely to survive.

And control requires power—the more powerful a Chosen, the more they can control.

"Chosen are drawn to the Game from the moment they gain awareness of what they truly are. Those at the lower levels of our society, the younger ones, compete to gain the favor of the Elders who can assist them in their maturation and development. The Elders compete among themselves for status and power, and increasingly larger regions to control.

"I don't know if you realize the position that you are in," Éva continues. "Because of Nicolas, you have joined the Game at the top, and there is nowhere to go but down."

This gets my attention, but not because of what she said about this game, but because of her reference to Nicolas.

"Can I ask a question?" I watch Éva with the hunter's focus.

"Yes, certainly. I imagine you have quite a few," Éva replies, her expression sharp.

"Who *is* Nicolas?" The question has been burning in my mind since I first saw him.

She laughs. "Why, he is the greatest Game player of all!"

But then her face becomes serious, and she says, "But you don't really know, do you? He hasn't told you? No, he wouldn't, I suppose."

She takes a breath, and her eyes flash.

"Nicolas is the Maker. Not just a Maker, but *the* Maker, the head of our lineage. He is one of the oldest surviving Chosen in the world, and one of the few of his age and power to still be in the Game. Most others like him have left our society and gone into seclusion. We call them the Old Ones. They are never seen."

I'm dumbfounded. I knew he was powerful. I can feel it emanate from him, ebbing and flowing in rhythm with his moods. But I had no idea he was their *leader*. And suddenly, everything about him falls into place—his bearing, his knowledge, his age. It all makes sense now.

Except the part about me.

I look at Éva, who is watching me closely. Her comments about the Game take on a new meaning, and I feel a chill wash over me.

"So why me? What does he see in me?" I whisper. My second most burning question.

"Because, my dear, you are the rarest of creatures. You possess all of the unsuspecting innocence of a human, but with the skills and needs of a mature Chosen. Your level of power and abilities are quite unusual in one so young, and yet you are completely unaware of it. Or of the Game." Éva studies me a moment as I consider this, then continues.

"So, as Nicolas sees it, your interest in him is pure and not tainted with the desires of one who seeks to manipulate and improve their position."

"Then why would he expose me to this *Game*? Isn't he afraid I might become . . . corrupted?"

Éva sighs. "I would imagine it is because he loves you and can't bear to be apart from you. And he cannot leave the Game. He has suffered much recently because his attention has been elsewhere." She looks pointedly at me.

He had said as much.

"So he really has no choice but to introduce you to our society. Though to be fair, Nicolas also relishes the Game. If he didn't, he wouldn't be the master of it that he is." She starts to say more, but seems to change her mind.

I become aware of steps outside the door, and Marie softly knocks. "Mesdemoiselles, I have brought you some tea."

"Come in," Éva says.

Marie enters the room carrying a tray.

"Bring it over here." Éva points to the small table between the chairs.

The French girl seems particularly subdued and tense as she quickly sets the pot and cups on the table. She curtsies and steps back.

"Will there be anything else?" There is a slight nervousness to her speech.

"No, that will be all," Éva replies imperiously. Marie practically runs from the room.

That's interesting. The poor girl was quite afraid of Éva. She's never shown any such fear of me.

I pick up the teapot and look at Éva, offering to pour her tea. Her mouth quirks and she nods. I fill her cup, then my own as I think over some of the things Éva has said. I wonder what my role in all this will be.

"We should probably discuss what will be expected of you tonight." She takes a sip.

Expected of me? What does see me as—a child?

I bristle, then relax. I probably am when compared to centuries-old Chosen.

"Tonight is a gathering of the Council. There are nine members, including Nicolas, who is the Council head. Each Council member is responsible for their own region and The Chosen that live within it. They meet every third new moon to give their reports and renew their ties.

"Once their business is concluded, they will spend time socializing. Nicolas will occasionally bring in a small orchestra or dance troupe to provide entertainment, or take the Council out to the theater or the opera.

"I don't know if Nicolas plans to have you attend the meeting or if he will have you come in once business is concluded. The latter, I would expect." Éva takes another sip of her tea, looking at me over the rim, then continues with her lecture.

"I would suggest you keep conversation to a minimum. If you are asked where you are from, be vague. If someone is rude enough to inquire about your lineage, tell them they will need to discuss that with Nicolas.

"Be strong. Nicolas needs you to be. You will be evaluated for weakness from the moment you enter the room, so don't show any." Her eyes narrow in emphasis.

I nod as she continues.

"Nicolas has told me little of your background, other than you were taken against your will by an unknown Maker and then abandoned. That is unforgivable in our world, but it's best if you don't reveal your beginnings. Rather than garner sympathy, it will raise a flag of opportunity to those who would seek to dislodge you from your position with Nicolas."

Éva doesn't say anything more, obviously allowing me time to digest what she has told me so far.

I quietly drink my tea and think about how all this fits so well with the Nicolas that has been hidden from me.

"Do you have any questions?" she asks, her eyebrows raised.

Does she know I don't hunt humans?

"What else has Nicolas told you about me?" I watch her face, but it reveals nothing.

"Very little, but he doesn't need to. I can feel what happens to him when he talks about you. This is a Nicolas that I have not seen in a very long time. You are good for him. In fact, you are more important than you realize. Because of who he is, his well-being is highly critical for the well-being of us all.

"And I pity the fool who makes the mistake of thinking he can get to Nicolas through you, because Nicolas will destroy anyone, and everyone around them, who even looks at you with ill intent." Éva tips her head as she looks at me.

I swallow and feel a glimmer of fear. Not for me, but for him.

"He loves you more than you perhaps realize. Do you love him?" Éva looks at me critically, and I sense that she would tear me apart if I did anything to harm Nicolas.

"Yes, I do. Very much."

"That's no real surprise. He's easy to love. And it's obvious to anyone in the same room with the two of you that you are practically bonded. But you have not done so, have you? Bonded?"

"I'm not sure what you mean."

She laughs.

"No one has spoken with you about this?"

I shake my head no.

"I see. Would it be safe to assume you know little of Chosen relationships then?" Éva raises her eyebrows.

"I know nothing." Embarrassed, I look away from her piercing gaze as it shifts from disbelief to pity.

"Nicolas, Nicolas," she says, shaking her head. She gets up and starts slowly pacing the room.

"For The Chosen, our world revolves around the blood. The blood of our prey, the blood of our Makers, the blood of our lovers. Everything is always about the blood.

"When two Chosen decide to pair, to bond, they will exchange blood. The blood of one flowing through the veins of the other, and vice versa, creates a connection between them. This connection is so strong that they can *feel* what the other is feeling, no matter how far apart. Our emotions are directly tied to the blood, so the sharing of blood is also a sharing of emotions." She stops and looks at me.

"This . . . blood exchange, how much do they . . . ?" I'm not sure how to finish the question.

"Why all of it, of course, so that the blood is the same in both of them. It really is quite satisfying, if you must know."

"Do they . . . uh, do anything else? Like humans?"

Eva laughs again, but it's not a kind laugh.

"Nicolas did not warn me I would have to explain the facts of life as though to a new-Chosen. I will have to thank him for that."

The condescension in her voice catches me off-guard. My embarrassment quickly shifts to pink-hazed anger.

Éva frowns. "I am sorry—I suppose that was unkind. No, we do not mate like animals and humans. Remember, for us everything is about the blood, the giving of it as well as the taking of it. Trust me, once you have done that, you will forget all about the clumsy rutting of your past human life."

Her continuing disdain pushes the hunter too far. A low snarl slips unbidden from my throat, and I stand and step away from the chair, glaring at her through a red veil.

My past human life? She knows *nothing* of it. There was no "clumsy rutting." It was the sharing of love, and I have my precious daughter because of it. We created life; we did not destroy it.

"Perhaps *your* experiences as a human were unpleasant. Mine were for the most part wonderful, and I *hate*—" I stop as Éva strides across the room toward me, her eyes dark.

"You hate what? What you are? Don't say it. And *never* say it where Nicolas can hear. We are The Chosen. *We* were chosen and offered this life because we were superior and above the rest. We are proud of what we are, and have no love for human life, except as sustenance." Her eyes flicker red, then back to dark gold.

"*You* may have been chosen, but I was not," I growl.

Éva hisses.

"Make no mistake. You *were* chosen. The real question is why, and why you were abandoned." She tilts her head. "And by whom."

Her words strike even deeper than before, dissolving my indignation. I take several breaths to calm myself. I really can't afford to alienate her.

"I . . . apologize for overreacting." I nod once, slowly.

Éva stands in silence for a moment, her golden eyes narrowed as she studies me.

"Nicolas said you were young, and that he needed me to teach you, so I will try to be more patient. I forget you were human not so long ago." She gives me a small smile and the visible tension in her body eases. "I do have one more thing to say about bonding. You need to listen carefully, and please, do not take this the wrong way."

Éva looks at me as she walks over to her chair and sits down. I follow her lead and take my seat again.

"Nicolas has not asked you to share blood yet—am I correct?" Her eyes have softened and show a hint of concern.

"No, he hasn't."

"As I said before, the blood is the center of our life. When we are attracted to another Chosen, the need to bond can be very powerful. We desire their blood, their essence, and we want to give them ours in exchange. This need can reach a point where even a simple caress can make either one lose complete control." Éva's intense gaze hardens again, drilling into me.

"So unless you are ready to commit yourself one hundred percent to Nicolas, I suggest you be very careful. And you should understand that if you do choose to bond with him, he will be extremely reluctant for you to ever leave his side. Bonding is total commitment, and once done, your life is no longer your own."

I look at her and slowly nod in understanding. I had realized that loving Nicolas meant my life was going to change. My question has been how much.

And now I know.

All of it, down to the very last drop.

CHAPTER 28

Nicolas walks into the library and his reassuring presence eases a little of my tension—but not enough to escape his notice. Concern flickers across his face as we both rise from our chairs, and raising his eyebrows, he looks at Éva. She blinks and shrugs, and he shakes his head.

"She'll do well, Nicolas," she says as she walks out to the center of the room. "She has a strong spirit and can stand up for herself. I believe she comprehends what is at stake."

Yeah, I do. Nicolas's position in their competitive society. And *my* life.

"However, she does have a bit of a temper, and needs to be careful not to display it in the wrong company. It can be taken as a sign of disrespect." Éva glances back at me with narrowed eyes as I cross the room.

He frowns at her, then his gaze softens as he walks over and takes me into his arms.

"Are you all right?"

"I'm fine. We just . . . don't agree on some things."

I sense that he wishes he could just hold me forever, sheltering me from the harsh realities of their world. But I realize that he has no choice, and I squeeze myself against him momentarily, then slowly push away.

"I'll be fine tonight. Éva made everything pretty clear." I try to keep the bitterness from my voice, but can't help but notice a sadness creep into his emerald eyes.

"Éva, please meet me in the study," he says, still looking at me.

She leaves the room without another word.

"You do not need to do this. It was unfair of me to expect you to be ready for Chosen social life so soon." He smoothes the hair back from my face. "There will be more opportunities to meet the others. Perhaps just getting acquainted with Éva should be enough for right now." His eyes darken in concern.

"You can't protect me from your world forever, Nicolas. Sooner or later I'll have to make a decision to join it—or not—and I rather it be sooner. I don't see any advantage in waiting."

"As you wish, then." He embraces me again. "I will not allow any harm to come to you. If I were able to walk away from them right now, I would. But to do so with no advance planning would be very dangerous for both of us."

He rests his cheek against my hair and takes a breath.

"I had hoped you and Éva would become friends, but perhaps it is a little soon for that. She is one of the few I really trust, yet I still never let my guard down completely—with any of them. Which is why I have survived this long," he says with resignation.

"I believe we got off to a good start. I just think she was a little surprised at how . . . ignorant I am. But she was patient enough and I never felt any ill will. I did, however, sense that she cares greatly about you and would defend you to her death."

"Ah yes, I believe you are correct. She and I . . . it was a long time ago."

I ease out of his arms and step back.

"I thought as much. You've lived for centuries. I would be a fool to think I'm the—"

"Sshh. This is not what I wish to discuss. Right now, my only concern is that you feel comfortable about meeting the others tonight." He reaches out, touching my cheek.

"I am. In fact, I'm looking forward to it. A few things Éva said intrigued me. I admit to being a little fascinated to see this Game of yours in action."

He drops his hand and gives me a wry smile.

"It bears little resemblance to most games, unless you count those that are to the death. Truthfully, I am a little weary of it as of late and am beginning to understand why the Old Ones have retired and gone into hiding."

"But aren't you like an . . . Old One, too?"

"Technically? Yes. But because I am still in the world and still playing the Game, I am not considered as such. However, I do have much of an Old One's power.

"So for now, we will play, and we will play well. The others jostle with one another to improve their status, but they can only go so high, and it amuses me to watch. Their Game with me is one of waiting. I hold all the cards, and will continue to do so until I am ready to call it, on *my* terms.

"And you, my sweet, are going to throw them all off balance. They will not know what to make of you, and will fall all over themselves trying to figure you out. And this I will enjoy watching, too." His smile becomes wicked, his eyes narrow, and the red blossoms within them.

Yes, Éva was right. He does love the Game.

And I can't help but wonder where I fit into it.

Soaking in a hot tub of water, I mull over Nicolas's words and speculate on what my role will be in tonight's gathering. I hadn't thought that I was going to be anything more than his arm candy for the evening, an ornament, meant to look pretty next to him and keep quiet.

And I don't mind that. I'd rather sit and observe their interactions with each other than engage in conversation myself. But I now think Nicolas has something else in mind, and I wish I had a better idea of what it is.

Unsettled by my thoughts, I stand up and grab a towel. So much for a relaxing soak.

"Mademoiselle?" Marie's voice is accompanied by her soft knock on the bathroom door.

"Yes, Marie?"

"Mr. Ambrus asked me to assist you in getting ready tonight."

"Okay. I'll be out in a moment." I finish toweling off and slip on a plush white bathrobe.

Wow. I'm really beginning to feel like a princess.

I step into the bedroom, noting her quiet, steady presence, and silently thank Nicolas.

"Would mademoiselle like for me to assist her with her hair before she gets dressed?"

"That would be wonderful. Do you have anything special in mind?" I'm relieved that she offered. Her hair is always cleverly arranged, and I haven't been able to come up with anything that would do justice to the dress and the jewelry.

"Yes, mademoiselle, I have several ideas that I think would be complementary."

"Great." I smile and sit down at the dressing table. I watch Marie in the mirror as she takes my hair down from its clip and begins brushing it.

"Marie, can I ask you something?"

"Yes, mademoiselle. I will answer as best as I can." She starts twisting sections and pinning them up.

"Earlier today when you came into the library, you seemed almost frightened of Éva. Why?" I study her face closely and she turns pale, just as I expected.

"Mademoiselle Éva." She glances down, her voice dropping to a whisper. "She makes me very . . . nervous. All of Mr. Ambrus's friends do."

"Why is that?"

She closes her eyes and shakes her head. "I cannot say."

Hmm. Unable to or forbidden to?

"Do I make you nervous?"

She looks up at me in the mirror. "No, mademoiselle, you are the only one who doesn't. You are not like the others." She blushes and slips a bobby pin into place.

Yeah, that's probably because I don't dine on humans, and they do. And she can tell the difference.

"Does Mr. Ambrus frighten you?"

"Sometimes. When he is very angry or upset. But mostly he is kind to me and takes good care of me. I know he won't hurt me."

But there's more she's not saying and I wonder just how much she actually knows about our kind.

"There, mademoiselle, how do you like it?" She seems anxious to change the subject.

"It's perfect. Thank you so much." I turn around and hold up a hand mirror. She has put all my hair up in elegant curls. It's just the right style for tonight.

"Then if mademoiselle is satisfied, let me add a few final touches."

I turn back around and watch in the mirror as she adds small jeweled clips, probably diamonds, to my hair.

"Thank you very much, Marie." I smile as I turn to admire my hair with the hand mirror.

"You are welcome. You look quite beautiful, mademoiselle." She smiles shyly in the mirror.

I start to ask her to help me with my makeup, but decide otherwise. She was fine when she was behind me, but having Marie's throat in my face might be a little more than I can handle. Since my paleness won't be an issue tonight, I focus on my eye makeup, keeping it simple.

Finishing, I turn to Marie and note her watching me curiously. Surely she realizes that I'm not only different from Nicolas's other guests, but different from her as well. I wonder again just how much she knows, but decide this isn't the time to find out.

"How soon do you think I should get dressed?" I ask, looking at the clock. It reads 8:10.

"Mr. Ambrus said you should come down at nine."

"And he doesn't like his plans changed, does he?" I ask, gauging her reaction.

"Oh no, mademoiselle," she says, lines creasing her brow. "You really shouldn't go down early."

"Perhaps you could check with him anyway?"

"I'm sorry, mademoiselle, but he asked that he not be disturbed. I am to wait here with you," she says firmly.

He is such a control freak, but with good reason, I guess. This would not be the evening to challenge him. He's probably timed my entrance for a specific purpose.

"Don't worry, Marie. I'll wait until the appointed time. Perhaps I should go ahead and get dressed in case things change."

"Yes, mademoiselle." Marie nods. "Would you like me to help you?"

"Uh, no, I can manage on my own. Thank you." I've had enough human scrutiny for one night. I give her a smile, head into the walk-in closet, and close the door.

The red silk brushes suggestively against my hand as I remove the black dress from the garment bag. I hang the black one on the closet bar and study its elegant lines for a moment, then take out the red one.

I'm tempted to put it on, if for no other reason than to see the expression he wore in the shop when I walked out looking as though I'd been dipped in blood.

But it's just not me.

I take the black gown off the hanger and slip it over my head. As I admire its stately lines in the mirror, my gaze darts one last time to the crimson fall of silk hanging behind me.

With a sigh of resignation, I open the door and step into the bedroom.

Marie takes in a quick breath.

"Mademoiselle. *Vous êtes belle!* Beautiful."

"Thank you. Nicolas picked out the dress. It's gorgeous, isn't it?"

She smiles. "Yes. Mr. Ambrus has very good taste."

Marie removes the black shoes from their box and holds out a pair of stockings. I take them and realize they are probably silk. I look at her questioningly.

"Mr. Ambrus had me pick them up this morning."

I frown. Does he think I'm such a barbarian that I don't even own a pair of stockings?

Suddenly irritated, I set them on the bed and get the ones I brought out of my bag. I look at them, then at Marie, but she keeps her expression neutral. Crap. The silk ones really are much nicer. I stuff mine back in the bag.

Once the stockings and shoes are on, I walk over to the table, pick up the black velvet-covered box containing the necklace, and open it. The sapphire's blue brilliance leaps to life when I take it out, reflecting the lamplight scattered about the room. I move in front of the mirror, put it up to my neck, and fasten it. Its beauty is mesmerizing, and I can't stop staring at it.

But it seems weird to have more around my neck than my annual income.

"Mademoiselle?"

Marie's reflection has joined mine in the mirror. She offers me a tiny box that matches the one for the necklace. I open it and take out a pair of small sapphire stud earrings.

I raise my eyebrows in question.

"Mr. Ambrus said that he ordered them when he purchased the necklace."

Shaking my head, I put in the earrings. Their addition to the image in the mirror completes the picture, perfect counterpoints to the necklace and the blue glittering in my eyes.

A faint noise at the door is followed by a crisp knock.

Marie walks over and opens the door, and Nicolas walks in. He stops, tilting his head, and nods his approval, his eyes bright.

"Marie," he says, without taking his gaze from me, "thank you very much for assisting Miss Martin. Your services are no longer required this evening. You may retire for the night."

"Yes, sir." Marie quickly curtsies and walks out past him. He closes the door and steps farther into the room.

"You are . . . absolutely stunning." His eyes darken as hints of red begin to shine through.

"And you as well. You're quite the dashing gentleman."

He's standing there in his black tuxedo, tall and dignified, and I realize I want nothing more than to rattle the cage of that calm exterior and free the beast that I sense is hidden within.

My vision colors as the one in me responds. Nicolas takes a sharp breath and moves, and I'm in his arms before I can blink. He growls low and deep, his breath cool against my jaw. I remember what Éva said, and I don't care. I reach up to his throat and nuzzle it, and he pulls me tighter, crushing me to him.

In a deep rumble, he says, "Aaahhh . . . no, my darling, not yet. But we will, if that is what you desire." He growls low again. "However, for now, we must wait."

I feel a surge throughout my veins as my blood reacts to his words with a mixture of anticipation and frustration, and I press myself hard against him, and my own growl quietly escapes my throat.

We stand immobile, our blood racing, the flows matching, and I can see no other future. He has completely subdued me. I am willing to give my life to him, no matter what it means.

Nicolas softly kisses my jaw, then brushes my lips with his, and relaxing his hold, gently shifts back. I don't want to let him go, but he takes a deep breath, forcing my arms to ease their grip. I relent and slowly release him.

"Now, as beautiful as you are in this gown, I think I would like to see you in the red one again."

"But . . ."

"Shh, my sweet. Humor me. Just try it on."

Torn between anxiety and elation, I nod and head back into the dressing room. I quickly change out of the black dress, swap shoes, then slide the red silk over my head and let it slither down around me.

I can't help but feel a sense of satisfaction when I look in the mirror, in spite of my misgivings. And I realize that once I step out of this room, I'm committed to wearing this dress, and so I better wear it properly.

With my head held high, I open the door, walk out, and pause.

Nicolas looks up and his whole body freezes.

Except for his eyes. His eyes turn deep crimson, and his gaze slowly travels up and down my body. His throat tightens, and with a deep inhalation, his mouth opens just enough to permit the tips of his fangs to show.

"Ahh . . ."

My blood racing, my body filled with yearning, I start toward him.

"No. Stop. Stay right there. Please."

I stare at him, at the hunger etched across his face, matched only by that within me, and force myself to do as he asks.

A shudder passes through him and, closing his eyes, he takes several deep breaths.

The steel tension in his body slowly eases, as does mine, and with a quiet sigh, he opens his eyes.

"You, my dear, are absolutely ravishing. No one will be able to take their eyes off you tonight."

I nod, suddenly embarrassed.

"You can come here now. I believe you will be safe—at least for the time being." He offers a quick half smile, but his gaze remains serious.

Feeling self-conscious, I cross the room and stop in front of him.

He reaches out and touches my cheek, his ruby eyes fading back to emerald, and starts to say something, but hesitates. He gently strokes my temple, then says, "Breathe. Relax. It is time to focus. I need you to be fully in control when we walk into the room and meet the others. Can you do that?"

I nod, take a breath and, stepping away, turn and face the mirror. My eyes are still bright crimson, made even more startling by the blue of the sapphires at my ears and throat, and the red silk draping my body.

His reflection watches me a moment, then he reaches inside his jacket and takes out a long, rectangular jewelry box, similar to the others.

"I have something for you."

More gifts? I *am* in a fairy tale.

Nicolas hands me the box and avidly watches as I open it.

The delicate bracelet nestled inside is a single row of glittering sapphires. There are nine of them, pea-sized, and they graduate in color from pale blue to very dark blue. Each of the spaces between the blue stones is filled with three small diamonds.

"Oh, how beautiful," I whisper.

"I am glad you like it. Here, allow me."

Taking the box, Nicolas sets it on the table, removes the bracelet, and fastens it around my left wrist.

He holds out my arm to admire his handiwork, then watching me in the mirror, bends to kiss the skin just above the stones. His lips linger a moment at my wrist before tracing the vein slowly up my arm.

"Uh, that is not going to help me 'be fully in control,'" I manage to croak. He raises his pink-tinged gaze to mine in the mirror as I gently pull my arm away, and gives me his playful smile.

That isn't helping either. I love that smile.

He steps behind me, placing his hands on my shoulders, and looks at my reflection.

"You will leave them speechless. You are a queen, and they will bow down at your feet."

I smile, thinking about facing that roomful of Chosen, and feel anticipation run through me, almost as though for a hunt.

Nicolas studies my expression in the mirror and, moving to my right side, takes my hand and slips it under his arm, resting it on the inside of his elbow. We both look in the mirror at the regal couple standing before us and his eyes momentarily flash red.

"We make a formidable pair. They have no chance, and they will know it. And they will see that we know it as well." His expression shifts, becoming dark and dangerous, and I am thrilled to accompany this magnificent being.

"Shall we?" He raises his eyebrows, and I offer a small, feral smile, my own eyes a crimson match to his.

"Ah, perfect," he says, and we leave our reflections and walk out the door.

CHAPTER 29

My hand still in its place on Nicolas's arm, we walk into the dining hall with its long ornate table full of seated guests. As we enter, The Chosen stand. The males, wearing tuxedos, bow, while the females in elegant gowns drop into deep curtsies. I try not to stare as we walk past them to the other end of the room. A mixture of tall and short, light-haired and dark, they are all trim and very attractive.

Tension fills the room as they hold their poses. Nicolas guides me to the head of the table and we remain standing next to his chair as he looks over the assemblage.

"Thank you," he says, finally releasing them from their courtesies. They straighten as their gazes stray to me.

"Please welcome Miss Martin," Nicolas continues. The Chosen again bow and curtsy briefly in my direction.

Nicolas assists me into the seat to the left of his, then takes his own, and with a flurry of quiet movement, the others return to theirs.

Éva, wearing a bare-shouldered gown in deep gold, is sitting across from me on Nicolas's right. She gives me a brief approving smile as she nods to me. I nod back, then look at Nicolas.

He glances at me and the corners of his mouth quirk. "Johan," he says, his voice slightly raised, "will you please bring us the wine?"

Burgundy draperies covering a doorway at the side of the room briefly sway, but no one appears. I watch the doorway for a moment, then slowly scan the table, taking care not to let my gaze linger too long on any of the guests.

They are all pale, beautiful, and elegant, and emanate an energy not unlike Éva's. All Elders, then. This is the Council of which she spoke.

There are eight of them, including Éva—four females and four males. It's interesting to watch their glances toward Nicolas, then toward me. Bewilderment slips across several faces and conversations spring up among them in a low hum.

The drapes at the doorway flutter open, admitting another Chosen, but he's dressed as a servant and carries a tray containing several decanters of wine. The servant, Johan I assume, sets the tray on a stand near Nicolas, then goes back through the doorway, returning seconds later with a tray full of wineglasses, which he sets on a second stand. He then becomes perfectly still, apparently awaiting further instructions.

I notice that his energy is very different; muted, one-dimensional, and almost non-existent in comparison to the others. Is he newly changed? He seems slightly tense and, darting his gaze to me, quickly drops it. I wonder what he senses of my energy. Does he question why one as young as me is in the company of all these Elders?

"Johan, I set aside a special bottle in the warmer. Will you please bring it, along with an opener?" The conversations stop as Nicolas speaks, but then pick up again as he goes silent.

"Éva, how was your afternoon with Miss Martin? Did you enjoy yourself?" Again, the quiet buzz instantly stops. Several of The Chosen shift forward a little in their chairs, their attention fixed on Nicolas and Éva.

"It was delightful. I found we have a number of things in common." She smiles at him and nods at me.

Yeah, what we have in common is *Nicolas.*

There's a faint ripple along the table as the others remark among themselves on the fact that Éva has already met me. I wonder if this gives her an advantage over them.

Johan reappears carrying a bottle of wine and an opener. He sets them on the decanter tray and steps back, becoming a statue again.

"Johan, please." Nicolas chooses a glass and moves it to the edge of the tray. Johan pours a small amount of wine from each of the decanters into the glass. Nicolas nods again to him, and Johan picks up the glass and drinks it down all at once.

Testing for . . . poison? Is Nicolas reassuring his guests, or himself, that the wine is safe?

Nicolas watches Johan for a long moment, then reaches over, picks up the corkscrew and the bottle, and opens it. He then selects another glass, pours the wine into it, and with a slight smile, hands it to me. As I take it, I become aware of another stir along the table.

When I glance at Éva, she is very still, and her eyes carry a slight warning. I continue to hold the glass and watch as Nicolas signals Johan to begin pouring the decanters. He quickly fills a glass and sets it in front of Nicolas, who raises it and slowly breathes in the aroma like any human connoisseur. I detect the scent of blood, human blood, yet it also looks and smells like wine, only spicier.

Interesting. I check my glass, but there is no trace of blood—just fine red wine.

Nicolas nods to Johan, who pours the rest of the glasses, setting the first of these in front of Éva. Johan then delivers a glass to the female sitting to my left and continues to distribute them down the table, alternating from side to side. Apparently there is a hierarchy at the table, with those sitting nearer to Nicolas having a higher status.

When everyone has wineglasses in front of them, Nicolas reaches over and takes my hand, then with a nod to me, he stands and I do the same. He picks up his glass and I follow his lead as everyone else at the table rises elegantly to their feet, their own glasses in hand.

Nicolas raises his glass.

"To the Blood."

As one, the other Chosen raise theirs and echo his words.

"To the Blood."

"And to the Game."

"To the Game," they repeat as a single voice.

His emerald eyes tinged in red, he takes a drink, and the others follow suit. He surveys the table, his gaze locking momentarily on each pair of eyes—eyes that lower in submission to him.

Power radiates from him in thick, heavy waves, and I see a Nicolas I have not seen before.

This one commands obedience with nothing more than his fierce attention and veiled promises of swift retribution should he receive anything but the highest respect.

Even the golden-haired Chosen across from me lowers her gaze and bows her head in subservience to him when he turns that attention to her. Éva holds her position until he sets down his glass.

"Please, sit." Nicolas motions everyone to their seats, then with a soft smile at me, assists me into mine and takes his. The others visibly relax and settle into their chairs.

"Éva, would you please introduce our guests to Miss Martin?" He takes another sip of his wine and leans back in his chair.

"Yes, Nicolas." Éva's golden-eyed expression is formal as she glances at me. "Miss Martin, I would like to present Miss Alina Dăneşti of San Francisco." Éva gestures to the petite, dark-haired beauty next to me. Her violet eyes shine as she murmurs a quiet "welcome" in an accent not unlike that of Nicolas and Éva.

The male sitting next to Éva is Lorenzo de' Medici of Chicago. His stocky build and darker coloring, along with his accent, remind me of Alfonso. Robert Williams of Los Angeles towers over Alina from his seat on the other side of her. With his sun-bleached hair and blue-green eyes, he could be a surfer poster boy if it wasn't for his milk-white skin.

Geneviève d'Orléans, from New Orleans, her dark hair cut short in a trendy bob, welcomes me in French. Elizabeth Wilson of Vancouver, a smaller, more delicate version of Robert, nods her greeting.

I recognize the Spanish in which Juan de Oñate Cortés of Mexico City warmly greets me, and I return his greeting in kind. Miguel Corte Real of Rio de Janeiro, his light-brown eyes gleaming, welcomes me in a language that sounds similar, but not really. Portuguese, perhaps?

They are all very gracious as they address me. Their accents lead me to believe that most of them may originally be from Europe. But they all share the bearing of nobility and I imagine they were probably lords and ladies in their human lives.

When the introductions are done, conversations spark up around the table. Nicolas leans over to talk quietly with Éva.

Alina, the Chosen seated on my left, looks at me curiously.

"So, Miss Martin, where are you from?"

I glance at Nicolas and Éva, but they appear to be deep into their discussion.

"The West Coast."

"Where exactly?"

I can't help but notice Robert, sitting on the other side of Alina, quietly sipping his wine as he listens in.

"Southern California, in the Glendora-Azusa area," I lie.

It's a well-practiced lie. Where I'm originally from—a small town in the northernmost part California—is only one part of my past that I refuse to share with anyone, *especially* a Chosen.

"Southern California. That's Robert's district." Alina turns to smile at him, but his glance at me is less than friendly.

"Do you ever visit the Bay area?" she asks, her attention back on me.

"Sometimes."

"Then you will have to let me know the next time you are in town."

"Yes. Yes, I will do that." I nod and glance at Nicolas, wishing he would rescue me.

"So how long—"

"Alina." Nicolas interrupts. "How are things in San Francisco?"

I lean back as they talk, relieved to be spared from further questions and, sipping my wine, discreetly observe the interactions among the various Chosen.

Johan walks quietly along the table, refilling the glasses. I watch his deference toward the others and wonder how much time he will spend as a servant, or if he even has a chance for upward mobility.

When all the glasses have been refilled, Nicolas once again stands and picks up his. The others all hasten to their feet, and as I tense to stand and join them, Éva quietly hisses, a look of warning in her eyes. I stay seated.

"I'd like to make a toast." Nicolas raises his glass in my direction.

"To my future Queen," he says.

Future Queen?

Stunned silence hangs in the air for a split second.

"To the Queen," the others belatedly respond, raising their glasses in salute to me.

What the hell? As enamored as I am by him, I didn't agree to this. At least not yet.

Determined to maintain my mask of confidence, I keep my eyes on Nicolas and accept the acknowledgment with a slow nod. He smiles and flicks his gaze to my glass. I raise it next to his, and in unison, we take a sip, followed by the rest of The Chosen.

I stand, suppressing my shock and anger with everything I've got.

"It has been a pleasure to meet all of you. I look forward to becoming better acquainted." I let my gaze sweep around the table. "I would also like to thank our host for arranging this gathering before I retire for the evening."

"To Nicolas, the King." I raise my glass in his direction.

"To the King," they repeat in a myriad of tones and accents.

As one, The Chosen raise their glasses and drink in tribute to their leader.

Nicolas gives me a sidelong glance, his eyes flashing red in admiration.

He holds his hand out to me. I set down my glass, step out from the table, and place my hand in his. The Elders immediately fold into bows or drop into curtsies as Nicolas parades us past the table and out of the room.

He walks me down the hallway and into the library. As soon as the door is closed, I release his hand, walk over to the fireplace, and plop down into one of the chairs.

"You were magnificent—" Nicolas begins, but I cut him off.

"Why didn't you tell me what you were planning?" My low tone only underscores my anger.

"Because if you knew beforehand, your fragile self-confidence may have interfered with your performance. As it was, it was perfect. I could not have asked for any better." His gloating smile goads me further. My resentment grows as I realize he set me up.

"So do they really call you 'king' or did I just embarrass them into it?"

"They need to be reminded periodically of exactly who I am, and you did that beautifully. You were so natural and sincere there is no way they could think I put you up to it. Even Éva was surprised." He chuckles. The smug look on his face infuriates me.

"And 'queen'? Tell me you're not serious, that it was just a matter of expression. That it was all just part of this Game that you and the others play." I glare up at him.

"Ah, but it was not. I *am* serious." His smile fades.

"Then why do I feel so used?"

I take a breath, but the anger is spinning out of control anyway. I slowly stand and face him.

"Don't you think you should have asked me first, in private, before announcing to the world that I am to be your queen, or whatever? Or do male Chosen just take whomever they want for a mate without asking her?" I hiss between my teeth, trying to keep my voice low. "And how presumptuous of you to assume that I would say yes!"

"You have not said no as of yet," he says, his tone shifting from arrogance to anger.

"You are absolutely right. I haven't. So there's no time like the present to begin." I take a deep breath. "*No*. No, I will *not* be a pawn in your *Game*, to manipulate and use against the other pawns in whatever twisted power struggle it is that you all seem to love."

My vision has now gone completely crimson, and suddenly the beast roars from my belly. I clench my jaw and glare at Nicolas as I stride past. He reaches out to grab my arm and I snarl and yank it back in a swirl of crimson silk. His eyes redden in fury. I can see him debate whether to stop me, but I keep walking, and he remains where he is. I reach the door and hesitate, but it's too late. The beast is rampaging inside me and I need to leave.

Slipping quietly through the door, I run up the stairs. As I tug the gown off over my head, the fragile silk tears. I rip the earrings out of my ears and pull open the catch on the bright blue necklace. I try to undo the bracelet, but I'm too out of control, and it breaks, sending blue sapphires and white diamonds bouncing across the polished wooden floor.

I throw my clothes on, my stuff into my bag, and turn to leave. The door opens, and Éva walks in, closing it behind her.

"I tried to warn him," she says quietly.

"You knew about this?" I say through my teeth.

"Not until this evening. I told him you might rebel, that you are too used to independence to be used in such a manner. He did not believe me. He is not accustomed to anyone defying him, and so was unable to consider the possibility of your reaction. I am sorry." The sadness in her tone seems genuine.

"So am I. He didn't even ask me . . ." I stop, and my jaw tightens as the hurt joins the anger.

"Then do not leave. Wait here and calm down. He needs to attend to the others for a short time."

"No. We need some time apart. This has all been too fast, so fast I haven't even had time to think." Trembling with rage, I start to walk past her, but she steps in my way.

"Do you not realize the honor he paid you tonight? That to pour your wine, and hand you your glass, he elevated you higher than himself? I have never seen him serve *anyone* in public, and neither have the others. They were astounded when he did that." Jealousy flares in her eyes.

"I . . . I . . . these things are all too subtle for me. I don't want to do this if I am to be as in the dark as everyone else." I take a breath. "Thank you, Éva, for everything you've done to help me. But I need to re-evaluate. And I need to hunt, so I'm leaving now."

"Hunt?" She looks puzzled. "But—"

"Don't ask. You don't really want to know." I walk around her and to the door.

"Please, Sunny, don't leave. Nicolas—"

"Nicolas will be fine. He's managed to survive over five hundred years, and I'm sure this is nothing more than a bump in the road to him. There will be others. With him, there always will be. I'm not blind."

"No, but right now you are being incredibly pig-headed and stupid. I ask again—" Her voice is now as laced with anger as mine.

"Good-bye, Éva." I open the door and walk out.

I go down the stairs two at a time and slip out the front door, closing it softly behind me. I run around the side of the house and am relieved to see my car parked at the end with nothing blocking its path.

Once inside, I'm further relieved to find my keys in the ignition where Alfonso had left them. I start the car and ease it down the driveway. As I pull up to the gates, they swing apart, and my getaway is clear. I head down the hill, and once I get some distance from the house, I hit the gas and waste no more time.

As I speed up the pass, I shake my head ruefully at the fact that I'm escaping from the evening, just as I feared. But that my escape would be from Nicolas rather than the party is not what I'd anticipated.

The Beamer screams up my driveway and I park, grab my bag, and head into the house. I quickly change into hunting clothes and the beast in me howls in expectation.

I leave the house and head straight up the mountain, breathing in the cold, pine-scented air. I stop partway up and let loose a deep roar, announcing to all that I am back, on *my* mountain, and that they best cringe at my passing.

It's going to take a whole herd to make me happy tonight.

CHAPTER 30

I track the small group of deer through the pines. They aren't the elk I'd been hoping for, but right now I don't really care. I haven't been this upset and hungry in a very long time, and I'll take anything I can get.

Pinpointing them up ahead, I quickly parallel their movement. When they step into a break in the trees, I leap onto the nearest buck and grab his large mule-like ears and, sliding backward to the ground, yank and flip him onto his back. I twist his head to one side, and sink my teeth into his jugular, and quickly lose myself in the trance of his blood.

A deep roar drowns out the sounds of his struggles, and I break away and look up.

A huge bear is charging straight at me.

I jump up and leap at him just as he stands, my sharp nails aiming for his eyes and my teeth going for his throat, underneath and away from those killer jaws.

All I get is a mouthful of the thick, shaggy fur. I try to reach under to slash his jugular open, but he nearly dislodges me, and I grab around the back of his neck and hold on.

Shock electrifies my whole body as his deadly claws rake down my back and I feel the skin and muscle part like tissue paper. The agony consumes me, but I hold on and shift my bite on his throat and try again. I taste blood this time, and shift again, trying to zero in on the artery.

But he's too strong, and I've allowed myself to get too weak. I scream as his claws rip down my back a second time, then the other paw swings up and gouges me down the side of my face and arm. He's now howling in pain, as I'm pretty sure I've blinded him on one side. Taking advantage of his distraction, I shove off and hit the ground rolling. I try to pop back to my feet, but blood loss seems to already be slowing me down.

There's no way I can outrun him now.

I push myself up and stand, looking for the best direction to go, when I realize he isn't interested in pursuit. He's backing up, roaring and whining, and wiping his bloody eye socket with his massive paw. He suddenly turns and takes off, and I hear him crashing through the forest as he makes a hasty retreat.

I sink back down to the ground in relief, but then realize I can't stand anymore anyway. A crushing weakness starts running through my body as my blood empties onto the forest floor. And then the fire of hunger ignites, and the agony in my ragged back is overshadowed as my veins start to feel like they are bursting into flame.

Crawling over to the dead buck, I draw every drop that I can get, but I need more. Lots more. The wounds aren't closing fast enough, and my lifeblood is still pouring out. I lay there, helpless, wondering if this is the end. Nicolas never said what happens if we don't get any blood to trigger the healing. I don't know if I'll die, or just become immobilized, lingering until the next predator comes along and devours me.

A part of me laughs, wondering what consuming my blood would do to a bear, or any other creature, as my mind tries to separate from the pain coursing throughout my body. But then another wave of fire flares through me, and I go completely limp. The red haze of my vision slowly darkens, and then it goes black.

április 15., vasámap

Éva arrived this morning. I am unsure as to whether or not their conversation went well. Sunny seemed tense when I returned to the library, and I do not know how much Éva told her. Éva is in great need of bond renewal, as I can feel her defiance growing beyond my limits of tolerance. But I need her to appear as independent as possible tonight. I will have to wait until after the others leave.

Though I could sense her doubts, Sunny claimed to be up to the challenge of tonight's meeting. I believe she is, perhaps more than she realizes, because what she does not realize is that the best hunters also make the best players in the Game.

It all went impossibly wrong tonight. I do not understand. She played her role perfectly, as I knew she would. But she suddenly became angry and unreasonable, claiming that she does not want to be with me, in spite of all indications otherwise. She had even shown me earlier that she is eager to share blood, and I was hoping that tonight would be our first time.

But all is lost now, as she will not answer the phone. I call and call, and she will not answer the phone.

PART III

THE TAMING

MONDAY

CHAPTER 31

I become aware of snuffling and licking at my back, and with a desperate burst of energy, roll and grab the creature with both hands. I don't even register what it is before its throat is in my mouth and I am biting down, seeking its life-giving blood. I drain it, and my vision slowly clears, and I let the dead coyote go. Fitting. This life started with a dog, and has started again with its wild cousin.

Laying there a moment, I try to sense what else is around me. I don't hear or smell anything out of the ordinary, so I carefully lift my head to get an idea of where I am. The carcass of the buck is laying about ten feet away, its torn belly a sign that it's been fed upon. I try to move and gradually regain an awareness of my legs and arms. But unfortunately the movement also reawakens the pain and it grips me in its iron fist. I freeze, waiting for it to subside.

It eases some and I attempt to get up before it comes back. Nothing is working right, and I end up sitting hunched over on my knees. Pushing my hands against the ground, I slowly stagger to my feet and stand there a moment, swaying. And then the next surge of electric agony arcs through my body. I grit my teeth and hold my position, determined not to go back down.

The hunger returns, and my belly and throat join my veins in flame. I gasp and try to ride it out, but the fire consuming me is unbearable. My body wavers and my knees start to shake. Bracing my hands against my thighs, I stand there, locked, not daring to move.

I'm not sure if the torment fades, or if I've just gotten used to it, but after a few minutes I'm able to slowly straighten. I manage a step, then two, and carefully work my way over to a nearby tree. Leaning against it,

I try to figure out what time of day it is. The sky is cloudy, and I'm thankful that at least the sun isn't adding its own brand of torture. But I don't know how long the sky will stay this way and have no idea if it's early or late in the day.

Finally getting my bearings, I start to head downhill. The pain makes a fresh assault on me, and I clench my jaw and keep setting one foot in front of the other. I stumble on a rock and go down, hard. After a long moment, I slowly struggle back to my feet. The dried flesh and blood on my back rips opens with the effort, and the scream that escapes me shatters the forest quiet. I take a step, then another, then another.

Staggering, and sometimes crawling, I slowly make my way down the mountain. I nearly pass out again at one point, but force myself to keep going. I need to find shelter. And soon.

Eventually I reach the clearing above my house and follow the trail that leads down to the back door. I start to weaken again, then fall, and lay there within shouting distance for what seems like hours. With a last burst of determination, I inch the rest of the way on my belly and finally reach the short step. I claw and pull myself up using the doorframe and open the door.

Fear of falling again immobilizes me, and I stand there a long moment, resting, then use the wall as support to move into the house. I creep along the walls and furniture to the bedroom, and gratefully collapse into bed, just in time for another crushing avalanche of agony.

As my scream fades, I hear the faint ring of a cell phone, and my world goes black again.

CHAPTER 32

I wake, it seems, for the millionth time. The phone is ringing again. It echoes in my head nonstop.

Answer it. I . . . need . . . to answer it.

My eyes search the room, finally stopping on my bag lying on the floor where I dropped it. But I'm afraid to move, and the ringing stops. The black begins to take me again, and I fight it off and attempt to get up. The movement immediately triggers the torture, and unprepared for its viciousness, I collapse back down on the bed.

After a while, I try again, this time steeling myself against the agonizing fire coursing throughout my body. I slide feet first to the floor and cringe as my back threatens to split apart. Crawling over to the bag, I find the phone, then prepare to work my way back into bed. But I drift off again, somewhat in relief, as that is the only time the pain is tolerable.

I'm startled awake again by a loud ringing and a vibration against my chest, and realize I'm holding the phone. I shakily flip it open, hold it up to my ear, and try to speak, but nothing comes out.

"Sunny. Why have you not been answering? Wait. I am sorry, please, do not hang up. I need to speak with you. Please." His voice cracks, and through the fog of pain, I realize he sounds like he is in pain, too, although of a different kind.

He pauses, then pleads again. "Sunny, please talk to me."

"Bear . . . ," I whisper, my voice as ragged as my back.

"What? What did you say?" he demands.

"Bear . . . ," I manage to croak a little louder.

"Bear?" He pauses. "By the gods of hell!"

Funny, I've never heard him refer to a deity other than himself.

"I will be right there. Stay with me!" He sounds frantic, and I hear yelling and loud noises in the background.

I drift off again, and am dimly aware that the voice in the phone is saying something. But I can't answer, as yet another onslaught of fiery pain flames through me. My body shudders with the intensity of it, and I gratefully pass out.

I feel myself being eased over onto my stomach, then hear a loud gasp. His arms cradle my body, and I'm lifted and gently set down. There is something soft beneath me, and I open my eyes enough to see the covers on my bed.

"Sunny, can you hear me? Sunny? Sunny?" I love his voice, and could easily die just listening to it.

"Sunny!" He is now almost yelling at me and his hand is moving my head to the side.

"Nic . . . ," I whisper.

"Sunny, take this." He is so insistent, and I just want to sleep.

Something's against my mouth—something wet. It's blood. Blood. I snap back awake as the sweet hot life drips on my tongue. I gasp, and grab what turns out to be an arm, pulling it tight against my mouth, and sink my teeth into it, and start gulping. I get maybe half a dozen good swallows, then shift to get a better bite, and the arm is pulled back. I try to hang on to it, but it's stronger than me, and I'm forced to let go.

I blink several times, trying to clear my head and my eyes, and the room starts to come into focus. A careful breath reveals that the pain has subsided a little. It's not gone, but it no longer owns me.

When I attempt to raise my head, Nicolas's taut face comes into view. I've never seen such a look of fear on anyone.

"Sunny, can you hear me? Can you understand me?" The panic in his voice is alarming, and I try to say something to reassure him, but can't seem to get anything out.

I feel myself being picked up again, then carried. A door slams, and the cold air of the night chills my skin. Gravel beneath his feet crunches with each step.

He shifts me in his arms and the sound of a car door opening seems far away. I'm aware of being lowered into the car, and then another wave of pain slams through me, though it's not as bad as the earlier ones. Nicolas reaches over, belts me to the seat, then closes the door. I try to move to a more comfortable position, but that aggravates the pain. The other door opens. Nicolas gets in and starts the car.

Curling more onto my side, I grit my teeth and reach over to him. I find his leg and hold on to it, squeezing it as each fresh round of flame washes through my body. His hand covers mine, rubbing it reassuringly.

The soft vibration of the engine is steady as the car races down the highway, and my body rocks to the gentle sway as we cut in and out of traffic. Soon amber lights flash by overhead—on, off, on, off. Streetlights. We come to a stop, then start again, then another stop. The crest on the gate streaks by, and then we stop again.

Nicolas gets out, opens my door, and unfastens the seatbelt. He carefully picks me up and quickly walks up the steps. The front door opens and Éva's face passes into and out of view. Nicolas carries me upstairs to the bedroom, and then gently eases me down onto the bed in a sitting position.

I start to slump sideways to lie down, but Nicolas catches me and holds me upright.

"Sunny, you have to sit up. Open your eyes."

I try to comply, but the lights are so bright and it seems like too much work.

"Éva, hand it to me, please. Sunny, you need to drink this." His tone is commanding now.

Something touches my mouth—a cup—and warm liquid washes over my lips. I lick them, startled to taste blood. The cup touches my lips again, and a little more sloshes into my mouth. Blood, it's blood, and I swallow, then start sucking it down as fast as I can. The cup tips up until its empty, and my eyes snap open.

"More," I croak, and another cup touches my mouth. I reach up and place my shaking hands around his as he holds the cup, and drink deeply as the sweetest nectar I've ever tasted bathes my tongue. I quickly drain that, then look up at him, silently pleading for more.

He smiles and offers another cup. I wrap my hands around his again and pour the precious fluid down my throat. I marvel at the flavor, its sweetness, its richness.

And then I realize what its source is.

Human. It's human blood. I have just duank *human* blood.

I release the cup and look up at Nicolas in horror.

"Sunny, we did not have any choice. You were so badly damaged and so bled out, there was nothing else we could do other than watch you waste away in racking pain. Believe me, this is not what I wanted." He stops, searching my eyes for understanding and forgiveness.

"Who," I whisper.

"No one died. It was given voluntarily in your behalf."

"Who," I repeat.

"Marie and Alfonso. They both wanted to help, and to be honest with you, it is part of their job to be emergency . . . donors. They are both fine and are anxious to see you when you are well."

I close my eyes in relief. At least my stupidity didn't result in someone's unnecessary death.

But I've just done something I swore I would never do.

And my body wants more.

It certainly feels better. The fire of my hunger has died down a little, and the pain from the injuries has faded a bit. I still burn, though, and I still hurt. I look at my arm, and the gaping wound down the length of it is very slowly closing in the deepest parts. I reach up and carefully touch my face, and can feel the furrows left by the bear becoming less raw as they begin to heal.

I move to stand up and Nicolas steps in close. "Perhaps you should wait a little while before you try to do anything."

Shaking my head in refusal, I carefully slide off the edge of the bed to my feet. I take a wobbly step, and Nicolas is there, supporting me under one arm.

"The mirror. I want to see my back," I say huskily. He helps me to the full-length mirror, and I turn around, trying to look over my shoulder. The flesh on my back pulls as I twist, and I inhale sharply through my teeth.

"I need the hand mirror." I start tugging at the rag that was my sweater, and the few threads that held it together across my shoulders separate. I hold the front with one arm and Nicolas hands me the mirror. I glance at Éva, noting the dismay written across her face as she looks at the reflection of my back.

I take a breath and raise the hand mirror. What I see is something out of a nightmare. My entire back is in ruins. The skin and muscle literally hang in meaty shreds; portions of my ribcage are exposed, the bones shockingly white in the raw pale flesh. In several places I can see the vertebrae of my spine. I watch them shift as I move. It's pretty gruesome, like a movie special effect come to life.

But none of the bones appear broken, surprisingly, and apparently he missed whatever internal organs still remain.

"Well, I must say that's impressive. I haven't seen anything like that before." A demented-sounding chuckle escapes my lips.

"No, what is impressive is that you not only survived, but somehow managed to get to your home. And I do not understand how," Nicolas says quietly.

As I examine my back, I can see minute changes occurring as it heals. But it's such a mess, I have a feeling it will take quite some time for so much tissue to regenerate. I peer closer at the dirt and debris that are embedded in it and wonder if infection is an issue.

"Shouldn't I wash it out?" I ask.

"It is not necessary. As with most foreign objects, the body will push them out as it heals. But if you would like to take a shower when you are a little stronger, I do not see a problem." Nicolas is still watching me curiously.

Facing the mirror, I inspect the two claw marks running from my temple down across my cheek and jaw, one of them so deep I can see my jawbone. Ugly.

I start to pick dirt out of the gouges, but it hurts to touch the raw flesh, and I stop.

"Will I have scars?" I ask.

"No, I do not think so, as long as we continue to help the healing process."

Great. Bet that means more blood, and I just can't see Nicolas pulling down an elk for me.

I turn sideways and look at the long ragged trails down my arm. They are deep, and I can see the tendons and bone from the shoulder to the elbow. But again, thankfully, nothing is broken.

A flood of pain suddenly washes through me, and I take a sharp breath and hold still until it passes. Nicolas and Éva both move to me, but I shake my head and wave them off. Unfortunately, though, the pain triggers a fresh hunger, and I feel the lick of flame start to move through my veins.

"Aah . . ." I close my eyes and clench my jaw. Nicolas grasps my elbow, and I hug the sweater with both hands as he guides me to the bed.

"Éva," he says, and she steps over to the table and fills the cup from a thermos.

"No," I say as she hands it to Nicolas. "No more human blood."

"Yes, you must, or you will end up right back where you were when I found you, in agony, helpless and mindless with the burning. Please, do not argue." He holds out the cup.

I take a breath and reach for it, part of me resisting, and part of me wanting to snatch it out of his hand. I start drinking, trying to go slowly this time, and feel the warm red nectar ease a little of the pain and the fire. I close my eyes in gratitude and reluctantly give the empty cup back to Nicolas.

He hands me another. I don't hesitate at all this time. Each swallow brings further relief, and the taste, well, the taste continues to blossom.

"How much more is there?" I ask, licking my lips clean.

"I have sent out to a blood bank. We should have a fresh supply within the hour. It will not be quite the same, as it has been processed, and your healing will be slower, but it seems to be our only option for now." He shakes his head and glances at Éva.

"Is there nothing else? I mean, my . . . needs are different than yours. Can't we find something . . . comparable to my normal diet?" I plead.

"Like what? I do not have any deer or elk here on the estate." He grows silent for a moment. "But perhaps—"

He takes a deep breath.

"Éva, stay here with her. I need to check on something." Nicolas frowns and leaves the room.

Éva walks over and sits on the bed beside me. She tentatively reaches out and strokes my matted hair.

"Sunny, my dear, can you please explain something to me?"

"I'll try," I reply, knowing what's coming next.

"What is this . . . reluctance of yours to feed on humans? They are our natural prey. I don't quite understand."

"I've never had human blood before. Until tonight," I whisper.

"Never? Not even when you were Changed?"

"No."

"But how? I mean, that is part of the Change. It is not complete until the human lifespark has been consumed. Are you saying you did not take a human when you Changed?"

"No, I've never killed anyone."

"But then, that would mean the Change was not complete—" She freezes, and a look of alarm crosses her face.

"That would make you still . . . ," she whispers, fingers pressed against her lips. "Oh Nicolas . . ."

CHAPTER 33

"That is enough, Éva."

Nicolas walks in as she finishes speaking and glances sharply at her. She gives him an unreadable look, gets up, and walks across the room.

He's carrying a long-sleeved dress shirt, probably one of his. He averts his eyes as I tear open the sweater neck and shrug out of what remains of the knitted mess. I hug it in front of me as Nicolas unbuttons the shirt.

He then tears off one sleeve, and with the shirt facing backward, leans over me to offer the other sleeve for my good arm. I slip it in and put the injured arm through the open armhole, leaving it exposed. He reaches around me and buttons the top button at the nape of my neck, leaving my back exposed as well.

"Thank you," I whisper. He kisses the top of my head and touches the undamaged side of my face, his face reflecting the pain that I feel. I hand him the rag that was my sweater, stiff with my dried blood and that of the bear. Horror flickers in his eyes as he appears to imagine how it got that way.

He looks over at Éva and quietly says, "There is very little human remaining in her. If there was much more, she would be dead."

Very little human? As in I'm still part human? Not a hundred percent monster?

"You knew?" I look at Nicolas in disbelief. "And you didn't tell me?"

"It took me some time to puzzle it out. Once I did, there did not seem to be any point in enlightening you. In fact, I feared it might shake your confidence."

"Damn it, Nicolas," Éva spits out. "This is so typical. When are you going to get past this obsession of yours with human females? No wonder you fell for her—she is the best of both worlds for you!"

"Éva!" Nicolas says harshly. "I will hear no more on this!"

Éva snaps her jaw shut, her eyes defiant.

"How did you know?" I demand, rising to my feet. "What—"

"Even though your skin blisters in the sun, your ability to move around during the day is not normally possible for one as young as you." Nicolas reaches out and gently touches my hair. "And you show an amazing tolerance to humans. You are able to spend long periods of time in close proximity to them, even interacting with them, without losing control. Again, this . . . behavior is not possible for a young Chosen. It takes decades of training to learn to maintain that much control.

"It was when you told me how your change occurred that I realized just how unusual you are. I had detected something odd when we first met. Your scent is quite different from other Chosen, and at first I thought this was due to your choice of diet.

"But there is something else. What makes you *so* unusual is that if the process of the Change is not followed precisely, the prospective Chosen dies. Every time. Every single time. You did not." He pauses.

"There needs to be a certain number of blood exchanges between prospect and Maker, and they need to occur at specific intervals. The final step requires that the candidate drain the blood of a human, all the way to the lifespark. It is taking in that spark that completes the Change."

I think about the dog, and I can see that Nicolas is thinking the same thing.

Great. I'm part dog. How disgusting. No wonder I thrill so much to the hunt of wild game.

"But you see, it has to be a *human* spark, because that is what we once *were.* So there must be another explanation, and I am still researching that."

Éva laughs, and it has a cruel sound.

"She feeds on . . . animals, right? So that makes her part human *and* part animal? Nicolas, that is revolting!" she says, disgust dripping from her voice.

"Éva!" Nicolas roars as he strides across the room to her. "That is quite enough! Remember about whom you are speaking, as well as *to* whom!"

She backs up, her face transformed in alarm. Nicolas grabs her by the shoulders and growls, "You need to leave this room. Now. I will talk with you later."

Éva nods, eyes wide, and Nicolas releases her. She turns and walks stiff-backed out the door, shutting it behind her.

"Nicolas, she's right. Don't hurt her," I plead. "She . . . she still loves you."

"I have no intention of harming her. She does, however, need a reminder that I am her Maker and that challenging me is not to be tolerated."

Part of me is suddenly concerned about what he just said. But that is quickly overwhelmed by a fresh round of agony, triggered by the emotional upset of the last several minutes. I close my eyes and prepare for the fire that seems to always be on the heels of the pain, and it follows within seconds. I inhale and grit my teeth.

"Damn! Where is that blood?" Nicolas swears as he empties the last of it into the cup.

I am lying on the bed, keeping as still as possible. But my mind races over the earlier discussion. Part human? The hunger flares, stinging my throat, and I realize my mind needs to keep still as well as my body.

Nicolas left a few minutes earlier to go check on the blood delivery. I wait for him anxiously, both in anticipation and in dread.

The taste of the human blood is something I don't think I'll ever forget, and a part of me knows this is what I'm supposed to be consuming, that the wild game has just been a substitute. But the other part of me, the part that remembers my daughter and my granddaughter, is not willing to destroy human lives, and I resign myself to the conflict.

Nicolas comes back into the room carrying a cooler and sets it on the table.

"The blood bank?" I ask with mixed emotions as I sit up.

"No, another possible . . . solution. I do not know if you will like it, or if it will even work, but it is worth a try." He tightens his jaw, his frustration apparent.

He pulls a large IV bag from the cooler and opens the valve on the tube. Bright red liquid streams into the cup, and he shuts off the flow when the cup is full.

I watch greedily, the hunger surging at the sight of the blood.

"Unfortunately, we were not able to keep it warm, and I must apologize for that." He steps over and hands me the cup.

Nodding, I take it. I sniff the blood—this is nothing I've had before. I gingerly dip my tongue into it. He's right, it's cool, and I shudder at the thought. But the flavor seems somewhat tolerable, and I take a swallow.

I look at Nicolas and nod, and begin drinking. It has a grain-like flavor and, the more I drink of it, the odder the taste becomes. It would be much better warm. Or ideally, hot, as in straight from the heart.

Finishing it, I hold out the cup for more. He brings the bag over and refills it, and I feel a thrill at the red stream pouring in.

Yeah, not much in me is human.

Downing the second cup, I realize the pain and the fire have both subsided slightly. This might work.

"What is it?" I ask. "And how do you keep it from . . . clotting?"

"I make a special preparation containing Chosen blood that has anti-clotting properties, among others. There is a very small amount mixed in with this blood."

"Which is . . . ?"

Nicolas closes his eyes, takes a breath, then looks pointedly at me. "I have a stable."

Stable. Horses. I am drinking horse blood.

The blood would come back up if it wasn't already being absorbed into my system.

"Oh Nicolas. I . . . I can't." Somehow killing horses for their blood seems almost as bad as killing people.

"I have a small number of them that we can use for donors. It is not necessary to kill them. In fact, I would not allow it. They are very special to me." His tone holds a note of warning, which is reinforced by the look in his eyes.

Recalling he was being trained as a horsemaster before he was changed, I suppose he's concerned I'll become a raving beast and go out and lay waste to the whole herd.

Gee, thanks for the vote of confidence.

"Nicolas, domestic animals . . . I just can't. Especially horses. It's just all wrong. And their taste . . . I'm a hunter. I need the chase, the fight, and the kill as much as I need the blood. Wild blood."

I had learned this early on, in the first few weeks after my change.

"Ah, well, you are not so very different from us. For us, it is the seduction and the willing surrender."

That's chilling. I shudder at the thought and catch a flash of amusement across Nicolas's face.

And then I realize he said *us*, and I am not part of the *us*. I am the other, the *not us*. The pain I feel at that has nothing to do with my injuries.

I hear a step outside the door, and Nicolas walks over to it as someone knocks.

"Mr. Ambrus? The delivery you were expecting is here." It's Alfonso, and I feel relieved to hear the normalcy in his voice. But I also feel something else, and it scares the hell out of me.

Even through the door, I can feel the call of his blood.

CHAPTER 34

"Sunny. Sunny, wake up." I feel his hand caress my hair, and I open my eyes and look up to see Nicolas looking down at me like a parent with a sick child.

"You need to sit up and drink this." Nicolas, beautiful Nicolas, is holding a large mug, and I can smell the blood.

Now that's a wake-up call.

I sit up, rousing further as the movement triggers the spasms. I grit my teeth and reach for the mug just as the fire starts. I gulp as fast as I can, wondering how soon the blood will work its magic to quench the twins of pain and flame.

"It's warm," I say as my mind begins to wake as well.

"Yes, I thought that reheated, as unpalatable as that can be, would be preferable to cold." He smiles, takes the mug, and sets it on the table that's been moved next to the bed.

I notice a group of large thermos bottles on the table, and look up at Nicolas in question as he selects one and refills the mug.

"It is a mixture. The blood from the bank is somewhat lacking due to being processed, but it is human and should expedite the healing. I added horse blood to help replace some of the vital life properties missing from the processed blood. I do not know if this will work as we need it to."

Nicolas hands me the mug, and I think about this as I practically inhale it. I don't slow down until the third mug to really analyze the taste. It's a strange combination, but the honey-sweet human blood helps to mask the oat-bitter horse blood.

He gives me mug after mug, yet after each one I still crave the next as much as I did the first.

By the end of the fourth or fifth mug, the pain of my injuries has reduced to a dull ache and my hunger to the heat of banked coals.

"How much more do you think I'll need?" I ask. It feels like the damaged tissue throughout my body is actually crawling as it starts repairing at a faster rate.

"I do not know. But you need to keep steadily taking it in as long as you feel any pain or a trace of hunger," he says as he hands me yet another full mug.

Drinking this one more slowly, I roll it around in my mouth, playing with the flavors. It's an odd bouquet, and I decide that I rather like it. Well, at least I can enjoy it while I'm still healing.

I laugh wryly, and Nicolas raises his eyebrows, wanting in on the joke.

"Well, I suppose it's all right to drink human blood, as long as it's for medicinal purposes. Oh yeah, and no one dies."

He doesn't seem to find this as amusing as I do.

Apparently he's not acquainted with the long human history of addiction that masquerades under the pretense of "medicinal purposes." Ironically though, plenty of people have died from that.

"Let me look at your back and see how you are doing." He takes the empty mug from me and sets it on the table.

Standing seems to halt my progress, and I catch my breath as the pain resurfaces, though it's not as vicious as it was before. Nicolas takes a long look at my back, and shaking his head, refills the mug.

I take it and gratefully swallow it down. I have no idea how much I've had so far, but the mug looks as though it holds about a quart. That would mean that I've had the equivalent of two humans so far, and it looks like it's going to take a bit more. I shudder to think how many people would've had to give up their lives for mine.

Leaving the mug on the table, I step over to the long mirror. I move in closer, using the hand mirror to look at the side of my face, and am grateful that the bear somehow missed both my eye and my ear. I don't know how long it would take to grow new ones, or if they would even be the same. Ugh. The twin gouges on my jaw are mostly closed now, but still have a way to go.

My shoulder and arm appear to be healing nicely as well. I move my arm around and wince at the soreness. It's stiff, too, which tells me I need to work on loosening it up.

Turning, I use the small mirror to look at my back. Thankfully, much of the inner damage has filled in, and all of the exposed bones have been covered. But my back still looks like a series of pale fleshy canyons, and I shake my head at the amount of damage the bear delivered so quickly.

I feel Nicolas watching me and look over at him, and a stab of regret pierces me deep in the chest. He's wearing that haunted expression of fear again, and I don't think I'll ever forget it.

Setting the mirror back on the table, I turn and cross the room to him. He touches my hair, and gently gathers me into his arms, being careful to avoid my injuries. His entire body is vibrating.

"I . . . ," he says hoarsely, but seems unable to finish.

I press into him and hold him, and he hugs me tighter.

Please, Nicolas, don't ever let me go.

We stand there a long while, our chests rising and falling in unison, until he slowly softens and relaxes his grip.

He leans back, combing my hair with his fingers, and pulls a pine needle out of the matted mess. He sets it on the table and says, "I think you are healed enough to take a shower if you feel up to it."

"Yeah, that would be great. But I don't have any clean clothes."

"I will ask Marie if she has something you can borrow. I doubt it will be a problem."

"Well, since she loaned me her blood, I would imagine she wouldn't mind too much. I'll be sure to return the clothes. The blood, however . . ." I smile, trying to lighten his mood.

Nicolas shakes his head, obviously not amused. He walks to the door, then stops.

His back stiff, his voice thick with strain, he says, "But first, can you please tell me how this happened? What did you do after you . . . after I forced you to . . . ?"

He turns, his eyes full of regret and sorrow.

"I was upset, and hungry, and just needed some time." I pause, unwilling to reveal that my disappointment and rage at his manipulations had made me nearly insane with hunger.

"I had just taken down a buck, and was not as alert as usual. I didn't hear anything except a roar. I looked up as the bear was coming at me, and all I could think was 'No, you don't, this is *my* kill,' and I . . . I attacked him." My vision reddens at the memory.

Stupid, stupid. All I needed to do was leap out of his way and attack him from behind. Then I could've enjoyed two meals. Instead I dove right into his teeth and claws, and nearly became his.

"You attacked him, instead of running." Nicolas shakes his head, frowning. "Part of me admires your fearlessness, and part of me is furious at your foolishness."

He looks up, and it's obvious the furious part is winning.

"Do you realize you nearly died? That he could have ripped . . ." He closes his eyes. When he finally opens them, their green depths are filled with pain. "That he could have ripped your head from your body?

"How soon after he tore your back did the weakness begin to set in from blood loss? Minutes, seconds? It is a wonder he did not finish you," he says through gritted teeth.

"I, uh, blinded him in one eye and he ran off," I admit in a low voice. I was damn lucky. I knew it then, and I realize it even more now.

Nicolas takes a breath.

"Chosen may be immune to the ravages of time, but we *can* die from grievous injury. Usually it is not the injury itself that causes death. That comes from the accompanying weakness due to blood loss and compromised circumstances." His tone is lecturing, harsh. "As you have likely determined, it is very difficult to defend yourself if you have lost your blood and cannot immediately replace it.

"Of course, if you lose your head, well . . . that is one thing that cannot heal." His voice fades to a whisper.

"And the head can live for some time, fully aware, until the tissues finally dry out," he says grimly. "It is a most unpleasant way to die."

Swallowing in horror, I look at Nicolas and see the horror reflected on his face as well. He crosses the room and roughly pulls me into his arms, my injuries forgotten.

He whispers, "I nearly lost you . . . forever. I do not know what I would have done."

The despair in his voice cuts through me like a knife.

"Nicolas, I am . . . so . . . sorry."

He leans back, holding my shoulders, and looks intently into my eyes.

"No, it is *my* fault. If I had not driven you away with my arrogance, this would not have happened." His voice is torn with emotion. "What I did to you was unforgivable. To use our relationship—to use *you*—in the Game in such a way was despicable, and I promise never to hurt you like that again. If . . . if you will still have me."

I swallow, trying to regain my voice.

"Yes, I will still have you. If you will still have *me*, part human and part . . . whatever." A *not us*. An *other*.

Nicolas, his eyes red, moves his hands to the sides of my head, cupping it gently. He kisses me, first on the mouth, then up the side of my face and across my brow. When he reaches the grooves in my jaw, he softly brushes his lips along the edges, giving tiny kisses as he works his way down.

He continues to my neck, and I feel fire light up in my veins, but it has nothing to do with pain. His mouth lingers there and opens, and I feel the graze of his teeth. I groan, and pull him closer. His lips move up alongside my ear, gently kissing my temple. He slides his hands down and, wrapping his arms around me, rests his chin on the top of my head.

"We will have to wait until you are fully healed. You are certainly in no condition to sustain any further blood loss, no matter how temporary. And there are things we need to discuss, as this is not a decision to be made lightly nor in the heat of passion."

I nod. He plants a last kiss on the top of my head and eases back.

"Now, drink another mug or two, and go enjoy your shower. I will return momentarily with clothes for you to wear."

The water runs over my skin, enveloping me in its soft warmth. It takes the stiffness out of my healing flesh, and I can finally take a deep breath without pain pulling at the tissues in my back. I almost have full range of motion in my arm, and reach up to feel the now shallow tracks in my jaw.

I rinse the last bit of shampoo from my hair, shut off the water and, grabbing a towel, step out and dry off. A quick wipe of the mirror allows me to examine my face and arm, and I feel pleased with how well they are healing. I wrap the towel around me, crack open the door, and stick my head out.

"Nicolas?"

He's not here, but a stack of folded clothing is on the bed. I walk out and pick it up, noticing it carries an exquisite fragrance. Hmm. I'll have to ask Marie what perfume she uses. It smells yummy enough to eat, even though I no longer do so.

The slacks fit well enough, though a little short. But before I put on the blouse, I need to see my back. I grab the hand mirror, then step over to the long mirror and turn around.

The deep canyons now look more like plowed fields, and I watch for several minutes as the pale flesh continues to magically form and fill in the gaps.

This is so amazing, but so creepy to watch.

I shudder, set the mirror down, and slip on Marie's blouse, buttoning it as I walk back across the room. The last thermos sits on the nightstand, calling me. Although I drank a mugful just before my shower, it seems to have already been used up by my rapidly healing body. My hand shakes as the thick red liquid pours into the mug.

It seems like I've been hungry for days, weeks, though it's only been a little over twenty-four hours since the attack. The need ebbs and flows wildly, according to my physical and emotional state from moment to moment. But the hunger has yet to abate completely, and it seems like it'll never be satisfied again.

That's pretty disconcerting.

Picking up the mug, I drink the red elixir slowly, savoring every drop as its healing warmth courses throughout my body.

Hope there's more soon.

The sun will be up in a little while, and though I'm not sleepy yet, my poor body's exhausted. Snuggling in bed with a book sounds really good right now, and there's an entire library downstairs waiting to be explored. Hell, I'll likely fall asleep just picking something out.

The faint sound of voices drifts through the foyer as I open the door and head down the stairs. When I near the library door, I realize Nicolas and Éva are in there. They're quietly arguing, and it's about me.

"But, Nicolas, I do not understand! If you really must have her, why do you not just take her, like you have all the others? Why not finish the Change? Then there will be no more nonsense over killing humans, and no more worries about her out there chasing wild animals!" Her voice, filled with frustration and anger, gets louder.

"Éva, please keep it down," he says, his tone low and irate. "I will not discuss this with you any longer. I have had enough. Your continuing protests and arguments indicate your time for renewal is quite overdue. Come here."

"Nicolas, no, not yet. Please, I beg you."

"Now."

Her soft footfalls pad across the floor.

Frowning, I knock on the door and hear Nicolas swear. He opens it, his eyes red and furious.

"Uh, I heard voices and decided to come down to see if I could borrow a book." I look at him innocently. His eyes narrow and I can see he's wondering how much I heard.

"Ah, you are done with your shower. Do you feel better?" His face and his voice both become neutral.

"Yes, I do. Thank you, and thank you for the clothes." I smile and purposely avoid looking at Éva, afraid I'll give away my eavesdropping.

"I will pass your gratitude along to Marie." The tension in him is fading, and I note out of the corner of my eye that Éva visibly relaxes.

"Éva. Please plan on staying a few more days." He turns to look at her. "We do have other business to finish up. But we are done for tonight."

Éva lowers her eyes in resignation and walks through the doorway. She nods as she passes me.

Nicolas looks at me, his expression unreadable. I look back at him with a hint of defiance.

I didn't fool anyone. They both knew I'd been there, listening at the door.

április 16., hétfö

I nearly killed her. She almost died, and it would have been my fault.

All because of my selfishness, my arrogance, my own stupid lust to win at the Game. I will never forget being overpowered by the scent of her sweet red essence as I opened the door, and seeing it painted, seeing her lifeblood smeared, all over the walls and the floor.

And her, lying in the middle of the red stain, torn to pieces, not moving. The agony I feel at this inerasable image is worse than any pain I have felt in my long life.

And now, I have done the one thing I promised her, that I swore, I would not do.

I have taken away her Choice.

TUESDAY

CHAPTER 35

Hunger is the first thing I feel as I wake up. Deep-seated, belly- and throat-burning hunger. Irritation sweeps through me at this endless need, and I hope the craving subsides once my body's fully healed. I throw off the covers, sit up, and look at my arm and shoulder. The gouges have closed completely, and now there's just a pair of silvery lines running down my arm.

Getting up, I go to the mirror and shrug off the nightgown borrowed from Marie. The twin lines on my face match that of my arm. My back is striped in silvery shallow furrows that run its entire length, from nape to hip. I count the lines—there are eight at the top, four for each swipe of his claws. In the middle of my back many of them merge, becoming wide, jagged ribbons of silver, deeper than the rest.

Damn. I can't get over what a mess he made of me, and how quickly. I just don't understand what happened. I should have been fast enough, strong enough. I should've been able to crush his skull when I went for his eye and tear a gaping hole in that shaggy throat.

Tightening my fists, I resolve to never let myself get that weak again, that helpless again. I catch a breath at the stabbing pain in my hands and open them to see blood welling where my own nails have pierced the flesh. Anger and frustration suddenly boil to the surface. My vision turns red, and the hunger explodes, flaming into every square inch of my body.

No . . .

A knock at the door penetrates the fiery need. It better be Nicolas with more blood.

"Come in," I say through gritted teeth, my jaw clenched tight.

He walks in, and his eyebrows lift as his gaze fastens on me.

"It . . . seems I may be a little late. This should help." He raises a steel thermos, and my body tenses as I walk over, resisting the urge to rip it out of his hand.

With an odd expression on his face, he opens it, and instead of pouring it into the mug, hands it to me. I grab it and slam down the whole thing without taking a breath.

I'm lowering the empty thermos when I realize that I am standing before Nicolas absolutely stark naked.

"Oh shit." I look down, and then look up into his blazing red eyes. His jaw is clenched as tight as mine was a few moments before, his body as rigid as mine had been.

"Ah . . . ," he says, and I see his fangs as he tries to speak.

I can't speak either.

Grabbing the robe from the bed, I walk into the bathroom. As I shut the door, I see him standing there, his eyes closed, body tense, and still as stone.

It takes several breaths for me to collect myself. When I finally feel like I can talk coherently, I slip the robe on, belting it tightly, and open the door.

He is gone.

It's been several hours and I can't stop pacing, back and forth, back and forth. I'm dressed now, and all I can think about is hunting. The pain from my injuries is gone, but not the hunger. Not the hunger. If anything, it's worse.

His step outside the door tells me he's here. He knocks.

"Come in." But I hear no movement to enter. "I'm dressed now."

Nicolas opens the door and walks in. His expression is tight as he strides over to the table and sets down a bag containing several thermos bottles. He steps back as I cross the room, take one out, and open it.

My eyes close in relief as the precious liquid runs down my throat and begins quenching the fire in my veins.

But this batch tastes a little different, more bitter, more oatey. I frown and look up at Nicolas in question.

He shakes his head. "I am sorry, but this is all we have for now. There is no more banked blood. You are drinking what little was left, mixed with that from the stable."

Is that why my hunger seems insatiable? Is it yearning for what I can't, *won't*, give it?

"You are still healing, even though it seems nearly complete. As long as you have visible traces of the injuries, there is still repair occurring at the microscopic level. The body's first job is to get back to an intact and functional status as a defense against further assault. All the real healing takes place once the major structural integrity is back in place." He pauses, studying me.

"I do not know if the horse blood will help much with this phase of the healing process. This is outside my realm of experience." His eyes soften, containing traces of sympathy.

"Well, since 'horse' isn't in my normal diet, maybe it isn't what I really need. Maybe what I need is what I normally feed on. Deer. Elk. Small game. My body is used to that and has been thriving on it since shortly after I changed." Irritated, I don't understand why Nicolas doesn't see the logic in this.

"Perhaps that is the case. However, you are nowhere near strong enough to hunt, so you will have to make the best of what we can find as a substitute. Do you agree?" His expression is grave, and I don't want to know what he's offering.

"The horse blood has gotten me this far, so as long as you have donors, I should continue to heal until I can hunt. Do *you* agree?" I frown, my mouth tight, and he nods.

"I have purchased a few more horses for that purpose. I have also sent out requests to other blood banks in the area, but unfortunately there seems to be a statewide shortage."

Great. I might not be killing the donors, but I'm taking something that someone else needs to live, and so I am indirectly responsible for their deaths.

And unfortunately, all this talk about blood isn't helping the hunger. I look at the bag.

Nicolas follows my gaze, reaches into the bag, and hands me a thermos. Conscious of making it last, I open it and pour it into the mug, then drink it slowly. But that only exaggerates its bitterness. I grimace and gulp it down.

"Would you like to get out of this room, perhaps go for a walk in the garden? It is cloudy today. In fact, it may rain on us, but we can take an umbrella." His green eyes look hopeful, and I nod.

Yeah, I need to get out of this room. I really need to get back to my mountain, but that will have to wait.

"How long do you think before I'm strong enough to hunt again?" I ask, hoping it won't be too much longer.

"I do not know. It depends on how well your tissues are able to utilize whatever blood we can supply. It could be several days, or several weeks." His expression is contemplative.

"How long would it take for a . . . normal Chosen?" I ask.

Nicolas takes a breath, and hesitates before answering.

He rolls up his shirtsleeve and slashes his arm open with his dagger-sharp nails. The skin and muscle part, then as the blood starts to well, the wounds close up without spilling a drop.

Oh.

"If a Chosen who had recently fed received injuries such as yours, the healing would have begun immediately. With a readily available source of fresh blood, their body would have finished the major structural repair within an hour or possibly two, with the rest of the healing completed a few hours or so after that."

Hours, not days. We are so much more different than I had realized.

"How many people would've died to heal them?" I ask quietly.

"It could take several donors. And they would not necessarily need to die. But the more blood available, the faster the healing." He seems reluctant to tell me this. He is aware of our differences, too.

I turn away, and part of me cringes inside, fearing we'll never be able to live in the other's world.

He comes up behind me, wrapping his arms around me, and rests his cheek against mine.

"We will make this work somehow. Please do not give up on me, on us. I love you more than you can imagine."

I turn around and look into those emerald eyes. "I . . . I love you too," I whisper, and he crushes me to him. But the crushing pain inside my chest has nothing to do with his embrace.

Nicolas holds my hand as we stroll through the garden. It's raining, and he's carrying a large umbrella to keep our clothes dry. However, the rain is gentle, and I let go of his hand to walk out into it. I look up and feel the drops falling softly on my face, and they become the tears I cannot shed.

As I look at Nicolas, a sadness comes into his eyes. He reaches out to brush away the drops from my cheeks and I kiss his hand. I kiss it a second time, then impulsively take a playful nip at it. His eyes widen, and I gently take hold of his hand with my teeth, and look mischievously up at him.

Oops.

His eyes are blazing red and his breath is fast, and he has crushed the umbrella handle.

I slowly let go.

"Um, maybe I shouldn't have done that. I'm sorry," I say, chagrined.

He takes a breath and holds it. The umbrella in his hand is vibrating.

"Ah, well, you seem to be doing your best to drive me insane today," he says hoarsely.

I look down in embarrassment. I'd forgotten about my little *display* this morning.

He reaches out and tousles my wet hair, then laughs. He grabs my hand and pulls me back under the umbrella with him and we continue walking. He has brought a pair of pruning clippers, and as we pass the living art of his topiary, he periodically snips off pieces and ties back new branches.

"Could we see your horses? I used to love them when I was a kid. That's why I could never . . . feed from one." I finish this last slowly, noting the sudden look of concern in his eyes.

"Not today. Perhaps another time." His face is neutral now.

"What, do you think I'll attack them? That I'll lose control? I may live off of animals, but I'm not one myself." Hurt and indignation quickly give way to anger. I pull away from him and step into the rain.

"I have no idea how you will react. I know how Chosen who are still healing from injury react to their food source, and they have little to no control. While in the healing process, the need for blood is too constant, too strong, and the ability to reason easily succumbs to the hunger." Not for the first time do I hear the experience in his voice in relation to injuries.

"Is that why I haven't seen Marie around? You've been afraid I would attack *her*?" I stare at him in disbelief.

"I felt you did not need the temptation, especially since you have been consuming human blood. And not just human blood, but *her* blood. Believe me, that does make a difference. We easily become sensitized to an individual's blood." His voice now holds a note of sadness that matches his earlier expression.

While I debate asking him what's wrong, his words sink in.

"But that will fade away, right? I mean, I wouldn't . . . harm Marie anyway. I really do like her." As confident as I feel, doubt creeps into my mind as I recall my reaction to Alfonso through the door.

"We shall see. But for now, it is best to limit your exposure."

"For how long?" I ask in a quiet voice.

"Again, I do not know. Days, at least. Possibly weeks. It all depends on how your system handles the healing process." His tone is subdued, his eyes holding a hint of concern.

Great. I feel the frustration mounting, and now I really do want to go kill something.

And of course, that thought stokes the hunger.

CHAPTER 36

Sitting in front of the fireplace, I scan the pages of a book Nicolas brought me, the one on The Chosen with his raven crest on the front. It's fascinating to read about their evolution and history, but I'm having difficulty focusing. This damn hunger is annoying, and the tension it's causing is aggravating it even more. It's a vicious circle, one I'm anxious to escape. At this point I don't know if I'll ever feel normal again, whatever that is.

Nicolas and Éva walk in, both relaxed and apparently over their argument from yesterday. Nicolas is carrying a cooler, and my vision turns pink in anticipation. I put the book down and get up out of my chair, trying to ignore the fire that has ignited once again in my veins.

Nicolas sets the cooler down on the table. He looks over at me, and I clench my jaw and walk stiffly to the table.

"I think we should dispense with the mug for the moment," he says as he takes out a thermos and hands it to me.

It's been several hours since the last one, which was straight horse blood and not very satisfying. My hand trembles as I raise it to my lips. Nicolas and Éva watch, their expressions closed.

I take several swallows before it hits me that this batch is different. There's very little horse in it, and the rest is richer, more full-bodied, and absolutely delicious. I stop briefly, and look at Nicolas in suspicion, but the hunger intensifies and I drink it down. I try to savor it and make it last, but that just doesn't work, and I quickly drain the entire thing.

I lick my lips and hand it back to Nicolas. I glance at the cooler, noting it holds three more, and Nicolas says, "Wait a little while. We need to be somewhat conservative for the time being."

"Where did it come from?" I ask. It's definitely human, and it does not taste like the stripped-down blood from the bank.

"I have made arrangements for private donations." He doesn't seem inclined to elaborate, and I don't feel inclined to know more.

But I do have one question, and as I open my mouth to ask it, he says, "No one died."

Relieved, I nod my head. I notice Éva looking at me curiously and a part of me bristles in defense.

"Sunny, relax. Éva and I have discussed your situation, and I believe she has a better understanding of it now." Nicolas glances at her and smiles, and she nods her head in compliance.

Something about her feels different, and I can't quite pinpoint what it is. But she certainly seems much calmer, almost serene. I note that her eyes are a pale gold. Maybe she's just fed.

Someone softly approaches the door, then knocks. Nicolas says, "Come in, Johan."

The young Chosen enters carrying a tray holding a carafe of deep red wine and three wineglasses. He sets it down and looks at Nicolas, who nods once. Johan fills the glasses and, looking at Nicolas again, steps back.

"That will be all for now." Nicolas dismisses the servant, and waits until Johan leaves the room.

His tone puzzles me. It's curt and condescending, with none of the kindness or even politeness he has with Marie and Alfonso. Interesting.

Nicolas picks up a glass and hands it to me, and takes another for himself. "Éva?" he says, indicating the wine, and she walks over and picks up the third glass from the tray.

Reminded of what she had said about Nicolas serving me, I realize the importance of paying closer attention to interactions between The Chosen, especially these two.

I wait to take a drink, watching Nicolas. He glances at me, then Éva, and raises his glass. "To the Blood," he says, green eyes sparkling.

I raise my glass in response. As I move it to my lips, I realize it's not just wine as the smell of blood reaches my nose. Nicolas smiles as I gingerly take a sip. The flavor explodes in my mouth.

It's definitely wine, perhaps a Merlot, but it's heavily laced with human blood. The combination is exquisite.

"How do you like it?" Nicolas asks, his mouth quirked, and a hint of amusement dances through his eyes. I haven't seen that for several days and am thrilled to see it back.

"It's wonderful, absolutely delicious." I have another taste and roll the flavors around in my mouth.

"Nicolas is known for his excellent bloodwine. It is a favorite among The Chosen." Éva smiles and takes a sip, savoring it a moment.

Nicolas looks back at her and takes a mouthful himself. He closes his eyes and smiles, then swallows. He opens his eyes and looks at me, faint red shining through his pupils.

"But why haven't I seen you drink it before, other than at the gathering? Is it only for special occasions?" I ask, wondering if this was one, and why.

"No, I actually enjoy it every evening. But you prefer tea, so that is what I drink when we are together." He smiles again and tips his head to the side.

I love that little mannerism and am momentarily distracted. I take another long sip of the wine and think about what he just said.

"Oh. You mean . . . you don't regularly drink tea?" I ask as embarrassment creeps in.

"Not really. But I do not mind the taste, and have certainly enjoyed drinking it with you." The warmth and fondness in his gaze melts my chagrin.

"The bloodwine, however, is not something *you* would have enjoyed—before now." He nods. "Which is why I had the bottle of Pinot Noir for you the evening of the gathering."

I take another drink and recall noticing the scent of blood when their wine was served, and being both concerned and relieved when I was served something different. It seems a lifetime ago, but in reality it's only been two nights.

In fact, everything before the attack seems like another life. Is that how I will mark time now—BB for before bear, and AB for after bear?

Suddenly feeling out of sorts, I drain my glass.

I had thought it would be BN and AN, revolving around the day I met Nicolas. But it seems the bear may have had a much bigger impact on my life than nearly causing my death. It was after the bear that I first drank human blood.

Sadness for my lost innocence grips me, and I wonder how much more of it will be sacrificed.

"Sunny?" Nicolas says, bringing me back to reality.

But it's not a reality I want. It's a freak show, a bad carnival ride, and I can't make it stop so I can get off.

"Sunny!" Nicolas walks over to me and the room spins a little. I'm feeling a bit woozy and lightheaded.

"I feel . . . odd," I say, my voice echoing as though from a distance. Nicolas takes my arm and guides me to a chair.

"Perhaps that is because you are a little drunk." Nicolas looks closely at my eyes as he sits me down.

"Drunk? I don' get drunk. Alcohol doesn't have any 'fect on me."

Did I just slur?

I recall the time I tried to drown my sorrows in alcohol instead of blood. After chugging the third quart of vodka, I threw it all up without ever getting any alcohol buzz. That sucked.

"This is not just 'alcohol.' In addition to the blood, it contains special ingredients that I infuse to enhance the effect of the blood. The wine is just a carrier, though important for the bouquet of scent and flavor."

Great. Drunk. On human blood. How nightmarish.

"Perhaps she would feel better if she had a little more of this. It might dilute the effects." Éva indicates the cooler with a nod of her head.

"Possibly." Nicolas looks speculatively at me.

Éva brings a thermos over and hands it to Nicolas. He opens it and offers it to me.

"Drink just a little bit," he cautions as I take it and raise it to my lips.

I take several swallows, then become lost in the blood and start gulping.

"Sunny." Nicolas reaches out as though to take it away from me.

Everyone, including me, is surprised when I growl and come half out of my chair.

"Careful, Nicolas," Éva says as she moves in as though to defend him.

I look up at him through a red haze and am having difficulty retaining control. The blood is calling me, and I look beseechingly at the thermos and back at Nicolas.

His eyebrows are raised, eyes intent, as he slowly withdraws it from my grip. I relent and let him have it, then sit back down and lower my face, ashamed.

"Oh. That was . . . weird." I feel disoriented, yet strong. Really strong.

I flex my scarred arm and move it around. It rotates freely, and seems to be as good, if not better, than before. The silver lines appear a little narrower and a little fainter.

I look back at Nicolas, feeling a bit more in control, and say sheepishly, "Nicolas . . . I'm sorry. I dunno what came over me." It sounds like a line out of a movie, though a bit slurred, and I laugh.

"The blood is what came over you, and that is what I have been trying to warn you about. Now do you understand about visiting the stable, and being around Marie?"

Uh-oh, Nicolas the lecturer is back. Great. I roll my eyes and laugh again, a little hysterically.

He raises his eyebrows. Again. They look like black caterpillars over his eyes. I giggle.

"Well, I feel stronger now. Can't ya just take me home so I can kill somethin'? This is drivin' me crazy. All I can think about is how hungry I am, and how much I want to hunt. In fact, I have a new prey in mind." Pausing for effect, I grin and push myself to a wobbly stand.

"Bear. Especially a certain one-eyed sonofabitch. I can take him this time." My feet somehow get tangled as I start for the door, and Nicolas catches my arm.

"This is the blood talking. You need to get control of yourself. Right now you are behaving like a spoiled, whining new-Chosen, and it is not amusing." His eyes are dark, his tone low and threatening.

"Let me go. I don't need your help." I try to yank my arm away. But it doesn't budge in his iron grip.

"I think you are done for the evening. You should go upstairs. Perhaps a hot shower will calm you down."

"Sure. Wanna join me? It could be quite fun." I laugh as his grip falters, and I nearly succeed in slipping out of it.

But he grabs tighter and, glancing at Éva, says, "Excuse us," and starts walking to the door. I laugh and let him half drag me across the floor. He shoots me a thunderous look, and I laugh again.

Wait until he gets me to my room. I know *exactly* how to disarm him, and I won't put up with him stopping this time.

He keeps hold of my arm as we climb the stairs. I go along meekly, but several giggles still escape.

We reach my door and he opens it. I go in ahead of him, but come to a stumbling stop when he lets go and doesn't follow me in.

Turning around, I look seductively at him and smile as I reach up to unbutton my blouse. He takes one step in, grabs the door, and pulls it shut. With him on the outside.

I hear the lock click.

"Nicolas! How dare you!" I scream, full of rage at his rejection. I pound on the door, then haul back and slam my fist through it.

I yowl in pain as it encounters an iron plate sandwiched inside the shell of the door.

That finally sobers me up. I rub my smashed fist and look at the door with the hole in the wood, the metal of the plate shining dully through it.

A shower sounds like a good idea after all.

április 17., kedd

She is mending, but very slowly. Too slowly. Her physiology is beyond my comprehension, and I am running out of options to keep her fed and healing.

She even reacted badly to the bloodwine, bringing her dangerously close to the brink of Chosen insanity.

But when she mentioned going after the bear, I did something horrendous to her. I could have stayed with her, and talked to her until she regained control. But I did not, because I feared that I would lose control. That my own lust and weakness would overrule my common sense, that I would take advantage of her when all she really needed was reassurance and comfort.

And so I abandoned her and locked her in her room, and I do not think I will be able to forgive myself for that.

WEDNESDAY

CHAPTER 37

I wake up, groggy and hungry. Always hungry. I get out of bed, walk over to the window, and move the blinds to the side. The sun is out, but it's partly cloudy, and I can only hope the clouds win the struggle for the sky.

Walking over to the mirror, I pull off the nightgown and look at my back. Most of the furrows are gone, and the silvery lines are now level with the rest of my skin. But a few run deeper, right in the area where several of them converge. I wrinkle my lip in disgust, realizing there is still enough unhealed damage that Nicolas won't let me go home yet. Crap. I really need to run something down.

The shoulder and arm still have faint silvery lines, as well as my face, and I wonder if those will ever go away. The scars give me a grim edge, which could be an advantage in certain situations.

I examine my hand and shake my head. The smashed knuckles are sore and still a little flat. Silver marks crisscross them where the skin broke.

Boy, did I get stupid last night.

But I don't really care right now. I'm hungry and cranky, and if Nicolas doesn't take me home, I'll walk. It's mostly mountains between here and there, with plenty to eat along the way.

A light step outside the door precedes a knock. Éva.

Hmm. Guess Nicolas doesn't even want to speak to me this morning. Serves me right.

Pulling on my robe, I tie the belt and face the door. "Come in, Éva."

She unlocks the door and opens it, and walks in carrying the cooler, closing the door behind her. Her eyes linger over the hole I punched in it, but she doesn't say anything. She walks across the room and sets the cooler on the table.

Well, at least he isn't going to continue punishing me with starvation.

I say nothing as I yank out a thermos and open it, then gulp it down without taking a breath. I set it aside and grab another, staring defiantly at Éva. I chug this one too, finally slowing as I reach the bottom.

The taste is different from yesterday, and I realize there isn't any horse blood in it at all. This is straight human. And I realize I don't even care as the wonderful-tasting elixir hits my system, cooling the fires that have been racing through me since Nicolas locked me in my room. I close my eyes in relief, and my whole body slowly relaxes.

I reach in to take a third and Éva says, "You might want to take it easy. Our supply is limited."

"I know where there's plenty more if Nicolas would let me go home," I say crabbily.

"Well, after your remark last night about hunting down the bear, I seriously doubt he is going to let you go home anytime soon. That was possibly the worst thing you could have said to him."

Oh. I did say that, didn't I? Crap. Pulling my hand out of the cooler, I sit down on the bed.

She's right, too. I feel a rush of guilt as I remember Nicolas's anguish and fear when he found me lying in my own blood after my encounter with that bear.

"Uh, well, then it seems I owe some apologies for my behavior last night." I shake my head and the remorse intensifies.

"You need to direct them to Nicolas. He is the one you hurt," she says, but without her usual tone of judgment.

She seems subdued, lacking her usual fire. I recall noticing it last night, too.

"Is everything okay, Éva? I mean with you. You seem rather . . . quiet. Did I say or do anything to you? I'm sorry if I did." I watch her face for her reaction.

"No, I am fine. Nicolas cleared up our . . . misunderstanding. I see his point of view now," she explains with little emotion, and my concern increases. But I decide not to push it.

"Perhaps you should get dressed. Nicolas is waiting in the library," Éva says. I nod and she turns to leave the room.

She stops at the door, looks at the hole again, and says, "Do not push Nicolas today. Last night was more difficult for him than you may realize.

That he felt it necessary to actually lock you in your room is an indication of the level of his concern. He has a . . . problem with locked rooms."

She opens the door and leaves, closing it behind her. She does not lock it.

Of course he does. I remember his story of being locked in a room during his Change. But worse, he knows mine, and that I behaved so rudely he felt it necessary to lock my door makes me sick.

Guess I better get this over with.

A fresh set of clothes had shown up in the closet sometime yesterday evening, after I'd gone down to the library to read. They're brand new, yet still smell of Marie and her lovely perfume. My throat tightens, and I feel a *craving* unlike any I have felt before.

Oh, no way. That's just a coincidence. It seems like I'm always hungry now. And even when I'm not, it's only a short time until I am again. I can't wait to get back on my mountain, where I can have as much as I want, whenever I want.

Dressing quickly, I stop in front of the mirror and steel myself to deliver the apologies I owe Nicolas.

I shake my head in disgust and leave the room. I ignore the hole in the door.

"Come in," responds Nicolas, a long moment after I knock at the library door.

Taking a deep breath, I open the door and close it behind me. I lean against it, reluctant to even face him now. He's sitting at the table by the window, paperwork scattered across the tabletop. He continues to write, his back to me. But I can see the side of his jaw, and it's tight, along with the rest of his body.

It's worse than I thought.

Pushing away from the door, I walk over and stand on the other side of the table. He sets down his pen, leans back in the chair, and looks up at me.

My heart clenches at the pain I see in his eyes.

"I'm sorry, Nicolas. I didn't mean what I said. About hunting the bear." I swallow at the shadow that crosses his face.

"Ah, but Sunny . . . you did. You and I both know you have been thinking about it. I see it in your face every time you look at your back in the mirror. The bloodwine only allowed you to admit it out loud." He tilts his head, but there is no amusement in his cool expression as he continues.

"You need to realize that I understand. To destroy any who threaten us is our natural instinct. It is what ensures our survival."

He stands, walks around the table to me, and places his hands on my arms.

"And that is why, when it is time, when you are completely healed and at your strongest, you will go hunt him down and protect your territory. And I will go with you."

"You will?" I hadn't expected this.

The tortured look crosses his face.

"What makes you think I could ever let you face something like that alone? To wonder if you are going to come back to me in pieces, or at all? No, I cannot even endure the thought."

He draws me in close and rests his cheek on my head.

"And now, I must apologize to *you*. For . . . locking you in your room. That was unforgivable." The remorse in his voice saddens me. He really had no choice. I lost control last night.

I slowly lean back to look into his deep sea eyes, and reach up to touch his brow, trying to ease the tension there.

"You did what you needed to do. I was not myself. I very easily could've headed out the front door for who knows where. I'm not angry with you, but I am disgusted with me. I'm sorry for my behavior, and for causing you pain." I stroke the side of his face and he turns his head to kiss my hand.

"There is no need to apologize. Your reaction to the bloodwine could not have been anticipated." He pulls me close again. "There is much about you that is different, and I should be more cautious. I tend to forget, as there is also much about you that is the same."

The same. I just wish we truly could be the same. But that would mean one of us has to give up our life as we have known it. And he has been living his so long that change would be impossible.

There is a third option, one I don't even want to think about.

I hug him close, hoping I don't have to give up . . . him.

We are headed up the highway to my home. Nicolas suggested we pick up some of my clothes and anything else I might need, and I'm eager to see my mountain again.

He pulls the red Ferrari up the driveway and we park at the back of the house. When he opens my door, I step out, my gaze locked on the mountainside. The hunger springs alive at the sight, even though I had another thermos just before we left. Nicolas notes the change, and his jaw tightens, concern written across his face.

I take a deep breath of the fresh mountain air, inhaling the myriad of scents wafting through the forest. The cloud cover is thick and heavy with the promise of rain. I look at Nicolas, then turn to go into the house.

As I approach the back door, my eyes widen at the bloodstains all along the doorframe and on the door itself. I pause, then grab the red-painted doorknob and turn it. What I see stops me in my tracks. I feel Nicolas behind me and realize this might not have been a good idea.

So this is what he saw when he came to get me. I shudder to think how I would have felt had the roles been reversed.

There is dried blood everywhere. It trails along the wall to the bedroom, and I follow it, appalled. As I walk into the bedroom, I note two things: the blood-soaked covers of my bed and the large dried puddle on the floor where Nicolas must have found me.

I look over at him and he's just standing there, rigid, his eyes filled with anguish. I walk back and wrap my arms around him, and a harsh sound escapes from his chest. My own chest aches in sympathy for him, and I resolve never to take the risk of doing this to him again.

Grabbing a suitcase from the closet shelf, I quickly throw some clothes and shoes into it. I gather some items from the bathroom and glance at Nicolas watching me as I pack. His expression is closed, his eyes so dark they are nearly black.

I shut the suitcase and nod at it. He steps over the bloodstain on the floor, picks it up, and takes it out to the car. As I go into the living room, his beautiful bookcase triggers another round of remorse. I've never even read any of the books he so lovingly picked out and brought up for me. I walk over and pull out several, and set them with my laptop, then get my other bag from the bedroom. After putting my stuff in the car, I go back to lock the door and grimace once again at the bloody reminder of how I almost died.

Nicolas is standing at the foot of the trail, staring upward, and I join him.

"What I do not understand is how you made it here." His voice is hoarse with emotion.

"Come on." I take his hand. "Let's go up there. I . . . I need to see where it happened."

He nods and we begin walking up the trail. Apparently it hasn't rained much here. I note dried blood scattered along the trail, heavier in places where I'd fallen or clung to a tree.

We keep hiking upward for some time and have no difficulty following the bloody trail. We're both silent as we climb.

Skirting around a cluster of trees, we enter a small clearing. Lying off to one side are the scattered bones and fur of a deer. A little distance away are the remains of a coyote, near a large bloodstained area. That must be where I collapsed after the bear took off.

Nicolas walks around looking at the carcasses, then steps over to an area where the dried grasses and ground are torn up. He runs his hand through his hair and shakes his head, then turns and looks at me.

"How did you do this? How did you fight off this bear and lose all the blood you lost, and then travel so far down the mountain?" The despair in his voice is palpable.

"I vaguely remember feeding off the deer afterward, then I must've passed out. I woke up to something touching me, and I grabbed it and drained it before I even knew what it was." I motion to the coyote. "His blood gave me enough energy to start down the mountain, and then I just kept going. All I could think about was getting to shelter, hoping the sun wasn't going to come out."

Nicolas is silent as he looks around at the scene, apparently trying to visualize the sequence of events. He finally speaks.

"You are the most complicated being I have ever encountered. You sustained enough damage and blood loss here in this clearing to render most young Chosen incapable of movement and mindless from the hunger, completely unable to function on any level." He shakes his head, his tone bleak.

"The outcome should have been eventual death, as you would have been unable to adequately defend yourself from predator attack.

"Yet you did. And you were able to figure out where you were, drawing on some unknown source of energy and power to get you down the mountain and into the house." He stops and looks intently at me.

"There is only one explanation for the mystery that you are, and I have been considering it for some time now. Your survival abilities confirm it." Nicolas pauses, looking thoughtful.

"I think I may know who, or at least what, your Maker is. I felt that unusual presence when it first came into my city—that is what led me to you. It seemed impossible at the time, but I have seen enough indications since then that it can be nothing else. The ramifications, if this is true, will send huge ripples through Chosen society."

"Who?" I ask in a whisper, half afraid to hear the answer to the question I've been asking for a long time now.

"One of the Old Ones, though I'm not sure yet which one. But none of them have been seen in over 360 years." He takes a breath.

"It would explain the uniqueness of your scent, the feel of your power, and your lack of normal newly Changed limitations. And it would explain why you were able to do what you did to survive. They are literally the most powerful beings on earth."

"And doesn't that include you?" I ask.

He looks at me and gives a slight nod.

"Yes, perhaps, but the others are much older, and much stronger. So you see, you and I are more alike than you realize. You need to stop focusing on our differences and start embracing our commonalities. Our dietary preferences are really of little consequence." He reaches out and strokes the scars on my face.

Well, they are of consequence to me.

But rather than argue, I focus on questions that have been haunting me since the attack.

"Then if I have this powerful blood in me, why was the bear able to do what he did to me? Why was I unable to kill him quickly? And why is it taking so long for me to heal?!"

"Because, dear Sunny, you are also part human. You never completed the Change. And it has left you in limbo. The blood of the Old One who made you is why you did not die then. Apparently it only needed a spark of life, any spark, for you to survive. Fortunately for you, the dog happened by right when you needed it."

"Then if I got that 'spark' as you put it, doesn't it mean the Change was complete?"

"No, as I'm trying to explain, it was only enough to sustain your existence, to keep you alive. The Changing spark *must* come from our former species, which is human, to fully become what we are."

What we are. Drinkers of blood.

Except . . . the blood he prefers is human.

And that abhors even a monster like me.

We walk back down the mountain in silence. No longer concerned with reliving the events of a few days ago, I've become aware of the wildlife in the forest going about their business. The hunter in me starts casting for scent, and the hunger flares in anticipation. A rabbit darts from the trail ahead, and I long to give chase. But not in front of Nicolas. Deer and elk are one thing, but I have no wish for him to see me feed on small game.

Catching a taste of deer on the air, my vision flares red as I instinctively tense for the hunt. I move in that direction, but Nicolas steps in front of me, breaking my hunter's focus. I frown and start to argue in a whisper.

"Nicolas, this won't be a problem—"

"You are right. This will not be a problem because it is not going to happen. You are not yet well enough to take down a deer. You risk damaging the freshly healed tissue, which will only make the regeneration process take that much longer. Besides, hunting up here will not be safe until we have eliminated the bear, and as we discussed, you are not quite ready to do that either." His look is determined, his voice stern, but I try again anyway.

"Well, knowing that he is up here will keep me that much more alert. He won't sneak up on me a second time." I ignore his comment about not being well enough, because deep inside, I can feel that he is right.

"He does not have to sneak up on you. He will walk right in and try to take your kill, like before. Are you telling me that you will just let him?"

I hesitate, because he is right on this as well.

"If you want to hunt that badly, I will go out and take care of this bear, and any others in the area. Is that what you want?" He raises those eyebrows and tips his head. He has me and he knows it.

"No." I shake my head and start walking down the mountain.

That's *my* bear. The beast in me growls in frustration, and I feel the burn of hunger beginning. Again.

CHAPTER 38

I shift position yet again, unable to get comfortable. Reading here in front of the fireplace sounded relaxing, but it's not helping. My gaze escapes the pages in my lap and drifts once more to the clock on the mantle—8:10. I wonder what's taking Nicolas so long.

Giving up, I set the book aside, shove myself out of the chair, and start pacing, unable to contain my impatience any longer. The simmer of my hunger is now boiling through my veins, and I hug myself in pain and frustration.

Nicolas left shortly after we got back to the estate to check on my blood supply for the evening. But he's been gone several hours now. I haven't had anything since around noon, and my skin is crawling with anxiety.

Part of the problem is that I only get a couple quarts at a time, so I'm never completely satisfied. I literally get gallons from deer and elk. And thinking about quarts and gallons stokes the hunger even more.

Damn it, Nicolas. You should've let me take a deer this morning.

The Jag pulls up out front, and I sigh as Nicolas gets out. He comes up the steps and in through the front door. But he doesn't stop at the library. I listen uneasily as he heads into the back of the house.

I continue pacing, and the flames continue to flicker throughout my body, slowly building into a bonfire in my stomach and my throat. Still Nicolas does not come. I debate going to find him, but that might not be a good idea, as there are definite sections of the house he has not invited me into. I speculate as to why and have a feeling his secrecy is his attempt to shelter me from the facets of Chosen life that I find troubling.

The fire spreads into my skin, and finally I curl up in the chair in flaming torment. I begin to descend into the pit of agony I'd spent time in only a few days ago and hug my knees tighter. I feel like I'm burning alive.

Nicolas, where *are* you?

Then I hear him come down the hallway and into the library. I sob in relief and look up as he walks over to my chair. My eyes shift, fixing on the cooler he sets on the floor.

"Ah Sunny, I am so sorry. We have encountered difficulties which I have been attempting to resolve."

He crouches down, opens the cooler, and takes out a thermos, then hands it to me. He helps guide my trembling hands to my mouth, and as the warm, red liquid begins to pour down my tortured throat, he starts speaking.

"I regret this is all that I have for you right now." His remorseful tone matches his words, and I look up into his emerald eyes brimming with sympathy.

It's straight horse blood and it tastes vile. I choke, and gagging, almost spit it out. But I need it too badly, and so I keep drinking, even though every cell in my body wants to reject it.

I barely force down the last mouthful. Swallowing over and over again to keep it from coming back up, I shakily hand the thermos back to him. He takes out another and I put up my hands in protest.

"No. No. I can't drink anymore of that. It's making me sick." And it's not helping either. The hunger rages on and I look up at him in fear.

"Why isn't it helping? Why can't I drink it? It was working before."

Nicolas winces and says in a low tone, "I am afraid this is my fault. As it seemed we had a plentiful supply of human blood, and I wanted to expedite your healing, I have been using less and less of the horse blood. The last several batches have not contained any. It appears your system has . . . adapted."

Adapted? No . . . My mind shies away from the implications.

"But what happened to the human donors?" I ask, thoughts whirling. Part of me hopes it was nothing bad, like dying, but the rest of me no longer cares.

"They have reached their limits and must rest longer before they can donate any more. I have been out trying to procure new volunteers, but have had no luck," he says worriedly, then with a deep breath, continues.

"I can, however, offer an alternative, but it will require you to be very open minded." He pauses, watching my reaction.

I'm pretty sure I don't want to hear it, and I'm pretty sure I'm ready to hear anything. If it will relieve my misery, I don't care. As long as I don't have to kill anyone. And right now, even that doesn't sound as objectionable as it has in the past.

As though he can read my thoughts, Nicolas nods and says, "I do have willing donors elsewhere in the city. I do not want to bring them here, but we can go there."

My body is already moving before my mind agrees. I stand up, Nicolas rising with me, and start for the door. I look back at Nicolas and see him watching me with a strange sadness in his eyes. My suffering seems like it's as painful for him as it is for me.

He joins me at the door, and we walk outside and get in the car. The Jag purrs down the driveway and I watch his garden creatures flash by, looking macabre in the thin moonlight. We drive through the gates and head down the hill.

Somewhere southeast of the downtown area, we pull into a parking lot next to a warehouse that's been converted into a nightclub. Nicolas gets out, opens my door, and extends his hand to help me out. Faint music thuds through the brick walls as we walk to a side entrance of the club, about halfway back along the building. Nicolas opens the door with a key, and as we step inside, he turns and enters a series of numbers into a keypad.

We follow a dark hallway to the door at the end, where he flips up the cover of another keypad. He enters another series of numbers, then presses his thumb onto a little window, and the red light of a scanner flashes by. He opens the door and we go in.

Through the haze of hunger, something in me says I should be a little impressed by the security, but right now I don't really care.

We walk into a room and it automatically lights up. It's an office, complete with desk, chair, and computer in one corner of the room. In the opposite corner is a forest-green sofa, matching stuffed chairs, and a couple of end tables with lamps.

Nicolas stops and caresses the side of my face, and I again note his look of sadness and regret. "Would you like to have a seat on the sofa? I will return shortly."

I nod and go over to sit down while he leaves through a door at the other end of the room.

My gaze wanders along the walls, covered in rich dark paneling and lined with paintings, and takes in the expensive furniture and plush carpeting. I shake my head. Even when he slums it in a warehouse, he surrounds himself with opulence. But the inferno in my belly and the flames in my veins reassert themselves, and I can no longer speculate about anything.

Nicolas opens the door and walks in, accompanied by a young man in his early twenties.

A human.

I feel myself snap to attention and a strange tingling overtakes my body. I stand up, barely able tear my eyes away from him to look at Nicolas.

"This is Skeeter, and he has volunteered to help us with your . . . situation." His green eyes are dark, and as he says this, the red flares through them.

Skeeter doesn't say anything, just nods, his light brown eyes bright and expectant. Nicolas walks him over to me, his hand on Skeeter's back. They stop in front of me and I'm nearly overcome by his warm human scent. The beast in me tenses in excitement and I close my eyes, my jaw clenching in frustration.

Somewhere in me alarms are going off, telling me that this is wrong, telling me to get out of here, telling me to run.

But it's too late. My mind fixes on the words "donor" and "volunteer," and my eyes open against my will and look at the frail young man through a red haze.

He rolls up his sleeve eagerly and offers me his arm—an arm riddled with small scars along his veins. His *veins*.

The beast roars in my head, and I squeeze my fists and look one more time at Nicolas, pleading silently to take this boy away.

But Nicolas only reaches out to support Skeeter's arm. Feeling as though I'm in a dream, I step up and take it in my hands. The silent wail in me is not from the beast, however. It is from the little slice of human soul that has guided my life these last five years. The pain that now lances through me has nothing to do with injuries or hunger, but I ignore it as my hands raise his arm to my face.

The beast springs and I sink my teeth into the soft flesh of his inner arm, just below the elbow. Sweet, hot, liquid ecstasy pours into my mouth and I begin to draw greedily. I'm dimly aware of his gasp and his groans, and then waves of pleasure wash through me. They begin in my mouth, move down my throat, and spread throughout the core of my being, following the path of the blood as it enters my system. I have felt nothing like this in the whole of my existence. I pull harder. Each mouthful brings a new flood of sensation that is beyond my comprehension, and the beast in me howls in rapture as I lose myself.

I'm suddenly jarred from my euphoria by Nicolas, his fingers wedging my jaw open and pushing my mouth away from this fountain of bliss. I snarl and try to take another bite, but Nicolas slaps me, hard, knocking my face away, and the shock that he would hit me is enough to break my blood focus. My grip on the arm loosens, and my hands are brushed off as though they were nothing more than mosquitoes.

As I war with myself to regain control, I hear them leave through the door.

"NO!"

But my cry is not just for the loss of the warm red ambrosia that has left the room and forever altered my life. It is also for the final remnant of my innocence, ripped away and washed from me in a river of human blood.

I sit curled up in the chair, trying to hold myself in one piece. I feel as though I've been split in two. One part of me is screaming and cowering in fear from the other part, the now dominant part. The one that is still caught up in the intoxication of the blood, the beast singing in triumph.

But my inner conflict cannot compete with the serenity and peace that permeate my body. No pains, no flames, no hunger. Only a warm, cozy feeling of floating on a soft cloud that I want never to end. I close my eyes and drift, and my turmoil fades away in the nothingness.

Nicolas opens the door and comes back into the room. I have no idea how long he's been gone, but it feels like I've circled the globe several times on my fluffy cloud of tranquility.

He walks over to the chair and looks down at me, his pale green eyes unreadable. I make no move to get up, but lethargy is not the only reason. I'm so furious with Nicolas that I can't even speak to him. I feel betrayed, by my own body and by him, but especially by him.

"I . . . *trusted* . . . you," I growl in a low voice.

He tips his head and says, "Stand up."

I don't want to, and yet I do. Very much.

I uncurl myself and get to my feet, facing him. He steps forward, and his expression is fierce, his eyes filling with red, and he roughly takes me in his arms. He kisses me, insistent that I respond, and I can't help myself, and I do. He then starts kissing all around my mouth, nipping at my lips, my jaw, and moves to my throat. I feel his teeth graze my skin, and then he moves to the back of my neck and down my shoulder.

My veins ignite, but not in hunger. It's a sweet fire, enhanced by my blood-induced euphoria, and I inhale the scent of his hair as he caresses my collarbone with his lips.

He moves his mouth up my neck, kissing and nibbling, and then in the hollow below my ear, right under the bone of the jaw, he slowly sinks the twin daggers of his fangs.

I don't have time to be shocked. He takes in one mouthful, and as he pulls, I am overcome with a wave of ecstasy. He swallows and pulls again, slowly, and I nearly collapse in pleasure. He tightens his arms, drawing me closer, and pulls again, and another wave washes over me. I hang there, helpless, waiting for the next onslaught, and he waits, growling.

Please, again.

And he pulls again, and I feel like I'm imploding, everything that is me being pulled into a molten core of rapture. He leaves me suspended above the fire, longing for more.

He waits, for eternity it seems. Then he slowly withdraws his fangs and kisses the wounds they made. He continues to hold me, softly growling, and I gradually come back to myself, once again forever changed.

"You see," he says huskily, "they do not suffer."

~

We are driving back to the estate and I sit frozen in silence. But that is only on the outside. Inside my mind is a raging maelstrom. I'm trying to make sense of how this happened, how I came to this. I fed from a human, a *person*. I keep thinking back further and further in time, trying to find the pivotal point in my life that brought me here. But they are all pivotal, and I can find no one to blame except myself.

I would weep, but it's impossible when I'm still trapped in the elation of the blood flowing through me and the memory of Nicolas's sharp caress. I finally reach over and touch his neck, all rational thoughts forgotten. His lip curls as he presses against my hand, and my blood begins to heat up again.

We pull into the driveway and park in front of the steps. As Nicolas helps me from the car, his touch electrifies me, and I look up at him through a red haze. His crimson eyes stare down at me and he takes a breath, and we walk up the stairs and into the house.

He leads me up to my room, opens the door, and ushers me in. He stops and just looks at me, and I feel myself melt as I look back into his blood eyes. He slowly takes me in his arms. His kiss is full of promise, and I am his. Completely.

As I lean in and press my lips to his throat, he gently pushes me back. He caresses my jaw with his lips, and then, in a voice hoarse with emotion, says, "We must wait a little longer. It is not time yet."

NO! I scream for the second time tonight, but this time in silence.

Don't do this to me again. Don't leave me wanting you so much I feel like I'm going to die.

"Nic . . . I . . ." But I can't get the words out because I don't have the words for what I want, what I need.

"Sshhh . . . ," he whispers. "Soon. Very soon. I promise."

He slowly releases me, kissing my forehead as he steps back.

Nicolas leaves the room without another word and closes the door behind him.

I look at the door, and at the hole I put in it, and wonder how much longer there will be closed doors between us. I realize that he's been opening them since we met, but I've been reluctant to step through. The door he took me through tonight was one I swore I would never enter, and now that I am on the other side, I would do it again. And again. And I don't know if it will open for me to cross back over, but tonight, I don't care. As long as I get to be on the same side of the door as he.

április 18., szerda

She has finally done it. Though she does not yet realize it, it was for the best. If she is to survive in The Chosen society, then she must learn to feed as we do. Yet a part of me mourns the wild innocent creature that she was when I first found her.

And I am the one who killed that innocence. I loathe myself for what I am doing to her.

And afterward, I crossed another line. I gave myself a pathetic excuse—that it was so she would understand. But I did not ask her permission, and that was bastardly of me. Yet I will never forget the exotic fire of her blood, and her sweet essence that was beyond anything I could have ever imagined. I cannot wait to drink of her again.

Yes, because if we stand here much longer, I'm going to tear your clothes off.

"That sounds great. Let me grab a few things and I'll meet you downstairs." Nicolas walks back to the door. He stops, looking at the hole, shakes his head, and leaves.

Curling my fist, I examine it from several different angles. The bones have knitted back together perfectly, but the skin over the knuckles wears a faint silver web. Huh. Another reminder to not be stupid.

I take a light jacket and my bag, hat, and gloves from the closet. Stopping on my way out, I look in the mirror one more time. Something in my face looks different. It's not the scars, and I can't quite pinpoint what it is. I shrug and head downstairs.

Nicolas helps me into the low-slung silver sports car, one I'm not familiar with. I study the interior as he walks around the car, and notice the Audi symbol on the steering wheel. He gets in and I say, slightly surprised, "This is an Audi?"

He smiles and replies, "Yes, it is. The R8."

I nod, trying to look impressed, but I'm sure he can tell that I have no idea what he's talking about. Amusement flits across his face, and I wonder what he has up his sleeve now.

We zip down the driveway, through the gates, and out onto the road. But when we reach the stop sign at the main road, Nicolas turns right instead of his normal left toward town, and we wind our way through the exclusive Broadmoor neighborhoods. We pass one of the many golf courses, then start heading up the mountain.

Guess he really meant a drive when he said it.

But we only go another half mile or so when the road ends in a parking lot with a sign for the Cheyenne Mountain Zoo. I look at Nicolas in surprise.

"The zoo?" I'm a little puzzled. And more than a little concerned.

He smiles and cruises the lot until he finds an empty space well away from the rest of the cars. It's not crowded, as it's early on a weekday morning.

I try again. "You won't show me your horses because you're afraid I'll lose control and attack them like some wild beast. Yet you take me to a zoo where there are likely exhibits containing the very animals I *do* hunt. I'm not sure I understand your reasoning."

"They have a rather nice collection at this zoo and I enjoy visiting it periodically." Ignoring my sarcastic remark, Nicolas gets out of the car, walks around to my side, and opens the door. "Since your recovery from the attack seems to be complete, and hunger is not an issue for you today, I thought it would make a nice outing."

Okay. Well, he is right about the hunger. Guess we'll see about the rest. But thinking about it, it occurs to me that I've never really been around any animals that I *wasn't* hunting, so this might be a bit interesting.

I peer at Nicolas suspiciously and wonder if there might be more to this visit than just looking at the exhibits. But he just raises his eyebrows and gestures for me to get out of the car.

Damn poker face. I can rarely tell what's going on behind that mask. Well, except for when we uh . . . yeah. Well, then he can hide nothing. Typical male.

With a glance at the sun, I slip on my gloves, grab my bag, and put on the hat, then get out. The jumble of odors that earlier wafted past the open door now becomes overwhelming. Some I recognize, or at least the family type, but there are many more which are completely foreign.

We walk up to the entrance, and Nicolas pays at the ticket window while I stand off to the side, taking in the scents bombarding me. The hunter, so far well fed and happy, stirs a little at the potpourri of smells, and I quickly shove her down. Interesting might be an understatement.

We pass through the gate and follow a broad walkway up the hill. I catch movement below us and to the right, and realize we're overlooking a pen containing quite a few giraffe.

I stop and watch as they move across the pen, their necks swaying rhythmically as they walk. I'm completely captivated by their long throats. I wonder how I would get to that soft spot under their jaws, or if I would even need to go up that high.

Nicolas laughs out loud, and I look over to see him watching me, his hand over his mouth as though trying to suppress further chuckles.

"You should see your face." He laughs again. "I can watch the wheels spinning as you contemplate that lengthy throat."

You sick bastard. You brought me here just to torture me.

I glare at him.

"Sunny, please. I had those exact same thoughts the first time I saw a giraffe, and I do not even hunt animals." He looks at me with an exaggerated air of pleading, and I give in and laugh.

It's actually pretty funny. We're always fascinated with throats, but one that long kind of boggles the mind.

He takes my arm and we continue up the path. We turn left toward the gorilla exhibit and my feet come to a dead stop. The corner pen contains several white-coated mountain goats, and the hunter snaps to full attention. This is a species I've researched, and have been eager to hunt, but they tend to be found more in the Rocky Mountains to the west. A big male jumps onto a rock and my muscles twitch. I drink in their musky scent, memorizing it for future use.

The mountain goats respond to my intensity by gathering together and moving up the rocky slope to the far end of the pen.

"Sunny," Nicolas says quietly and gently takes my elbow. I allow him to guide me up the path, finally tearing my eyes away from them.

I take a breath and say, "Those are on my list. Now I know what scent to hunt for."

Nicolas sighs, and irritation flickers through me. What did he expect?

We continue up the path and encounter a pen containing a large pond. A massive hippo lumbers across the concrete and flops down next to a second, even bigger one. He yawns, and those bone-crushing jaws and huge teeth send a shudder through me. Definitely a fight I would avoid, no matter how much blood they have.

It's not like I haven't seen zoo animals before. I remember taking my daughter a few times when she was young. We loved to watch the animals go about their business. But I haven't been to the zoo in *this* life and my perspective is quite a bit different now. Now it's all about their suitability as prey, their strengths and weaknesses, and their delicious scents. And the scent of their blood.

I glance at Nicolas as we continue up the hill and wonder if he assesses these creatures the same way I do, or if he merely finds them entertaining.

We enter a cinder-block building with a wall of glass along its length overlooking a large, densely vegetated habitat. The hillside is covered with grass and trees and dotted with clusters of boulders. On the other side of the window, a baby gorilla is playing with a stick, and about twenty feet past him, a large silverback male is eating a piece of fruit.

The silverback suddenly tenses, staring in our direction. He lunges to his feet with a roar and charges toward us as the baby screams and runs up the hill. A female appears from behind a rock and the baby leaps into her arms.

Other gorillas rush from all corners of the pen to the mother and baby. The male stops about ten feet from the glass, appearing confused as he tries to catch our scent. He can see us, though. He thumps his chest, resulting in a series of hollow pops punctuated by deep grunts.

My initial response is defensiveness, but nothing else. I don't see them as prey, and I don't understand their behavior. I look at Nicolas.

"Do they normally react like this?"

The group begins to move up the hill to the far end of the enclosure while the male continues to posture and growl.

"As far as I can tell, they only behave this way when I enter the exhibit."

"But they don't seem to be able to smell us through the glass."

"I believe they sense our energy. There may be enough physiological similarities between gorillas and the humans that I normally . . ." He pauses. "Obviously they feel threatened."

He reaches out to take my hand and we leave the building. We follow the path back past the hippos and down the hill. The ribbon of concrete winds through a food service area and then curves up and around a playground. Several mothers are here with small children, and I feel a strange tingle in my blood as the hunter peers at them with abnormal interest.

Nicolas slips his arm around me and softly nuzzles my ear, and I inhale sharply as my blood heats up in reaction to his caress. I close my eyes a moment, enjoying his sudden affection.

When I open them, we're turning onto a path that leads up a hill. And in a flash of irritation, I realize what he had just done.

"You did that to distract me!" I try to pull away, but he just laughs and holds me tighter.

"I did that because I love you." He smiles, or smirks—I'm not sure which—then says, "And yes, I did that to distract you. Your body may react more strongly than usual to food sources for a little while longer, and I did not wish this to upset you."

Food sources? People aren't a food source to me.

I frown as it seems my body may feel differently. But that's only temporary, and this new appetite will be a thing of the past once I get back on my mountain.

I hope.

The path up the hill takes us into the Rocky Mountain habitat area. As we pass a large pond, a young moose walks to its edge. My feet stop dead in their tracks while I memorize the scent of another Colorado species I've been anxious to try. The moose notices my intense focus, but seems to care less as it bends to nibble algae and grasses from the rocks in the water.

"The bulls can be anywhere from eight hundred and fifty to fifteen hundred pounds. Animal blood is typically five percent of body weight, which would calculate out to be about five to nine gallons." I grin, then laugh at the image forming in my head. "That could feed the whole Council."

Nicolas doesn't respond and I glance over at him. His expression is speculative, and I wonder if he realizes that I'm joking—at least about the Council part.

We continue up the hill and a canine scent I noticed earlier gets stronger. At the top is a forested pen, and as with the gorillas, glass separates the occupants from the spectators.

But there is a section off to the side barricaded with chain-link fence, and it's in this area that several wolves suddenly appear. They raise their muzzles, scenting the air, and then start pacing and snarling, hackles raised.

My body tenses and a low rumble erupts unexpectedly from my chest.

I quickly shut it off and glance at Nicolas in embarrassment. But he has also tensed, his eyes dark, and then red sparks through them. I look back at the wolves, and they continue to pace by the fence, bristling and growling.

My tension grows and I fight myself to relax.

"Nicolas, what's going on here?"

"There are ancient rivalries between our kinds, as between most predators. I believe you may have experienced that with the bear, yes?" He breaks his gaze away from the wolves to look at me.

"You mean he wasn't just after my deer?" I think back on the bear's ferocity.

"I suspect there may have been a territory issue. This is the time of year they come out of their dens, which may be why you hadn't encountered him before.

"Come." He reaches out his hand and I take it, and we continue on around the trail, the growls fading in the distance.

It's a good thing there haven't been any other visitors near these last couple of exhibits. Of course, since most people are pretty oblivious, I doubt they would have noticed anything unusual anyway.

The next exhibit contains animals I am familiar with, or at least their scents. Fortunately that is the extent of my contact with them, although in a fight with one, I think I would fare much better than I did with the bear.

The two mountain lions resting on a sunny rock ledge snap to attention as we walk up. They lie there a moment, tails lashing, and one opens his mouth in a silent hiss. Two more appear from the back of the pen, mouths wrinkling as they taste our scent and hiss. I am instantly captivated by them, and yet feel none of the aggressive response I did with the wolves.

I glance at Nicolas and he seems to share my admiration. The cougars continue to watch us intently, occasionally showing us their fangs. I realize this gives me an opportunity to ask a question I've been dying to have answered. I double-check to be sure no humans have come into the area while I was distracted by the cats.

"Nicolas, can I ask a . . . personal question?" I continue to watch the cats as several begin to pace along the ledge.

"Yes?"

"Why is it that you have fangs, and I don't?" This has bothered me since I first felt their touch on my throat.

He waits a moment before speaking.

"That is a question I have had since I saw you take down the elk. But I believe we answered that once we began to solve the mystery of your Change." He reaches out and brushes his fingers against my lips.

"You mean because I'm still part human?" This makes sense to me.

"Yes, that is the conclusion I have come to." He looks at me curiously and smiles.

Good. I was afraid he was going to say it was a male-female thing, and then I'd feel awkward, as though I'd asked about his more personal parts.

"So, how do they work? I mean, most of the time they aren't visible. I was quite shocked the first time I felt—" I stop in complete embarrassment.

He smiles at my discomfort.

"They reside in special grooves in the upper gum, just before the eye-teeth. Would you like to see?" His eyes grow dark and his smile takes on a wicked glint.

And my blood suddenly heats up. There is certainly something I find very attractive about his fangs.

"Uh, maybe not right now. I'll . . . I'll take your word for it," I say with a catch in my voice.

Nicolas laughs and gives me a knowing smile.

Damn him. He knows what he does to me. He asked that on purpose.

"They descend as part of a biochemical reaction that occurs whenever we anticipate a need for them." His mouth quirks.

Right. For anything that involves taking in blood, and apparently not limited only to feeding.

I look back at the mountain lions, and again several open their mouths and hiss. I decide we should move on, as thinking about fangs right now has become a bit distracting.

But no such luck, as the next exhibit is the lynx, which has a similar reaction to us. However, we seem to make him more nervous, and after hissing at us, he gets up from his resting spot and disappears behind the rocks.

Just beyond the lynx, we pass an enclosure with a pair of otters playing at the edge of a pond. They are too cute to consider as prey. We watch for a few moments, then move on down the hill.

As we round a curve in the trail, we come to a tall structure with a sign naming it the Fire Tower, and another proclaiming it the grizzly bear exhibit.

I look at Nicolas, and he's wearing that calculating smile I see anytime he's surprised me.

"This is one of the reasons I brought you here today. We need to discuss your strategy if and when you hunt the bear that attacked you. I thought it might be useful to observe their anatomy and movements."

Nicolas. Every time I question his motives, he flips my suspicions upside-down and shows me that he really does care.

I nod, and we climb the tower stairs, exiting onto a wooden boardwalk that weaves through the tops of the trees above the exhibit. The beast in me roars to life, fueled by the pungent bear scent. Grunts and growls accompany the sounds of scuffling somewhere below us and off to one side. My body immediately tenses, and I can feel that Nicolas's reaction matches mine.

As we walk out farther, two young bears come into view about forty feet below. They're mock-fighting and the sight brings me to a halt. This was what Nicolas meant. I watch as the bears circle around one another, then stand on their hind legs and grapple each other like two wrestlers. But unlike wrestlers, they constantly seek a hold on each other's throats with their teeth. I'm struck by the similarity to my own engagement with the bear.

"Well, I certainly attacked him as another bear would have," I quietly observe. I'm feeling a bit unnerved at the scenario below me. "I'm imagining myself as one of those bears—but a lot smaller."

"Yes, they seem to prefer to fight on their hind legs. I suspect it was your speed that allowed you to get inside his defenses so quickly. He was probably not prepared for that."

Nicolas's voice carries a note of strain. This must be difficult for him as well.

"Your only good avenue of attack would be from above. You would have just a few seconds to tear out his throat with your hands." He lifts my arm and examines my sharp nails.

"This would not be the same as taking an elk or deer. His hide and fur are much thicker, and his reactions will be much different." Nicolas stares down at the brawling animals.

Yeah, I already figured that out.

He takes a deep breath, and we walk out a little farther along the boardwalk. The grizzlies break off their sparring and look up at us. All playfulness evaporates as one scents the air, growling, while the other bellows and drops to all fours. Snarls rip from our own throats, one much deeper than the other. I drop into the hunter's stance and watch through a red haze as they thunder across the ground toward us.

Five to six hundred pounds *each* of angry muscle, teeth, and claws should be intimidating. But all I can think of is how much I want to leap down there and which one to take first.

Nicolas lays a hand on my shoulder, bringing me back to rational thought.

"I wouldn't have jumped," I say hoarsely.

"Of course not," he replies. "But we have company, so I suggest we leave now."

I glance over just as two young women push strollers out of the elevator and onto the platform connected with the boardwalk.

Calming myself, I nod to Nicolas, and we head back to the tower platform. The bears rush along the ground below, roaring, their gazes locked on us.

The mothers each let out a shriek of terror, spin the strollers around, and head straight for the elevator. We pause to allow time for the elevator doors to close behind them while the bears continue their rampage at the edge of the fence. The shouts of zoo workers add to the snarls as they rush to the pen, and we quickly take the stairs down to the bottom.

As we walk away from the tower, several employees run past us and up the stairs. I look at Nicolas and burst out laughing. He smiles and we start to walk down the hill.

"Are your visits always so exciting for the zoo?"

"I do limit them so as not to attract attention." He smiles again, his eyes flickering with amusement.

I laugh, stand on my toes, and plant a kiss on his cheek. He's so damned adorable.

He looks down at me warmly, puts his arm around my waist, and pulls me to his side. We walk a few more feet, and then he stops.

"But on a more serious note, I want you to consider something for me." His eyes are now somber.

"Okay."

"We need to remove the bear from your territory to eliminate any future problems, yes?"

"Yeah."

"Then I would ask that we, you, handle this in a different manner." He takes a breath. "Have you ever shot a rifle?"

Handguns—yes. There's one hidden in my car.

"Uh, no."

"Then I will take you to the shooting range and you will learn. I can see no other safe way to rid yourself of this bear." His tone brooks no argument, but I try anyway.

"Nicolas—"

"Ah. Do not argue. This is the way it must be." His eyes grow dark along with his tone as he continues. "I watched how you reacted to these bears. You give me no reason to think it will be any different with your bear."

Damn right it's my bear.

"Nicolas, please hear me out. First of all, the bear that attacked me was a black bear and weighed several hundred pounds less. And he was not nearly so tall when he stood. I would guess he was about five and a half feet."

"Sun—" Nicolas tries to interrupt.

"No, let me finish. Second, I was extremely hungry, to the point that my strength was compromised. I had just brought down the deer and started to feed when the bear charged." I take a breath.

"And third, I was very upset—no, I was furious—with you, for, well . . . what happened at the Council meeting. I was overemotional, overhungry, and not paying attention to my surroundings. Otherwise, I would have sensed the bear's presence before ever taking down the deer. For all I know, he was hunting the herd too, and I took *his* kill, or the one he was planning to make."

Nicolas's expression is tight, and I instantly regret bringing up the meeting. He had already admitted that he felt responsible for my flight from the estate that night and my subsequent brush with death.

"I'm sorry . . . I didn't mean to say that," I whisper.

"No, you are right." He pauses, flexing his jaw. "But none of what you said makes any difference. Our natural prey is humans, and we've evolved with the abilities and skills for hunting *them*. That means, in addition to being attractive to them, we surpass them in the areas of strength, speed, and the senses. We are not designed to fight bears.

"But I have one other point you seem to consistently forget. You are still part human and your Chosen physical abilities and senses are not fully developed. And they will not be until you complete the Change." His voice is grim as he continues.

"So unless you are ready to do that, you need to be aware of your limitations. Shoot the damn bear and get over this vengeful combat you seem to lust for." Now he is angry, the red flashing through his eyes.

I don't know what to say. As usual, he makes perfect sense.

"All right." I sigh.

"All right, what?"

"All right, I'll learn to shoot a rifle. And I'll hunt the bear . . . with a rifle," I say in defeat.

"No, *we* will hunt the bear with a rifle. You are not doing this alone." His tone is adamant.

Yes . . . sir. And the beast in me growls in defiance.

We walk in silence down to the next exhibit area. Nicolas stops and turns to me, placing his hands on my shoulders.

"You must understand how much I care for you. If you could feel what I do when I think of any harm coming to you . . ." He closes his eyes and draws me close, and I cannot help but respond to his embrace with one of my own.

"But now," he says, "I want to show you my favorite exhibit. It is the main reason I visit here, and the other reason we came today."

We turn and walk a little farther. A sign announces we are entering the Asian Highlands, and as we pass it, a large tiger strolls down the vegetated slope in his pen. He stops and looks at us, flattening his ears and baring his teeth in a snarl. The tiger hops down onto a rocky shelf, separated from the front of the cage by a pool of water, and stands, sniffing the air.

I can't believe how big he is—about nine feet from his nose to the tip of his tail and around six hundred to seven hundred pounds. The sign says he is an Amur, or Siberian tiger, the largest cat in the world.

He snarls again, and I marvel at the size of his fangs, at least two to three inches long. I glance at Nicolas and he's smiling.

"Beautiful, is he not? Brings the term 'fang envy' to mind." He chuckles and I look at him surprise.

Oh my God, was that a joke? From Mr. Serious?

The tiger watches as we leave the exhibit but, like the mountain lions, doesn't show the aggression of the wolves and the bears.

We pass a small enclosure with a Pallas cat. He is tawny and long-haired and about the size of a large housecat. He hisses from the shelter he's lying in and retreats deeper inside.

A little farther up the path is one of the most beautiful cats I've ever seen. The sign states it's a female snow leopard. She has a thick, ash-grey coat with dark spots, and pale, yellow-green eyes.

She sees us and snarls softly, then gets up and walks to the front of the enclosure. She stands there staring at Nicolas, who is staring back just as intently. The cat's tail slowly swings from side to side as she gives little hisses, showing her fangs. Nicolas softly hisses back. It seems like they have some kind of connection.

"She is the reason I visit this place. Snow leopards are magnificent hunters, and I have met only one other huntress I admire more." He glances at me, his dark eyes flaring red, and I smile in embarrassment. He looks back at the leopard and continues.

"When I first escaped from my Maker, I headed east into the mountains of what is now Kazakhstan. I ended up in a situation that necessitated I vary my diet from my normal preference. I learned where and how to hunt the various antelope, wild sheep, and goats from watching a young female snow leopard. She grew to tolerate my presence as long as I kept a respectable distance. She was the only companionship I had for many months." His tone carries a hint of longing.

"You almost sound as if you miss those days," I say carefully.

"The solitude and simpler life I do miss sometimes. Living off the land in less than adequate shelter? Surviving off of wild animals? No, those things I do not miss." He tips his head and looks at me.

I try to imagine him living in those rugged mountains, and to my surprise he fits, in spite of his current-day GQ image. I remember when I took him hunting, how he moved so gracefully, like a big, sleek cat.

"So *you* have hunted *animals* in the past? Then the idea that I do is not so, well . . ." I stop, unwilling to verbalize what he might think of my primitive and barbaric hunting practices.

"Sunny, I have never had any judgment regarding your dietary choice. It is *your* choice. I do feel however, that it is a difficult one to manage, and that it is far easier and preferable to pursue the prey we evolved to hunt." He reaches out and caresses my jaw.

I hate it when he talks about people like that.

"But," he continues, "other Chosen are not so . . . understanding, and it would be best to keep your preferences to yourself. That is one of the matters I needed to clarify with Éva. She has sworn to make no mention of your situation."

He looks at me in question and I nod my agreement.

Nicolas turns to the leopard sitting quietly and watching us. She silently hisses as his gaze falls back on her and he hisses softly back. Then, ready to leave, he holds out his arm for me to take, and we walk on.

Apparently having shown me all he felt was important, Nicolas speeds up the pace. We quickly pass the Australian exhibit area and the elephant yard, and head back toward the entrance. On our way, we pass the giraffes again, and I laugh out loud at the image of trying to bring one of those beasts down.

Nicolas looks at me and smiles. "I visualize using a ladder, and asking whether it would mind if I just took a few samples to see if there was any variation in taste as I scale the rungs."

I burst out laughing again, and not just at the image he's painted. That's the second joke in less than an hour, and I'm glad to see his good humor finally resurfacing. He smiles, pulling me close as we exit the zoo.

CHAPTER 40

The Audi hugs the curves as it climbs the winding Pikes Peak road, and I feel like we're flying. We dance through the turns in a smooth, effortless rhythm, one after another. Nicolas's skill, paired with the graceful Audi, is pure artistry in motion. I'm fond of driving and consider myself to be pretty good behind the wheel, but I'm in awe as I watch him.

Nicolas glances over and smiles. "You appear to be enjoying the drive."

"I'm in love with this car, and the way you handle it. I don't even care about the scenery right now." I look at him, my vision pink with emotion.

He glances back at me again with a flash of red in his eyes. I reach out and put my hand on his leg as we continue to wind up the mountain.

"I bought the R8 specifically for this road and come up here anytime I need to unwind, especially in the evenings. I enjoy the cleansing focus of the drive, and the serenity I find on top of the Peak."

I quietly laugh.

"I've made those kinds of drives myself."

Shifting my attention from Nicolas and the road, my eyes settle on the view rotating past the windows as we glide through the S-curves. I look out below us and marvel as I have before on the beauty of the Colorado landscape. I can see for hundreds of miles—forests, meadows, lakes, distant peaks, all in shades of greens, browns, and glittering blues, splashed with snow and set against the backdrop of a clear azure sky. I feel a bit like an eagle as the earth spirals beneath us, the car floating through the turns.

The road abruptly changes from asphalt to a compacted dirt surface. I look at Nicolas, surprised he would take this silver beauty on such a road, but he just slows the pace a bit and smiles.

"It is only a car," he says, his eyes glinting with humor. "Why limit such a fine-handling machine?"

I laugh, fairly sure he's accustomed to ignoring limits of just about any kind.

We stand gazing out at the peaks in the far distance that make up the Continental Divide. Nicolas is unusually quiet as he stares at the western horizon.

"Sunny, I want to talk with you about last night." His tone is unreadable.

The lid on the black box slams open, and I'm instantly assaulted with the images and emotions of the previous evening.

I hesitate for a moment, then ask a little coldly, "What part?"

Nicolas takes a deep breath, then says, "You were . . . very upset with me."

You mean when you fed me that pitiful boy? Or when you left me facing a closed door?

Sudden outrage chokes me, its bitterness sending a wave of nausea through my belly.

"Sometimes we have to make choices when options are limited, and they are not necessarily choices we would make under better circumstances." The muscles in his jaw flex as he stares out into the distance. "You must know by now that I cannot stand to see you suffer in any way. I will do everything in my power to bring that suffering to an end, even though it may cost me your . . . goodwill."

He turns to look at me, his green eyes dark and intense.

Though I feel like I was manipulated last night, the spark of doubt ignites as he speaks, because I have seen him agonize in the face of my pain.

"I am sorry if my actions to end your hunger were not necessarily what you would have wished. But it was the only option I felt open to me, and to you. I tried to present it in the least objectionable manner possible.

"I want you to understand the humans who offer themselves to us do so in full knowledge of what it may mean. They do not object to the price of the pleasure we give them. Skeeter has been a donor for quite some time now. He seems unwilling to live any other life."

His tone is no longer apologetic as he studies me.

"Is he . . . is he all right? His arm, my teeth—" I whisper.

The image of the ragged mess my bite made swims into view again and it sickens me.

"He is fine. I attended the wound and it healed, leaving no scars." He watches me as I consider what he just said.

"It's already healed? Without any scars?" I ask, my anger dissipating against my will.

"My blood is very potent. I used it to seal the wound."

As he says this, a new image bursts into my head, of a different arm, in a different place. My place. The night Nicolas found me in the center of a red flower created by my blood.

I frown. "When you came for me, after the bear . . . I remember an arm, your arm . . ."

"Yes, I needed to preserve what little blood you had left in your body." The shadow of that painful moment darts across his face.

"But didn't I take a lot?" I remember drinking and drinking. "Why didn't it heal *me*?"

"Because I only allowed a small amount. Enough to stop the bleeding and take the edge from your pain and hunger." The serious expression on his face shifts, becoming tinged with worry. "And that brings us to the other matter about which we need to speak.

"When a Chosen takes in the blood of another Chosen, they also take in the emotions, and some of the essence as well. The more blood is taken, the more the taker is tied into the emotional state of the giver. It creates a connection, one that will slowly diminish with time. Unless, of course, the connection is renewed." Nicolas steps closer and gently grasps my shoulders.

"When two Chosen take in the blood of one another, the connection is both ways, and much stronger. Should they prove compatible and choose to make a commitment to each other, they will make a complete blood exchange. We call this bonding. Bonded Chosen each experience emotionally what the other is feeling, and find it extremely difficult to function independent of one another. But they rarely wish to, as they feel . . . complete, like a single entity, when they are together. It is very rewarding, and no Chosen should go through their time here without experiencing this at least once."

His green eyes search mine, and I have no answer, but the blood in my veins is beginning to heat up. I feel like I'm drowning in his dark emerald gaze and am dimly aware of my awe that *he* would have this conversation with *me*.

"Sunny, I have been alone a very long time, and had lately reached the point where retreat from Chosen society seemed more and more attractive. Until the day you came into my city, and I saw you standing across the street.

"And since then, my life has centered on you. I have, minus the actual physical act, bonded to you, and that is something I thought not possible at this stage in my existence.

"I love you beyond all reason, beyond all doubt, and wish to spend the remainder of my time with you, if you are willing."

Oh God.

It feels as if the world has dropped out from beneath my feet. Though I haven't imagined any other future since I met Nicolas, hearing him say it aloud is . . .

"I, uh . . ." I can't seem to choke the words out.

"Sshh." he says, placing his fingertips gently on my lips. "Do not answer yet. I want you to take some time to think about this.

"You need to understand the depth of the bond to one another. The bond becomes the primary reason for existence. Each Chosen becomes the center of focus to the other, to the point that it seems free will is no longer available." He brushes my hair back from my face.

"And this is why you and I must not . . . why I must be very careful. Last night, I almost gave in." He pauses, his jaw clenching, his eyes blazing red.

"Under the circumstances, it would have been quite easy to go too far in our first sharing, which could have destroyed everything. Bonding without your knowledge, your understanding of what it truly means . . . the guilt I would have felt would have overwhelmed us both." He pulls me close, hugging me tightly.

But that wouldn't have mattered to me. This is where I belong. Right here in his arms. And I'm beginning to think I might be ready for forever.

"I want you to have this Choice, along with all the others that will come from sharing a life with me. It is a Choice you do not have to make now, and I would prefer for you to give it very careful consideration." But the longing in his voice tells me he hopes I do this soon.

I nod, unable to speak, and he holds on to me as though he will never let me go.

~

Twilight on top of the world is absolutely amazing. The color changes first in the eastern sky, shifting from pale blue to medium blue, then deeper, until finally a dark indigo blanket is drawn east to west over the earth. As the sun starts to drop behind the Continental Divide in the west, the peaks of the Rockies are silhouetted by the golden glow. And then night literally falls as the sun is rapidly swallowed by the mountains.

I watch the sky, first in one direction, then the other, and am aware of Nicolas watching me.

"My sweet Sunshine. This is one of the things I love about you. Your zest, your enjoyment of new experiences and your surroundings are a gift to me. It freshens the world for me and enables me to look forward to the future once again." His eyes contain a gentle hint of that amusement I love as he begins to speak, then they quickly darken with emotion.

"So did taking my blood last night . . . do you feel what I'm feeling?" I face him, curious.

"Yes, to some degree. I took very little as I only wished to demonstrate that you need not be concerned about the boy feeling any pain. I knew you would not believe me if I tried to explain it." His eyes are soft as he strokes my cheek.

"Was it . . . enjoyable for you?" I recall the ecstasy of his fangs in my throat and the heat in my veins rises again.

"Ah." Nicolas inhales sharply, his eyes flashing. "It was extremely so. As much for me as for you."

My blood bursts into sweet flame as I grasp the implications of this.

He tenses, his eyes now blazing red.

"The concurrent exchange of blood between Chosen is indescribable. I can only say that it will surpass any experience you have ever had."

"Oh." It's all I can manage to say through my own crimson haze.

He grows very still, then takes another breath, and carefully steps away from me to face the distant peaks.

My thoughts fade as the memory of his embrace last night sweeps over me.

Nicolas shoves his hands in his pockets and walks to the far end of the parking lot, his back stiff. I try to calm myself, as my reactions only seem to be making things worse.

Wow. This is interesting. I think I have an idea now how Chosen spend much of their time.

I suddenly giggle with embarrassment and my tension eases. Nicolas turns around in the distance and I can see that he's relaxing as well. And grinning.

He wouldn't need to be tapped into my emotions to guess what I'm laughing about.

CHAPTER 41

Nicolas gets back in the Audi after closing the gate near the bottom of the mountain. Apparently the Pikes Peak Highway closed several hours earlier and, apparently, Nicolas has special arrangements, along with the key to the gates.

The life of the rich and powerful. They follow no rules but their own.

"Nicolas, I have a question about what we discussed earlier."

"I will do my best to answer any questions you have. Please, do not hesitate."

"You gave me your blood when I was hurt. Why don't I feel what you do?" I have been wondering about this since he explained about sharing blood.

"I only gave you enough to ensure your survival until I could get you back to the estate. What you did take in was immediately used to seal your veins and facilitate the healing process." He frowns, as he does anytime we talk about what happened. "The crisis you were in—the pain, the hunger—was extreme enough to overpower any emotional effect such a small amount of my blood would have had."

"Oh." I pause, then take a breath. "Well, then, I have another question."

"Go ahead," he says, his voice straining to sound patient.

"How long do the emotional effects last, when there are any?"

"Ah. Well, it is dependent upon the amount of the blood taken in. Small amounts . . . a day or two maybe. The more taken, the longer the emotional tie." He pauses and shifts the gears.

"Bonding is different, because it is a total exchange. I am not sure how long the effects actually last, because the pair finds frequent renewal of the bond to be very satisfying." He takes a breath as I vividly recall how he made me feel last night, and his hands tighten on the wheel.

I frown. This could get complicated if he reacts to my every random feeling.

"Sunny, my reactions . . . this is not quite typical. You do not have my blood to help moderate your responses, so right now I am a little at your mercy." His mouth quirks as he glances at me.

I get to control Nicolas for a change? Seriously?

"For how long? Several days? This could be quite fun." I laugh at the chagrin on his face.

"Or it could be dangerous if you can't control your impulses. I may find it difficult to resist ravishing you if that is all you think about." Now he's smiling, a devilish smile.

"Me? You're one to talk." I shake my head, remembering the library, the garden, and the feelings that blossom anytime he holds me.

"Ahh . . . Will you please stop?" He looks at me, eyes blazing red.

I snicker and try to think of something else.

"Oh, I suppose. I'd hate for you to crush the steering wheel of this fine car." I laugh, reach out, and muss up his hair.

He laughs as well, catching my palm and kissing it.

God, how I love him.

As we head back to the Springs, Nicolas says, "Do you mind if we stop by the club? I have some business that requires my attention. We do not need to stay long."

A tingle races through my blood at the thought of the club and what, or who, is there.

I don't like to think about what that means.

"I . . . uh, yeah. Okay." The lid on the black box cracks open.

I watch the lights flash by the windows as we drive through the city. They remind me of the thoughts flashing through my mind, thoughts of what might lie ahead intertwined with the guilt-ridden memories of last night.

We pull into the parking lot at the side of the club and park. Nicolas gets out and opens my door, and I feel uneasy as we walk to the side door of the building. He stops and takes me by the shoulders.

"Please, do not worry so. I have several matters that need to be taken care of, and then we will leave immediately thereafter, if that is what you wish. All right?" He brushes the hair back from my face and looks at me expectantly.

"All right." But I don't feel reassured, and he frowns as he reaches out to unlock the door.

I wait in the short hallway as Nicolas keys in the codes for both boxes and my uneasiness grows. He opens the door to the office and holds it while I walk through and into the room.

The room where I fed from a human.

I freeze as the panic takes hold, but Nicolas comes up from behind, wraps his arms around me, and whispers in my ear.

"Sshh, calm down, my love. Everything is going to be fine."

But why do I feel like it won't, like *I* won't?

Nicolas gently turns me around and looks at me with dark emerald eyes. "There is nothing to be worried about. Wait here while I meet with my club manager. I will return as soon as I can." He touches my cheek and I reluctantly nod.

With a kiss on the top of my head, he walks out the door at the other end of the room.

I sit down on the couch, but almost immediately get back up and start pacing. The anxiety twisting in my gut has awakened the hunger, which alarms me even further.

Déjà vu. I swear if Nicolas comes back in here with another *donor*, I will run all the way back to my mountain.

My throat tight with fear, I continue to pace and, after about a half hour, finally hear him touch the doorknob. I stop, tense and poised for flight, but when he opens the door, he's alone.

The tension drains out of my body and I breathe a sigh of relief.

Nicolas, on the other hand, hurries into the room, his face strained. But when he sees me, he slows his approach and stops, and takes a deep breath. I marvel again over how much he seems to react to my emotions.

His pale green eyes search mine, and they contain a sadness that I vaguely remember from last night.

"You were ready to run. I could feel it, and I feared I would not get back here soon enough." He grabs me in his arms and holds me tight, as though he would physically keep me from running.

A wave of emotion washes over me, a jumble of love, concern, and guilt. Especially guilt, as I remember that the last time I ran from him, it ended up costing both of us in ways I could never have anticipated. And ultimately was responsible for me being in this room, terrified of a choice I don't want to make, ready to run again.

What a screwed up mess.

I take a breath and gently push back out of his arms.

"I'm here, I'm okay. And I'm sorry that I caused you to worry." I look up at him and touch his jaw, and he kisses my palm.

"No, it is I who has caused you to worry. I would like to remedy that if you would allow me.

"I would like to take you on a tour of the club so you can see that it is not this . . . den of murder and horror that you seem to imagine. Does this sound acceptable to you?" His eyes search mine and I finally nod my agreement.

"Good." He steps back and holds out his hand, and I place mine in his. I can't help but compare my hand to my trust—and I can only hope it's not misplaced.

Nicolas opens the door that he came through moments earlier and holds it for me. I hesitate, then sigh as I step through, because I realize I will do anything to be on the same side of the door as he is.

The hallway stretches in both directions. A faint thudding is coming from the left, and it's in that direction we head. As we get closer, I recognize the beat of dance music.

I'm surprised I couldn't hear it from the office, but I suspect everything in this building is well insulated, because Nicolas doesn't do anything halfway. This proves to be true as he opens the heavy door at the end of the hall, and sound hits me like the blast wave from an explosion.

He grimaces and follows me as I walk through the door. We veer left and go down a narrow aisle, past stacks of boxes and cases of beer. Turning right, we go through a heavy black curtain. Standing on the other side is a very large man dressed in a well-tailored black suit. He steps aside as we pass, nodding to Nicolas, then resumes his position in front of the curtain.

The music is nearly deafening as we make our way past the door of a walk-in cooler and then stop at the end of the bar. Looking out over the dance floor, the scene is a typical techno club, its darkness broken by the lights pulsing to the rhythm of the music

Even though it's a Thursday night, the dance floor is packed with bodies convulsing in every direction in response to the onslaught of electronic sound. I start to feel edgy, and the hunter in me goes on alert, making me tense even more. This is unsettling. I don't like this new reaction my body keeps having to people.

I stand and watch the dancing while Nicolas speaks with the bartender, and then realize not all of the dancers are human. I detect auras of Chosen energy scattered throughout the crowd, and I quickly pick them out. Their beauty, graceful movement, and air of superiority are alluring, and the people gravitate around them, planets to their brightly burning suns.

There are three that I can spot, two males and a female, and none of them have a shortage of admirers of either gender. Young men and women dance in small groups around each one, yet maintain a respectful distance so that The Chosen dance as though in a bubble on a sea of bobbing humanity.

I glance at Nicolas to find him watching me, perhaps to gauge my reaction to The Chosen in the midst of the human crowd. I raise my eyebrows, and he tips his head, then indicates that we should leave back through the way we came.

The mountain-sized human guard pulls aside the curtain to allow us through. We wind our way back to the heavy door, and I wait while Nicolas enters the access code. The noise fades as he closes the door behind us, and I breathe a sigh of relief as we start back down the hallway.

Nicolas continues past the office, stops at a door just beyond it, and quickly presses the buttons on yet another one of the multiple keypads that seem to guard every doorway.

In spite of his aversion to locked doors, they are everywhere in this place. They appear situated to keep the uninvited out, but I wonder if they also keep them in.

The room we enter is a quiet lounge with subdued lighting and soft classical music playing in the background. There is a small, unattended bar, though it appears well stocked, along the same wall as the door we came in. I notice another door at the far end of the room. Along the walls are black-curtained booths, and in the middle are several small round tables with chairs to seat four.

A couple of the booths on the far wall are occupied, their drawn curtains muffling the low voices within. I sense the presence of several Chosen, as well as human men and women.

"Shall we sit?" Nicolas asks, stopping at a booth next to us. I slide in and around to the back while he heads over to the bar. He returns a moment later with two glasses of what appears to be wine.

He puts them on the table, sits down, and slides around to sit next to me. He picks up one of the glasses and sets it in front of me, and smiles at my wide-eyed expression.

"Do not worry, yours is not bloodwine." His eyes glint with amusement. "Although, if it was, I suspect we could have a very interesting evening."

"Maybe." But I'm too distracted by my returning anxiety to joke around.

Nicolas purses his lips, his expression becoming serious. I wonder if he can feel my hunger.

I take a sip of the wine, but it tastes odd, too thin, the wrong kind of sweetness. My tension raises a notch as I realize there is only one thing that will taste right at this point.

Taking a deep breath, I brace myself for an argument. But I can't look at him as I begin to speak and instead stare down at the table, my fingers curled tightly around the wineglass.

"Nicolas, can you . . . can you please take me home? To *my* home? I need—I would like to—go hunting. And I don't really want to be here. I don't belong here." My voice fades to a whisper and I finally look up at him.

He's frowning at me and something dark passes behind his pale eyes.

And then the door opens, and a scent that I am intimately familiar with tumbles in. I look at Nicolas in alarm as I realize who it is. Nicolas's expression shifts to neutral, and the thought hits me like a hammer that I have been set up . . . again.

Skeeter walks into the middle of the room with a young woman, also human. As the hunger fully ignites, I remember what Nicolas said about blood one has had before.

I clench my jaw, and as the beast rages, I say in anguish, "Nicolas, how could you—"

But before I can finish, a male Chosen follows through the door that hadn't quite closed behind the humans. He's tall, well built, and with his blond hair waving to the tops of his broad shoulders, devastatingly handsome. He walks up between the couple and places an arm around each waist, then moves them toward one of the curtained cubicles at the back of the room. Skeeter glances at Nicolas, and guilt paints the boy's face before he looks away.

The Chosen stops and opens the curtains, revealing a private sitting area with a large semi-circular sofa and a low table. As the couple sits down, he looks at Nicolas and nods. His intense blue eyes spark as he fastens them on me, then with a smile he closes the heavy draperies.

Oh. I thought the boy was here for me, to tempt me. I turn back to Nicolas to find him staring at me through a mask of pain and disbelief.

"Do you really think so little of me? Do you really feel I would deliberately—?" He doesn't finish, clamping his jaw shut with an audible snap.

"No, I don't know. I'm sorry. I just thought when he walked in . . ." I can't finish either, ashamed that I would be so suspicious of the one I love.

"I checked the club before I came back to the office to ensure he was not here, as I knew the strain it would cause you." His eyes, dark and angry, bore into mine as he continues.

"He should not even be here tonight. We have rules as to the frequency of their visits for their own safety. If they donate too often, they cannot recover properly and will grow weak and susceptible to illness. And we do not accept them here if they are ill. Again, for their benefit.

"You seem to think I am some kind of—" He stops. "Ah. Never mind. We will discuss this later, in private," he says coldly.

I feel like a paranoid idiot.

"I'm sorry," I whisper, staring down at the table. I can't bear the look on his face.

He is silent a moment, then says, "Wait here." He gets up and goes out the door.

Sitting with my eyes closed, I try to contain my whirling emotions. I then become aware that the voices coming from the blond Chosen's booth have stopped. What I hear now are moans of pleasure, and my embarrassment is quickly overshadowed by my own hunger and need.

Great. As irritation flashes through me, I shift in my seat and notice Nicolas's untouched glass of bloodwine on the table.

Picking it up, I smell it. The soft aroma of the blood, enhanced by Nicolas's special spices, floats up and caresses my nose.

Oh, what the hell.

I take a drink, savoring the flavor as it blooms in my mouth. I can feel the liquid trace its way into my system, exactly the way fresh blood does when taken directly from a vein.

Now I understand why this would be a preferred drink among The Chosen. Somehow I missed this benefit the first time I tried it.

I take a second drink and hold it before swallowing. It soothes every surface it touches as it makes its way through my veins and slowly begins to calm the hunger.

It doesn't seem to be affecting me the way it did last time, so I continue to take small swallows. The glass is nearly empty when the door opens. I look up as Nicolas walks in accompanied by a pretty young brunette. A human.

He walks to the table and, with a raised eyebrow, notes the glass in my hand. I take a breath and look up at him, and realize about the same time he does that I am no longer upset.

He visibly relaxes, then turns and gestures to the young woman behind him.

"Sunny, I would like you to meet Charlene. Charlene, this is Sunny." His voice is now warm and, to my relief, carries no trace of his earlier anger.

"Hello," she and I say at nearly the same time. Charlene nervously giggles, and I force a smile as I slap down the beast that has taken sharp notice of the girl.

"Charlene, please sit down," Nicolas says. As she settles into the booth on one side of me, he takes the seat on the other. "Charlene has volunteered to speak with you, hopefully to ease your concerns about the role the humans have in our society. I trust you will give careful consideration to what she says."

Scooting a little closer to Nicolas, I try to put some distance between me and this human. Her dark brown eyes shine as she explains how much she loves to come here and spend time with The Chosen. My attention fixes on her arms as she enthusiastically waves them about. They bear some fang scars, but not as many as Skeeter's.

"So, anyhow, Nicolas just wanted me to tell you that, you know, our experiences here are something we look forward to. In fact, I hate the nights when I am not allowed to come in because I'm supposed to be 'resting.'" She gazes adoringly at Nicolas. "I know, I know, the rules are for our own good."

I feel a sharp flash of jealousy at the way she looks at him, and glance up to see him notice it. Amusement crosses his face and my breath catches, as his expression is my favorite, and he smiles at me knowingly.

"So, you know, it's been, let's see, about nine or ten nights since I was here. So I'm okay now. Do you want a taste?"

Her words jar me back to the conversation, and as I look back at her, I see the arm she's holding out to me.

Her arm.

My eyes lock onto the bluish veins beneath her skin. The beast in me suddenly crouches, preparing to spring, and I jerk my gaze away as Nicolas wraps his arm around my shoulders.

"I'm sorry?" I say to the table while I scramble to regain control.

"I said would you like to try me? It's been long enough, and I really, well, I really need . . ." Her voice tapers off, and I glance up to see tears begin to pool in her eyes.

Lucky her. She can cry for real.

"Doesn't this hurt? Aren't you afraid?" I ask in a panic, trying to buy time. But the beast and the hunger are both raging, and I realize that it's me who is afraid.

"No. Not at all. Just the opposite. That's what I've been trying to tell you. We *like* it, I mean, really *like* it. It's kinda like doing drugs, only I'm not putting harmful stuff into my body." She stares at me hopefully.

No, you are just having the life drained out of it, drop by drop.

Shocked, I turn to look at Nicolas and his carefully composed expression, and she says, "Please? Nicolas said he won't, and, well, a couple of the others here *do* scare me. They're not gentle like he is."

I look back at her, my fear shifting to anger. The beast in me roars, my vision reddens, and I can barely speak without growling.

"And what makes you think *I* will be gentle?"

Her eyes grow wide and she swallows before answering.

"Because . . . you're *with* him, you know? Like a couple. I've never seen Nicolas with anyone else except people like me, but that's not the same. I know he wouldn't be *with* someone who was mean or anything." Her voice is sincere and hopeful, and my resolve begins to crumple.

She holds out her arm again, and I yank my gaze from it to look at Nicolas. His expression is soft, with that hint of sadness, and I realize that I am going to do this. And that this time it is entirely my choice.

"Nicolas, my . . . teeth." I have no wish to mangle this girl's arm, but the beast is impatient and my control is continuing to slip.

Nicolas stands, his eyes growing dark and unreadable. He walks over to the bar, grabs a small bottle of liqueur and a burgundy glass from the back shelf, and returns to the table.

"Come." We both get up and follow him to the door at the rear of the room. My body is vibrating as I try to restrain it, while Charlene is grinning in anticipation. He opens the door and waits as we pass through into a hallway that has several more doors lining it.

Nicolas punches in a code at one of the doors, and we enter a room that looks like a hotel suite but with no windows. He motions for the girl to sit on the bed and sets the liqueur and glass on the nightstand.

"Drink up," he tells her, and she nods and reaches for the bottle.

Nicolas turns to me, takes my arm, and leads me back out into the hallway, closing the door behind us.

"Are you sure you want to do this? It is not too late to change your mind." He looks at me with concern, as I'm sure he is aware of what this may cost me.

But it is too late. And I'm tired of fighting it, of fighting his way of life, of fighting him.

I nod, and the beast roars in elation, while the human part of me sobs and crawls into the black box.

"As long as no one dies," I whisper. "Please promise me that you won't let me kill her."

He takes me in his arms and holds me. But I'm sure he can feel my impatience and overwhelming need, and with a kiss to my forehead, he releases me and opens the door. He looks back at me, giving me one more chance, and I reach out to take his hand, and we walk through the door together.

április 19., csütörtök

I felt alive today for the first time in many days. She is finally laughing again, and my blood races at each small sound she makes, each smile she graces me with.

Her blood, deep within me, makes my soul sing, and I embrace every flash of anger, every rush of desire that she feels. But more importantly, now I know. Now I know that she loves me beyond my expectations, beyond any hope I could have had.

I only wish that I deserved it.

The Choice she made tonight—was not really hers.

FRIDAY

CHAPTER 42

I wake a bit earlier than usual and take a long stretch, feeling every muscle spring alive, and get out of bed. Just as I've done for the last four mornings, I go over to the mirror to inspect my scars. But they are unchanged from yesterday, and so it looks like I will wear them for the rest of my . . . life, or whatever it is.

My life. I can't believe how much and how fast it has changed. Last night was the final step to yet another new way of existence. I think about Charlene and the incredible pleasure we both experienced as I took her blood.

Nicolas was very supportive as he showed me how to use my nails to create small wounds so that I did not cause her unnecessary pain or damage. And Charlene was right, he was very gentle as well. Keeping a hand on her for reassurance as I took her arm, Nicolas encouraged me to go easy and not give in to the frenzy. He talked soothingly and stroked my hair, as though he was calming a frightened horse or a wild beast. His calming influence somehow kept me from losing my head to the rapture of feeding, and when he felt it was time, he was able to stop me without resorting to force.

I recall basking in the glow of her blood as I watched Nicolas use his own to seal her wounds. Charlene was in a similar state of bliss, all but oblivious to his ministrations, but she did manage to squeak out a thank you. The wounds healed completely, leaving no scars, and I was puzzled over the scars she did have, but decided to leave the question for another time.

I shake my head to clear it of last night's memories and walk over to the closet to pick out something to wear.

As I open my door, the soft sounds of a violin float through the air. I head down the stairs to the music room and stand outside for a moment, listening to the caress of the bow on the strings. Smiling, I think of myself as the violin, and Nicolas as the bow, and how well he plays.

The music stops and Nicolas says, "Please, come in, Sunny."

I open the door, grinning, and see him standing there, a wry smile on his face, eyes faintly tinged with red.

"Don't tell me you can still feel what I feel," I say in disbelief.

"As a matter of fact, yes. I can. To a small degree. Unfortunately, that is all it takes to get my own thoughts heading . . . in certain directions." He smiles.

Oh.

"So last night was . . ." I try not to snicker, but I'm not successful.

"Very enjoyable, yes. It is interesting living vicariously through your emotions. It is an unanticipated experience that I am finding quite entertaining." He smiles, slightly wicked this time.

"Well, thanks, I'm glad I keep you entertained. Speaking of, what was that beautiful piece I heard you playing?"

"Just a little composition on which I am working. I am pleased you like it." He smiles, walks over to the Strad's cabinet, and puts the violin and the bow away.

"Oh, you don't need to stop. I didn't mean to interrupt."

"I had completed that particular movement. Your interruption is quite welcome, in fact. I have been waiting for you to arise." He closes the cabinet and walks back over to me.

He gently takes my shoulders, his green eyes warm, and says, "I trust you slept well?"

"Yes, I slept very well, as I have every morning since I've been here. I seem to need much less sleep than at home. Must be that wonderful bed. I'll need to see about getting one."

Nicolas nods and smiles, one of those secretive smiles that drives me crazy.

"What?" I look at him, trying to figure out what he is thinking.

"You are so . . . human sometimes. I find it most endearing." He smiles and brushes my hair back from my face.

I step back and blink.

"Human? What part?" Surely not the part that feasts on blood.

"Ah. I suppose I could best explain it as your freshness and joie de vivre." His knowing smile has a slight air of satisfaction, and now I'm feeling pretty clueless.

"O . . . kay." Guess he can't help being Mr. Mystery.

Strolling to the door, he says, "I need to go to Denver this afternoon to attend to some business. Would you like to come?"

"Yeah, that would be nice. Though I was kind of hoping we could go to my place so that I could get my car. I have a few errands myself that I need to take care of." I notice a shift in his expression. "But we don't have to do it today. Tomorrow would be fine."

"May I ask why you feel it necessary to pick up your car? I have a whole garage full available. You are welcome to use any of them for your errands. Take the Ferrari. Or the Audi. Just let Alfonso know which one, and he will get it out for you." He smiles, and whatever had bothered him the moment before seems to be gone.

I guess I could drive one of his cars. Though I do wish I had brought the BMW back with me the other day. But I haven't really had any time to think about it, let alone anything else from my life before. Before Nicolas. Before the bear.

"We will likely not return until tomorrow, so you may want to pack a few things. I have another club there that also requires my attention, which will give you the opportunity to meet some of the Denver Chosen."

I take a deep breath. Another club. And if Chosen are there, so will be their donors.

I force a smile.

"All right."

"This will be a little different than your formal introduction to the Council members. These Chosen, as well as The Chosen here in the Springs, are at a . . . lower social rank. They will regard you as they do me, so please do not be overly concerned about meeting them." He watches as I nod.

"Now I need to gather a few items myself and will meet you in the library when you are ready."

I nod again, mulling over what he just said about The Chosen, and start to walk past him.

Nicolas reaches out and grabs my arm, and pulls me to him. He kisses me, softly, then with more urgency. I respond, pressing closer to him. His lips drift along my jaw, kissing a path to my temple, then into my hair. He softly inhales, breathing in my scent, and electricity runs up and down my body. With a final kiss on my forehead, he steps back, his crimson eyes full of emotion.

I take a breath and try to collect myself, and watch through a pink haze as he does the same.

"So, just for the record, as far as I know, I did nothing to instigate that," I say, half-smiling.

Nicolas purses his lips, then smiles in defeat.

He caresses my jaw and I kiss his palm as it leaves my face.

"I will meet you in the library shortly," he says as we walk out. I nod in response and hop back up the stairs.

~

The elevator across the aisle of the parking structure whirs and clanks to a halt. The doors open, revealing Nicolas, and I watch in admiration as he strides toward the car, briefcase in hand. He smiles as he approaches, looking every inch the GQ man in his black three-piece Armani and tieless burgundy dress shirt.

"How did it go?" I ask as he gets into the car.

"It was a typical board meeting, filled with debate about which companies to buy and which to sell and who to fire. Like all meetings, it took more time than necessary. But I find the board members tend to be more cooperative if allowed to have their say before voting. It makes them much more supportive of my decisions."

His decisions. I shake my head.

The sleek red Ferrari roars to life and he pulls out of the parking space.

"And you? Did you enjoy your book?"

"It was nice to have some time to read." I'd elected to read in the car rather than wait in his office in the prestigious Denver high-rise. Too many people between here and there, and I just don't trust myself around them right now. He hadn't pressed it.

As we head toward the outskirts of Denver, I recall something I meant to ask him earlier.

"Nicolas? Where's Éva? I haven't seen her in the last couple of days."

"She returned to New York yesterday. She had been gone longer than planned and had urgent business she needed to attend to. She wished to say goodbye, but her plane left early in the morning while you were asleep."

"And the other Elders? When did they leave?"

"They returned to their respective cities the next morning after the Council meeting."

"So they didn't know about my . . . accident?"

"No. They stay at the hotel when they visit and had already left for their homes when I finally reached you on the phone."

Good. Hopefully they weren't aware of the fight we had.

"Like the Elders, The Chosen you meet tonight will be curious, as they will be able to instantly detect that you are not of their lineage. Please keep in mind that your energy is quite unusual. It is similar to an Elder in its intensity, but not the same. They will be fairly intimidated and likely not to speak to you, in spite of their curiosity." He glances at me as he guides the Ferrari through the traffic, then continues.

"But, if any do, it would be best to be vague as to your origins, and mentioning the West Coast will be sufficient." He glances at me again, apparently trying to gauge my reaction to the idea of interacting with the others.

"Éva had cautioned me to be very careful of what I say with the Council members. I just assumed it wouldn't be any different with other Chosen," I reassure him.

"Good. I think you will do just fine." He downshifts as he gets off the freeway into an industrial area. This club must be in a warehouse, too.

"Nicolas, I do have a question about the lineages. If I understand correctly from my reading, anyone who has been changed by the same Maker is of their lineage, right?"

"That is correct."

"So will The Chosen that I meet tonight all be from one lineage, or from several, or . . . ?"

Nicolas chuckles.

"They are all from one lineage. Mine. As is every Chosen you have met so far."

Every one of them?

"So, are there any other lineages in the area?"

"No, none in this part of the world. The others are mainly in Europe and Asia."

I think about the various cities and countries his Elders are from.

"Are you saying that *all* of The Chosen in North and South America are of your lineage?"

"Yes."

Wow. That is nearly . . . half the planet.

"Sunny, when I came to this country, I brought a handful of my Elders with me from Europe. I placed them in strategic cities in this hemisphere with the understanding that I would not allow any competing lineages. They swore their allegiance to me and regularly renew their vows. They *must* get my approval, and my participation, in order to bring any prospective Chosen into our lineage."

My God. His need to control everything is stronger than I realized. I frown, suddenly feeling unsettled as I once again realize that he is someone who seems to always get exactly what he wants.

Nicolas glances at me and scowls.

Damn, he reads me just like a book.

"You need to understand that the situation in Europe became very chaotic and dangerous at one point. When Chosen are at war, it tends to engulf the human community as well. I came here with the intention of maintaining a peaceful existence and preventing a recurrence of the mayhem that had run rampant in other parts of the world."

Oh.

I feel embarrassed as I realize—again—that I may have misread Nicolas's motives.

He pulls the car over to the side of the road and turns his dark gaze on me.

"Are you finished judging me yet? Am I still found wanting?" His tone is deathly quiet, but it doesn't hide the anger lying underneath.

"I, uh, I'm sorry," I whisper, feeling mortified.

He shakes his head and pulls the car back out into traffic. We drive the rest of the way to the club in silence.

CHAPTER 43

Nicolas is strangely distant as I walk beside him to the front of the club, which appears from the outside to be nothing more than another warehouse. As we pass a line of people waiting to get in, they react with excited gasps and whispers. He nods to the two large bouncers at the entrance and one of them opens the door to let us in. Nicolas uncharacteristically goes through first, leaving me no choice but to follow.

We are immediately swept up in the sound and flashing lights of electronica music. I glance at Nicolas, expecting to see the disapproving expression I'd seen at the club in the Springs. But what I see instead brings me to a dead stop—and all I can do is watch.

What I see is Nicolas on the hunt.

He slowly walks through the dancers, stopping here and there, his dark eyes shining with intensity. His expression is openly predatory and yet the women dancers are drawn to him like moths to a flame. Several rub up against him as they dance and he softly snarls, but he doesn't push them away. He continues to part the sea of dancers as he saunters through. They trail in his wake as though swept up in a net.

Once again he reminds me of a cheetah as it walks along the edges of a herd, sizing up the most likely target. He literally radiates danger, but the humans are falling all over themselves to get next to him.

A buzz ripples throughout the club as everyone becomes aware of his presence, and the highly charged atmosphere feels like it will explode.

Electricity races through me and the hunter springs to full alert. I fight to retain control as I watch Nicolas cross the room.

Other Chosen appear in the crowd that Nicolas left behind. The dancers quickly gravitate to them, seeking whatever they had hoped to get from the tall dark one who has just passed through their midst.

I'm suddenly surrounded by humans of both genders, their expressions and movements promising me unspoken delights, and the beast in me roars to life. I clench my jaw and try to walk in the direction Nicolas has gone.

A light-haired Chosen is instantly next to me, and he extends his elbow as he looks at me in apparent fascination. I accept and take it, grateful for the distraction from the willing bodies full of blood, and we work our way through the crowd.

At the back of the room, we pass between two large bouncers, through a black curtain, and into a darkened lounge populated with couches and low tables.

I breathe a sigh of relief as we stop and free myself from the Chosen's arm. I look at him in gratitude and am startled by the intensity of his grey-green eyes.

"Thank you," I say as my tension eases and control slowly returns.

"You are quite welcome. Mr. Ambrus said he'll be here momentarily." A nervous smile plays at his lips, then with a glance around, he continues.

"Your first time here at Club Vér?"

I thought that would've been obvious.

"Yes," I answer in a neutral tone.

"It can be pretty overwhelming the first few times. The other clubs I've been to require a lot more discretion. Since this is invitation only, all of the attendees have been pre-screened." He warms to his perceived role as guide and continues to talk.

"They come from all over the country. The selection of donors here is one of the best in the U.S. Even *we* have to apply in advance to get in, and most usually wait months to be accepted. But it's so worth it. I usually—"

"Thank you, Will. You may go now," Nicolas says as he enters through a door at the far end of the lounge.

"Thank you, sir." Will bows to Nicolas. "Miss." He nods to me as he leaves through the black curtain.

I watch Nicolas as he approaches. His pale green eyes tell me what he's been doing since I saw him disappear into the crowd, and I feel the hunger stir again at the thought.

"Why did you just leave me—" I demand.

"Not here. Come." His clipped tone irritates me even further.

But instead of arguing, I nod and follow him back the way he'd just come and into a long hallway. Just a short distance down the hall, we enter a stairwell that leads to a second level and ends at a door. I follow him upward and wait silently on the landing while he just as silently keys in the access code.

This room is much larger than his office at the other club and much more luxurious. The opposite wall is darkened glass from one end to the other and overlooks the main dance floor, its pulsing lights illuminating the writhing bodies below. Several elegant sofas line the window, bracketed by small round tables.

I continue to the center of the room, arms folded, then turn around to face him and wait for his explanation.

Nicolas quietly closes the door and pauses with his back to me, his hand resting on the wall. He then slowly turns and looks at me with a red-laced intensity that sends a chill down my spine. He approaches, his piercing gaze locked onto me. Then, too fast for me to even register, he picks me up and cradles my body against his chest, his crimson eyes never leaving mine.

He strides across the room to a door at the far end that's slightly ajar and shoves it open as we pass through. The room is lavishly decorated in deep reds and black, but all I really notice is the large circular bed in the middle. He reaches back with his foot and kicks the door shut.

Éva, despite all of her centuries, had no idea what she was talking about.

I arch my back and stretch my arms and legs, enjoying the feel of the silk sheets on my naked skin. Nicolas left a few minutes ago and I think back over the last several hours. He's had five hundred years to hone his skills in bed, and I'm pretty sure they're unmatchable.

Human-type lovemaking was something that Éva said The Chosen don't care to do. But obviously Nicolas doesn't seem to mind, in spite of the fact that I don't think it was as fulfilling for him as it was for me. I guess maybe he wanted to see just how much of me was still human. Well, we both found out that some parts very much are.

But his Chosen passion for me was kept under restraint—a restraint that left him nearly vibrating as he fought to keep his teeth from my throat, and a restraint that was sorely tested by my eagerness to feel those fangs again. When I protested, he murmured something about the preciousness of human lovemaking and how he wanted me to enjoy it one last time before I discovered the raptures of Chosen love.

And then he very quickly made me forget why I protested at all.

The door to the office opens. His soft footfalls are accompanied by human ones, two sets of them.

I sit up as Nicolas walks into the bedroom alone, closing the door behind him. He crosses the room and extends his hand. I take it and stand, and he pulls me to him and envelops me in his arms. I can feel his breath on my neck as his lips part, and he gently draws his fangs across my skin. My blood reignites and I press my throat against those daggers. He inhales sharply, then slowly pulls back until he is holding me by the shoulders.

"Get dressed," he says huskily.

I'll jump off a cliff if you ask me like that.

Picking up my clothes that he had thoughtfully gathered and placed on a chair, I'm conscious of him watching me dress. It's nearly as exciting as when he watched me undress.

I finish buttoning my blouse, and Nicolas takes my hand and raises it to his lips, then kisses the inside of my wrist. He pushes up my sleeve, opens his mouth, and traces the veins of my arm with his fangs. Thin lines of blood appear, and he gently follows the red path with his tongue. I take a sharp breath and can't let it out. He smiles wickedly as he rolls my sleeve back down and lowers my arm.

Keeping hold of my hand, he leads me to the door and opens it. Two people—both human—are standing in the outer room. The young man and woman are both quite attractive and wearing the latest in club fashions. They try to act nonchalant as they sip from burgundy wineglasses, but their hammering hearts give away their anticipation.

I look questioningly at Nicolas, but he all he answers me with is a seductive smile, his emerald eyes glittering as they change color. He leads me to one of the sofas and nods to indicate that I should sit down. As I do so, he signals the man over with a flick of his fingers and points to the spot next to me.

The beast, already quite aroused, leaps within me, and I can barely restrain myself as the man quickly finishes his drink. He sets his glass on the table as he walks over and takes off his jacket. Eyes bright, he rolls up his sleeve and sits down close to me. I grit my teeth, struggling to maintain some sort of composure.

Nicolas leads the woman over, takes her empty glass, and has her sit next to the man. Her eyes are shining, almost feverish, and her breathing is fast and shallow. Nicolas sits down on the other side of her, facing me. She turns to him and raises her arm, and he gently grabs hold. With his crimson eyes locked onto mine, he slowly sinks his fangs into the inside of her upper arm.

She gasps, and the man beside me begins to breathe faster as he watches them. He then faces me and, quivering with excitement, raises his arm. I can barely keep control while I carefully slice it just above the elbow with my nail, then raise it to my lips. I take hold and look up to see Nicolas still watching me, waiting for me, and as I draw in my first mouthful, so does he.

The savory nectar explodes in my mouth, and closing my eyes, I feel its heat bathe my throat as I swallow. The man groans in delight, and I open my eyes as I pull again. I realize that Nicolas has waited, watching, and is timing his pulls with mine, and I can hear her soft moans in response. The liquid ecstasy floods my system, working its way into my veins and bathing them with a sweet fire that flames anew with each mouthful. I watch Nicolas, his eyes crimson with pleasure as they watch me.

Again I draw, harder, and the man moans as he climaxes. His reaction surprises me, but then I'm overcome by a wave of intoxication that breaks over me as I swallow his precious lifeblood. I close my eyes and draw again, and again, and slowly begin to lose myself to the rapture of the blood.

Something is pressing hard against the side of my mouth and my eyes snap open. Nicolas is bending over me, increasing the pressure of his hand, and comprehension finally dawns. I reluctantly let go and the man slumps against the back of the couch.

I look at him in alarm, but Nicolas shakes his head and pulls me to my feet. He kisses me, long and deep, and I can taste her blood in his mouth. He moves from my mouth to my jaw, and then with no warning, sinks his fangs into my throat. As before, I nearly collapse in ecstasy, and each mouthful he takes sends me further into euphoric oblivion.

I am dimly aware of him withdrawing, then picking me up and carrying me into the bedroom. He gently lays me on the bed, and with a last kiss, leaves the room and closes the door.

I drift off into a crimson world and fade into unconsciousness.

április 20., péntek

Tonight she finally met the Bastard. That unprincipled prick wasted no time in seducing her fully to our way of life. I do not think she realized who she was dealing with, and I cringe at how thoroughly he took advantage of her trusting nature.

Even after all these centuries, he can still find a way to slip past my guard and take over.

I can only be grateful that he stopped her from killing the human at the last moment.

SATURDAY

CHAPTER 44

I wake and find myself still in my clothes. Confused, I start to sit up, and then the memories come flooding back. I sink back down with a gasp and relax into the soft haze of blood that still caresses my system. After a moment I force myself to sit up again, and as I move, my head begins to clear a little. The haziness fades and is replaced by an unbelievable energy. I stand and stretch, and every fiber in my body comes instantly alive.

What an amazing feeling—to go from sweet lassitude to high octane in a matter of seconds.

I survey the room, really seeing it for the first time. It's a classic playboy den, though decorated very tastefully, and as I look around, I realize it's meant for only one thing. Seduction.

Smiling wryly, I recall what Nicolas said about Chosen hunting, and how the chase for them is the seduction and willing surrender.

And then every hair on my body stands on end.

Because that is exactly what Nicolas has been doing to me.

Oh . . . my . . . God.

Unnerved, I hug myself as doubts begin to swirl through my head. Panic floods through me and the memories of the last month begin to take on a different hue.

The door opens and Nicolas comes in, his face taut, tension rolling from him in waves.

"We need to go. Now. Something has come up, and I must get back to the Springs immediately. Are you ready?"

Struck mute by my revelations, I can only nod in agreement.

The Ferrari feels practically airborne as we speed south. I fight to quell the fears that keep surfacing, both the old ones and the new. I don't know if I killed the young man from last night, and if so, that would mean Nicolas let me do it intentionally. He had me so aroused beforehand that I was no longer able to think, and all he had to do was point me in the direction he wanted and let go. I shudder at how easily I may have been manipulated—and desperately hope that is not the case.

The image of the limp body sagging against the back of the couch surfaces, and I take it, stuff it into the black box, and slam the lid. My collection of memories that I don't want to remember is steadily growing. I grimace and look out the window.

The sun is just above the mountains to the west, and I wonder why I slept so long. How odd.

I glance over at Nicolas. I had thought his agitation was in response to mine, but I can tell it's much more than that.

He's tight-lipped, his eyes once again dark and faintly tinged with red. He hasn't said a word since his announcement in the bedroom. My fears for myself soon become overshadowed by my concern for him.

I finally reach across the chasm that separates us and touch his leg. His gaze flickers, and he places his hand over mine.

We continue the remainder of the trip like this, unmoving and unable to speak to one another.

~

The sun is setting when we pass through the gates. As we approach the house, a black sedan parked in front of the steps comes into view, and Nicolas curses under his breath. He pulls in ahead of it and shuts off the Ferrari.

He sits for a moment, then says, "I have an unexpected, and frankly, unwelcome visitor. I think this might be a good time for you to visit your home as you have spoken about doing. You may take this car." His whole body is tense, his eyes dark and unreadable.

"Okay." Discussion does not seem to be an option right now.

He opens his door and gets out, and as I grab the latch for mine, the front door of the house opens. Nicolas growls, then bends down and says, "Stay in the car."

A tall, statuesque female Chosen descends the steps, her dark red hair floating in waves around her shoulders. She's wearing deep emerald slacks topped by a similar-colored satin blouse, a stunning contrast to her pale complexion and red hair. The surrounding porch lights cast shadows beneath sharp cheekbones and a bladelike nose, adding to the haughtiness of her expression.

Copper-colored eyes, like those of a Persian cat, narrow as they fix their gaze first on me, then shift to settle it on Nicolas.

"Nicky, Nicky. It is *so* good to see you. I am so glad you returned from your trip. You are just in time."

He walks up the steps and says, "Katarina, what are you doing here?"

"Nicky, don't be like that. Why, I am here to see you, and to meet your new lady friend. Is that her in the car?"

She continues to walk down the stairs, but Nicolas stops right in front of her.

"Nicolao, please be civil. I did not come here to fight." Katarina makes a pouty face, which somehow looks very dangerous.

"She was just leaving. She has important business she must attend to and cannot stay." His stiff tone matches the ramrod-straightness of his back.

"Well, surely she has enough manners to introduce herself before she leaves. I cannot imagine you would tolerate such rudeness." She arches a red eyebrow and looks at him.

I can feel the debate raging in him, and I don't even have any of his blood.

Opening my door, I start to get out. Nicolas turns, frowning, and is suddenly back at the car. Shaking his head, he reaches out his hand and I take it. His eyes are full of warning, and I realize why as I stand up. Powerful Elder energy is rolling off of Katarina, and it feels foreign and threatening, completely unlike Nicolas and his Council members.

Not of his lineage. I remember what he said about The Chosen wars.

The hunter in me snaps to attention, ready to defend her territory and her mate.

Nicolas smiles tightly in response. He took my blood last night and can feel everything I feel. I smile back, suppressing a growl, and shift my focus to Katarina.

As we start up the steps, she looks me over, then redirects her attention to Nicolas.

"My, she *is* pretty, isn't she? And such beautiful eyes. Nicky, you've outdone yourself this time. She is an admirable specimen." Her voice drips with condescension.

Nicolas bristles. "I'll remind you this is *my* home. *You* are to be civil as well. Agreed?"

"Yes, yes, Nicky, you are right." Looking at me, she haughtily adds, "Forgive me, my dear. I tend to forget my place, as Nicky has been forever reminding me. Oh, but wait, I *have* no place as far as he is concerned. He made sure of that long ago."

She directs a dark glare back at Nicolas, her lip curled.

He clenches his jaw and a faint growl rumbles deep in his chest.

We haven't even made it up the stairway and these two seem ready to tear each other apart. This is going to be interesting.

Nicolas stops when we reach Katarina, then he guides me behind him and to the next step above them, keeping me close.

He takes a breath and stares disdainfully at the red-haired Chosen. "Miss Martin, may I present Katarina Habsburg, of the Austrian Habsburgs."

That's a name from the history books. Remembering my protocol lessons from Éva, I only nod in response.

Katarina tenses as she scowls back at Nicolas. "I believe you have it backward, Nicolao."

"No. I have it exactly right." He squeezes my hand.

Éva had explained to me the lower ranking Chosen is always presented to the higher ranking in formal situations. It's obvious Katarina believes she holds the higher station.

Her copper eyes narrow as she looks at Nicolas, then at me.

"I see. I have heard rumors that you had named a . . . 'queen.' But I imagined someone more regal. She just does not seem your type, Nicky." Her lip curls to one side and she looks at me as though I'm something she'd have to wipe off her shoe.

That does it. I've had enough of her crap.

"*She*," I snarl as Nicolas braces, "is standing right here. I have done nothing to you, yet you have been insulting me since we arrived. You need to stop." I stare at her through a deep red haze. Katarina studies me, pursing her lips. To my surprise, she bows her head.

"Well, perhaps I have . . . underestimated you. Please forgive my rudeness." Her voice is careful and I nod in response.

Turning to Nicolas, she declares, "Now, Nicky, I am absolutely *dying* for some of your renowned bloodwine. I've traveled half a world so I can enjoy a glass with you." She smiles sweetly, yet the look in her eyes is anything but.

Nicolas gestures for her to proceed back up the steps. We follow her through the still-open door and into the foyer, Nicolas tightly gripping my hand.

Marie is nowhere in sight.

And the strange scent of another foreign Chosen lingers heavily in the air.

Katarina stops. Nicolas strides past her and to the library door, opens it, and steps back to allow her to enter first.

She nods as she passes us, and we follow her into the room. The fireplace is lit, but appears to have been burning only a short time.

"I took the liberty of having your servant light a fire in here. The room is so much more pleasant with a flame, don't you think?" She smiles.

It could be my imagination, but it seems everything she says and does is a veiled threat.

"Which servant?" Nicolas asks quietly.

"Why, the young blond," she replies, watching Nicolas.

He goes very still.

"I believe he said his name was Johan, or something like that." She pauses and tips her head. "Do you have others? I did smell the rather heavy scents of several humans. It would be so like you to have humans for servants. You seem to be so fond of them." Her voice contains a strong note of derision.

Nicolas softens, and I realize he was concerned it had been Marie. I have a feeling that would have been very bad for Marie.

"Now where is that bloodwine? I've been waiting for some time now, Nicky, and have developed quite a thirst." Her imperious demand grates on my nerves.

Nicolas clenches his jaw, watching as she strolls to the window. He walks me to the library door and says, "Will you please go to the kitchen and ask Johan to bring us a carafe and some glasses?"

But he does not let go of my hand.

Opening the door, he stops and looks at Katarina and asks, "Do we need more than three glasses? Did anyone accompany you, or are you alone?"

I'm sure Nicolas had smelled the presence of the other Chosen the moment we stepped into the house. But apparently we are now deep in the Game.

"Why, Nicky, you know I never travel without a companion. He is with your servant, I imagine." She smiles. "I'm sure he would enjoy a glass of your bloodwine as well."

"I see. Then perhaps we should have my special reserve." Turning to me, he says, "I will go down to the wine cellar if you will speak with Johan."

I nod and we both leave the room.

Nicolas closes the door and takes a deep breath. We walk toward the back of the house, and he opens a door off the hallway, just outside the kitchen. A staircase leads downward into the cold air of the wine cellar. We step onto the landing, and he closes the cellar door, locks it, and leads me downstairs.

At the bottom of the steps, he finally releases my hand that he has been clutching since I got out of the car.

"I would kill her where she stands if it would not create a war." His anger boils to the surface, and I see a more deadly Nicolas than I've ever seen before.

"And I do not know yet who she brought. His scent is unfamiliar to me." He paces the cellar floor. The tension emanates from him in huge waves as he continues.

"I can only hope Johan had enough time to send Marie and Alfonso away." He glances at me with concern. "I think this would be our best opportunity for you to leave and go to the mountain. I already explained you had business to take care of, and that will have to suffice."

"I'm not leaving you here alone with them. No way." I frown and steel myself for the ensuing argument.

"Éva is on her way from New York. It is she who alerted me that Katarina had flown into the country. Lorenzo, Robert, and Alina are flying in as well. They will be here shortly."

"What's 'shortly'? A few hours? No, I'm not going anywhere. I'm staying right here with you."

His jaw tightens. "I need you to leave. I need you to be safe, and you will not be while you are here. Please, for me, go home."

"No. I will not. I'm staying . . . unless, of course, you want to leave with me."

He swears, walks over to the wine racks, and picks out a bottle.

"Nicolas, I don't understand. What can she do? I thought you were, well, like an Old One."

"Yes, but I am not the *only* one. There is another in Europe, and we have long been rivals. It was to him that Katarina turned when I . . . rejected her . . . centuries ago. They are bonded." Nicolas uncharacteristically runs his hand through his hair.

"Just so you understand the depth of her animosity, I courted her when she was human. I thought with her family's power and wealth she would make an excellent mate. But she proved to be deceitful and overly ambitious, and I grew intolerant of her treachery. When I refused to Change her, she offered herself to my enemy." He takes a deep breath.

"She has never forgiven the insult. Every century or so she feels the need to remind me of what she thinks I lost when I declined to make her my consort." He looks at me, dread filling his eyes.

"Apparently she heard about you and is here to attempt to destroy whatever happiness she perceives I might find. I fear you are in much greater danger than you realize." His eyes flash red and he pauses.

"As to what else she can do? She generally wreaks havoc among the human population wherever she goes and has enough money to smooth over her . . . indiscretions, should she choose to do so. Katarina could make my life in this city very difficult, and I have no wish to relocate.

"She also will tamper with The Chosen of my lineage, which is why I must get back upstairs to ensure that Johan is still completely mine. And why you must not be alone with either Katarina or her companion. I fear she will attempt to take you into her lineage."

He looks at me imploringly. "So will you please reconsider going home?"

"No, my place is by your side." And as I say this, I realize it's true, no matter what has happened or what will happen.

I take the bottle of bloodwine from him and wait.

Nicolas draws a deep breath and nods. "Very well. Then that is exactly where you will stay. Do not leave it. I do not know what I would do if anything happens to you."

He kisses my forehead, then takes my other hand and we start to head back upstairs.

But as we reach the bottom step, Nicolas inhales sharply, and then we are running up the stairs.

CHAPTER 45

As we enter the kitchen, the first thing I see is the massive back of a huge, pale-haired Chosen at the rear of the room. The second is Johan's face, frozen in fear, as he peers anxiously out from behind the six-foot-nine figure towering over him. The servant is pressed back against the counter with nowhere to go, trapped by the menacing Chosen.

Johan's face fills with relief as he sees us. The giant's back stiffens and he looses a growl of frustration.

"Johan, come here," Nicolas says quietly. Johan sidles away from the counter and hurriedly crosses the room.

The other Chosen starts to turn in our direction, and faster than I can even grasp, Nicolas leaps across the room and slams the giant back up against the pantry. The wooden doors splinter and burst inward, and as their bodies crash down to the floor, Nicolas lands in a crouch and grabs the pale hair with one hand. He cocks back his other arm, fingers spread and nails fully extended, and aiming directly for the throat of the massive Chosen.

Fear ignites in the Chosen's face, and he radiates absolute terror as Nicolas roars at him, fangs and red eyes flashing in rage.

The Chosen goes completely limp in submission, and Nicolas drags him out of the pantry wreckage and across the room. Johan and I glance at each other and follow them to the library.

As we get to the door, Nicolas throws the giant across the room where he lands in a crumpled pile at Katarina's feet.

"Ah," she says without batting an eye. "I see you've met Lars. Apparently he was not minding his manners, and obviously you handled him with your customary Magyar grace. Well done, Nicky," she says scathingly.

"Tell him next time I will take his head. I will not tolerate any aggression from him or from you," Nicolas snarls, the fury dripping from his voice.

"Now. I will once again ask . . ." He takes a deep breath. "*Why* . . . are . . . you . . . here?"

Lars pushes himself up from the floor, and Katarina glances at him before speaking.

"Gilles wanted me to deliver a message, but it is impolite for you to abuse my associate *and* expect to discuss business without refreshments," Katarina says firmly.

Nicolas sighs, then glances at Johan. I give him the bottle that's still in my hand and he leaves the room.

"Sooo, my dear," Katarina says, looking at me. "Where *are* you from? And *who* are you from? You have a most unusual aura, and I can't quite place it. You feel rather . . . odd." She watches me speculatively, her copper eyes narrowed, and a sudden wave of disorientation leaves me a bit unsteady.

I feel like prey trapped in the fiery gaze of the predator.

Not a nice feeling.

"She is from the West Coast," Nicolas replies before I can.

"Well, she is obviously *not* of your lineage, which raises other questions." She turns to Nicolas. "What are you *up* to, Nicky? Forming a new alliance? We've noticed that you seem to be building an army, and that makes us *very* uncomfortable."

Her flame-colored glare could melt steel, but Nicolas only tips his head and allows her a slight smile. His eyes are not smiling.

The silence lengthens, and I watch, fascinated with the stakes of this Game being played before me.

Johan comes back into the room carrying a tray with a carafe and five glasses, and sets it on the table.

"Finally." Katarina signals Lars, who's regained his feet and somewhat recovered his dignity, and he walks across the room to the table.

Johan visibly braces himself, and I wonder how long Lars was harassing him before we showed up.

Lars picks up one of the glasses and sets it to the side. Johan pours a small amount of bloodwine into it, then picks it up and takes several swallows. Everyone watches for a minute, then Katarina nods and Johan proceeds to fill the remaining glasses.

This looks similar to the procedure that was followed when the bloodwine was served to the Council members. I realize there must be a poison to which they are susceptible, and wonder what and just how lethal it is.

Nicolas walks over to the table and Lars quickly backs several steps. With a black look directed at the large Chosen, Nicolas chooses a glass and takes a sip himself.

"Very good. Thank you, Johan. You may go." Nicolas speaks in a surprisingly gentle tone to the young Chosen as compared to his treatment of the servant at the Council meeting. I suspect it's in response to Johan's trauma at the hands of Lars.

Nicolas then picks up a second glass and walks over and hands it to me. I catch something flicker in Katarina's expression. Surprise, and jealousy, perhaps. She has obviously never gotten over Nicolas.

Huh. First Éva, and now Katarina. Interesting.

Lars picks up the remaining two glasses and walks over to Katarina. He hands her a glass and she reaches up and caresses his cheek. He catches her fingertips and kisses them, then looks back at Nicolas. His expression is almost gloating, like he is saying, "see what I have that you gave up."

Nicolas snorts. He actually snorts. I hold my face as still as possible.

Katarina rolls her eyes and, raising the glass to Nicolas, takes a sip. Her eyes close as she savors the red liquid, and she takes another swallow without opening them

I take one as well. The spiced bloodwine coats my tongue, and I swish it around in my mouth and swallow. Every drop leaves a path of sweet fire as it spreads into my system. I am struck by how powerful this is compared to what I had the other night. It really is just like drinking blood from a hot vein, and as a wave of pleasure washes over me, I look at Nicolas. He smiles and lifts his glass to his lips.

"My God, Nicky, how do you make this? This is absolutely exquisite!" She swallows another mouthful and softly moans. I glance at Lars, and see red flicker through his eyes as he takes a drink and watches her.

Hmm. Her boy toy appears to be quite in love with her. But from what Nicolas said, she is bonded to someone else, someone of Nicolas's status. This Chosen seems to be rather young and nowhere near as powerful as Nicolas. I almost laugh out loud at how effortlessly Nicolas dragged and threw the giant around.

The gleam in Nicolas's eyes tells me his thoughts are running along the same lines. I suspect he will know exactly how to use this little piece of information.

"Well, business does not seem to be quite so pressing now. Perhaps we can wait and have another carafe of this fabulous bloodwine. It is well worth traveling around the world for." Katarina smiles, the copper of her eyes pink hued.

She really is quite beautiful. It's understandable how Nicolas might have been attracted to her, at least until she opened her mouth.

"No, we need to discuss whatever it is that brought you here." He curls his lip. "Now."

Katarina narrows her eyes, then smiles.

Nicolas looks pointedly at her. "I'm sure you have a flight to catch."

"Nicky, you really can be quite rude sometimes. I am in no hurry to leave." She languidly waves her hand and takes another drink.

Nicolas sets his glass on the reading table next to the bookshelves. He's barely drunk any.

Good idea—it's pretty potent.

I watch Katarina and Lars finish, their eyes slightly glazed as though on a blood high.

As Lars walks back to refill their glasses, Nicolas asks, "What does Gilles want?"

"Why, your head, of course. Vacuum-sealed in a jar of blood. What else?" she says, smiling nonchalantly.

In a jar of blood so the tissues don't dry out? Conscious? Oh, that's just . . . ghastly.

"You say this to me in my own house?" His words ooze with disgust. "You really are quite a witch, Katarina, and Gilles deserves you."

Katarina laughs. "Well, you asked me what he wants. I am just being honest."

"You do not know how to be honest. However, this once, I do believe you." He sighs. "What did he really send you here to say?"

"Now, you see? A different question. A more precise question. Really, Nicky, I think you have fallen out of practice."

Lars hands her back a full glass. She takes a long drink, closing her eyes as she swallows.

Nicolas takes a deep breath and waits.

Katarina opens her eyes and looks at Nicolas. "Explain why you are increasing your ranks. It seems obvious to us, but we would like to hear what you have to say about it."

"How I manage my lineage is really none of your business. In fact, I might ask *you* the same question." He watches, but her face reveals nothing.

She takes another drink, then walks across the room toward us. Nicolas steps closer to me, and I set my glass down on the reading table next to his.

"But what I really want to know is . . ." Katarina stops about six feet from us. "Who is *she*? What role does she play in this? You have not bonded, yet you have named her your queen. Who are you aligning with? The Egyptians? The Chinese?" Her look grows dark.

"You appear to be preparing to move against us, Nicolas. And I am here to tell you that we are aware of it, and we are making preparations ourselves. So if it is full-out war you want, we will gladly take you up on your offer, and take your head and your lineage in the process."

Nicolas clenches his jaw and takes a breath. "There is nothing I can say to dispel your unfounded paranoia. But what I can say is, if *any* of you step foot in this hemisphere, it *will* be war. The heads will roll, and yours will be the first should you be foolish enough to come here again."

"You would take *my* head, Nicolao? You who once loved me? Who once desired me? But wait, I forget. There have been so many others." She looks at me and continues.

"Has he told you how many times he has fallen in love? How many times he has seduced wealthy young women into loving him, and then just disappears and leaves them heartbroken . . . forever? How many young women he has Changed, only to abandon them once they became Chosen—"

Shock races through me at her words. The doubts I constantly fight to keep buried explode forth with renewed energy.

And I'm shocked again as the slap that cracks across her face echoes throughout the room.

I don't know if I'm more surprised at the slap itself or the fact that Nicolas would actually strike a female.

Lars, growling, leaps to her side to defend her.

But she is an Elder, and very strong, and though she staggers, she manages to stay on her feet. She places a hand on Lars to restrain him, and he complies.

Smart boy.

Massaging her jaw, she smiles. "You will regret that, Nicky."

"Probably," he says, but beneath his frustration and anger there is a hint of satisfaction in his tone.

"Well then, I think we are done here. I'm famished. Where are you taking me to dinner, Nicky?"

Weird. She's so mercurial—like a bipolar on steroids.

He stands silent. I suspect he is wondering how long before Éva and the others show up.

"Come, come, Nicky. This is one Game you don't want to play with me. Either take me to dinner, or I will go out and find my own. And I know how much you hate it when I do that. Lars and I are especially hungry tonight, and you can thank yourself for that. You and I both know how physical abuse whets the appetite." She grins seductively, then looks at me.

I keep my face still as I try to suppress my imagination.

Nicolas purses his lips and nods. "Very well," he says quietly.

And I realize with a chill that tonight some of Nicolas's donors will likely die.

CHAPTER 46

"You should stay here or go home. You do not want to come to the club tonight." Nicolas says as he paces the cellar floor.

We came down here to talk privately. Apparently the wine cellar's second purpose is to serve as a soundproof room against sharp Chosen ears.

"As I told you before, I'm not leaving you alone with them." No matter what Katarina said, I still feel very strongly about this.

"Do you doubt my ability to handle them?" He laughs quietly and brushes my hair back from my face.

"Then why did you call the others if it wasn't for reinforcements?" I'm a bit puzzled, as Nicolas does seem to be physically superior to both of them.

"I need them to escort Katarina and her friend out of the country. Robert and Alina are both pilots and will fly my plane. Éva and Lorenzo will keep Katarina company and out of the pilot compartment." He looks at his watch before continuing.

"Alina and Robert's flights have already landed in Denver and they are on their way here. Lorenzo should be touching down momentarily and Éva is about twenty minutes behind him."

"Then can't we just wait here and not go to the club?" I hate the thought of those two predators prowling among the club's trusting donors.

"Unfortunately not. If I do not take them to the club soon, Katarina will go hunt on her own. She is rather sadistic, and delights in taking the lives of innocents." He tightens his jaw. "And she has been known to take children."

I look at Nicolas in horror. Children?

"As she knows this is especially offensive to me, I can almost guarantee that is who she will hunt if she is loose in my city. And she would take special pleasure in leaving evidence pointing toward me or any of mine." His dark eyes flash in frustration.

"Well, can't you . . . force her to stay here?" My desperation increases as I try to come up with some kind of alternative.

"It would be a very ugly fight. And I am afraid once things get physical, I would not stop. If I kill her, Gilles would unleash his whole lineage on this country, and it would jeopardize the very survival of our kind." He takes a breath and frowns.

"Sunny, please. I understand what you are feeling, which is why you should go home. I will be doing everything I can to minimize her impact at the club. I will have no time to protect you from some of the aspects of Chosen life you find disturbing."

Like killing people.

"I need to get back to the library now. You make your choice. But remember, you will have to live with it, so make it with no regrets."

In other words, I better not whine about it if I don't like what I see.

I nod and we head back upstairs together.

The limo pulls out through the gates, speeding toward the downtown area. Sitting across from us, Katarina leans against Lars, playing with his hair and laughing at their quiet private jokes.

I sit close to Nicolas and hold tightly onto his arm. My anxiety is mounting, and he glances at me and takes a breath.

Right. I forget he's so tuned in to what I'm feeling. This will definitely make things more difficult for him at the club. I try to calm myself down.

"You need to relax, Nicky. Perhaps find a new partner. One who does not make you so tense." Katarina laughs. "Oh, but as I recall, you always were too tightly wound and never had any concept of *real* fun."

Katarina laughs again as Lars nibbles on her ear. He then bites through it with one of his fangs and she gasps, her face lit with pleasure.

Great. A live Chosen porn show in our own back seat. Well, maybe not exactly "live."

Too soon, we pull into the club parking lot, drive around to the back of the building, and park. Johan gets out and opens the rear passenger door. Katarina steps out first, lightly dragging a nail across his throat as she passes him. Lars follows and growls menacingly at the servant.

Faster than I can track, Nicolas is out the other side and two inches from Katarina's face.

"Behave yourself and keep your goddamn dog on a leash," he snarls.

"Nicky, Nicky. Open the door, or we go for a walk. Your choice." She smiles that sickly not-so-sweet smile she favors.

Nicolas grimaces, then quickly keys in the access code for an entrance I've not been through before, and we enter a hallway lined with several doors on one side. I realize this is similar to the hallway leading to the private rooms, but on the other side of the building.

We walk down the hall, past the lounge and the office, to the door leading to the dance area. Nicolas opens the thick door and stands back as they go through.

But before I can follow, he closes it and takes me by the hand. He leads me into the office.

"Please do this for me. Please stay here. You will not want to see this." He brushes the hair back from my face. "I had the club closed to all but our long-time donors. They understand the risks of being here tonight. But many of them enjoy the danger, and some of them come here hoping that they will not leave alive. I know that may sound harsh to your ears, but that is the reality of it."

I start to argue, but then realize he is right. I don't want to see.

"Katarina and her dog will be quite involved in feeding and will not give me any trouble. And while they are so occupied, my Elders will arrive, and their little game will be over."

"Okay." I reluctantly nod my agreement.

Nicolas breathes a sigh of relief and crushes me to him. I hug him tightly as well, then with a kiss to my forehead, he says, "I will be back to check on you shortly." He opens the door to leave.

The voices of Katarina and a human male reach me as they pass by in the hallway. Fortunately, I don't recognize the man's voice, but sadness descends over me when I realize I'll likely never hear it again.

Nicolas glances back at me and shakes his head, then closes the door.

It's been about half an hour and I wonder if the Elders are here yet. I check the other door, the one leading to the parking lot. But when I peer down the short hallway, my eyes zero in on the keypad next to the outer door.

Without the code, I can't even *look* outside, let alone leave. I return to my pacing.

Concern for Nicolas writhes in my belly like a coiling snake. I hope Katarina and Lars didn't get a couple of feedings in them and decide to go after him. They'd be strong and high from the blood, and between the two of them, they might cause Nicolas some problems.

I don't like this. He should've been back to check on me by now. He said he would.

The hunter whines about her mate. The beast joins her, its growls rumbling in my chest.

I've waited long enough.

Hell, I hope I haven't waited too long.

Opening the door to the hallway, I peek out and taste the air in both directions. I don't hear or see anything, and that could be good—or very, very bad.

I let the door close and grab a stapler from the top of the desk, then step into the hall and wedge the stapler against the jamb, leaving the door cracked open. Just in case we need to get somewhere safe in a hurry.

Not sure which way to go—the door to the lounge is locked, like everything else in this Fort Knox of a club. Frowning, I head down the hall toward the main club and open the heavy door.

The smell of human blood hits me like a jackhammer.

The beast and the hunger roar, and I take a breath and try to regain some measure of control. Grabbing a case of beer, I prop the door open with it and go in.

The music is blaring, and as I wind my way through the boxes to the black curtain, the smell gets stronger. I clench my jaw and open the curtain. Lying on the other side of it is the bouncer. Despite his size, he would have had no chance against Lars. His throat is torn out, but very little blood is dripping from the gaping wound.

Staring at the far wall, I brace myself against the overpowering smell and sight of the blood, then leap over the body. When I walk out to the bar, the bartender is lying behind it in a crumpled heap. My jaw tightens in response to the smell of *his* blood, and the beast in me threatens to break loose.

I quickly retrace my steps and kick the beer out of the way, and the door clicks shut behind me. Leaning against the wall, I shove the beast down and try to regroup. I can still smell and taste the airborne blood particles from that room, but at least I'm not confronted with the liquid form, or what was left of it.

As I manage to restore some sense of calm, a loud boom echoes down the hallway. I shove off the wall and race down the hall to the lounge door and yank on it, but it won't open. Another loud crash from inside the lounge sends both the hunter and the beast into a frenzy.

Nicolas!

Just as I'm about to try to punch through the door, it vibrates with a loud thud. I leap to the side as it bursts open and Lars's body hurtles through the air and slams against the hallway wall.

I look inside the room to see Nicolas standing, disheveled, apparently having just thrown Lars for the second time today. Katarina is crouched off to one side, her blouse torn and her hair in disarray. She looks ready to spring at Nicolas.

But before she can launch herself, I am on her.

I grab that red hair and yank her head around, trying to slam her body onto the floor like she's a deer. But she manages to latch onto me, and we both go down.

She's *strong*, and suddenly I'm hanging onto her hair for dear life, fighting to keep her bared fangs out of my throat. Her crimson eyes blaze with hatred as she snaps at my face.

But then her head is jerked backward, and I let go as Nicolas pulls her off of me.

He has her firmly by the hair and has one of her arms pinned behind her back. He shoves her facedown onto the floor, puts one foot on her back, and grabs her head with both hands.

"Nicolas!" I scream. "Stop! Please, stop!" Frantic, I leap to my feet and wave my arms.

He hesitates, then slowly releases her head. He turns and looks at me, the gratitude in his eyes warring with his anger.

The door leading to the hallway with the private rooms opens and Robert walks in.

"Holy shit," he says as he comes into the room, closely trailed by Alina. They're both staring at Nicolas, who still has his foot on Katarina's back and once again has a fistful of her hair.

I'm betting that right about now she's wishing she wore it short.

"Nicolas, are you sure you want to do that?" Alina's calm voice penetrates the deathly silence that has descended over the room.

Nicolas snarls and gestures around the lounge. As the others scan the room, so do I.

At the same time, I become aware of the overwhelming scent of blood. The draperies and walls are splashed with it, like some grotesque abstract painting, and the floors are smeared and sticky. Broken and twisted bodies are scattered about what is now a chamber of horrors.

There is no chance to feel revulsion, as I am instantly fighting to rein in the beast and the hunger that are once again raging inside me.

Nicolas looks at me, and his eyes redden as I look at him through a pink haze.

"Ah. Sunny. Please. Do you need to go outside?" He still has hold of Katarina, and guilt flickers through me for distracting him.

"No," I say hoarsely. "I'll be okay." I hold my breath and focus on him and try to block out the hunger.

"Good."

He glares down at Katarina, and his face is grim as he steps off her back. Still gripping her hair, he pulls her up while she struggles to her feet.

Nicolas looks over at Robert and Alina.

"There are several more bodies in the private rooms. And while I was discussing Katarina's excesses with her, her dog slipped up front and killed my bouncer and my bartender, who were expressly off-limits." His voice is deep with hatred and rage as he again focuses on Katarina.

"But the most unforgivable act was attacking me as I came back into this room. You tell Gilles he had better hope I do not come hunt him down. I am tired of his games—and yours." Nicolas pauses as he leans in, bringing his face closer to hers. She hisses.

"I promise you, Katarina, the next time I lay eyes on you, I *will* kill you. The truce is the only reason you are still alive."

He straightens and gives her a deadly smile. "However, for what it is worth, attempted assassination voids the truce, so I am well within my rights to end your miserable existence." He smiles again and tips his head. "But I have a better idea."

She glares at him, but for once keeps silent.

I hear a groan out in the hall and glance in that direction before looking back at Nicolas.

He shakes his head and says, "His neck is broken and I suspect his back is as well. He won't be giving anyone trouble for a little while.

"Robert, Alina." Nicolas indicates the hallway with his chin. "Grab that piece of garbage and bring him back to the lockup. These two can wait in there until Lorenzo and Éva arrive."

Katarina's eyes grow wide at the mention of Éva's name, and Nicolas coldly smiles.

"Ah yes. Someone who despises you even more than I do. She will be your escort home. It should be an interesting flight." His laughter has a cruel sound to it. "Sunny, come with me."

I follow him as he forces Katarina down the hallway, glad to escape the bloody room and take a breath of somewhat clear air. Nicolas stops at the last private room, the one closest to the outside door.

He opens the door, and I notice it's several times thicker than a normal door and is lined with steel. The walls inside are also lined in thick plate steel. Heavy-duty rings, chains, and manacles are mounted at various heights on three of the walls.

Nicolas walks Katarina over to a corner with several odd-looking garments hanging from hooks. Her eyes grow wide, and she growls and tries to twist out of his grasp.

He laughs and wrenches her arm up behind her back.

"Do you want it broken? I will even break the other one so you have a matching set."

She stops struggling, but her eyes are blazing red and furious.

"Sunny, grab one of those jackets and hold it up."

It's heavier than it looks. It appears to be a type of straitjacket, lined with a thick, hard, plastic-like material, maybe Kevlar, and reinforced with steel bands.

I hold it open as Nicolas jams her free arm into one sleeve, then pulls it behind her and thrusts the other one into the remaining sleeve. He motions with his chin, and I grab the chain hanging from the end of the sleeve and hand it to him. He yanks it around her waist, then moves the arm he's holding so I can grab its chain and hand it back around to him in the opposite direction. Nicolas pulls both chains tight, forcing Katarina to hug herself, and shoves her up against the wall. He quickly tightens all the fastenings up the back of the jacket just as Robert and Alina carry Lars in.

Spinning Katarina back around, he asks, "Now, are you going to behave yourself or do I have to hang you from a hook until the others get here?"

"You will *pay* for this, Nicolao," she snarls, hatred pouring from her voice.

"Oh, I already have. You tormented and slaughtered everyone in my club, including my bartender and my bouncer, both of whom had been with me for a long time. You are despicable animals, and I question why I am even leaving you alive.

"But I do have a reason. I will be sending a message to Gilles explaining how fortunate he is that I am sending your head back to him with your body still attached. And I will include a little note about you and your special relationship with your dog." Nicolas smiles as a look of fear crosses Katarina's face.

"I thought so. I am not quite sure how you have been hiding it, or why you thought you could get away with flaunting it here. But I am sure Gilles will be thrilled to know he shares blood with someone who also shares with an underling. Double-bonding is still frowned upon in Europe, is it not?"

"Nicolao, no . . . he will kill me." Her terrified whisper indicates this is no exaggeration.

"That, Katarina, is exactly my point."

He turns to me and places his arm around my waist and, with a last look at Katarina, walks us out of the room.

We head back to the lounge, and I pause to take a breath before we go in. Nicolas looks at me questioningly. I nod that I'm okay and we enter the room. The raw, coppery smell of human blood permeates the air, and my throat tightens as both the beast and the hunger grab hold.

Nicolas frowns. "Are you going to be able to handle this? Or would you prefer to wait in the office?"

I grit my teeth. "I'll be okay."

"All right. But you can leave anytime you need to."

I nod again in response.

He walks farther into the room, grimacing as he surveys the human wreckage.

"What a waste," he says, shaking his head. His eyes narrowing, he looks over at me.

"What were you thinking, attacking an Elder as powerful as Katarina? She could have easily killed you. You know less about fighting Chosen than you do fighting bear. Do you not have *any* common sense?" Frustration is thick in his voice, but no real anger.

"She . . . was getting ready to attack you."

"And I was waiting for it."

"Oh."

He reaches over and smoothes my hair.

"Come here." He pulls me close and holds me tight. He nuzzles my ear and whispers, "I love you."

And I wonder for how long as Katarina's words about all the women he's loved echo in my head.

Nicolas pushes himself away from me and looks searchingly into my eyes.

"Why I am feeling doubt from you? Do you still question me? What do I have to do to prove myself to you?" His voice is pained and the hurt in his eyes is unbearable.

"She said . . ." I can't finish, as the possibility that it was true is crushing me.

"And you believed her?" he whispers, incredulous. "This cannot go on. We need to resolve this, but unfortunately, we have other matters to deal with right now."

He touches my jaw and, shaking his head, walks away.

No, don't walk away. I believe you. I need you.

The hunger surges with my torn emotions. I try to slam it down as Nicolas's back stiffens.

"Perhaps you *should* wait in the office," he says without looking at me, his tone cold.

"No, I'll be fine." I suddenly can't bear to leave him, especially now. Not with this . . . this *thing*—whatever it is—between us.

He walks to the nearest body and, bending down, rolls it over. Shaking his head again, he walks to the next and looks at it, and to the next, and to the next. He curses as he approaches the last one, and out of morbid curiosity, I go over to where he is standing.

The arms and legs are contorted, bending where they should not, and the back is obviously broken. I can't see the face because the neck is bent at an odd angle. Fang scars line one arm, and about that time I recognize the scent of what's left of his blood.

It's Skeeter, or was, and I look up in horror at Nicolas. He glances at me and nods, and I turn away and hug myself. Poor pathetic boy. Whatever he was missing in this life, I hope he found it on the other side.

I look around the room, feeling sorrow for the rest of them. Then I realize all the victims are male.

"You sent the women home." I look up at Nicolas in gratitude, my love for him resurfacing from beneath the doubts.

He closes his eyes and the tension visibly drains from his body. He walks over to me and gently takes my face in his hands.

"I am not the brute you seem to think I am. I do what I have to do to survive, but I am not cruel, and killing is something I try to avoid. And yes, I sent the women home to protect them."

"I love you, Nicolas," I whisper, silently weeping.

"I know." And he takes me in his arms and holds me while I cry the cry with no tears.

CHAPTER 47

Éva walks into the bloody lounge, and the expression on her face as she assesses the carnage is murderous. She stands a moment watching Robert and Lorenzo stack the bodies near the rear door, then looks at Nicolas.

"You are all right?" Concern creases her elegant features.

He gives her a feral smile. She matches it with one of her own, and I am once again reminded of their shared history.

"Are they in the holding room?" she asks.

Nicolas nods, and with a glance at me to follow him, we go back to the room where Katarina and Lars are being held.

Nicolas opens the door and Katarina is sitting in the corner next to the curled-up form of Lars. She sees Éva and slowly gets to her feet, her face wearing a look of sheer hatred.

Éva lets out a soft laugh, but the animosity in her eyes is even stronger than that of the red-haired Chosen. She saunters across the room to Katarina.

Golden eyes stare into copper, then both flare into violent red. With no warning, Éva's hand whips out, and she rakes Katarina across the face with her nails fully extended.

Katarina reels back in shock and hisses. Four deep, bloody gashes trail across her cheek.

Éva growls. "I normally would not assault someone who is helpless, but you . . ." She opens her mouth and bares her fangs. "If your blood was not so foul, I would drain you right here, then take great pleasure in separating your worthless head from your pathetic body. Very slowly. And I hear your bonded favors jars. What a lovely fate, one you would rightly deserve."

Katarina snarls. "Oh, but you and I have much in common, dear—"

Éva slashes Katarina across the other cheek.

"You and I have *nothing* in common, and never did. He *never* loved *you*," Éva spats.

Nicolas becomes very still while I fight to keep my face expressionless.

Éva walks over to a cupboard and opens it. After rummaging around, she pulls out a ball gag and walks back over to Katarina.

"I do not wish to be subjected to the venom that spills non-stop from your mouth." She shoves the ball between Katarina's bloody teeth as Katarina snarls and tries to twist away.

"Double-bonding? Are you serious? With Gilles and that?" Éva points to the blond Chosen, who is growling at her but otherwise making no movement. "I look forward to seeing Gilles's reaction as I pass that little tidbit along. You best say your goodbyes to loverboy while you can."

She laughs and walks back over to the door where Nicolas and I stand.

"Johan and Alina should be back with the van by now. Once they have finished loading it, you and the others can take the limo back to the airport," Nicolas says.

Éva reaches out to touch Nicolas's cheek, but glances at me and her hand drifts down to her side. Regret flickers in her eyes, and I wonder again what happened between these two. She steps past Nicolas and we follow her out into the hallway, closing the heavy steel door behind us. He takes the lead and we go back into the lounge.

"You are sure you are all right? I was worried sick the whole way here." She glances at me again, then looks back at Nicolas.

"Éva, you know I can—" Nicolas begins, but she cuts him off.

"And if they had taken *her*? If they were holding her hostage?" Éva shakes her head.

Nicolas tenses and a low rumble vibrates in his chest.

"You are more vulnerable in a way you haven't been in a long time. You need to keep that in mind. The next assassins may not be so arrogant or so stupid." She turns to me.

"And you need to make some hard decisions. If you are going to be with Nicolas, you *must* be able to hold your own and not be a weak spot in his defenses." Her tone is harsh, but her words ring true.

"Éva!" Nicolas growls.

"I will stop now, but it needed to be said, and be said so that you *both* hear it. It's time you face the reality of your situation."

Giving each of us a last hard look, Éva walks out of the room.

Nicolas is silent as we head home in the rental car that Robert brought from the airport. Johan has taken the van loaded with the bodies somewhere. To where, I don't know. And I don't want to know, but I grieve for all those lives that were cut short.

Nicolas reaches out and rubs my leg reassuringly as we pull through the raven gates and up the driveway.

We park in front, and he gets out and opens my door. I step from the car, and as I look at the house, I feel the sadness take hold. And it's more than for the lives lost tonight. It's for the fact that I can stare calmly at bloody human bodies piled in a room and not go into hysterics at the sight. That I am becoming more and more like The Chosen and I don't know where it's going to end.

Nicolas pulls me to him and hugs me.

"This . . . melancholy." He shakes his head and sighs, then takes my hand. "Come."

We go in and he leads me up the stairs. But instead of turning left toward my bedroom, he veers right, and we go down a long hallway that ends in a set of double doors.

He opens one of the doors and we walk into a huge bedroom. The colors are rich and dark: burgundy, deep forest green, black, with touches of gold here and there. The bed is a large elaborately carved poster bed and hung with heavy black and burgundy draperies. It's fit for a king and looks to be centuries old. Hell, it probably belonged to a king. A sitting area next to the window contains a sofa, chair, and small table.

He walks us past priceless art lining the wall to a door at the other end of the room. It leads into a bathroom, which has a room-sized Jacuzzi and a huge, glassed-in shower with multiple faucets on the three walls. All of the fixtures in the room are gold, and the intricate porcelain tiles appear handmade.

He takes me inside, then stops on an elegant rug in the middle of the floor. Facing me, he strokes my hair, then looking into my eyes, he starts unbuttoning my blouse.

My breath stops.

He very gently brushes the blouse from my shoulders and runs his hands down my waist. My blood heats up as his hands move to the front of my jeans and he unfastens them. He slowly pushes them down past my hips and, bending his knees, to the floor. He unzips and pulls off first one boot, then the other, and the jeans are next. He shoves the pile of clothing out of the way.

He then stands very slowly, his hands retracing their path up my body, followed by his lips. I gasp and can barely breathe. When his hands reach my shoulders, they continue up to my jaw, and he gently holds my face. His lips brush mine, softly.

I break the spell he has me under enough to reach out and unbutton his torn and bloody shirt. He takes it off as I undo his slacks. I push them to the floor, and he steps out of his clothing and shoes and kicks them to the side.

We stand completely naked, and I wait, blood flaming sweetly in my veins. He smiles and strokes my hair again, then leads me over to the shower. Turning on all the faucets, he pauses a moment for the water to heat up, then leads me in.

The water is deliciously hot and pummels me from three sides. I close my eyes as it washes over my body, and then I feel Nicolas's hands, slick with soap, slowly rub my back.

I can't recall the last time I had my back washed.

Standing there, I relish his touch, my eyes closed as he washes me all over. He stops a moment, then gently moves me underneath the spray. I tilt my head back and enjoy the sensation of the water running through my hair.

I straighten and open my eyes to see Nicolas watching me, his eyes flaming crimson. The tips of his fangs press against his bottom lip, and my blood flares again in excitement.

I take what's left of the crushed bar of soap from his hand.

"Turn around," I say, my voice rough with emotion. He does so and inhales sharply as I touch his back and begin washing it. I massage it top to bottom and can feel his soft growls in response. I move my hands around his ribcage to his chest and soap it as well, pressing myself closely against his back.

As my hands move to his waist, he grabs and holds them for a moment, then turns back around.

He slowly pushes me up against the wall and pins me there with his body, then bends to kiss my shoulder. He shifts and the sharp points of his fangs trace the veins across the top of my breasts. The water hitting the shower floor is now pink and my excitement surges. I move my mouth to his shoulder and take hold of it with my teeth.

He groans and I bite harder. He gasps, and then slowly pulls his body back, and I let go.

Watching my face, he reaches up and slices the inside of his upper arm, where the bicep curves and meets the shoulder. Blood wells, and I can feel his eyes on me as I first lick, then bite the gaping wound. I start to draw in his blood and can feel *him* in it as it fills my mouth. Everywhere that his blood—his essence—touches is a caress, and it brings instant bliss. The liquid *him* bathes my throat, then floods into my system and finally traces its way throughout all my veins. His blood now mingles with mine. *He* is now part of *me*.

I stop breathing. His body wraps around mine, and he slowly sinks his fangs into the side of my throat. The sharp pain is exquisite, and a soft moan escapes from deep within me.

He waits, and I wait, then I pull, and he pulls. The feeling of him drawing my blood *out* as I am drawing his *in* is surreal. It's an ecstasy beyond words, making all the recent pleasures in my life pale into insignificance. I gasp, and as my knees give out, we slowly sink to the floor.

The hot water continues to bathe our outsides while the hot blood bathes our insides. I can feel him in every tissue of my body, and for the first time in my entire life, all my lives, I feel complete.

I pull again as he pulls, and feel us descending into a bottomless rapture. I am enveloped by him inside and out, and groan with the rightness of it. He growls and holds me tighter, nearly crushing me, and I revel in it.

I start to draw again, but his hand pushes gently against my mouth. He releases my neck.

No, don't stop, I don't want to stop. Not ever.

I let go and start to cry as I am completely overwhelmed by emotion, both mine and *his*. I can *feel* his intense love and protectiveness and need, and I'm awed by the depth of his passion for me, and by the profound love it triggers for him. He holds me tighter as he feels my response, and clinging to him, I cry even harder. My chest aches with my sobs, but oddly, so do my eyes, and then I realize they are wet, and it is not from the water.

Tears. I have tears. I reach up to touch them, and when I look at my fingers, they are covered in blood.

And part of me weeps harder still, for tears of blood can only mean that what's left of my human side is slowly fading away.

Nicolas strokes my hair, and whispers, "I am sorry."

április 21., szombat

Tonight we became as one. Nothing in my long life had prepared me for the intensity of our emotions, and I wept in rhapsody, as did she. And like mine, her tears were bloodtears. She is Changing, and I can feel her fear so strongly now. I wish I could ease it, but this is something we all must go through.

I do know this—after five hundred years of searching, she is the One.

SUNDAY

CHAPTER 48

I slowly open my eyes, and reaching for Nicolas, I already know that he's not here. I roll over and look around the room, but the heavy drapes are drawn, and I have no idea what time of day it is. My robe is lying across the foot of the bed—he must have brought it from my room before he left.

Blurry memories of last night surface and reawaken my longing for him. I barely remember Nicolas lifting me out of the shower and drying me off as I was still too caught up in our emotions and unable to move. He carried me to his bed, then curled up around me as I drifted off to sleep. I have a vague recollection of him slipping out of bed sometime later.

Getting up, I peek through the drapes to look out at the day. It appears to be late morning and the sun is shining brightly. Hmm.

I throw on my robe and head to my room to get dressed, wondering what Nicolas has planned for the day.

Quickly slipping on a long-sleeved blouse and a pair of jeans, I walk back to Nicolas's bathroom to get my boots and clothes from yesterday. The boots are sitting by the door, but my clothes are gone. They must be in the laundry, which would mean Marie is back.

At that thought, the hunger perks up a little, but then fades away. That's odd. I frown and go back to my room to get a pair of socks. As I walk in, Nicolas's cell phone rings from my bag on the dressing table. Last I saw it was in the Ferrari. Guess he must've brought it in.

I fish the phone out of my bag and flip it open.

"Hello," I say warmly.

"Good morning," he says. My blood thrills to the rich sound of his voice.

"Good morning."

"You slept well." He says it as a statement rather than a question.

"Yes, I did. I just got up a few minutes ago. Are you at the club?"

"Yes. It will take some time to put things back in order. We will likely not be able to reopen for a day or two, which is a bit of an inconvenience."

Yeah, I'll say. Where do Chosen eat when their only restaurant gets shut down?

"Do you need any help?" I ask.

Except—cleaning up might give me a bit of a problem. The thought of the blood spattered from one end of the club to the other stirs the hunger again, and again it fades away.

God, I can't even *think* about blood anymore without a reaction.

I need to go hunt. Run something down, wrestle it to the ground, and feed until I can't take in any more. All I've been doing is snacking for the last few days. Hell, since the damn bear attacked me. My frustrations surge and I squeeze my fists.

But not too hard.

"Sunny? Are you there?" Nicolas has a note of concern in his voice, and it seems like I can *feel* it as well. Weird.

"Um, yeah?"

"Is everything all right? You did not answer my question, and you seem to be upset about something."

"I'm sorry. I was thinking about the club. I'm fine." And for some reason I *am* fine . . . now.

What's *wrong* with me? Talk about mood swings.

"Hmm. I asked if you would like to drive the Audi into town to take care of the business you mentioned the other day." His quiet tone is laced with amusement. I can almost feel it.

"Oh. Yeah, yes, thank you. That would be great."

The Audi. Cool.

"I had Alfonso park it out front for you. The keys are in it." His voice is warmer now, and I definitely feel some of that warmth in my blood.

"Thank you . . . Hey, Nicolas? Can I ask you something?"

"Always."

"Is it possible that I can tell what you're feeling? I mean, last night . . . I didn't think I took . . . very much." Embarrassment flushes through me. What we did last night is even more intimate than sex, and I'm not sure how to talk about it.

Then I feel his echo of amusement.

This is really weird.

"Yes, it is possible. That is why I stopped you. My blood is very . . . potent." Again I feel the amusement as well as hear it in his voice.

"Oh. No matter how far apart we are?" I ask. This is going to take some getting used to.

"The effect does lessen with distance. Speaking over the phone seems to temporarily strengthen the connection, probably due to the sound of the voice. But it is not quite as strong as if we were in the same room or building."

"Okay." I frown. "So . . . can I tell what you're thinking, too?"

'Cuz it sure seems like he knows what *I'm* thinking, especially after he's taken my blood.

"No, only what I am *feeling*. However, since emotions are influenced by thought, it can seem the same sometimes." He pauses, and I feel a flash of amusement. "For example . . ."

And I feel a rush of desire, and my blood sweetly flames in response.

Oh, shit.

"Oh, uh . . . thanks." I squeak out sarcastically. "How am I supposed to get anything done if I'm feeling that?"

He laughs.

"Now you know what tortures you have been inflicting upon me for the last week," he says, and I can hear the smile in his voice as well as feel it in my blood. His warmth washes over me again, and I recognize it as love.

As my own feelings of love add to his, it feels like I'm literally glowing from both.

"Ah. Yes, this is what I tried to explain. There really are no words for it." His voice is husky, and my blood begins to heat up even further.

"But, unfortunately," he continues, and the glowy feeling begins to fade. "This is not a good time to indulge ourselves. We both have things to do today."

"Okay. Then, I guess I'll talk to you later?" I can feel him withdrawing, like he's leaving the room.

"Yes. Please call if you need anything."

"I will. And thank you for the use of the Audi." I focus on my feelings of gratitude and love.

He takes in a breath and holds it a moment.

"You are welcome." And I feel his answering warmth and passion flow through me, and then he hangs up.

And leaves me with a small echo of his feelings, sitting snugly in my core.

Wow. This is amazing.

I put on my socks and boots and walk over to the dressing table to brush out my hair. Again something seems different when I look in the mirror, and I don't think it's the fine silver scars that trace their way down my jaw. I can't quite put a finger on it.

Oh well.

I rub on some heavy sunscreen and decide to add foundation since I look a little paler than usual. Didn't think that was possible.

As I'm applying the makeup, the sound of footsteps drifts up from the hallway below, then proceeds to head up the stairs. The step is human and light.

Marie.

Tensing, I listen as she reaches the top and walks in the direction of my room.

I go completely still in response to the tremor that runs up my spine. She pushes open the door that is ajar and walks in carrying my folded clothes.

Her scent, the one I've been savoring in her borrowed clothing, swirls into the room and wraps itself around me.

And I can taste and hear the song of her blood.

The beast and the hunger roar to life, my vision turns pink, and I stop breathing. She freezes when she sees me, and I clench my jaw as a look of fear crosses her face. The hunter snaps to attention and waits to spring.

We are suddenly locked in the classic poses of predator and prey, and we both know it.

The cell phone rings, shattering the deathly quiet, yet neither of us moves.

I continue to hold my breath and try to shove the beast back down. It responds a little easier than I would've expected, and its scream is quickly muted to an impatient growl.

"Hello, Marie," I say hoarsely.

She glances at the still ringing cell phone, then back at me.

"Good morning, mademoiselle." Her voice is thin and nervous. "How are you feeling?"

Brave girl. Smart. Make me think and behave civilized so I won't leap across this room.

"I'm much better. Thank you very much for your . . . gift when I was so ill," I say as gently as possible under the circumstances. I try not to think about what her "gift" was.

She relaxes slightly, and the hunter in me does so as well. That's good. If she were to run, there's only one response the hunter would have.

"You are welcome, mademoiselle. I am glad I was able to help. You have always been very kind to me." Again she knows exactly what to say. I'm able to leash both the beast and the hunter a little more tightly.

The phone is still ringing and I glance at it.

"Would you like for me to answer it, mademoiselle?"

Good idea. It would reassure Nicolas to hear your voice.

"Yes, Marie. Please do."

I watch as she slowly and carefully walks to the small table in front of the window where I left the cell phone. She sets down my clothes and picks up the phone.

"Hello?" she answers.

"Marie?" I hear Nicolas's worried voice on the other end and can feel his concern.

"Yes, sir," she says, sounding nearly normal. His relief washes through me.

"Is something wrong? Where's Sunny?" he asks quietly, radiating calm through both voice and blood, which I can now feel soothing my whole system.

Thank you, Nicolas.

"She is right here, sir. Would you like to speak with her?" She looks at me, trying to hide the fear still showing in her blue eyes.

"Yes, please." He coughs. "Marie . . . you are all right?"

"Yes, sir." Her eyes are big as she starts to walk forward and hand me the phone.

I tense again.

"Just set it on the table, Marie," I tell her, and she stops and sets it down. "Thank you. You may go."

She nods, then bravely turns her back on me and leaves, shutting the door behind her.

Sure wish she would lock it right now.

Taking a big breath, I feel the hunger surge again in reaction to her scent still hanging in the air.

I walk over and pick up the phone.

"Hi," I say in relief.

"Are *you* all right?" he asks quietly, and again I feel his calm run throughout my body.

"Yeah. I, uh . . . had a moment when she first walked into my room." A really long moment.

But I don't have to explain that. He knew exactly what had gone on.

Lying to him now is absolutely impossible. I frown as this sinks in.

"Do I need to come back to the estate?" The concern in his tone weaves through my blood. I take a breath before answering.

"No, I'm fine. I was just getting ready to leave anyway," I declare as steadily as possible.

"In that case, I am confident you have the situation under control. Call me when you are on the road. I would like for you to stop by the club before taking care of your errands." His tone is neutral, but I can feel his worry along with his impatience.

Interesting. Lying to *me* now may be a little difficult as well.

"Okay," I answer. The phone goes silent and so does our other connection.

I toss the phone into my bag, grab my hat and gloves, and stop to take a last look in the mirror. And now I realize what seems different.

Whatever has been staring out of my eyes for the last five years has become more intense, more lethal, and I feel a ripple of fear as I look at that creature.

Great. Always did scare myself, but terrify now seems like a more appropriate word.

Disgusted, I walk out the door and head down the stairs. I'm acutely aware of Marie's lingering scent and hasten across the foyer to the front door, anxious to get out before anything else happens.

Just before I reach it, the library door opens, and Marie walks into the foyer.

Though I'm better prepared this time, I still have to fight the beast as it jumps to the surface, screaming its hunger and frustration.

I grab the door handle and twist it down. Holding tight to the door, I pause and look at Marie.

She's wide-eyed and holding onto the library door.

The phone starts ringing.

Damn you, Nicolas. Leave me alone. I can handle this.

I hit the off button.

"Marie, I'm sorry if I scared you upstairs," I say quietly.

"Mademoiselle, it was my fault. Mr. Ambrus suggested I stay in my quarters until he returned, but it was so quiet, I thought no one was here."

I nod and turn to leave.

"Mademoiselle?"

Don't stop me now, Marie. You've been really smart so far.

"Yes?"

"If you don't mind me asking, what happened to you?" Her curiosity and concern apparently win out over her sense of self-preservation.

"I, uh, was injured in an accident, but I'm better now."

"Yes, Mr. Ambrus told me that night. But your recovery . . . it has not gone well?"

"Well enough. Why do you say that?"

"It is just that you do not seem to be yourself," she says softly.

I clench my jaw and try not to think of the reason for that, but the thought breaks through my defenses anyway.

Her blood. Her blood is the first that made me not myself, at least the self I've been since my escape from the warehouse a lifetime ago.

I close my eyes, focusing on beating back the hunger that now has flames racing through my veins. The beast roars impatiently and I shove it back down.

"What do you mean?" I carefully open my eyes, grateful that my vision is clear again.

"You are . . . more like the others now. You . . . you frighten me," she whispers.

"Marie . . . I frighten myself," I admit, and giving her a sad smile, head out the front door.

CHAPTER 49

As I pull the Audi through the black raven gates, I mull over what Marie said and agree with her. I have seen and felt the changes, and am aware that I'm becoming more like The Chosen. It's just a bit disturbing that it's noticeable to someone else, especially a human.

I think back over the time that's elapsed since I crawled off the mountain. It's been exactly one week. One week. And in that short amount of time, I have walked dangerously close to the cliff I've been avoiding for the last five years.

And now that I'm away from Nicolas, away from his influence and his overpowering presence, it seems as though I can finally think, finally breathe. I question the decisions I've been making—and am not too happy with them.

Yet if I want to be with him, to love him and be loved by him, I can't see any other way I could've made them.

Frustration blossoms as I weigh my choices. It basically boils down to two realities: I give up myself and who or what I am, and become something I don't want to be.

Or I give up what is likely my only shot at love and companionship, and resign myself to an eternity of loneliness.

~

The silver sports car is halfway up the pass before I remember to turn the cell phone back on. I debate whether or not to do it. But the consequences will probably be pretty unpleasant if I wait any longer, so with a sigh, I pull it out of my bag and press the button.

Wow. Nine missed calls and three voicemails. Crap. He must be bent.

Good. The rebel part of me is feeling a little exhilarated at the unexpected freedom, and I laugh at the idea that I get to pull his strings for a change.

But then I remember his fear of losing me, and the depth of his feelings, and the guilt starts to creep in.

Oh, this is going to hurt.

I press "1" and push SEND.

"Where are you?" His anger and frustration pour through me.

"Taking care of some things." I wince at the sound of my own defensiveness.

"You did not answer, and you did not call me as you said you would." His voice is tense, and I feel his anger rise a little more.

"I, uh, turned off the phone and forgot to turn it back on," I admit then wish I hadn't.

"You what? You were having a problem, and you turned off the phone?" He's now furious. And so am I.

"I don't *need* you to call every single time you think I might be having a *problem*. I am capable of handling things myself. Frankly, the ringing was distracting me and making it more difficult for me to focus!"

"Focus on what?" he asks quietly.

"On . . . on not attacking Marie," I answer in defeat.

His silence seems to be a reprimand, but I can feel it in my blood as well.

"I take it you also did not go to the club as I asked."

The feel of his rebuke literally nauseates me. I fight to block it, along with the regret and conflicting rebellion it's spawning in me. I struggle to answer him.

"Uh, no, I didn't go to the club." His words suddenly hit me. "What do you mean by 'go'? Aren't you there?"

"No, I am here at the house. When you would not answer, I feared the worst."

I remember how the deaths at the club affected him, and know that he is far more attached to Marie.

Crap. My guilt begins to take a stronger hold.

"Ah." He takes a breath. "Well, at least you recognize that you caused unnecessary concern with your disregard of what I had asked. Perhaps next time you will listen to me, as I generally have very good reasons for what I say."

His annoyed parental tone irritates the hell out of me, and I rebel again.

"Well, I'm sorry that I am so . . . difficult. Maybe you need a break from having to manage every little aspect of my life. I'm sure it can be quite exhausting." My guilty feelings evaporate as my temper flares, and I feel his flare back in response.

He stays silent, and I have nothing further to say. But our angers chase each other around, and as they escalate, the beast wakes up and I am now livid.

The phone goes dead, and relief courses through me as our other connection cuts off.

Wow. Guess that's one way to calm down a fight, at least a long-distance one. But I'm still torqued, and the Audi whips between the cars on the pass like they were standing still.

I pull up the driveway, park next to the BMW and, slapping my hat back on, get out. I take a deep breath of the mountain air, and it begins to dissipate the assortment of negative emotions raging throughout my body.

As I stand there breathing and looking at my mountain, I want nothing more than to go tearing up there at a dead run. But I have other things to do and must wait until the sun goes down anyway.

Resigned, but in a much better mood, I go into the house.

I give up and stop scrubbing. There's no way the blood is going to come out, and it looks like I'll have to replace the carpet.

Damn. I wonder how much that's going to cost.

Getting to my feet, I pick up the bucket and walk over to the sink. As I pour out the pink water, I think again about how much my life has changed. I don't know if I should blame that goddamn bear or Nicolas. Hell, I guess it's both, and I better include me in there, too.

I walk around the house with the sponge and the spray cleaner looking for any spots I've missed, then step outside. I already scrubbed the door and doorframe, but I give them another wipe-down just to be sure.

The sun is finally getting lower in the sky, and a thrill runs through me at the thought that I will soon be running on my mountain. With one more glance up the slope, I go back inside to the bedroom.

The bed is ruined. I shake my head and strip off the bloodied covers, and look at the stained mattress in disgust.

Great. More money. I wonder how much the rental company will charge to replace it.

I flip the mattress over for the time being, then gather up the bedding and take it into the living room. As I dump it in front of the fireplace, I try to ignore the elaborate bookshelf that overpowers the room.

Just like its owner, dominating everything. I snort, realizing that even though Nicolas gave it to me as a gift, I still think of it as his.

Grabbing a pair of scissors from the desk drawer, I plop myself on the floor next to the bedding. The fire I'd built earlier is pleasantly dancing in its little space, and flares up in appreciation as I begin to feed it snippets of fabric. I cut out all the bloodstained material and watch as it hits the fire. The dried blood burns in a shimmer of color, and I think about how it burns in my veins when I'm hungry—for either a meal or for Nicolas.

Bad thought. My blood answers it, and I feel both hungers flare up, mimicking the flames in the fireplace.

I shake my head to try and clear it, and get up to look out the window for what must be the ninth time. The sun is definitely low enough on the horizon now—I'll be safe from its direct rays, especially if I stay in the shadows until true dusk. I turn back to the fireplace and quickly shred the remaining bedding, burning anything with blood on it.

I'm not sure why my instincts demand I destroy all traces of my blood—I just know I have to. As for the mattress and the carpeting, I'll need to pick up a sharp knife and a blowtorch.

Gathering what's left of the unstained bedding, I take it outside to the trash bin. I look one more time at the sky, and then skip back inside and head to the bedroom.

I quickly change into dark brown hunting clothes and pull my hair into a pony tail. As I come out of the bedroom and head to the back door, the cell phone rings.

I stop and take a breath and, resigned to hearing a lecture, answer it.

"Yes?" I say, trying to keep a neutral tone.

"Please be careful." His tone is neutral as well. But it holds a hint of concern, verified by what I'm feeling from him.

"I thought you couldn't read minds." It sure seems like he can read mine, and I'm not sure I like it.

"I can sense your anticipation for your hunt, and frankly, it is a bit overwhelming." His amusement weaves through me, and I start to relax, but then I realize how far apart we are.

"You can feel me at this distance without being on the phone?" My suspicion flares, and he can't hide his frustration at it.

"I have been feeling your anticipation all afternoon. You forget last night was not the first blood you have given me. Our sharing of feelings is still quite one-sided." The feel of his frustration gives way to loving warmth, and I'm suddenly at war with myself.

"I need to go, Nicolas. The sun is almost down."

"As I said before, please be careful. And keep in mind that your pain is mine as well." His warmth and caution flash a moment, then both phone and emotional connection go dead.

Nice parting shot. Thanks for the guilt trip.

Growling, I open the door, and with a last check on the dwindling sun, race up the mountain.

~

The bouquet of scents embraces me as I sprint up the trail. The smell of the pines and the earth, mixed with that of the small and large creatures, is heavenly. I drink it in, searching for the specific scents of my prey.

I run all the way up to the top of the mountain, and when I reach it, turn and look across the valley. Pikes Peak stands there, imperious and magnificent in the twilight, its snow-covered sides pink from the setting sun. I can't help but think of Nicolas, his arrogance and his beauty, his cold hidden side and the heat he shows me, and a little of my resolve begins to break down.

The war inside me threatens to cut loose, one side fighting for me and the other for him. I try to shove the conflict away, and fortunately for once the beast jumps to the rescue. As it starts to rampage, I let it go and give in to its rage and frustration. Its roar explodes from my chest, and as it booms across the valley, the mountain and its denizens go silent.

In the fading echoes of my outburst, I hear a distant answering scream from a big cat and smile as I think again of Nicolas.

Yeah, hope you *felt* that, you bastard. You're tearing me apart, and I want you to *feel* every bit of my pain.

With a last glance at the darkening Peak, I work my way across the mountain, angling down toward the meadows where I hope to take out some of my pent-up anger. I keep my nose in the air as I travel, looking for a tendril of scent that will lead me to my quarry, and finally I catch one.

I eagerly follow it, and the hunter in me thrills to be back in action. This is how a real hunter is supposed to hunt, using stealth, power, and violence to take down and subdue its prey. The scent grows stronger, and my thoughts fade away as the instincts take over.

The smell of the sweet grasses in the meadow below floats toward me, and I slow my pace. I approach the clearing warily, and spot a small band of bull elk grazing in it. I watch for a few moments, then carefully circle the area, casting for the scent of any other predators who may have targeted this herd as well.

I finally reach the place on the far side that I'd noted earlier. It will give me good cover from a position above and to the side of the herd, and I study the several animals I've already selected. As I hoped, one of them takes a few steps closer to me, his head down as he nibbles on the short spring grasses. He must be a two-year-old, weighing only four hundred and fifty pounds or so, not much larger than a muley buck and quite a bit smaller than the other elk. I change my strategy.

Muscles coiled like springs, I crouch, watching as he takes another step forward, then another. He raises his head and looks at the herd he has strayed from.

Now.

I launch, grabbing high around his throat as my body slams against his neck and shoulder. My nails sink into his windpipe as he staggers under the force of my impact. I throw myself backward, his throat still in my lethal grip. As my feet touch the ground, I take a step back and yank. Hard. Already off-balance, his front legs rake the air as he topples toward me. I release him and dance back as he crashes into the ground at my feet.

Before he can raise his head to get up, I leap onto his neck, grab his muzzle, and wrench his head to the side. His neck breaks, and my teeth are in his throat before he even stops kicking.

The hot thick fluid pumps into my mouth, and I blissfully swallow several mouthfuls before I realize something is wrong. It tastes . . . *wrong*. I push back and spit out what's left in my mouth, and stand there watching as it pours out uselessly from his throat and onto the ground. My hunger rages in frustration at the sight of the waste.

What the hell? I bend down and dip my fingers into the red stream, bring them up to my face, and smell the blood. It smells okay, but not okay. I taste it, trying to isolate the problem. It tastes weak, and, well, just . . . not . . . right.

I bend down and examine the dead elk, looking for signs of disease. I go over him from head to toe, but can find nothing unusual.

Huh. This is really weird. I remember once taking a sick deer. The blood had a slightly odd taint, but was still palatable and satisfying, and I'd had no trouble draining him dry.

I stand there puzzled, and finally decide I might as well clean up. I have no desire for the red life that is trickling out of the elk's body. I snort in disgust and walk to the pond at the lower end of the meadow to wash.

Shit. Well, I just have to find another one. Maybe I'll try a mule deer, my old standby. I trot back up the slope, feeling remorse at the unnecessary death I inflicted tonight. But it won't be a complete waste. That carcass will feed many mouths for a while.

I work my way up and across the slope for several miles, then turn down and cross back. But I'm not having any luck, and the beast growls in anger.

Finally I catch a whiff and quickly make my way to its source. However, it turns out to be several does with fawns, and I regretfully move on. I absolutely refuse to kill females or babies.

I keep moving, and at last pick up another trace. I follow it, slowing to a near crawl as the scent grows stronger. I stop on the edge of a small clearing and finally spot a mule deer buck bedded down under the trees on the other side.

Quietly maneuvering around the clearing, I come up behind him. I am on him before he can even get up. I pin him and viciously tear out his throat, and bury my face in the hot red flow. As it splashes over me, I realize it tastes foul as well.

Nooo . . .

Screaming in frustration, I give in to the beast. My hands grab the dead buck's head and savagely wrench it from his body, then I stand and fling it across the clearing.

Goddamn it, Nicolas! What have you done to me? What the hell have you done to me?

I take several steps, then sink back to the ground, weeping in fury. The hunger, already flaming, spreads to scorch my veins and starts to rage out of control.

Oh, no, no . . . I don't understand. It's only been two days.

I try to rein it in before it completely takes over, and thankfully begin to have some success. As calm slowly descends, I take a shuddering breath in gratitude. Peaceful tranquility continues to warmly work through me, and suddenly I recognize it.

Nicolas. He is here, or at least very near.

The bloodtears begin to flow again, partially in relief, and partially in resignation.

Damn you, Nicolas. I'm sorry I ever met you. And I can't imagine living without you.

I get up and start traveling back in the direction of the house.

The Ferrari is parked at an angle behind the Audi and the BMW. Making sure I can't leave.

I take a deep breath and walk into the house.

Nicolas is sitting in the living room, and his eyebrows raise as he takes in my appearance. I clench my jaw and storm into the bathroom, then slam and lock the door, hoping he gets the hint.

I look in the mirror and a sick laugh escapes my bloody lips. I truly look like something out of a horror movie. My face is smeared with blood and darker trails run down from my eyes. My hair and clothes are covered and sticky with it, and my hands and arms look like I'm wearing red evening gloves.

Awesome. Hope you liked it, Nicolas.

I realize the calmness he shared with me has faded, along with everything else he was feeling. Interesting. Apparently he can shut off the flow. I wonder if I can.

Shedding my ruined clothes, I step into the hot shower. The water runs pink as it courses over me. I start at the top, washing my hair first, then rinse it and grab the body scrubber and some soap and get to work.

While washing, I look for that place inside me I use when hunting, the one of absolute stillness and focus. I let the hunter loose a little, and she helps me find it. I zero in, then practice holding on to it.

A few moments later, Nicolas knocks on the door.

"Sunny, are you all right?" His voice holds a note of concern, but I don't *feel* it. I don't *feel* anything.

"Yes. I'm perfectly fine." I try to hold the stillness, but it slips as I lose concentration. And now I can feel his concern, along with bewilderment.

Interesting.

He stands quietly on the other side of the door. After a moment, I hear him walk away and return to the living room.

I think I'll be practicing that a lot from now on.

Finishing my shower, I get out and towel off. I quickly comb through my wet hair, then open the door and walk to the closet.

His heat runs through me, and I glance back to see him standing at the door, watching. My blood starts to respond, and I tighten my jaw and return to picking out my clothes.

He cranks the heat up. I shudder as the sweet flames of desire race along my veins.

"Nicolas, please stop. I'm really not in the mood right now." I keep myself from turning around, because if I look at him again, I'll be finished.

His breath is suddenly on the back of my neck, and he starts kissing and nipping the side of my throat. I close my eyes as my body surrenders, and he wraps his arms around me and pulls me close.

His warmth wraps around me and through me; and against the last little bit of will that I possess, my body responds with a warmth of its own.

We stand there, bathed in our feelings for each other, and I wonder why I ever considered any other future.

With a last nip at my neck, he pulls back and says, "Get dressed. We need to go."

I nod and quickly put on a pair of black slacks and a red sweater, slip on my boots, and grab my leather jacket. Ducking into the bathroom on the way out, I pick up the pile of bloody clothes and head into the living room.

Nicolas is spreading the logs out in the fireplace, but steps back as I walk up and toss the clothes in. I close the screen as they catch fire and watch for a few moments while they burn. When the flames begin to die down, I look at Nicolas. He nods, and with a glance at the door, indicates it's time to go.

I walk to the back door, open it, and wait while he passes through. As I close and lock it, I wonder how long it'll be before I return. A while, I think.

Turning, I look up the slope, and a sadness comes over me at the changes in my life. I'll miss my mountain, and the life of the hunter I've lived for so long. I wonder if I'll ever get to experience it again.

Nicolas moves to my side and his sympathy washes over me. He gathers me in his arms and holds me, and his warm love traces its way through my veins. As it does, mine answers, and I realize a Choice has finally been made.

I'm just not sure I was the one who made it.

CHAPTER 50

We drop the Audi off at the estate and head out again in the Ferrari. I'm surprised when we pull into the parking lot of the club.

"Nicolas, how did you reopen the club so quickly? I thought it would take another day or two."

"It is not open. I made special arrangements," he answers, his tone neutral.

"Oh." The hunger reawakens and begins to burn once again.

I wait impatiently as he gets out and comes around to open my door. With a resigned sigh, I step out and we go into the club, passing straight through Nicolas's office and into the lounge. Nicolas stops at the bar, hands me two glasses, and grabs a couple bottles of bloodwine. Together we walk back to one of the private rooms.

Setting the bottles on the bedside table, he opens one and fills both glasses. He hands me mine, and quickly downs the other. I feel his relief when the bloodwine hits his system and realize that some of my edginess has been his as well.

I follow his example and close my eyes as the sweet nectar traces its way throughout my body, then give him a weak smile along with my empty glass. He refills it, then does the same to his own.

"Drink up. You need to mute your hunger before you feed, or you risk killing your donor. I know how powerful your need has been this evening, and I do not think I will be able to help you control it, as it is affecting me as well."

Oh.

I don't argue. We keep drinking until both bottles are gone, and I'm sitting in the happy glow of the spiced blood.

"I will be right back. You will stay here?" His question is really more like a demand, but I nod my head in agreement anyway.

I wait, enjoying the warm buzz of the bloodwine. The door opens, and Charlene and another girl walk in, followed by Nicolas carrying a small bottle of liqueur and two burgundy glasses.

My hunger, which I thought was safely drugged, slams awake at Charlene's scent. I hold my breath, wrestling to maintain control, and glance at Nicolas, his jaw clenched as he deals with my beast as well.

Charlene's eyes grow wide, but the other girl seems oblivious. Nicolas ushers them over to the couch and has them sit down. He opens the small bottle, fills the glasses, and hands them to the girls.

He walks over to me and takes me in his arms. His calmness seeps into my blood and I welcome it.

"You can do this," he whispers in my ear. "Do not doubt yourself."

He pulls back, holding me by the shoulders, and looks at me. I stare into his dark green eyes and nod. With a kiss to my forehead, he takes my hand and leads me to the couch where the girls are sitting.

"This is Annie. She is fairly new here. I trust you will be gentle with her. Yes?" He looks at me expectantly.

Nodding, I watch the slender blonde as she finishes her drink. She smiles dully, still apparently unaware of the beast raging behind my eyes.

I glance over at Charlene, and so does the beast, and from the look of fear on her face, I can tell *she* sees it. I suddenly feel ashamed, and strengthen my resolve not to harm this girl.

When I sit down next to the girl, she seems unsure of what to do. I frown and look at Nicolas, but he just raises his eyebrows and nods for me to proceed.

"*Annie*. Your sleeve," Charlene says. She rolls her eyes, as though she's a pro at this. Which I guess she is—at least compared to Annie. And me.

"Oh. Yeah." Annie pushes up her sweater. Her arm has scars running along the vein, but only one set of fang marks.

Junkie. I look up at Nicolas, frowning, and glance at Charlene. She shrugs.

Wow. This is a new low. But I'm unable to dwell on this as the girl raises her arm expectantly. The beast growls and the hunger demands I address it now.

I carefully press my nail into her vein and she sharply inhales. I quickly pierce it again, and then raise her arm to my lips. I gently take hold, keeping the beast tightly leashed, and draw in the first mouthful.

She gasps in pleasure, and I nearly do as well. Her blood coats and soothes the fire in my mouth and throat, and as I swallow, the ecstasy begins to move through my system. I pull again, and again, and again. She groans, and I answer it as the rapture builds. I start to lose myself, then fighting to stay aware, pause to regain control.

"Don't stop," she mumbles, and the beast strains against its bonds. I wait a moment longer, then slowly begin again.

I watch her face, and as it starts to go slack, reluctantly withdraw. The beast growls, but doesn't insist. I glance up at Nicolas, and he nods. I gently release her arm and ease her against the back of the couch.

"Is she okay?" I ask in a whisper, brushing her hair back from her face.

"Yes, you did well. That was a good time to stop." Nicolas is sitting on the other side of Charlene, and they are both watching me.

I realize that he didn't feed, and look at him in question. Charlene glances at him and he nods. She gets up and sits on the other side of me.

The beast leaps up in glee, anxious for this blood it has savored before. I clench my jaw and look at Nicolas.

"You need this, Sunny. We both know it. I have other resources and can wait. You should not." His voice is quiet but insistent.

I look at Charlene and she nods. The hunger begins to rage again, in spite of the limp, barely breathing body next to me.

"It's okay. I'm not worried. You won't hurt me," she says, her brown eyes childlike and full of trust.

Is this what you look for, Nicolas; this innocence, this giving over of the self?

Because right now, I am revolted by it, and by the deception used to gain it. This is . . . despicable.

I shift my gaze away from her and stare across the room. I don't want this.

And then Charlene turns her back to me, pulls her hair to one side, and tips her head, exposing her naked throat.

Over the roaring in my head I barely hear Nicolas shout, "Charlene, no!"

The beast leaps up at the same time I do, only I lunge in the opposite direction that it wants to.

I stand facing the corner on the other side of the room, my arms wrapped tightly around myself, and try to blot out Charlene's words.

"But Nicolas, it'll be okay. She's already had some, and she was nice about it. I've heard it really is the most awesome way to do it. Please?"

"Charlene, she is not ready. And you do not know of what you speak." His voice is strained. I feel his anxiety, and none of his calming influence, as he battles my beast inside him.

"But I want to do this. Please?"

"Charlene," I growl. "I have already ripped out two throats tonight, though they were not human. This way is not something I'm capable of with you. I'm telling you that I would not be able to stop, and you would end up like those bodies I left in the forest."

Only . . . you would be drained down to the last drop.

The room is silent, except for the sound of her breathing and the irresistible thump of her heart. Its rhythm increases as my words seem to finally register.

"Nicolas, she needs to leave. Now. Please." My voice is still hoarse as I fight to control the hunger and the beast that threatens to take control of my body.

She offers no further argument. I listen as Nicolas scoops up Annie's semi-conscious form, and he and Charlene leave the room.

I slowly collapse in the corner, shaking with my sobs. Nicolas comes back in, and then he is wrapped around me, whispering reassurances.

"I can't do . . . this, and I can't hunt anymore. What the hell am I going to do?"

"Sshhh. This will work out. It is always difficult in the beginning when one is learning how to maintain control." His voice is quiet and soothing, and I feel his calming influence in my blood as well.

I focus on that feeling, and on his ensuing warmth. I hold tight onto that, and the beast finally succumbs in defeat.

"Nicolas, how many of your Chosen begin their lives with killing? I've been killing with little restraint since the beginning. That is what I do, how I hunt, and how I feed. I don't think it'll be possible to change." The desperation in my voice is answered by his confidence as it flows through my system.

"It *is* possible to change, because I have done so. Only, my prey in the beginning was *not* animals, and the throats I ripped out were uncountable." His remorse sounds old, tired.

But his words sink in and begin to smother my doubts, and finally I nod my acceptance. He stands, pulling me up with him, and turns me to face him. He frowns as he looks at me, takes a handkerchief from his pocket, and starts wiping my face.

The handkerchief is covered in blood when he stops and I grimace at it.

I remember being so disappointed when I had no tears. Now I wish they'd never started. Guess I'm going to have to learn to stop crying altogether.

Stepping around Nicolas, I go into the bathroom to wash up.

It's been quite a while since Nicolas left, and I finally get out of the chair and start pacing for the third time. I really need to learn to pack some reading materials in my bag.

He opens the door, looks at me, and beckons, saying, "Come."

And I do what I always do when he commands me like that.

I follow him out and down the hall to the next room. Nicolas ushers me inside and shuts the door behind us.

The room is dark and filled with the scent of a human male. The hunter perks up in anticipation of a chase, and I smack her down, but the beast is waiting as well, and it is not as easily controlled. Nicolas walks me to the chair in the middle of the room where the man is seated. Despite the lack of light, I can see that he's average looking, older, and a little rough around the edges. The beast growls.

"Who's there? Did you bring her? Can I see her? Is she beautiful?" His voice is thick with lust, and part of me feels disgusted.

But the other part couldn't care less, and the hunter whines to be released, anxious to subdue this prey in the dark.

I glance at Nicolas, and he gestures for me to go ahead. I silently circle the man in the chair while he's still peering forward, trying vainly to see in the inky blackness.

He's wearing a flannel shirt with the sleeves cut off, and is well-built with large biceps. I feel myself start to heat up with a strange combination of hunger and desire.

I step up behind him and quietly crouch down. As I reach out and softly stroke his muscular arm, he gasps. I grab it with both hands and, rotating it toward me, sink my teeth into the inside of his upper arm, and I *pull.*

"Holy mother of God!" he cries out, half in pain, half in pleasure. I swallow, and feel the tangy nectar of his blood go down my throat and into my system. I draw again, and he moans.

"Yes . . . yes."

I pull again, and again, and again, and the beast takes over. I shift my bite slightly and pierce his vein in new places, and then I'm gone, lost in the blood.

He slumps just as Nicolas touches my face, and with a shudder, I reluctantly let go.

There's no movement from the slack figure as I slowly straighten. "He's not dead, is he?" Alarm flickers along the edges of my blood haze.

I hope he isn't, but I feel no remorse over how I treated him. He's not some innocent kid looking for attention and thrills. This is an adult with baser needs, who came here to play adult games. He probably didn't figure that he *was* the game.

"No, just unconscious. There is some leeway between unconsciousness and death."

"And the others? Annie, the couple from the other night? They are okay?"

"Yes. I ensure they do not die."

Relief allows the soft, warm bloodcloud to embrace me once again. The beast is content, the hunger quenched.

Perhaps I just need to choose my new prey more carefully.

I turn to Nicolas and he's just standing there, watching me. He looks . . . magnificent, and I'm thrilled that he's chosen me to be his partner in this life. I reach up and pull his face to mine, and kiss him long and hard. He wraps his arms tightly around me and returns my kiss, and our mutual flames of love and desire ignite deep within my veins.

április 22., vasámap

This morning's incident with Marie could have been a major setback had it turned out differently. But my Sunny's will is strong, and she kept control and did not give in to the bloodlust. I am pleased to see how nicely she is coming along and enjoy watching her as she learns how to manage herself with the humans. I still feel her doubts, but I think today's experience up on the mountain finally proved to her that she is truly a Chosen, and that it is time to embrace her rightful destiny.

This evening showed that she is progressing quickly—more quickly than I expected. Unfortunately I had to resort to using a human I knew she would bear no sympathy toward, but she responded perfectly, and without a trace of her normal regret.

It won't be much longer until she can join me. She is almost ready.

TUESDAY

CHAPTER 51

We walk through the black curtains into the front portion of the club, nodding to the new bouncer as we pass by. The loud music pounds in the rhythm of a heartbeat, and excitement pulses through my veins in perfect time with it.

At the end of the bar, we stop while Nicolas speaks to the bartender. I scan the dance floor and notice the tall blond Chosen I'd seen with Skeeter. He stares at me intently, then curls his lip and smiles. He's dancing with a pretty young brunette and, watching me, he pulls her to him and nuzzles her neck. His eyes redden, and he smiles at me again as he caresses the body of the human, who is now suggestively rubbing against him as she dances.

My blood starts to heat up as I watch them, and then Nicolas is behind me, quietly growling. The blond Chosen's expression quickly shifts to neutral, and he turns his partner and moves farther back into the crowd.

I start to ask who the Chosen is, but think better of it as Nicolas's jealousy flares through me. He reaches up and caresses my neck, as though to remind me of the pleasures he brings me, and it works. I close my eyes as my body responds to his touch, then inhale sharply as his heat hits me. I turn to look at him and feel the amusement that's dancing in his emerald eyes.

He leans in and whispers, "I . . . do not . . . play fair."

No, you sure the hell don't. I smile to myself.

"Do you see anyone on the floor who looks interesting? Besides that Chosen, whom I will kill if I ever catch him looking at you like that again?" His last words take on a lethal tone.

I swallow.

"Um, no, I haven't really looked yet," I stammer.

"I noticed," he says quietly, all humor gone.

Mine is suddenly gone as well, replaced with a flicker of irritation and rebellion.

He laughs and tousles my hair.

Bastard.

"Come, shall we see if we can find you someone . . . suitable? You are always so prickly when you are hungry." He leans in and kisses the top of my head, grabs my hand, and walks toward the dance floor.

I resist momentarily, and he stops, looks back, and gives me that amused smile he knows gets me every time. This time is no different.

Smiling, I shake my head and accompany him to the floor.

We stroll through the gyrating humans, who seem to instinctively avoid bumping us. I spot another Chosen, a dark-haired female, dancing with an attractive Latin-type guy. She nods to Nicolas and glances at me, then grabs her partner by the wrist. He grins and eagerly follows as she leads him in the direction of the black curtain. The beast growls, wanting to follow as well, its attention locked on the willing human. I slap it down and focus on the crowded floor.

I watch the various dancers, but this is just not working for me. Nicolas talked with me about what to look for, but all I see are people. People out having a good time with each other, some of them hoping for more, but all of them just people.

I can't see them the way he does. As food.

Nicolas bends to my ear and whispers, "I will return momentarily."

He moves off through the crowd.

Suddenly I'm under attack from my two selves, the one that's thrilled he may have spotted someone, and the one that's terrified he has.

I don't want to do this. There must be another way.

Shaking my head, I walk back to the curtain. The beast growls hungrily as a dancer gets a little too close, and I flinch away from any accidental contact.

"Oh, I'm sorry," says a young, redheaded goth in metal-accented black. Shoving back the dancers jostling him, his eyes grow wide as he looks at me again. "Hey, you're new here, huh?"

The glare I give him is full of warning, but he just smiles. He lifts his arm and strokes the inside of it with his other hand, raising his pierced eyebrows in invitation.

The beast understands perfectly and leaps up with a roar. I swallow and tighten my fists as I work to stay under control.

"Yeah? Come on, I'm ready. Right now." He grins eagerly, his blue eyes bright with excitement.

Without waiting for an answer, he heads for the black curtain. I stand there watching him, struggling to contain the wildness rampaging inside me.

"You should go with him," Nicolas says quietly behind me. "He is quite experienced."

Still I hesitate, trapped between my two natures.

"Waiting another night will not help matters. You know this," he says steadily.

He's right. As he's explained, and I'm finding out, the only way to keep the beast manageable is to feed it frequently.

Looking down, I nod and walk to the curtain. The boy is shuffling and fidgeting, and keeps glancing at the bouncer, who has no intention of letting him pass through the curtain. He looks at me, then back to the bouncer, as though to say, "See? She's coming. You can let me through." But the bouncer ignores him and watches me as I walk up.

I glance at the redhead, then back at the bouncer, and nod once. He moves to one side and pulls back the curtain. The boy steps through, trying to remain nonchalant, but he's practically shivering with expectation. I follow him and the curtain drops down behind me, and I pause a moment for Nicolas. But the draperies remain still.

Guess I'll see him in the lounge.

As I walk past the boy to the door guarding the private area of the club, he says, "So what's your name? Mine's Terry."

But I barely hear him as I contemplate the keypad. Nicolas had given me the code earlier, before we left the house.

This is my first time using it. My first time doing something of my own volition that I swore I'd never do—feed from a human—with no one standing beside me, helping me, encouraging me. Changing me.

With a ripple of unease, I enter the numbers, one at a time. Each feels like another nail in the coffin containing the old me.

The click releasing the lock sounds the final one, and I swallow down my misgivings and open the door.

The boy saunters beside me as we make our way down the hallway. He reaches for my arm, but I just give him a cold stare, though my irritation is more with myself than with him. He stuffs his hands into his pockets, and we walk the rest of the way to the lounge door in silence.

This time I have no hesitation as I quickly punch in the code.

The boy follows me inside, then strolls over to the curtained cubicles. I walk past him to the door for the private rooms, open it and, pausing, look back at him, expecting him to join me.

His feet are unmoving, his body rigid, his shoulders hunched up, and his face pale with terror. The female Chosen and her human partner are talking in low whispers in one of the cubicles, but no one else is here. His obvious fear puzzles me.

I motion him over and his eyes widen further, like a deer trapped in the predator's gaze. The hunter in me springs to the surface, anxious to give chase to this prey that is obviously ready to bolt. I slap her down and walk back to the boy.

"What's wrong?" I ask him. The other Chosen and her partner stop talking.

"I don't want to go back *there*," he says loudly, his voice shaking.

"Okay. Why not?" My curiosity overrides the beast that is impatiently waiting.

"Because . . . because . . ." He swallows.

The female Chosen comes out from her cubicle, walks over to us, and looks at him critically.

"You know the agreement. You've been here long enough to know how it works," she says matter-of-factly.

"But it's supposed to be my choice! I didn't ask to go back there!"

"What agreement? Why don't you want to go back there?" I ask, quite concerned now.

"Because . . . most people who go . . . back there . . . don't come out again," he whispers.

What the hell?

I grit my teeth against the flash of rage.

Damn you, Nicolas, for keeping this from me.

"Well, Terry, I believe there's been a misunderstanding on my part. As you mentioned, I'm new, and not well-acquainted with all of the guidelines here." I glance at the Chosen, then place a hand on Terry's shoulder. He trembles beneath my touch and the beast strains to break loose, but I lock it down.

I look at Terry, keeping my expression as gentle as possible.

"I apologize if I frightened you. I had no intention of . . . harming you, and was only seeking the privacy to which I'm accustomed."

He peers searchingly into my eyes, and a little of his fear seems to subside. I look at the Chosen, and she's staring at me, her expression hard. I don't know what her problem is, but she needs to stay out of this.

I narrow my eyes and curl my lip slightly, and she lowers her head and gives me a slight bow. She turns without another word and goes back into her cubicle. I look again at the frightened boy in front of me.

This is just wrong. I can't do this to someone who's afraid.

Wanting to ease this boy's fears before taking him back up to the front part of the club, I ask, "Would you like a glass of wine? You may sit anywhere you choose."

He nods, turns to the cubicle he's standing next to, and pulls back one curtain, securing it open in a large ornate hook. He looks at me again, goes in, and sits down at one end of the couch.

Taking a deep breath, I go to the bar and grab glasses and an opener, a bottle of wine for the boy, and a bottle of bloodwine for me. I think I'm going to need the whole bottle.

Soft moans start issuing from the other cubicle, and I turn back and grab a second bloodwine.

I set everything on the low table in front of the couch, then hand the bottle opener to Terry and move the wine bottle in front of him. He struggles unsuccessfully to open it. I'm not sure if he's still upset or has little experience with opening wine.

"Here, let me." I take the bottle, finish peeling off the wrapper, open it, and set it back in front of him. I open my own and pour a much-needed glass of bloodwine. Swallowing it down quickly, I feel the beast begin to quiet. I refill my glass and drink a little more slowly, savoring the feeling as it soothes my tissues and veins.

Grabbing the bottle, I move to the other end of the couch and settle into the corner.

Terry seems much calmer now and a little of his swagger returns.

"Thanks. Uh, this is pretty cool." He watches me over the rim of his glass as he takes a sip.

"You're welcome. Again, I'm sorry for upsetting you." I finish my glass and pour another. The beast is restless sitting this close to the boy, and sedation seems my only option right now.

The door to the hallway opens and Nicolas comes in. He stops a moment, watching us. Turning to the bar, he grabs a small bottle of liqueur from the back shelf along with a burgundy wineglass and walks over to our cubicle.

His eyes are pale green, which explains why he wasn't here any sooner. That's odd—I didn't even feel him feed.

"Hello, Nicolas. Terry and I were just having a little talk about the private rooms," I say carefully, watching him.

Nicolas gives me an unreadable look and says nothing.

"He . . . didn't want to go back there. After he explained why, I felt his reluctance was justified and decided that here was just fine. I think *someone* should've mentioned the rules to me earlier." I give Nicolas a steely look and let my anger slip free, watching as he feels it.

Terry finishes his glass and pours another, wisely opting to stay out of our discussion.

"I see," says Nicolas, his tone neutral. But I feel an answering flare of anger from him, and I smile a not-so-nice smile at him.

He sets the liqueur and glass down on the table with a pointed look at the red-haired boy. Terry winces and nods.

"Well. I have phone calls to make. You can find me in my office when you are ready to leave." He purses his lips and looks thoughtfully at me, then turns and leaves the room.

I resist the urge to growl and instead drain my glass. Terry snickers and I turn to see him offering to refill it. The beast quivers at the sight of the deep red liquid streaming from the bottle, but otherwise stays still and watchful.

Terry sets aside his wine and opens the liqueur Nicolas brought, then pours it into the burgundy glass.

He holds it up in my direction.

"Can we start over with a toast to a new friendship?" he asks, smiling.

I frown. Friendship? These people really are delusional about their relationships with us.

But I shrug, not wanting to upset him any further, and hold up my glass. He clinks his to mine, then quickly empties it. I do the same and the warm glow of the spiced blood finally starts taking effect.

He seems to be getting more and more relaxed as we continue to drink. I, unfortunately, am unable to do the same, as his proximity is keeping me on edge. The beast is subdued for the moment, but it's also waiting.

"So you never told me your name," he says as he sips his drink. His eyes are bright with the alcohol, and their previous excitement is returning. The beast sits up and growls.

"You're right," I say, keeping my tone distant. Friendship is not what I want.

"O . . . kay. Well, I just have to tell you, I've never seen anyone, like, get in *his* face before." He gestures with his chin toward the door that Nicolas left through. "I mean, he's polite and treats us good, but truth be told, he scares the shit out of everyone. Including the others like you."

He laughs and takes another couple swallows.

Yeah, well he used to scare me, too. Not so much anymore.

Glancing at the now empty bottle of bloodwine, I reach over to grab the second one.

"You don't need to open that," Terry says quietly.

My body freezes as I focus on containing the beast that's now lunging in anticipation.

"Well, I mean, now that I know you don't want to, you know, kill me, I'm totally down for a little blood action." His hip banter doesn't hide the desperate longing in his voice.

I continue to stare at the bottle. This is so weird. I'm not used to having conversations with my dinner beforehand, let alone having them beg me to feast on their blood.

"No, seriously dude, I mean, miss. I'm pretty much in the mood right now. I mean, if you don't mind me saying so, you're really *hot*, and well, you know, they say I'm *real* unique. Something about my red hair makes me taste kinda special." Out of the corner of my eye, I see him nodding to himself as he shoots me a hopeful look.

Letting go of the bottle, I straighten and look directly at him. The beast is in full rampage right now, and I want Terry to see it. But instead of being frightened, he smiles his cocky grin and pushes up his ragged sleeve.

My vision shifts from pink to red as he gets up and releases the curtain from the hook. He walks back over and kneels on the floor in front of me, holding up his arm.

"C'mon, it'll be good. You'll see," he says in a low voice.

I carefully take his arm, frowning as I concentrate on keeping the beast under some sort of control.

"Is it okay if I touch you?" he asks hopefully.

"No," I say, and pierce his arm with my nails.

The drive home is interesting. Neither of us has spoken since our curt exchange in the lounge. I'm feeling pretty mellow at the moment and don't want to ruin my peaceful state with a fight.

Terry was right. There is something a little different with his blood, a spicy flavor mixed with the typical human sweetness. Maybe that's what gives redheads their feistiness. Fascinating.

We pull up in front of the house and Nicolas turns off the car. I open my door and get out before he does, then head up the steps and inside without waiting for him. I feel a flash of anger from him, but like earlier in the evening, it's faint. The effect of his blood must be wearing off.

I go directly upstairs and am already closing my door when I hear him shut the front door. Then the library door opens and closes, and I breathe a sigh of relief. I really do not want to deal with a confrontation right now.

I'm partly relieved that our blood connection is fading, because it can be overwhelming at times. But I also miss being able to read Nicolas better, and I'm especially missing his warm flashes of affection.

He's probably missing this as well, although he may still be feeling more from me just because he's taken my blood several times over the last week. And as I think about that, I'm not entirely sure that's a good thing. Talk about being able to keep tabs on someone.

It's nearly dawn and the lassitude that typically accompanies the sunrise starts to settle over me. I strip and crawl into bed, still cozy in the afterglow of Terry's blood.

I'm drifting off to sleep when Nicolas comes in.

Opening my eyes, I see him standing there, watching me. I fight back an automatic smile as he walks up to the bed. He kneels on the floor and brushes the hair back from my face.

"Do not be angry with me. I am only trying to make this as easy for you as I can. And that means I may not tell you everything, at least for now." His eyes are full of regret and traces of it echo within me.

My tears threaten to well up, and I swallow, suppressing them the best I can.

"I love you. Please understand." His green eyes search mine for the forgiveness he seeks, and I cannot help but give it. He closes his eyes and whispers, "Thank you."

The sleep is taking me over, but I perk up a little as he stands and takes off his clothes. He pulls back the covers and, slipping in behind me, wraps his body around mine.

I fall asleep with him cradling me and cannot imagine anything more right.

április 24., kedd

She fed on her own tonight, with little assistance from me. Her confidence is growing, and I feel such a strong sense of pride as I watch her blossom. She will truly surpass all of us as she comes fully into her birthright.

I believe I have identified her Maker, but cannot surmise what drove him out of seclusion and why he chose this particular human. And I cannot imagine what might have occurred to have interrupted her Change. Robert and Alina have not been able to find any trace of him, and so I am left with the endless mystery of her.

THURSDAY

CHAPTER 52

I draw another mouthful and feel her lifespark flare like the sun, then wink out.

An explosive rush of fantastic and absolute power ignites in my core and expands outward, gaining strength as it bursts through every cell in my body. My entire being shudders as the energy rolls from me in wave after monstrous wave. I'm staring through a bright white veil and can see everything down to its smallest molecule.

I feel like a true goddess. Undefeatable and unquestionable and immortal.

Draining out the last of her blood, I drop Marie's body on the floor.

And I wake up in horror, my vision red, the beast wreaking havoc inside me, and I feel like I'm about to explode. My mouth aches and my body is burning alive with hunger.

Nicolas bursts through the door in a panic, looking around the room as he strides over to me in the bed.

"Oh my God, Nicolas! What have I done? Did I kill her? What the hell is happening to me?" I rip off the covers and leap to my feet.

He holds out his arms and I gratefully crush myself to him. I can't stop the tears and try in vain to keep them off his shirt.

"Sshh." He strokes my hair, holding me tight while I sob. "It was only a blooddream."

"It was Marie. Her lifespark . . ." And I feel him tense, then forcibly relax. His calmness washes through me, but I'm so agitated it's having little effect, even though we shared blood again last night.

"What's happening to me?" I shakily ask again.

He's quiet a moment, then says, "You are Changing. The blooddreams are common as the Change nears completion."

Changing.

Oh.

I feel like I'm losing everything that is . . . me.

Sitting in the library, I stare out the window at the surrealistic shapes in the garden. I feel a kinship with them, as they have also been twisted and tied to fit Nicolas's image of how they should be.

I thought that I wanted him. I thought that I wanted to share my life with him, enough to make the sacrifices, to be what he needs me to be.

But for each step forward I take physically, I mentally run back two.

I'm nearing the end of this journey, and I don't know if I can finish it.

Living in two worlds has proved impossible. But I'm not sure it's possible for me to live in his, and as mine now seems closed to me, I have nowhere to go.

I can feel Nicolas, his worry, his fear, his attempts to reassure me. But it's not helping. Nothing is, and I haven't been able to speak, in spite of his frantic questioning, since early this morning.

Since I killed Marie in a dream. A dream inside a nightmare I can't seem to wake from.

A dark blue sedan pulls up the driveway and parks in front of the steps. Éva gets out, glances at me through the window, and walks up to the front door. Nicolas greets her in the foyer, his tone low. Their footsteps echo down the hallway toward the back of the house.

The mythical creatures on the other side of the glass beckon me to join them, and I slip outside and down the steps to the garden. Pegasus is magnificent in his flight to the sun, and I walk to him and reach up to his perfect wing. Its green feathers dance in the light where the afternoon rays kiss it. I touch the vines that have been lovingly woven around the wire form, then take hold of one, and pull it loose. I grab another and pull it, and another, and another . . .

"Sunny," Éva says quietly.

"I don't want to be bent and shaped anymore. I don't even recognize myself in the mirror."

I stop pulling the vines and turn to her.

"Look at me, Éva. I'm not even burning. The sun is hitting me and I am not burning."

The bloodtears leak down my face, following the dried tracks of those that went before.

"You are killing him," Éva says, her voice filled with pain.

"And he is killing me," I whisper.

Literally.

She's quiet a moment, then reaches up and touches a loose vine.

"Sunny, as difficult as it is for me to admit it, you and he belong together. I have known Nicolas for nearly all of his existence in this life, and I have never seen him this way—with anyone." Éva's words fade into a whisper. "Not even with me."

Her admission only makes it worse.

"But Éva, will he still love me once I am like you, like him? Because who he fell in love with almost doesn't exist anymore. Will he want me once she's completely gone?" My voice sounds like my insides feel—ragged and torn.

"I cannot answer that," she says quietly.

I close my eyes and think about his soft caresses, the heat he shares with me, the laughter that dances in his eyes and in his smile, and I don't know if I can bear to be apart from him.

Éva continues. "But I *can* tell you that you have changed him as well. I do not know this Nicolas. He is gentler, more tolerant, and more patient. His coldness has been replaced with a warmth I've never seen."

And if I let myself, I can feel that warmth. But I'm able to block it, and block mine, and I'm grateful to the hunter for helping me discover how.

"Sunny, do you understand why the two of you have not bonded yet? Why he has only given you small amounts of his blood?"

She knows this? He told her? Anger twists in my throat that he would share something so intimate with another, even her, and I turn away from her words.

She persists. "It is because he is a Maker, and his blood has unique properties that tie his lineage to him. One of those properties is control."

Control? I look back at Éva.

"Explain what you mean by 'control,'" I say in a low voice.

"Those of his lineage—those who carry his blood—are compelled to follow his wishes. They are physically unable to do anything counter to his purposes or desires. This ensures their allegiance remains strong, and that they are not able to rebel or try to take control of the lineage."

I look at her in disbelief.

"And that is why every third new moon his Elder Council meets with him. That is when we renew the blood ties, assuring him there is no threat of takeover from within."

"He gives you, all of you, his blood?"

"Since he is our Maker, it only takes small amounts to reinforce the ties, as long as it is done regularly. And he takes our blood in exchange, although in larger quantities, as insurance that we remain loyal. He'll know if we're tempted to plot against him."

Holy shit. My thoughts are racing so fast I can't even track them. And now all I want to do is join them and run.

I turn and start to walk away, fighting to keep the rising panic from overwhelming me. I lose my focus and am instantly inundated with Nicolas's feelings of love and anguish. I feel them shift to frustration and regret, then abruptly shut off.

I pause, then keep walking toward the gates.

"Sunny!" Éva calls and I ignore the concern in her voice.

I hear her running, and then she is in front of me. She grabs my shoulders. "Sunny, you did not let me finish! Please listen. This is important."

"Get . . . your . . . hands . . . off me."

She drops them, but continues to stand in front of me.

"You do not understand—"

"I understand he's been manipulating me since the beginning, and now I find out he's even been controlling my feelings!"

"That is not true, and not possible. You are not of his lineage. His blood could not have the same effect on you. He only allowed you small amounts so he could be sure that it did not."

"Move, Éva." I growl and curl my lip for emphasis.

"Do you love him?" She stands her ground.

"Do I love him? Or does he *make* me love him?" The words shudder as they leave my lips, because I know the answer.

He makes me love him by trapping me with his fierce gaze, his amused smile, his comforting arms. He makes me love him every time he looks at me. He makes me love him just by being *him*.

"And when did you know? Wasn't it *before* he gave you his blood?" she demands.

I've loved him since I saw him standing across the street staring at me.

Stepping around Éva, I start walking again toward the gates.

I hear the rental car start up at the house, then roll down the drive, its tires crunching against the concrete as it approaches. The gates open and the car stops beneath the raven crest.

Nicolas gets out, and in a neutral voice asks, "Would you like a ride home or do you prefer to walk?"

Swallowing, I feel myself begin to crumple inside.

I stop, and I can't look at him, and I can't speak.

All I can feel is the overwhelming emptiness inside me, the place he normally occupies, the place he belongs.

His voice is cold.

"We cannot keep doing this. *I* cannot keep doing this. I have done everything I know to show you that you have nothing to fear from me. I have even given you my blood so you could understand the depth of my feelings for you. And you still doubt me, question me, question my love for you.

"I do want you to know I have absolutely no control over you. If I did, it would make my life so much easier." His laugh is sick and despairing. "But I do not *want* to control you. And I do not want you to feel as though you are an . . . unwilling partner . . . in this relationship."

He takes a long breath and continues.

"And so I believe it is best we take some time apart. You need to decide what it is you really want, and if you really want to be . . . with me." His voice cracks. "Because I do not want this if you are not sure. I cannot take it any longer."

I feel like I'm going to die.

"Come back to the house and you can collect your belongings. Éva will drive you home." He takes another breath. I hear him step away from the car and then . . . nothing. I look up and glance wildly around, but he is gone.

Vanished. Just like the first time I saw him.

Oh God. What have I done?

Nicolas . . .

Éva walks up, purses her lips, then says, "Get in the car."

Not knowing what else to do, I nod and sink into the passenger seat as she slips into the driver's. She starts the car and drives it back up to the house. I get out and run up the steps and fling open the door.

He's not here. The emptiness of the house echoes that which is inside me.

Disbelief becomes shock as the reality of what just happened settles in.

I take a breath and head upstairs. In a fog, I pile my clothes and shoes in the middle of the bed. I stuff it all into my suitcase, then walk over to the dressing table to get my makeup bag.

Lying on the table next to my bag is the blue sapphire bracelet that I broke the night of the Council meeting. It has been repaired, but it's different now, changed. Like me.

The tiny diamonds separating the sapphires are gone. The palest blue sapphire is now paired with an emerald of pale green, and followed by a small ruby. Each succeeding pair of stones is a shade darker, and joined to the next by a single one of blood red.

I pick it up and clutch it to my chest, then hear Éva at the door.

"He was going to give that to you on your bonding night."

My insides feel like they're going to collapse from the void that just got even emptier.

I set it back on the table, grab my suitcase and the rest of my stuff, and look up at Éva.

Shaking her head, she leaves the room. I follow her down the stairs to the front door, and she waits as I walk through.

She closes it behind me, and a little more of me dies.

When I finish putting my stuff in the back seat of the car, I turn to look once again at the house. I think about the first time I saw it and all the fears it triggered.

And now I fear I'll never see it again.

I fight to hold back the tears, then get into the car. Éva is already behind the wheel, and she starts it up and we head around and down the driveway.

I watch the leafy creatures as we pass. There's a slight wind and they seem to be waving. But I can't tell if they're congratulating me on my escape, or begging me to stay.

The gates close behind us as we pass through, and I look back at the twin raven crests, proud and unyielding. I close my eyes and clench my jaw, then stare straight ahead, looking back no more.

We pull up the driveway and Éva parks next to the BMW. We haven't spoken since we were in the bedroom, other than me giving her directions. She gets out and looks up the mountain while I unload my stuff from the back seat.

A cell phone rings and Éva pulls it out of her sweater pocket. Glancing at me, she walks slowly down the driveway. I hesitate a moment at the door, then carry my stuff inside.

As I come back out, Éva is standing next to the car.

"Nicolas said that you are welcome at the club, but to let him know what evenings you plan to visit so that he can ensure there's a selection of donors that will be acceptable to you. But please call first so he can make the necessary arrangements."

The additional ramifications of our separation abruptly hit me, along with an instant awareness of sharp hunger.

It's the first thing I've felt in hours.

Éva gives me a sad look, and shaking her head again, gets back into the car. I watch as she turns the car around, then listen as it goes down the driveway. I look up at my mountain in the evening sky, seeking its companionship, but there is nothing there.

Just a bunch of dirt, rocks, and trees.

The hunger starts to burn silently in my veins.

április 26., csütörtök

Agony is the core of my existence now. The place where she belongs, inside, is empty, a flaming black hell, and I deserve every ash it makes of me.

It is all my fault for pushing her too fast, for not acknowledging her insecurities and allowing her to work through them at her own pace.

And so I have driven her away once again, and once again I cannot find her.

PART IV

THE WILD

CHAPTER 53

I pull out the first black sweater in the drawer. It's cashmere, one meant for work, but I don't care. I yank it over my head, slip on my black running shoes, and head out into the darkness. Racing up the trail, I cast about for scent. Any scent. A part of me pities the creatures that are unfortunate enough to cross my path tonight, but the hunter and the beast laugh in delight at the prospect of the chases and the bloody kills.

A rabbit darts out from under a bush and is instantly a steaming ragdoll of fur and ruined flesh. I toss its remains off the trail, wrinkling my nose in disgust at the bitter taste, and keep moving up the mountain.

I reach the top of the tree line and intentionally avoid looking back at the Peak. I need no reminders of *him*, and, unfortunately, I've made too many comparisons between his cold stony form and the arrogant mountaintop.

With a growl, I continue climbing. I reach the crest, and instead of heading across the slope, I race down the backside of the mountain. I've only been over here one other time. Conquering new territory will be a welcome distraction.

I run for what seems like hours, but am unable to outpace the demons that seem to be in my head now. These demons are not the mythical ones, but the emotional ones. Grey regret, black sorrow, white loss, red anger. They all have their own voices as well as colors, and the maelstrom of sight and sound threatens to incapacitate me.

But I refocus on my hunger and embrace its agonizing fire coursing through my system. For once I'm grateful for its presence and gladly give free rein to the beast that accompanies it.

The scent of deer catches the hunter's attention, and I veer my course to follow it. I slow as the scent gets stronger, then see a clearing up ahead through the trees. The moon won't be full for another week, but it's still bright enough to beam down into the clearing. I see the deer and their shadows, and without pause, burst into the middle of the herd.

My nails slash open the throat of one deer as I pass it to grab another around the neck. I pull it back toward the body of the first as it lunges desperately and when I get it close, flip it to the ground and pin it there. I reach over, grab the first one, and bury my face into the hot red river pumping from the gaping wound. The second one is thrashing madly, and as I finish draining the first, I reach over and break its neck, ending its terrified struggles. I quickly drain it as well, then stand and shrug the two carcasses off of me.

The taste of the blood I've just inhaled finally registers, and I nearly throw up. But I clench my jaw and resolve to keep it down.

A chill ripples my skin as I realize the blood has done nothing to blunt my hunger. My veins are still crawling with agonizing fire, and in my stomach, the hunger wars with the nausea.

As I step over the bodies, I glance down and stop. They were both does. I've just broken my cardinal rule against killing females.

Damn you, Nicolas.

No.

Damn me.

Damn my indecision, my unwillingness to change.

Damn my inability to accept what I am.

A killer. A taker of lives. It doesn't matter what they are.

Two-legged or four-legged, none of them want to die. None of them want to be food for another.

And the human part of me peeks out of the black box she crawled into so long ago.

But such is the fate of all who live, she quietly whispers.

The cow in the slaughterhouse, the fish in the stream, the deer in the forest, and yes, the human in the casket.

All needed to consume in order to live. All become food for another.

The best you can do is to minimize the suffering of those whose lives you must end. And be grateful for what they give you.

Do not hate yourself. You are no different than any other creature.

But I have fed from humans. From *people.* And that *does* make me different.

And have you ended their lives? Did they suffer?

No . . .

Then accept what you are, and use your knowledge and strength wisely.

Bullshit.

The beast in me leaps up in rage, and the hunger blazes anew, and the remnant of my human self quickly ducks back into the black box.

I take off running across the mountain again.

I open one eye and squint up at the sun beaming through the leaves. It looks to be about midmorning.

Sure am tired of these erratic sleep patterns. One day I wake up only a few hours after crashing, the next day I sleep until nearly dusk. Too weird.

Stretching on the branch that was my bed, I automatically test the air for whatever might be nearby. I hop down out of the tree and walk to the lake at the bottom of the slope, then slip off my shoes and dive in, clothes and all. I've found this is the easiest way to wash them. I swim halfway across the lake, then turn and head back to shore. Getting out, I strip and lay my ragged and soggy clothes on a flat rock to dry.

I find a neighboring rock and stretch out to do the same. The sun feels good and I marvel again at why I do not burn now. I don't know if it's because I'm closer to finishing the Change, or because of *his* blood. And I immediately cringe away from that thought, from any thought of him.

Jumping up, I run back into the lake, this time swimming all the way across to the other side. I climb out and begin walking along the shore, casting for scent.

I don't know why I bother. I've lost track of how many days, or maybe weeks, I've been out here, and lost track as well of how many deer, elk, and other assorted forest creatures I've killed. I've drained every one of them, and no matter how much blood I take, it never seems to quench the fire of my hunger.

But I keep hoping. I keep hoping I can reprogram my system, to make it forget the human blood it so easily became addicted to. Sometimes, like now, the hunger is just a mild burn. But other times I'm nearly overcome with waves of flaming agony, and I'm reminded of how I felt after the attack by the bear.

I've thought about looking for him. I can take that one-eyed brute now. I'm not *weak* from the hunger, just unsatisfied. But I am far from home, and not quite ready to head back to it. I don't know when or if I ever will be. Part of me is afraid of whom I might find there, and the other part is afraid I won't find anyone at all.

God. Not again.

I run and dive back into the lake, embracing the freezing water as my body slips through it. I welcome the numbness it brings to my head and my thoughts, and swim ever downward into its black depths.

The mountain lion snarls and hisses at me, and I drop the deer and snarl back. I crouch, arms spread and nails ready, and growl again. I can see he's calculating whether or not he can take me, or at least my deer. I stand a little taller and let the beast roar at him. He cringes and hisses, then turns and runs.

Smart cat. I pick up the deer, finish draining it, and drop its lifeless body.

I laugh. You should've had more patience, cat. You can have it now.

Testing the air for the direction of the pond I passed earlier, I head back to it to clean up. I walk out to a rock on the shoreline and bend down to rinse off the stag's blood.

I figure I'm only a day or so from home and am looking forward to a hot shower. And some clothes that aren't falling apart.

Then I'm going to pack up the car and head west to the Rockies. Think I'll try some mountain goat, maybe some moose.

But first I have a score to settle. I've been looking for his scent for two days now, and won't leave this mountain until I find it. I've already started laying bait by leaving carcasses next to well-traveled trails, which is why the cat and I had a little face-off.

It's getting close to dawn and I start looking for a suitable tree to bed down in. Spotting a high branch, I scramble up the trunk of a big pine. As I stretch out on the limb, I think about my bed, and how good it will feel, and fade away into sleep.

It must be late afternoon, I decide, opening first one eye then the other. Stretching, I shift slightly and have to grip the branch as I slip a little. I have no idea why I don't fall off while asleep. Just another mystery I'll never figure out.

Clambering part way down the trunk, I drop the last twenty feet and land lightly on my feet. I stretch again, glance up the mountain, and start climbing.

I reach the top just before dusk. As I take the last few steps, Pikes Peak looms into view, as do the memories I've been suppressing since returning to the wild. Pain and emptiness whisper in my belly, threatening to grab hold, and I take off running down and across the slope. I hit the tree line and the Peak disappears from view behind the tall pines. I stop a moment and close my eyes, my breath shuddering, and focus on the hunter's coldness, then continue through the trees.

It does feel good to be on my mountain again. Crossing the familiar trails, I follow one as it angles west. I'm so focused on searching for tracks and other animal sign that I almost blow right past it, but a particular tree catches my eye, and I come to a dead stop.

This is the clearing where I fought the bear.

Glancing on the ground, I spot a couple of sun-bleached ribs, all that is left of the deer I nearly died for. I look around me, but there's nothing unusual about this particular clearing.

Except that this is where my life was forever altered, forever torn open, just as my body was. My body healed, became whole again. I fear my life never will.

With a growl, I taste the air, seeking him, but it holds nothing of interest. I resign myself to methodically crisscrossing the mountain, hoping to stumble across his scent, and start working my way across the slope.

I've been hunting for sign of the bear most of the night with no luck. My constant hunger sharpens as the scent of deer drifts through the forest, and I veer off to follow it. But as I track it, the smell of blood permeates the air and I leap forward to its source.

I stop at the edge of a meadow, and down near the pond, a bear is feeding on a freshly killed fawn as its mother watches in terror from the safety of the forest. When he looks up, he has only one eye.

Everything in me freezes.

He's bigger than the last time I saw him, more filled out. Must be getting his weight back after hibernation.

I watch as he feeds, noting his proximity to the trees. Fading back, I slowly creep around the meadow, hoping a breeze doesn't pop up and carry my scent to him.

Now I'm about thirty feet from him and the beast is yowling in excitement. I give it full rein, take a quiet breath, then explode from the trees, leaping, and leaping again. The bear whips around at my first impact and rushes open-mouthed toward me. My second leap carries me over his back and I land behind him. Before he can turn, I slash his rear legs with my nails, trying to hamstring him. But his fur is too thick to get deep enough, and he spins, howling with rage. I am already in the air and land back toward the trees. He charges and I dart into the forest.

Roaring, he crashes through the underbrush and downed limbs as I spring up the trunk of a medium-sized fir. He loses me for a moment, his vision handicapped by the loss of his eye from our first encounter.

I drop down onto his back, and he tries to shake me off, then throws himself upward to stand on his hind legs. My hand slides beneath his throat, and I grip tight and squeeze, penetrating the thick hide. He slings his head around and slams backward into a tree, and I vault off just in time to avoid being crushed. Leaping into a gap between the tree trunks, I pause and growl, taunting him.

He drops to all fours with a snarl and charges, and as he nears, I step behind a tree and come up behind him. I slash at his hindquarters and he roars as he turns. I hop backward, and he rears up and lunges forward. I dive under his front claws and hit his midsection, hard. His breath goes out in a whoosh, and as I flip away, I drag my nails through the soft skin and fur of his belly, and draw the first real serious blood. The beast in me gets frantic at the sight and smell, and I fight to maintain my head as I regain my feet and leap away.

The bear doubles over briefly, then straightens and blindly charges in my direction. I dance easily out of range, noting the trail of blood he's leaving. Spotting a large pine, I stay just out of his reach as I work toward it. The last twenty feet, I turn and run, and can hear him running behind me.

I launch myself up the trunk and start scrambling upward. He is right on my tail. I keep going, staying just ahead of him, and listen to his breath grow shorter as he tires. About fifty feet up he stops, and I reach down and slash his face. With a roar he climbs up higher, trailing me by only a few feet. But he's worn out, and he stops again. The tree trunk below him is coated in blood, and he's weakening by the second.

Starting to slip, he tries to climb back down. But he's too tired and has lost a lot of blood. He stops, apparently focusing on just hanging on. I feel a little sorry for him, as this has not been as quick or noble a death as I would've wished.

I reach down and slash at him again. As he tries to swipe back at me, he slips, then loses his grip entirely. He slides downward a few feet, then topples backward and falls, seemingly forever, before finally crashing onto the rocky ground. The forest shudders with his impact, and he doesn't move.

I scramble down the trunk and leap to the forest floor, then cautiously walk up to him. But he is unmoving, still. I watch his blood begin to pool beneath him.

You son of bitch. You owe me this for the way you helped destroy my life.

And I reach down, yank his head back, and open up his throat. I kneel down and bury my face in it, and drink until I can drink no more.

A warm haze washes through me, and for the first time in weeks, the hunger quiets, the fire in my veins goes out, and the beast is satisfied.

FRIDAY

CHAPTER 54

It's near dawn, and I'm coming down the trail above my house. As I exit the trees, I stop.

His Jag is parked next to the BMW.

Oh God.

The wild part of me wants to turn around and run back up the mountain. Instead, my body slowly sinks to the ground. The emotions I buried in the wilderness claw their way to the surface, and I'm helpless as they rip my chest apart. The tears start and I know they will never stop. I will lie here and cry out my lifeblood until I'm nothing more than a dry husk and the wind carries away my paper-like flesh.

As the rising sun puts me to sleep, I feel him gather me into his arms and pick me up. He starts walking, and my body softly rocks as he moves down the hill.

He shifts me into one arm and I hear the familiar sound of the back door opening. The forest noises dim as we move inside, then he gently sets me down. He tugs off the rags that were once my clothing, and brushes my tangled and matted hair back from my face.

"Sunny. Open your eyes." His warm and gentle voice caresses my very soul.

I can't, because I am asleep. This must be a dream, and if I open them, he won't be here.

"Are you injured anywhere?" he asks.

I can't talk in my dreams. I try to shake my head no.

The sound of the shower startles me. Cradling me like a child, he lifts me up and steps in. The warm water is soothing as he shifts my body, his hand running over my skin and through my hair. I crack open an eye and watch the water-borne dirt and bear blood flow down the drain.

He finishes washing me, and then stands there, holding me in the comforting spray. I drift back off to sleep, or maybe I'm dreaming that I drift off to sleep. A pleasant coarseness strokes away the moisture on my skin, then I fade again to the sound of his quiet footfalls as my body sways in his arms. I hear rustling, like the brush of leaves against one another, and he releases me to float on clouds. My body sinks deeper into their cushiony surface and I sink deeper into sleep, and as I lose the last of my awareness, I hear my dream say, "I love you."

The first thing I become conscious of is that whatever I'm lying on is not hard. I cautiously reach out, expecting to feel air, but instead touch softness and fabric.

I open my eyes and lift my head to look around. A bed, my bed. Not a tree branch.

Or maybe it is still a dream, I realize, as I turn and see Nicolas stretched out next to me, leaning on his elbow with his head propped up on his hand.

"Good morning," he says, his voice low, musical, his emerald eyes shining.

As before, words stick in my throat, unable to escape. So this must be a dream after all.

He reaches out and brushes back the hair from my face, then softly strokes my lips.

But that felt pretty real.

He shifts, then leans over and kisses me on the mouth.

Oh, this is definitely real.

And I feel my body respond, and then he crushes me to him. He holds me tight for a long moment, then slowly releases me and leans back. He reaches out again and starts working the tangles from my hair with his fingers.

"I was unable to comb all of these out earlier, as you were sleeping on this side."

"You carried me off the mountain," I croak, my voice finally breaking free.

"I did," he says quietly as he continues to pick at my hair.

"You are here."

"I am."

"How long have you been here?"

"Since the night you left. A month ago." The raw pain in his voice is unmistakable.

"A month? I've been gone a month?"

It's all a blur of mountains and forests, lakes and meadows, blood and more blood.

He purses his lips, but does not answer. His face, his green eyes, fade away as the wilderness sings in my soul, calling me, seducing me with its untamed melody.

He touches my cheek, jarring me back to the present.

"You waited here," I whisper. "All that time. For me."

"Yes. I could do . . . nothing else." Again I hear the pain, accompanied by loneliness, and wonder how he survived.

Because the only way I did was to give myself to the blood and to the wild.

Once more it calls, and I shut my eyes and remember the colors and smells that caressed my senses, and the wind that softly brushed my skin. Life is so simple out there. Hunt and run and swim and sleep. No complicated emotions to manage, no one to argue with, or be disappointed in, or be embraced by, or be loved by.

My eyes grow damp as tears begin to well up beneath their closed lids.

"Sunny." His voice is calm and soothing. Feather-light fingers again touch my face.

Startled, my eyes fly open. Yes, he is still here. This is not a dream.

But my body needs to move, to stretch, to run. It's not used to being so still for so long. Slipping out of the bed, I back across the room, watching him. He gets up as well, and part of me starts to panic. I turn to the closet, take out a pair of jeans and a sweater, and slip them on.

"I need to go," I whisper to the floor on my way out.

"Will you come back?" he asks, his voice strained.

"I don't know. Maybe." I take a long, slow breath. "Yes. I just need . . . a little more time."

The back door is before me. As I open it, I hear him behind me.

"I'll be here," he says.

I step outside and breathe in deeply, inhaling the pine and other scents that make up the forest, and take off up the mountain at a dead run.

It's nearly dark when I walk down the trail to the back door. I take a last breath, then open it and walk in.

He's watching me from the chair by the fireplace, its low flame casting shadows over his face. Closing the book in his lap, he sets it on the table as I walk over and take the other chair.

"I have questions that need answering." My voice is hoarse from lack of practice.

"I will answer them." His voice is steady.

"Do you kill people?"

"On occasion."

"Do you care anything about any of them? Marie? Charlene?"

"Some. The ones I have become . . . acquainted with. I will protect them from any harm."

"Is that because you care or because they belong to you?"

He is silent.

"And how do you keep all these people from revealing what you are?"

"The same way I manage my lineage."

"With your blood." I get up and start pacing the room.

"For humans, only small amounts are necessary, and it can be from any Chosen."

"So if you can control your lineage and your . . . humans with your blood, why should I think that you don't control *me* with it." Fighting to stay calm, I turn and stare at him.

"Because the control always belongs to the dominant Chosen, which is what I am to my lineage. You are *not* of my lineage, and you have little human left in you. Your Maker was a very powerful Old One, and he somehow passed a great deal of that power on to you.

"In many ways, you and I are evenly matched. I discovered this when I took your blood the first time. You had a rather significant influence over me, and I was not prepared for that."

I turn to hide my involuntary smile as I think about the times I drove him crazy with my longing for him.

"It was only when we took equal amounts of each other's blood that some sort of balance was reached," he continues.

And it felt so *right*.

"In Chosen society, the most successful matches are between equals. If one is more dominant than the other, it is difficult for the pair to find any kind of true harmony."

"So you gave me your blood to see if I was a suitable mate." I turn back to him, frowning.

"I gave you my blood because I love you, because I wanted you to *know* it, and because the sharing of blood is a consummation of that love."

My throat tightens as wisps of emotion threaten to escape their tomb. I focus on the hunter's stillness, trying to snuff them out.

But then another thought occurs to me and coldness returns. I watch him carefully and ask my next question.

"Éva said you take the Elders' blood so you can monitor them. Is that why you took mine?"

A look of embarrassment crosses his face.

"Ah, no. That happened because I was going insane from wanting you, and I, ah . . . lost control. Several times."

Oh.

My resolve crumbles and heat starts flickering though my veins.

"And it is with great restraint that I am still in this chair, watching you, the way you prowl, with that wild look in your eyes." His darken, then blaze into smoldering crimson.

My vision turns pinks as my blood ignites into sweet flames.

He tenses, but does not move from the chair.

A growl rumbles from my chest as the beast, accustomed to being in charge, takes over. I leap at him and he meets me halfway, and we collide with a force that knocks us to the floor. I tear wildly at his clothes, ripping fabric and skin, and feel his nails rake my body in answer. Slicing the front of his shirt open, I sink my teeth into the hard muscle of his chest.

He groans, and then he shrugs me off and stands, pulling me up with him. I slash at him again, and he catches my arm, then grabs the other. He shifts them to one hand and pulls my face to his and kisses me savagely, his fangs tearing my lips. I bite down on his mouth, and he growls, then ducks and picks me up, throwing me over his shoulder. He hisses as I claw his back, and I gasp as he sinks his fangs into my thigh. He carries me to the bedroom, turns, and dumps me on the bed.

And then he is on me, grabbing and nipping as I tear at him. He takes hold of my hair, then bends over my face and exposes his throat. I bite down hard, and his blood starts to flow, and I draw it out in strong pulls. His fiery essence explodes through me, filling me with his love and his passion and his yearning. I feel his fangs pierce my shoulder, then he draws me into him, mouthful after mouthful, matching my tempo.

Our rhythm sends us further into ecstasy, and we slowly drown in the euphoria of sharing blood. I feel *him* inside me, running through my veins and bathing every cell. Completing me. As his lifeblood spreads throughout my body, I slip into the oblivion of total and unending rapture.

május 25., péntek

She has come back to me. There are no words for what I felt when I carried her off the mountain, safe once again in my arms.

She is completely wild, and this time I will not try to tame her. I will let her run free, and will stay by her side no matter where she chooses to run.

Tonight we shared blood, truly shared. But I stopped us short of bonding, because it should be planned and something special that we look forward to. I want us to knowingly embrace each precious moment of that experience. And I want her to be ready, with no doubts, and so I must wait a little longer.

SATURDAY

CHAPTER 55

I wake to find him watching me, his face inches from mine. His eyes are paler green than I've ever seen, and there is a thrumming deep in his chest, almost like a purr. I have never known such contentment, and my breath catches as a wave of his love washes through me. It triggers an answer in my blood, and as he feels it, the thrumming gets stronger, and I feel myself humming in response. I close my eyes and revel in the shared vibration of our bodies.

He pulls me to him, and our love is gentle now. I fade away and become part of the *we*, slipping outside of reality itself.

I feel his fingers tracing paths around my face, and my eyes open as awareness of the outer physical world takes hold.

His emerald eyes are shining as he gazes at me. I reach out to touch his cheek and he kisses my hand, his eyes never leaving mine.

"Thank you for coming back," he says in a soft voice. "I was not sure you would."

I wasn't either.

"The pull on you of that world up the mountain is strong."

I nod as memories of pine-scented breezes and the music of the forest spring up. The hunter rouses, alert and restless.

And I can see in his eyes that he feels her as well.

He sits up and gets out of the bed, then reaches his hand out. I take it and join him on the floor.

Brushing my hair back from my face, he asks, "Would you like to go for a run?"

I nod again as anticipation ripples through me, and he smiles.

"Then get dressed," he says. "You can show me where you like to go."

Elated, I head to the closet and paw through it. I finally pull out a pair of jeans and step into them, trying to ignore the weight of his stare behind me. I stop as my blood begins reacting to the heat in his.

"You're supposed to be getting dressed, too," I manage to choke out.

"I enjoy watching you."

My voice is muffled as I slip a black tank over my head.

"Well, you better hurry. I'm not waiting . . ." I look up to see him standing by his suitcase, fully dressed in a pair of black jeans and a dark green sweater.

"How the hell do you *do* that?" I ask, amazed as always at how fast he can move.

Rolling my eyes at his smug smile, I shake my head and walk toward the door. He reaches out and grabs my arm as I pass, drawing me to him. I don't bother resisting.

"It appears *I* am waiting for you," he breathes into my hair as his heat hits me again.

"What?" My blood smolders and I shove away from him.

He smirks and glances at my bare feet. "Your shoes?"

"Don't need them. Are you ready?" I don't wait for his answer as I head for the back door.

It's evening and the hunter is impatient. I step outside, filling my lungs with the fresh mountain air, and let her take the lead as usual. With a last glance at Nicolas, I spring across the driveway and set out at a fast clip up the trail.

It feels good to be back outdoors, and I start to lose myself to the wild as I run. His footfalls are close behind, and I increase my speed as we charge up the mountain. Veering off the trail, I leap over brush and downed limbs, and use the scattered boulders for springboards as I weave up the slope. I feel satisfaction at the sound of him pacing me, and sense his thrill as he runs. He catches up, and then we are running parallel, darting and ducking through the forest. I look over at him and grin, exhilarated at our high-speed dance up the mountain, and feel his enthusiasm in response.

We burst through the edge of the tree line and I keep going, Nicolas beside me. I get partway up the bare rocky slope, stop, and turn around.

The Peak is standing tall and noble in the evening sky, and I look over at Nicolas as he gazes at it. I am once again struck by their similarities and feel a rush of pride and love as I watch him. He looks at me and his warmth echoes throughout my body.

He walks over and strokes my hair, then leans down and kisses me. As I respond, he grabs me around the waist and pulls me close. Our veins mutually ignite, and he begins to kiss me harder. I feel his fangs slowly descend, and nipping him on the lip, I break away and sprint up the slope.

He is instantly on my heels, and now our chase has a new element of excitement to it. I reach the crest of the mountain and launch myself over the edge, landing halfway down the rocky slope, then jump again. He is right behind me and I make several more leaps, alighting each time in a spray of gravel and dust.

I hit the forest edge, hurtling over limbs and rocks. His hand brushes my shoulder, and I duck away and scramble up a large pine. I laugh at the feel of his surprise, and as I reach the first large limb, walk out toward its end, then dive for the ground. Twisting to land on a rock some distance away, I push off and leap again.

I feel his amazement and realize that he's stopped. I pivot and tilt my head, then snarl at him and continue down the slope. Slowing a little, I allow him to catch up, then take off through the forest.

Breaking out of the trees, I head for the small lake at the bottom of the slope. I shrug off my tank as I run, then stop and watch for him. I'm stepping out of my jeans as Nicolas bursts through the trees, and laughing, I sprint for the water. As I reach the rocks at its edge, I launch into a low dive, knifing through the cold surface far from shore. I angle downward, pulling through the water, exalting in its chilly caress. Farther and farther I swim, then pop up to the surface. I fling my dripping hair back and allow the beast to let loose a roar that echoes across the lake.

Nicolas is standing on the shoreline watching, his admiration flooding through me. I close my eyes and focus on wanting him, here, now, and open them to see him stripping. I crank up the heat, and he catapults from the beach, slicing into the water halfway from the rocky shore.

I radiate my warmth and can feel his getting nearer. I wait, my blood thrilling, and he slides up the front of me and explodes through the surface. Before I can swim away, he grabs me, wrapping his body around mine. We sink, and so do his fangs, right above my breast. I catch his upper arm and bury my teeth in it.

The twin sensations of each other's hot blood threading through our veins is a delicious contrast to the icy cold water slipping past our skins as we fall to the bottom.

Bellies down, we lie next to each other on a flat boulder at the edge of the lake. The three-quarter moon reflects across the water, its light dancing on the restless surface. The breezes weave through the pines and the trees sing their songs for all who care to listen.

Nicolas reaches over and strokes my hair.

"You killed your bear."

I look at him with raised eyebrows.

"I recognized the smell of his blood on you."

Oh. Guess he would. It's not the first time he's found me covered in it. But at least it wasn't mixed with mine this time.

"As I watched you in the forest today, I realized you are more than capable of handling anything out here."

I feel his admiration again and respond with warm gratitude at his acknowledgment.

"Can I ask how you did it? How you killed him?" The curiosity shining in his eyes floats through me.

"I, uh . . ." I pause, trying to gather the words. Thinking and speaking still seems difficult, especially when I am out here in the wild, the wild that is trying to lure me to stay.

I take a breath and begin again.

"I made him angry and he got reckless. He was bleeding—a lot—when I finally led him up a tree. He climbed until he was tired and weak from loss of blood. I kept egging him on, and he kept climbing until he couldn't hang on any longer. He fell."

"And was your vengeance satisfying?"

"Yes. And no. His blood was the first that quieted my hunger." I pause, remembering. "But I didn't feel good about his death, or at least how he died. I realized he was just a dumb creature acting purely out of instinct, and I had so many advantages over him that he had little chance."

"Do not downplay his abilities. He almost killed you the first time you met." The anguish in his voice that is there every time we talk about it is now matched by that in his blood, and I shudder.

But the bear is no more. It's time to put all that behind us.

"How . . . how did you know I was up on the trail when you found me?" Hazy memories of drowning in sleep and tears thankfully dim the echoes of my chaotic emotions.

The combination of his agony and relief is *not* muted, though, and I quiver inside with its rawness as he answers.

"I felt you up there. I have been feeling you for the last two days."

My God. How we've both suffered.

I reach out and take his hand. His fingers stroke mine as we stare out across the moonlit water. He sends a warm serenity through me, and squeezing his hand in appreciation, I continue.

"I don't understand how you could've felt me. You said I was gone a month. I thought the effects of the blood didn't last that long."

He reaches over and softly brushes the tip of my nose with his finger.

"You forget I felt you the first time you came into my city. Your energy signature is quite unique and very strong. And it is even stronger now than it was then."

That was nearly two months ago. I think about everything that's happened since that day, since I first saw him. How every time things between us seem perfect, something tears us apart.

I roll away onto my side and lean on my elbow, frowning as my mood darkens again.

"You said we needed time away from each other. Why'd you change your mind so soon?"

The same evening I left, as I recall from my dream that wasn't a dream.

His expression shifts to neutral, but he can't hide the pain and regret in his blood.

"You . . . have quite an ally in Éva. She reminded me how volatile the emotions are when one is Changing, and threatened to tear off my head if I did not regain my senses and go to you."

My eyebrows arch in surprise.

Éva. Huh.

"But her words mattered little. Because I realized after you were gone that I would rather have you driving me insane than live with the emptiness you left inside me." His voice catches and his despair explodes through my veins.

I close my eyes and lie back down on my stomach as I fight to suppress my own memories of hollowness and loss.

His fingers trace the scars across my back as his warmth and reassurance drift through me, forcing away our mutual pain. I mirror his feelings, and we lie there on the rock, bathing in the moonlight and each other.

After a while, I remember something else I've wanted to ask him.

"You were at my house the whole time?"

"Yes."

"Didn't you go home to get clothes, and, well, to feed?"

His mouth quirks and he shakes his head.

"No. After a few days, Éva packed my suitcase and brought it to me. She was concerned that I would continue to wear the same clothes until they were rags. Not unlike someone else I know." His eyes glint in amusement.

I smile. I'd gone far enough wild to give them up completely if I'd stayed out here much longer.

But then I frown as I think about the second part of my question.

"What did you live on?"

"I hunted."

"Animals? Deer?"

"And the occasional elk."

I roll back onto my side and look at him in surprise, then laugh.

"I wondered why there was such a scarcity of game as I got closer to home."

He grimaces.

"And how *was* that?" I ask with a smirk.

"A bit disgusting at first, and never satisfying. But it kept me from starving. I became somewhat used to it."

"Yeah. I had a similar experience. But the last week or so the hunger did seem to ease a bit after feeding. I think with more time I might be able to adjust back to my regular diet."

He opens his mouth to respond, then closes it in a silence that is matched by my own.

Oh Nicolas. You don't need to say it. I feel your revulsion, and it's doubtful you could ever adjust. You've been on your diet for far too long. You will never change. And I accept that.

I gaze out over the water, and then remember the one thing that did relieve my hunger.

"Except for the bear. That came close to quenching the hunger entirely, and killed the fire in my veins. I felt quite satisfied after taking him."

"Perhaps that was because you had tasted his blood before, and the hunger always wants to finish what it started. Or possibly because he was a predator, not unlike humans."

Hmm.

"But I do not like the idea of you adding bear to your menu. I would ask you to promise not to, but I see how well you kept your last promise regarding bears." His wry smile fades.

Defiance flashes through me and the hunter tenses in rebellion. I grab on to her stillness and feel his surprise, then nothing as I block out all emotion, both his and mine.

I sit up and glare at him.

"I am not the same as I was then."

"No. You are not." He frowns, then regards me thoughtfully.

And then I ask him the question that has been eating at me since the beginning.

"So how do you like *this* me? The one with the mountains and the forest in her blood?"

The one that learned how to live without you.

"Or do you prefer the one that walks beside you, feeds beside you, when we are in your world?"

The one that could not say no to you.

He purses his lips and takes a deep breath.

"I prefer the one who doesn't shut me out, no matter where she is or what she feeds on."

There is sorrow and pain in his voice, and I relent and let him back in. The rush of his twisting emotions sickens me.

He tightens his jaw and says, "Please . . . do not do that. It is an agonizing punishment, and one that should not be used lightly. Do you not remember the day you left?"

I remember when he shut me off, and the hole that opened up in me that day, nearly swallowing me into complete blackness.

"Yes," I whisper, forcing back tears.

"It is far more powerful now that we are nearly bonded. We came much closer to complete exchange last night, and I barely had enough presence of mind to stop us. We need to learn to respect each other, now, before we bond, or the consequences will be devastating to both of us."

"What do you mean? What consequences?"

"Once bonded, any . . . disharmony . . . is extremely painful and can be somewhat incapacitating. And a complete break of the bond can sometimes result in the final death of one or both. This is something I planned to speak with you about before I formally ask you to bond."

Oh.

He leans over and touches my jaw with the back of his hand.

"And I have not yet asked because you have not been ready to consider such a decision. There is still much you need to learn about Chosen life, and it did not seem fair to bring you into it unprepared." His emerald eyes are soft, and a fresh wave of his love courses through my veins.

"I would bond with you this very moment if it were entirely up to me. But it is not, and only you can decide when you are ready. Until then, we should use this time to grow accustomed to each other's feelings. And to learn how to talk with one another when we do not agree."

Part of me feels a little resentful about being lectured, but I know he's right.

Amusement tugs at his lips. "And I will try to offer explanations in a way that does not make you feel like a schoolgirl."

Embarrassment flickers through me at being caught reacting like that schoolgirl. I laugh out loud and climb down off the rock.

"Then I will try not to behave like one."

Walking to the edge of the water, I collect his clothes and toss them to him, then retrieve my own.

I watch him dress as he watches me, feeling the desire rising in both of us again.

This is ridiculous. I finish dressing with my eyes closed. As I pull the tank down and over my hips, I feel a strange combination of heat and humor. I open my eyes and Nicolas is standing just inches in front of me, laughter lighting up his face.

I shove him backward and he pretends to stumble, then leaps forward and tackles me around the knees, and I go down. He is on me faster than I can register, and kisses me hard on the mouth, then just as swiftly, leaps away. As I jump to my feet, he disappears into the forest.

Oh really.

Taking off after him, I spot him through the trees momentarily, but then he is gone. I stop, wary of him circling back behind me, and let the hunter slip free. I use the stillness this time to open my senses to their fullest, and slowly pivot to see if my awareness of him is stronger in one direction than another.

I was right about him trying to come up behind me, as that is where I feel him. Looking around, I spot a large pine and silently move to it, keeping check on his position. I quietly climb up about sixty feet to a good-sized limb, then stretch out on it and wait.

A few minutes later, he appears out of nowhere across the clearing from my tree. I watch as he glances around, puzzled, and then finally looks upward. His eyes trace up the tree trunk and stop as they reach my branch.

"Do you have any idea how much you look like a leopard up there on that limb?" he calls to me.

I snarl for him, then laugh and scoot back to the trunk. I scramble halfway down and jump, landing next to him.

"So . . . do you want to see if you can make me purr?" I say seductively and, laughing, take off for home.

We walk hand in hand down the trail and into the house. It's almost dawn and I'm starting to feel lethargic. Nicolas leads me into the bedroom, strips off my clothes, and lifts me into bed.

"I need to go into the Springs to take care of business. Will you call me when you wake?"

I nod, and he bends over and kisses my forehead. The last thing I see is him standing there watching me, and as I fade away into sleep, I feel his warmth caressing my very core.

május 26., szombat

She is different now. Stronger, more sure of herself, and less willing to succumb to my every wish. And I love her even more for that.

We ran today through her forests and her mountains, and swam in her deep, cold pools. A part of me understands why she is so attracted to that carefree life.

But it is not for me, and I sense that she knows. So now I find myself waiting once again as she makes her decision about which life to lead. I can only hope it is one that includes me.

SUNDAY

CHAPTER 56

I wake, and the first thing I feel is that he is not here, and I am missing him, almost painfully. His answering longing weaves through me, accompanied by his warmth, and I resign myself to waiting for him. I get up and pick up the cell phone, and it rings.

"How can I call you if you call me first?" I ask teasingly.

"You were taking too long. I felt you awaken several moments ago and decided you needed extra motivation to get out of bed," he answers, amusement lacing his voice.

"Maybe I require other motivation, like you being here." I send him a blast of heat.

"I will be momentarily. Is that a suggestion or a promise?" And I feel his heat in answer.

"Too late. You're not here now, and I'm already out of bed," I say mockingly.

"Good. Then get dressed. I have something I want to show you." His voice takes on a mysterious tone.

Oh, not that game again.

"Fine. Do you want fancy? Casual? Blue or white, or maybe pink? Anything else you would like to order? Might as well get it out of your system now, 'cuz you only get one shot at it today."

"Ah . . . I see. Then don't wear anything. That will suit me best."

Crap. Lost that one.

"That's not—" I stop as I hear his car come up the driveway.

I look down at myself and realize I'm wearing exactly what he requested. How is it that he always manages to make me do what he wants?

With a wry smile, I walk over to the closet to at least put on a robe. He's in the bedroom before I can even find it.

Leaning against the doorway, he says, "I am glad I brought one of the convertibles. Your outfit today will surely turn some heads."

I snort and pull out a pair of khakis and a white blouse, then get dressed and do my best to ignore his desire that's beginning to heat up my blood.

Finished dressing, I walk over to him. "I'm ready. Where are we going?"

He smiles and starts picking at the tangles in my unbrushed hair.

"Not running in the forest, so you may want to consider wearing shoes."

I feel embarrassed as I look at my dirty feet and realize what a barbarian I've become.

"Uh, well, then I guess I'm not quite ready. Give me a minute?"

He nods, green eyes laughing, and says, "I'll be waiting in the car."

We roar up the highway, the growl of the yellow Cobra echoing off the mountainsides lining the road. The sun is playing hide and seek with a few pale grey clouds in a sapphire sky. I look back at the Peak, and as usual, it takes my breath away as I notice how it dominates the horizon. We slow down through the village of Woodland Park, then speed up as we head west out of town.

After traveling several miles, Nicolas takes a right onto a dirt road. A-frame mountain homes are nestled here and there in the pines, and we make a series of turns as the road gently climbs past them. A few miles in, we approach the end of the road and pull up to a pair of wrought-iron gates.

Each gate is adorned with a crest of a rampant lion wearing a crown, the lions facing each other in the classic royal pose. Next to the gate is a polished piece of marble engraved in script that reads The Rose & The Lion Castle, accented with the etching of a simple rose.

Nicolas reaches over and presses the button on the electric gate panel. He announces himself and the gate opens less than a moment later. The Cobra purrs up the gravel road as two red foxes scurry across and into the brush.

As we round the curve of the driveway, a European medieval castle comes into view. The upper edges of the grey stone walls are toothed in the style of an ancient fortress. A tower at each end contains windows at several levels. The back and sides of the entire structure are surrounded by an ornate wall in the same grey stone as the rest of the castle. We park in an area off to the side as an older gentleman walks up to the car.

"Mr. Ambrus. It's nice to finally meet you. I'm Richard—Ric—Lyons."

"Hello, Ric. You may call me Nicolas, and this is Sunny." Nicolas nods toward me and gets out. I smile at Ric and wait while Nicolas walks around the car to open my door. He reaches down to help me out as I look up at him, unable to hide my puzzled expression. I have no idea what he's up to, and he's giving me no hints.

"Pleased to meet you." Ric smiles at me, his grey-blue eyes sparkling. "Come, let me show you around before we go inside." He gestures and heads up the path.

Thankfully the beast stays quiet, unaffected by the first human I've seen in over a month.

Ric explains how he and his wife traveled Europe extensively when they were younger. When it came time to build a home, they decided to model it after the castles they had toured and loved so much. He escorts us through natural-style landscaping, pointing out exotic marble and granite boulders tucked between the plants and scattered around the pond.

Ric continues to talk with Nicolas about building the home as we walk around to the front and up a red flagstone stairway. The steps are flanked on each side by a low wall as they lead up to an arched entrance. Sitting atop the walls, embracing the archway, is a pair of grey stone lions nearly five feet tall. They sit with one paw raised, mirroring each other, and their mouths are open as they proclaim their kingship of this magnificent castle.

"Ric, I noticed the name of the castle on the stone outside the gate. What is the story behind The Lion and The Rose name?" I ask.

He laughs, his eyes twinkling.

"My wife loves roses, and I love lions."

So simple. And so sweet. I smile at him in recognition of their partnership.

"Come inside, but please be careful of the cats," he says as he opens the door.

Cats? I glance at Nicolas, but his face is neutral. This should be interesting.

We pass several of them crouching on a cat tree as we come into the entryway. They sit as still as the stone lions outside, eyes wide as they watch us go by.

Ric mutters something about how they're usually much friendlier. I bite back a smile as we follow him through double etched-glass doors into the parlor. Half-listening, my eyes sweep the stunning interior and note the ornate fixtures and furniture, much of it gilt and antique.

Ric proudly explains the history behind the various artwork and furnishings, most of it imported from Europe and several centuries old. From the crown moldings that edge the ceiling and doorways to the burgundy-veined grey marble floor and pillars, this place is a small but perfect replica of the European castles of old. It is truly suited for a king, and I can see why Nicolas wanted to show it to me.

"But," Ric says patiently, "as I explained to you over the phone, our home is no longer for sale. We did have it listed, but decided not to sell and took it off the market."

I look at Nicolas and see the glint of amusement as his surprise is unveiled.

"Do you like it?" he says to me, pointedly ignoring Ric. "It is surrounded by hundreds of miles of forest, most of it federal land and not subject to development."

I love it, and Nicolas would be right at home in its opulence. And I could hunt to my heart's content.

Glancing at Ric, I see worry on his face. Hmm.

"It's pretty far from the Springs," I say guardedly.

All it would take would be one word from me, and Nicolas would pay many times over the original asking price. But I don't want to be responsible for parting Ric from his beloved castle.

"Perhaps we should talk about it." I look at Nicolas and try to project my concern for our host.

Pursing his lips, he gazes at me thoughtfully and says, "All right."

He looks over at Ric. "Thank you very much for showing us your magnificent home, and for your time. Here is my card. Should you ever reconsider selling, please give me a call. Price is not a consideration."

A look of relief crosses Ric's face, and he nods as he takes the card.

I suspect he was afraid Nicolas would name a figure he couldn't turn down. By keeping his offer vague, Nicolas gave him a way out, and Ric seems to have gladly taken it.

"Well, my dear, shall we?" Nicolas extends his elbow and I weave my arm around his.

Ric hastens to the entryway and opens the double doors. We walk through, then wait while he closes them and opens the front door. The cats have not moved and stare stonily at us as we pass by.

As we walk down the steps, I look back at the twin lions guarding the entrance. I glance again at Ric and can still see the lion in him. He must have been quite something in his youth, and I admire the woman who captured his heart.

We bid our goodbyes, get in the Cobra, and head down the driveway. I look back one more time and shake my head regretfully as we go through the lion gates.

"Other than the distance from the Springs, it was perfect," I say, staring straight ahead.

"Yes, it was. It would have been quite suitable as a second home."

"But I couldn't part him from it. His soul is in every stone." The thought almost brings tears to my eyes.

"Yes, it is." Nicolas glances at me and a wave of his warmth floods through me. He reaches over and brushes his fingers against my jaw.

"And that is one of the things I love about you, Sunny. Your concern for others is something I so rarely encounter, and it reminds me of how I once was." His voice carries a trace of sadness, and I wonder about the man he had been.

"But it's still there," I say gently. "I see it with Marie and Alphonse, and even with some of the donors. They are more than just food to you."

He glances at me with a wry smile, tousles my wind-ruffled hair, and turns onto the highway.

CHAPTER 57

Nicolas pulls up the driveway and parks next to the BMW. He gets out, walks around, and opens my door.

I love this gentlemanly stuff.

He takes my outstretched hand to help me out of the car.

Me. The one who can face down mountain lions and kill bears.

Biting back a smile, I walk into the house.

Nicolas heads into the bedroom and the sound of luggage zippers drifts out, signaling the moment I've been dreading. I hug myself and lean against the doorway, watching him walk over to the closet and remove a garment bag hanging at the back.

My throat grows tight as he stops to look at me with regret in his eyes. I can't hide the whirlwind of emotion now spinning through my gut.

"Ah Sunny. I am sorry. I have much neglected business that I must return to. Éva has been trying to manage my affairs here as well as her own in New York, but she could stay no longer and returned home this morning. I must get back to the estate."

"I understand. I'll be fine." I take a deep breath and calm myself, then change the subject.

"Can I ask you a question? What happened with you and Éva? She obviously still cares for you, and you seem to rely on her much more than the others." This has bothered me for a while, both for her sake and mine.

Nicolas lays the garment bag down on the bed and takes a long breath.

"We were once bonded, for a very short time. We were both quite new to this life and did not fully understand the meaning of the bond. The pursuit of power and the temptations that accompany it proved to be more important than maintaining our commitment to each other. Our selfishness quickly drove us apart, and we mutually agreed to break the bond." His voice is grave as traces of his regret flicker in my blood.

"But . . . I thought . . ."

"I spoke from experience when I tried to explain that breaking a bond is extremely painful. It is only because it was what we *both* wanted that we were able to recover and move on. Should either of us have not been willing to break it, that one would have suffered greatly, with death as a possible result. Again, we were young and did not realize the risks of breaking any more than the importance of nurturing the bond." A shadow passes through his gaze and is gone.

"But she still loves you."

"Yes, she does. And I still care for her. But that time in our life was centuries ago, and we have been comfortable in our relationship as it is for a long while now."

I wonder.

Nicolas's eyebrows raise and he laughs.

"You have only seen one Éva, the one who is protective of me. You have not seen the Éva who delights in playing the Game, with both Chosen and human. You are fortunate she likes you, otherwise you would not feel so sympathetic toward her."

I recall the Éva that laid open Katarina's face, and realize the few occasions I was around the Elders, they all deferred to her, almost fearfully.

Huh.

"Now, I really must get back to the Springs." He takes a deep breath. "And that means I have a question for you."

I knew this was coming. I've been considering the answer since my return from the wild.

But he doesn't ask the question and stays silent, waiting.

This will be the third night since I killed the bear, and I've been remarkably free of hunger since then. I felt no reaction to Ric at the castle today, but I'm not sure if it was due to my absorption in his story or Nicolas's calming influence.

Of course, thinking about the hunger wakes it up, and I feel a slight stirring in my belly.

I also can't deny the fact that thoughts of human blood have been stalking me off and on all day.

"Not tonight. Perhaps tomorrow," I answer the unasked question.

He nods, his expression thoughtful.

"Then I will try not to be gone too long. I at least need to get some fresh clothes." He smiles, but again I feel his remorse as we both contemplate the temporary separation.

Nicolas picks up the garment bag, walks around the bed, and grabs the suitcase. I follow him out to the car.

He stands there a moment looking at the two-seater Cobra, then glances at me.

"You are sure?" he asks.

"Yes, I'm sure," I answer, amused at his dilemma. Me or his wardrobe.

"Because I am perfectly willing to leave these here and wear rumpled clothing." He waits, eyebrows raised.

"Go, so you can take care of what you need to do and get back. I will be fine." I laugh.

He sadly smiles as he wedges the suitcase and bag into the passenger seat.

"But *I* may not be fine. Just, please, do me a favor, and do not get angry with me for asking," he says gently.

"What?"

"Please be careful? That is all I ask."

"Yes, I will be." My amusement wilts beneath his concern.

He looks at me for a moment, and his eyes flash red as his heat surges through my veins.

I quickly step back. "No, don't start that. I'll be here waiting for you when you get back." I fold my arms and attempt to look unapproachable.

He laughs, takes a step forward, and says, "Then do not look at me like that. You know I cannot resist a challenge."

"Whatever." I shrug, feigning indifference.

The air sighs as he appears inches from me and plants a kiss on my forehead. Just as quickly, he is sitting back in the car.

"Will you teach me to move like that?" I ask in amazement.

"Maybe." He laughs and the Cobra roars to life. He backs out and around, then waves as he heads down the driveway.

I listen to the thunder of the engine as it hits the highway and fades off into the distance.

Crap. I miss him already. And I feel his longing, as well as his warmth, wane into the distance like the sound of the yellow car.

But not all of it. There is still a little warm spot of him deep in my core, and it's enough to hold me a while.

Because I remember what it felt like when it wasn't there at all.

Hell. A black, empty, lonely hell.

Draining the last of his blood, I drop the buck's carcass, shaking my head in disgust. It just doesn't seem to taste any better, no matter how much time has passed.

I try *not* to think about the club, but the more I try, the more I do.

As much as I hate to admit it, I'm really looking forward to going there tomorrow night.

I was fine while living in the forest, because I just gave myself over to the wild and didn't do a lot of thinking. It helped not being around people and those who feed on them.

But unfortunately, the call of human blood is far stronger than the call of the wild.

Its coppery sweet smell was crisp and appealing in Nicolas when he returned from the Springs this morning. I was aware of it at some level all day today. It was on his breath and on his clothes and in his very pores. It was only because I made the decision earlier to wait that I was able to tell him I wouldn't be going with him tonight. It was more difficult than I thought it would be.

I just wanted to hunt one more time out here as a confirmation. A confirmation that, as much as I might like to pretend we can live in both worlds, we both know we can't. I can live wholly in one, or wholly in the other.

And I do not want that place in the center of my being to be empty anymore.

I run the mountain one last time, crisscrossing its slopes before finally climbing to the top. I turn and stare at the Peak in the light of the moon, just a few nights from being full. It's been two months since I first saw that incredible mountain from here, its snowy mantle vivid in the full moon of early spring. It still wears a bright blanket of snow, even though the surrounding mountains below it now stand naked, cloaked only in trees.

So much has changed, and yet, to the timeless Peak, nothing has.

I am still sitting at the top of my mountain, basking in the dwindling night, when Nicolas walks up. He sits down beside me, and together we watch the moon fall and the sun begin to rise, and the Peak watches with us.

Nearly asleep, I feel him pick me up and cradle me as he carries me down the mountain. I snuggle against him, and my last thought is that his arms are my most favorite bed of all.

május 27., vasámap

I showed her the castle today. I was sure she would fall in love with it, and I was looking forward to surprising her with it as my bonding gift. It would have been perfect for her. But her compassion for the human who lived in it overruled her desires, and she asked me not to purchase it. I will not—for now.

I can finally breathe easy. She has made her Choice—and she chose me.

I nearly wept while she said her farewells to her mountain, as an element within me deeply regrets taking her away from a life she so clearly loves. But her rightful place is by my side, to be my Queen, and to share with me the leadership of all The Chosen.

MONDAY

CHAPTER 58

I put the box of clothes into the back seat of the BMW and head into the house to make a final check. Everything that couldn't fit into my car is boxed, taped, and waiting in the living room for the movers. The empty bookcase is waiting as well, its guardian bookends and their printed treasures safely packed and taken home by Nicolas earlier this morning.

With one last look around me, I realize that I am finally done.

I am done here.

Closing my eyes, I say goodbye to my simple little house and to the simple life I so briefly had, and to the life I might have had if I hadn't seen a black-haired stranger staring at me from across the street.

I fight back the tears and pull the curtains closed, then head out the back door for the final time.

My eyes trace the little trail I'd worn as I take one last look at the mountain above me. It is no longer mine—I said my goodbyes to it last night. Perhaps the next tenant of the little house will discover the wonder waiting for them in their backyard, and will love it as I did.

I just hope they don't run into any bears.

The slender young man is eager as he follows me back to the lounge area. He waits, shifting from foot to foot as I punch in the code and open the door.

"Relax," I say to him, but it is just as much for myself. The beast is vibrating in excitement, and I feel Nicolas's attempts to calm me, but I don't think they're doing much good.

"Wait for me in that booth." I point to one of the draped cubicles, then walk over behind the bar.

I grab a bottle of bloodwine and debate whether I should waste time with a glass. I hear the keypad being pressed and the door opens.

Nicolas walks in and joins me at the bar. Smiling, he opens a cabinet and takes out a large glass mug.

"Here, this is a little more civilized than drinking from the bottle." He reaches for the bloodwine and I hand it to him, watching as he opens it.

"How did you know . . . ?" Damned mind reader.

"Because that is what I would have done if I felt like you do and no one was here to watch." His emerald eyes glint with his customary amusement as he pours.

I snort and take the mug. I look up at him and start to drink, then close my eyes as the bloodwine begins to trace through my system.

Draining it, I wipe my lips and hold the mug out for more. Nicolas finishes filling his wineglass, then empties the bottle into the mug. I drink it a little slower this time, and can feel the calming effects of the blood and spices as I start to unwind.

"It's been awhile. I'm a little worried." But I don't have to tell him. I know he can feel it.

"You will do fine. I will be right outside if you have a problem," he says, his voice and his presence steady and reassuring.

"Does it ever get any easier? Maintaining control, I mean?" It was never an issue when I hunted in the forest.

"Yes, with time and practice. Eventually you will be able to go longer between feedings without risk of losing that control. But for now . . ."

Yeah, I get it. Welcome back to the world of the addict.

The dry rasp of a cough escapes the booth. That addict is waiting impatiently as well.

"Here." Nicolas hands me a small bottle of liqueur and a burgundy glass. "Always remember—they must drink this first. It enhances their pleasure and ensures they feel little pain."

Vague memories of burgundy glasses in human hands surface, but my questions fade as the beast starts pacing anxiously.

I drain the mug, grab the small bottle and glass, and walk across the room to the booth. As I close the drapes, I glance back at Nicolas. His face is unreadable.

The coppery nectar is even sweeter than I remember. All thoughts of life in the wild fade as I lose myself to the bliss of feeding. I can feel Nicolas outside the curtain savoring it with me as our pleasure echoes back and forth between us.

And any regrets I might've had are swept away in the crimson current of human blood.

május 28., hétfö

She showed me tonight that she is truly ready to assume her position with me in Chosen society. She handled the human as though she has done it all her Chosen life, and I was bursting with pride for her. She will be truly remarkable as my bonded. I am eager to start planning our ceremony.

This weekend we go to Denver where she will start learning a little about our selection process. I have a special couple in mind, and cannot wait to share in the feeding with her.

SATURDAY

CHAPTER 59

We slip through the traffic as we head north to Denver. It's Saturday night, an invitation-only evening with specially selected guests. I remember the last time we were here, the energized atmosphere, both Chosen and donors barely able to contain themselves. And I remember how they treated Nicolas, like the king that he is, and I understand that he periodically needs this.

I reflect over the last four or five days and how easily I've adapted to Nicolas's life and feeding at the club. It feels natural now, and I'm no longer so afraid of killing the donors. How odd to think that a little over a week ago I was running wild in the mountains gorging myself on gallons, yet still unsatisfied. Now I'm content with just a few pints.

And nothing dies.

Nicolas pulls the yellow Lamborghini up to the curb and a pair of valets open our doors. He gets out, and the people in line whisper excitedly as he walks around to my side. He reaches for my hand and helps me up from the low-slung sports car.

We walk past the waiting patrons, their muffled voices quieting as they stare. I can feel their hunger for us and what we represent, and my own hunger answers in anticipation.

The doormen nod to us and open the doors. The flashing lights and pulsing music are electrifying and my excitement rises. Nicolas shifts my hand to the inside of his elbow, and we walk into the maelstrom of bodies writhing to the beat.

Guess he's not going to leave me standing at the door this time.

The mob of people splits as we stride through. But there's confusion as they register that he is not alone. I see looks of surprise and jealousy, especially from the women, and one dancer arrogantly decides to ignore my presence. She sways her body closer and puts herself in Nicolas's path, seduction painting her expression.

I step in front of him and unleash both the hunter and the beast, just a little bit. She looks at my face and the color drains from hers, and she stumbles as she tries to back up. I lift a corner of my lip for emphasis and everyone before us moves back.

"Easy now. Frightening them serves no real purpose here," Nicolas whispers in my ear, but I feel his pride rush through me. I smile and compose my expression, then press back against his side. He surveys the crowd and nods. I watch as they relax and begin dancing again.

We continue to the rear of the club and I notice the young Chosen I met the first time here. Will was his name. He nods to me and grins, and I smile in response. We reach the black curtain and Nicolas looks back over the crowd. I spot several other Chosen as he gives one an intense stare, then he turns once again to the curtain, now held open for us by a pair of burly bouncers.

We walk down a dim hallway and stop outside one of several locked doors scattered along the hall. Mounted on it is a sign bearing the words, Club Orgia in an ornate script. When Nicolas opens the door and ushers me inside, I'm expecting a lounge similar to the one in Colorado Springs. I'm totally unprepared for what's inside this lounge.

The candlelit room is host to an orgy of blood and sex, and no one is bothering to hide behind curtains. The beast slams into high gear at the smells and moans of the entangled bodies. I swallow and glance up at Nicolas as we walk around the perimeter to a door in the far wall, and as he punches in the code, his face is carefully neutral. But he can't hide the excitement in his blood and mine cranks up even further in response.

As we enter another hallway, I mutter, "Thanks for the warning."

"And what would you have liked me to say? The buffet is open?" He smirks, eyes bright.

"That's not funny." But, in retrospect, it kind of is. I've always thought of the clubs as Chosen restaurants.

I shake my head and bite back a smile. Nicolas glances at me and smiles as we stop outside another door, which opens into a private room.

Again, as everything else here at the Denver club, this is a luxury suite, with several elegant rooms and a wet bar.

I've had less than a minute to absorb the surroundings when there's a knock at the door.

"Come in," says Nicolas.

Will walks in, followed by an attractive and well-dressed couple in their late thirties. He nods to Nicolas, then smiles at me and leaves, closing the door.

The man steps forward with his hand outstretched.

"Hello. I'm Peter Butler, and this is my wife, Anne. We're pleased to meet you."

"Good." Nicolas ignores the man's hand and remains standing where he is, arms folded as he appraises the couple. I glance at him, then my eyes drift to examine them as well.

The man's confident bearing, along with his well-tailored suit, speaks of money. The woman's black evening gown is couture, but it's her glittering ruby necklace that sends the beast into a frenzy. I wrench my gaze from the crimson-colored stones draped around her throat and look at Nicolas. The arousal in his eyes is new to me, and I feel it in his emotions as well, but it's not just anticipation of blood. There is something else going on here, and I use that puzzle to distract and hold down the beast.

"I, we, have been looking forward to this for some time now. I trust you've found our assets to be acceptable?" The man slides his hand into his pocket as his wife latches onto his arm.

Assets. Invitation only. Oh.

These are not just donors. These are prospective Chosen.

"Upon initial examination, yes. But there are several more steps involved in the screening process. You do understand you can be rejected at any time," Nicolas says, his tone stern and his dark green eyes hard.

"Yes, we . . . we understand." The man strains to keep his voice steady. His wife, wide-eyed, nods in agreement. Red light sparkles off the rubies as she moves.

"And you understand the consequences of rejection should that occur."

The air thickens as the man shifts beneath Nicolas's lethal stare. Fear permeates the room.

"Y-yes, we do. But we're confident you will find us to be of benefit to your . . . organization." His words seem a vain attempt to keep the discussion focused on business.

But we all know the discussion is really about life. Theirs.

So much for sheltering me from Chosen realities. Guess Nicolas has decided I don't need to be babied anymore and that it's time to grow up.

"The bar is there if you would like anything to drink." Nicolas indicates it with a nod of his head, and the woman's eyes flicker greedily in that direction.

Hmm. Drinker. I examine her scent and can smell the alcohol that seems to be embedded in every cell in her body.

I glance at Nicolas, but his face remains expressionless as the man walks over to the bar. He finds a glass and, with a little searching, a bottle of bourbon. Filling the glass nearly to the brim, he walks back over and hands it to his wife. She eagerly takes a swallow, then another.

"You may make yourselves comfortable in there." Nicolas motions toward one of the bedrooms. "On the table is a bottle of specially prepared liqueur. I strongly suggest you *both* drink it as it will make your experience much more pleasant." He smiles, but it does not quite reach his eyes. "We will join you shortly."

Nodding, the man wraps his arm around his wife's waist as she takes another drink from the now half-empty glass. They walk into the bedroom and close the door.

"What if only one of them passes?" I ask quietly. This is my first concern, among others.

"They have both made it this far. Not many pass the screening process my Chosen conduct. Most are thanked and sent on their way if there is anything found amiss, none the wiser as to what they were really being screened for." His tone is low and he is very still.

"But what if only one?" I insist.

"Then only that one is allowed to take the next step."

"You would break up a couple?" That shocks me even more than the risk of their deaths.

"This couple is not as attached to each other as you would assume. Furthermore, I have yet to see a couple survive the Change as a couple. Human relationships cannot withstand the demands the Change and

Chosen life places on them. They never even look back as they begin their new lives."

"Never?" I look at Nicolas in alarm. I'm not thinking about the couple in the other room. I'm thinking the couple in this room. Us.

"Ah . . . Come here." He walks over to me and gathers me in his arms, holding me tight as he speaks.

"You should not be worrying about this. You and I are different. We are already Changed, and have adapted well to both this life and our differences. This will not be a problem for us."

"But I'm not. I'm not . . . done," I whisper, fighting to hold back the damned red tears.

"You are more Chosen than most Chosen. Any further Changing you do will only make you more you, a stronger you. And I will stay by your side no matter what. I am not some flighty human discovering power and immortality for the first time." His voice, his arms, and his blood reassure me in every way they can. I begin to relax.

As my mind works through his words, I feel him breathe in the scent of my hair, and his embrace changes from one of comfort to one of demand. I gladly give in as our blood heats up. He nuzzles my neck and my thoughts start to melt away.

Thank you, Nicolas. I get tired of my worries and fears, and for most of this life, only hunting and the forest could subdue them. This is much better.

He kisses my throat, then brushes it with his fangs. I grab his hair and hold him tight, but he gently pushes himself away.

"My sweet, save that passion. I have a treat for you in the other room. I want you to enjoy it."

I frown.

"No killing?"

He quietly laughs. "No killing. But enjoyable nonetheless." He leans in and nips my mouth, and I reach for him.

But he is no longer there. He's now standing at the door waiting for me. His eyes are blazing red, and his body vibrates with the same excitement I feel in his blood. I waste no time joining him.

We open the door and walk in side by side.

Nicolas was right. The rapture of the blood was magnified by experiencing it through each other. My every mouthful was its own wave of euphoria, enhanced by feeling Nicolas's pleasure at the same time. The humans, gasping in ecstasy, seemed to be caught up in our sharing as well. As they passed out, I drifted into ruby-colored rhapsody, only vaguely aware when Nicolas gathered me up and carried me from the room.

He gently places me in his bed and undresses me, then a moment later climbs in. I snuggle against his blood-warmed skin and fade off again into the red fog, embraced inside and out by Nicolas and his unfathomable love for me.

SUNDAY

CHAPTER 60

I wake slowly, still blood-drugged, and realize Nicolas is still here in bed with me. He's curled around me much as he was when I passed out, but is now motionless, inert. I feel him take a breath and stir as my awareness returns.

"Nicolas?"

"Hmm?"

"Were you asleep?"

"Something like it."

"Does that happen very often?"

"No."

His odd tone catches my attention.

"Ever?"

He hesitates.

"No."

Oh. Huh.

But before I can ask anything more, he pulls me in closer, and I feel his blood in me start to heat up. Mine responds, and like lightning, he is all over me, nipping and growling. He slices his upper arm, and as I take it, his fangs bury themselves in my throat.

We drown in each other's blood, and go further than ever before. And we keep taking, and taking, and then I feel a strange flutter in my core, and everything starts to go black.

And then he is shouting and shaking me, and I don't have the strength to respond, and I feel myself slipping away. He slaps me and jars me back a little, and I fight to stay, but it's too hard. I feel him pick me up and then hear faint sounds of doors opening and slamming.

Ice cold water stings as it sprays my skin, startling me. He's rubbing me frantically all over, and through a black haze I see his face contorted in terror, his mouth moving as though speaking. I focus on his wild eyes and try to hold on to them, and slowly the black fades away. My vision starts to clear a little, and I realize that bloodtears, diluted by the water raining over us, are washing down his face. I take a breath and inhale water from the shower spray and cough.

"Sunny?! Sunny?! Are you with me? Sunny?!"

I can finally make out what he's saying.

"Yeah," I whisper.

"Oh, thank God." And he crushes me to him, his body shaking as he sobs.

I fight to reconnect to my senses and slowly become aware that he's quieted. He holds me tight while the icy shower washes over us.

"You are still with me?" he asks, his voice broken.

"Yeah. What happened? Did we bond?"

All that comes out is a strangled groan.

He takes a breath and tries again.

"No, we did not bond." He tenses and hugs me tighter to him.

"What happened?"

"I . . ."

A shudder wracks his body.

"I . . . I almost killed you."

Oh.

I feel strange, like I'm floating in nothingness. There seems to be a war in my body, and for some reason I'm not absorbing Nicolas's blood. Instead, it feels like my veins have clamped shut, refusing to let his blood in. It weighs heavy in my belly, and his emotions have nowhere to go, no way to travel in my system. So they're swirling, all the guilt and fear and self-loathing, round and round in my gut, and they're making me sick. I curl tighter around myself as Nicolas brushes damp hair back from my face. He pulls the bedcovers closer to my chin, then begins his pacing again.

"Are you sure? I have donors waiting in the other room." The rising anxiety in his voice adds to the churning chaos in my belly.

"Nicolas, please. I need a break. Just for a little while. Please, can you shut off?" I open my eyes to look at him, and he stops his pacing long enough to nod.

I feel him slowly withdraw as he struggles to shut down the flow of emotions. I close my eyes again and find the hunter where she's defensively crouched, and encourage her to come out. As she surfaces, I grab on to her stillness and hold it tightly.

All emotion, his and mine, abruptly stops, and I take a long deep breath.

But my relief is short-lived as flaming hunger blazes up my throat and scorches my empty veins. I can actually feel them quivering under my skin. My stomach continues to roil and the nausea intensifies. My veins spasm, then spasm again.

I bolt from the bed and into the bathroom, slamming the door.

"Sunny? Sunny!"

"Stay out."

Bending over the toilet, I heave up all of his blood. I know he can hear me, but I have no choice. Everything in me is telling me to get rid of it, *now*. That it's a threat to me. I don't know how I know this. I just do.

When I've thrown up every last drop, I sink to the floor. The inferno of hunger is now raging throughout my helpless body. It's as bad as when the bear nearly tore away my life.

But I know how to fix it this time. Gritting my teeth, I grip the toilet and force myself to my feet. I stagger to the sink and wash my face, then stumble to the door and open it.

Nicolas is standing right outside, his face a mask of horror.

"Ah Sunny. Please . . . forgive me," he whispers as he guides me back to the bed.

"I'll take those donors now."

CHAPTER 61

The Lamborghini weaves in and out of traffic on the busy highway. I watch as Pikes Peak approaches in the distance and feel grateful for its anchoring presence in the southwestern horizon.

We haven't spoken much. I'm still lost in the time warp of what happened, and Nicolas is lost in his excruciating guilt. I want to let him back in, because there's still some of his blood woven in my system from before. But neither of us seems ready. My self-preservation is still too protective, his anguish still too raw.

As the Peak begins to loom over us, I reach out and put my hand on his thigh. A tremor goes through his palm as he grips my fingers.

"Do you need for me to stop at the Club?" he asks, his voice strained.

"No, I should be fine for a while longer. Maybe later tonight."

It took five donors and everything I had in me not to kill them. And Nicolas still had to help me stop.

I remember how incessant the healing hunger was after the bear attack. Its demands, though strong, are different this time, maybe because there's no damaged tissue to repair. Yet my system is undergoing some sort of rebuilding. I can feel a strange internal crawling not unlike the sensation of knitting flesh.

I have no idea what kind of effect this latest experience will have on my ever-evolving Change, and I don't think Nicolas does either. I feel like some sort of lab experiment and can picture the notebook in his head as he records the data of my bizarre life.

The gates open and we pull up the driveway. The forest of creatures is welcoming in the twilight, and I decide a walk among the greenery might feel good.

He parks in front, gets out, and opens my door. His face is taut as he reaches down for me, and I resist the urge to snap at him, to tell him I'm fine and to just leave me alone. I let him help me from the car, then gently pull away from his clinging grasp and look at him.

"Nicolas. Please. I'm all right. You need to take a breath and try to relax. I'm here, and I'm alive, and we have both survived. We will get through this as we have everything else."

He seems so fragile right now and I don't really know how to handle it. This is a complete role reversal from our previous crises.

He nods and steps back, then heads up the stairs. He opens the door and holds it, waiting.

"I'll be in shortly. I'm going to walk in the garden awhile," I say, trying to sound gentle and strong at the same time.

What a strange balancing act. Now I know how he feels whenever I'm having some sort of emotional breakdown.

He nods and goes inside.

Crossing the driveway, I walk out into the garden. I wander among the creatures, tucking a stray vine back into place here and there. Pegasus beckons me, and I drift over to him and run my hand over his outstretched wing. Strands of greenery still dangle from where I tore them loose so long ago, and I work to re-weave them back into place.

When I've done as much as possible to repair the damage, I take a last look at his shape embracing the sky, then continue my walk through the manicured forest.

I reach what must be the center and come to a dead stop in front of a new topiary sculpture. As I examine it, I realize it is actually two.

Two life-sized leopards.

They're entwined around one another, and it's difficult to tell whether their embrace is one of affection, or one of battle.

Tears well up as I wonder when he put them here. They appear to be newly planted, yet their forms are filled and covered with mature vines and leaves. I doubt he had them made—that is not Nicolas's way. He must have a greenhouse somewhere on the grounds, as they speak of his carefully crafted work.

I touch them gently, noting the details he somehow managed to reproduce with living plants. The talons on the outstretched paws curve to slender points and I can even make out the shape of the pads on the bottoms of their feet. I walk around to the front and stop, stunned by what Nicolas has woven. My throat tightens as I look at their faces.

One is fierce, his mouth gaping, his long fangs poised over the throat of the other. His body is large, almost coarse in its shape, with foliage so dark green it's nearly black. The other is slender, sleek, and her foliage is variegated, mostly silvery green with darker green spots on the leaves. Her lips appear to be curled, but no fangs are exposed, and her expression seems softer. One lethal paw is inches from his throat, the extended claws sharp and deadly.

Nicolas steps up behind me, and I close my eyes and let the tears fall as he gathers me into his arms. He rests his cheek against my hair and we stand there in the rising moonlight. I stare at the living statues he created of us, and slowly release the stillness I've been holding.

I feel him tentatively reach out as my emotions begin to function again. I focus on my feelings for him and welcome his answering warmth, heavily laced with worry and guilt. My sense of him is muted though, and I realize that other than what I threw up this morning, I have not had any of his blood for several days.

He, however, had nearly all of mine, so I need to manage my emotions carefully. I gently take a little bit of the stillness back, hoping to provide some sort of buffer without shutting off the flow entirely.

Some of the tautness drains from his body and I rub his arms, trying to ease him further.

"They're beautiful," I say quietly as I look at the cats in the moonlight.

"Yes, they are," he replies.

Modest as ever. I force a smile and face him.

His expression is unguarded, and I see pain that he is somehow blocking from me. He quickly smoothes his features and brushes the hair back from my face.

"It's not your fault. We didn't know," I say, trying to project reassurance. But I don't think it'll do much good. He's going to eat himself up about this for a long time.

"I should have known. I . . . I did know. But I foolishly thought *I* could somehow work around it. Your Change seemed so complete I let myself grow complacent. No . . . arrogant. I believed I could somehow circumvent the laws of Chosen nature." His pain shifts to anger, and the tension mounts again in his blood and in his body.

"And then I tasted your lifespark, your *human* lifespark, as it started to come apart . . ." His voice breaks as his body shudders.

"But it's still here, inside me. I can still touch my human part. You did not damage it. Besides, wouldn't that just have furthered the Change?"

"No. You would have died. Ceased to exist in any life. We do not consume the lifespark of those who are being Changed."

Oh. He really did almost kill me.

His anger melts back into anguish. I try to cope with his needle-like agony and self-reproach that's now rushing through my system.

"But I didn't die. Whatever it is that I got from my . . . Maker . . . protects me somehow. I'm not as fragile as you seem to think."

He looks at me and touches my jaw.

"No, perhaps not. But there is one thing you are not." He pauses, takes a breath.

"You are not immortal. You *can* die."

Not immortal.

I step back and turn around. I look at the cats immortalized in mortal greenery.

Huh.

I don't know when I started assuming I was. Maybe from the beginning, when I looked down at the drained body of the dog in my arms. I haven't aged in the five years since that night. Even when he said I was still part human, I thought I was like him and the other Chosen. Timeless. Like the Peak.

"Then why didn't I die when I lost my blood from the bear attack? How is that any different?"

"Because your blood drained freely. Your Chosen safeguards maintained enough reserve to protect your lifespark." He takes another breath and continues.

"It is not the same as having your blood forcibly withdrawn from you."

You mean having the life sucked out of me.

Not immortal. And he is.

Aging. Able to die. And he is not.

My throat tightens and I walk over to the leopards. I reach out and stroke a fang, then look over at Nicolas. His eyes reflect the horror I feel, but he makes no move toward me.

I close my eyes and focus on the hunter, seeking a little of her calculating coldness while still keeping the connection with Nicolas open. It seems to work and, calmer now, I redirect my attention to something he said a few moments earlier.

"So, if you don't take the lifespark of someone who is undergoing the Change, how is theirs any different from mine?"

"The lifespark of a Chosen is permanently altered, becoming immortal, when they consume their first lifespark from a human. *That* is the final moment of their Change."

When they kill their first human.

And I feel the chasm that's been lurking between us since this morning open even farther.

We get back from the club just before dawn. It took another four donors to calm down the hunger fires that started building again about midnight. But it went a little better this time. At least I was able to stop on my own.

Nicolas accompanies me upstairs to our bedroom and watches while I undress and get into bed.

"Aren't you going to join me, even for a little while?" I ask. I'm starting to crave him. The distance he's been maintaining all night is only making it worse.

He looks at me with sorrow in his eyes, and I feel it in his blood, and he is starting to scare me.

"Nicolas, you have to talk to me. You have to tell me what is going on. We need to work this out together, isn't that right?"

He nods. "I must make some phone calls and try to get some answers. We will talk when you wake."

"Promise?" I ask . . . no, I demand.

"Promise." With a last look at me, he leaves and closes the door.

He is really starting to spook me. I drift off to sleep with knots in my stomach.

június 3., vasámap

My world collapsed today. All my careful planning, all my precise preparation, was undone by my arrogance and lack of control once again. In spite of my own intentions, I went too far. The need to bond with her has been driving me insane, and in a moment of weakness, I gave in to it.

And I nearly killed her—again. But this time it was directly by me, not by some poor dumb beast. This time it was by my lust, my need, my fang.

I will never forgive myself, and I can never trust myself with her again. I have proven time after time that I have little control when I am with her. I know that I will eventually remake her, or worse, kill her, as long as she remains in this shadow-state of a Chosen.

And so I am left with my final Choice—to take away hers, or give her up entirely.

MONDAY

CHAPTER 62

I wake, and he's sitting in the chair, watching me.

"Come here." I pull back the covers.

He takes a breath, then gets up and walks over and kneels on the floor. His hand hesitates as he reaches out and touches my face.

"I miss you," I whisper, clutching his hand to my cheek. "I can feel you fading, and I don't like it. Please, don't leave me with this . . . this emptiness that's starting to grow in me."

Bloodtears blur my vision as a sob escapes.

He closes his eyes and clenches his jaw. I can feel him nearly vibrating with tension, and I release the last bit of stillness I've been holding on to. I focus on my love and worry for him, and can see its visible effects as he catches his breath. I can barely feel his response. My fear of its loss rips through me and then into him.

His eyes open and my pain is reflected in their dark green depths.

He whispers, "I am sorry. Please, only a little."

My tears spill in disbelief as he unbuttons his sleeve, rolls it up, and offers his forearm. His *forearm.* Not his chest, or his throat, or anywhere intimate. Shaking my head at his determination to keep distance between us, I pierce his vein and take a small mouthful, waiting to see how my system reacts. I can detect no threat and take more.

The inner conflict in his blood is overwhelming, a swirling chaos of longing and love, guilt and fear. I pause, then take a little more and his out-of-control feelings continue to intensify.

This is almost too much to bear. I reluctantly stop.

I slowly let go of him and roll back down onto the bed. He leans back, pushes his sleeve down, then stands and walks across the room. I get up as alarms go off throughout my body.

"If you are ready to get dressed, we can talk in the library," he says.

I'm relieved to see a brief flare of familiar red as he looks at me. But he quickly masks it, and without another word, leaves and closes the door.

This is really bad.

Dread tightens my throat and I dress and go downstairs.

Several bottles of bloodwine are sitting on one of the tables next to the fireplace, along with two filled glasses. I cross the room to where he's standing as he stares at the low flame in the hearth.

He turns as I approach, gestures to one of the chairs, and takes the other.

My panic edges toward hysteria and he grits his teeth.

"Nicolas, please tell me what's wrong. What have you found out?" I choke back a sob.

He says nothing. Instead he hands me one of the glasses of bloodwine and quickly downs the other. I do the same. As I finish my glass, he offers to pour more. I gladly accept and drink while he refills his glass.

By the second bottle, I'm starting to regain some composure as the blood and spices work to soothe my system. I can feel his tension easing as well.

We continue drinking in silence, scarcely daring to look at one another. At the end of the third bottle, I'm starting to get a real blood high. I close my eyes and focus on the warm pleasure the bloodwine brings, and feel a mutual calmness finally take hold of us.

"I'm afraid we have a rather serious problem," he says.

I keep silent and beat down a flutter of fear.

"It seems with your current stage of Change, it will, ah . . ." He pauses and takes a breath. "It is not possible for us to bond."

Yeah, I kinda figured that out.

"It also seems we may have upset the balance in your system between the blood of your Maker and my blood. Your instincts were correct. It was critical that you cleanse yourself of my blood, and if I had not been so panicked, I would have realized what was starting to happen."

"Meaning?" I ask.

"Meaning that since your Change is unfinished, you are more susceptible to being taken over by another Maker, including me. The blood of your Maker has been strong enough to keep this from happening, at least until I took nearly all of yours. There was not enough left to resist mine for much longer, especially since you had so much of mine. If you had kept my blood, you would have become part of my lineage." His jaw tightens.

The spasms in my clenched veins were the final warning, I realize. If I hadn't vomited his blood, it would've overpowered my system. My veins would've opened and . . .

"And you would have become my Maker," I whisper.

"Yes. You would be subject to the same influences as anyone in my lineage." He frowns.

"Besides the control issue, how bad would that be?" As abhorrent as it seems, part of me is willing to accept whatever it takes to keep us together.

"We would no longer be equals. It would make our relationship very . . . difficult."

"That's why it didn't work out between you and Éva."

"Yes, that is a large part of it." The ghost of regret slips across his face and is gone.

I think about this for a minute and watch as he sips his bloodwine.

"Why didn't my blood have a similar effect on you?"

Amusement flickers through his eyes for the first time in days, and his answer is accompanied by a brief smile.

"Because I am a 550-year-old Maker, and your blood is young and, in spite of its power . . . is second generation, for lack of a better term."

Makes sense, I guess.

"So what now? What can we do?"

His expression becomes serious again, underlined by a crushing sadness that resonates deep inside me.

My panic bubbles to the surface and I nearly choke.

"Very little. I now fear the effect my blood will have on you. It was only because I could not bear for you to be in pain that I gave you any today."

No. No. Don't say that.

"And I am finding it extremely difficult to be around you and not touch you. I am afraid if I take hold of you I will never let you go, and will do anything to keep you with me. Including forcing you into my lineage," he says, his face rigid. "And I could not live with myself if I lost control and did that."

Anguish slips through his mask and twists his blood into knots throughout my body.

And I know what I must do. And I don't know if I can.

"So that leaves only one option," I whisper.

He visibly strains to keep his face neutral.

"If we are to be together, I need to complete the Change."

He nods, and I feel the conflict in him echoing mine. Same conflict, different reasons.

I get up and walk over to the window, but rather than seeing the garden, I see my faint reflection in the glass. The details may have changed, but the general outline is the same.

Just like the Choice I've been facing since I met Nicolas. That hasn't really changed, either—only the way in which I've reached it.

I've been sitting here in the library for several hours, watching the garden creatures tremble as a nighttime breeze plucks and pulls at them.

Nicolas has been gone for some time. He left when it seemed like we had nothing more to say to one another.

The library door opens, and he stops beside my chair, his expression unreadable.

"I have to go to the club and take care of some business. It is possible I may need to go out of town, and I must make arrangements to ensure things run smoothly while I am gone."

Out of town? Is he the one running this time?

I stand, and the panic I've been fighting to control all day takes over, filling my eyes with unshed tears. My anxiety hits him and I feel him brace as he tries to deal with it along with his own.

"Sunny, Sunny. Come here." He gathers me into his arms, hugging me close.

My chest heaves over and over as I weep. The cries of a wounded animal fill the air, and I realize they're coming from my throat. Nicolas holds me tight and his hand trembles as he strokes my hair.

"Ah, my love . . ." His voice cracks.

"Nicolas, can't we . . . can't we keep trying to make this work? I mean, it has so far, sort of." The words waver as they come out in a jumble, like the thoughts and feelings inside me.

His hands move to my shoulders and he eases me back. His green eyes are full of pain.

"I do not know. Because what I feel now when I look at you, when I hold you, is fear. Fear that in one way or another I will destroy you if we stay together."

Yes, I know. Because that fear is dominating the love you usually share with me, killing it with sharp daggers of anguish and guilt.

"And how will you feel, Nicolas, when *my* blood fades from your system? Have you thought about that? Because I am ahead of you in that . . . in that process, and I can tell you it will be far worse than any other concerns you may have right now." My voice quivers, and I feel myself shrink back from the thought of the looming emptiness.

He pulls me close again and says nothing.

"Please, let's just give this a little more time. We . . . we just can't let this go so easily." I can barely choke out the words.

He still says nothing, but finally he nods in agreement.

"All right," he whispers. "We will keep trying, if that is what you want."

More than anything I've ever wanted.

He gently releases me, brushing the hair back from my face. His eyes flicker red and he steps back.

Still not trusting himself.

"But it does not change the fact that I may have to go out of town. The relationship with Europe has deteriorated this past month, and I need to meet with my allies and do what I can to repair it. Or we may be facing a Chosen war, which is something that cannot happen."

I don't even hesitate.

"Can't I go with you? I mean, I think separation right now is not . . ." I can't even finish.

He takes in a sharp breath and frowns.

"The last place I want you to be is among my enemies. This is not a good idea." His voice has an edge to it, and I feel his apprehension swiftly change to a bestial and primitive protectiveness.

"Then before you say no, please, let's discuss it further. I'm sure we can figure this out."

"Perhaps. But no promises." He shifts his hardened gaze to the fireplace. "Now, I really do need to get to the club. Would you like to meet me there later?"

As he says this, the hunger breaks through the emotional chaos and starts to simmer in my veins.

"Yes. I'd like to shower and change first."

"Call me when you leave."

Yes, Nicolas. I'm relieved to see a little of the old bossy self come back to the surface.

"I will. I promise." And I mean it. I need him to be *him*—not this tortured creature that's lived in his body for the last two days.

He steps forward and, gently taking my head between his hands, kisses me on the forehead. He then quickly steps back and walks out the door.

I'll take anything I can get right now, as long as it's in the direction of normalcy. Whatever that is.

I call Nicolas when I leave the house, just as I promised. Our conversation is even briefer than usual, which doesn't help my anxiety level. At all.

After parking the BMW beside his Jag, I enter the club through the side door. As I step into his office, he rises from the chair behind the desk and walks up to me. I wrap my arms around him, not giving him a chance to be distant, and can feel his relief as he hugs me back. But the relief is still laced with tension, and he takes my arms from around him and moves back.

Baby steps, I remind myself.

"Come, I have something a little special for you." His face is unreadable. I get no sense of what he is feeling, other than the whirlwind of emotions that have been battering him since he . . . since I almost died.

I reach out my hand. He hesitates, then takes it.

Baby steps.

He leads me down the hall, into the empty lounge, and to the door leading to the private rooms.

"Bloodwine?" I ask. The hunger is feeling a little unmanageable, and the beast has been throwing itself around since I left the house.

"No, you will be fine. I will be there." His steady and reassuring voice eases some of the tension squirming through me.

We walk into the third room down the hall, one I haven't been in before. It's different from the other two, darker, more somber.

"I will be right back. Make yourself comfortable." And he exits the room.

The beast is in full rampage right now, and the hunter is alert and watchful. Something about this room has brought her out, and it puzzles me.

The door opens and Nicolas walks in, followed by a dark-haired young man.

"This is . . ." Nicolas pauses and looks at him.

"Dominic. My name is Dominic. I'm from New York. Éva's my sponsor." He strolls up to me and reaches for my hand as though to shake it. I'm shocked when he brazenly raises it to his lips. I snatch it out of his grasp, unkissed, and step back. He smiles insolently, his grey eyes mocking.

I can feel Nicolas raging. When I look over at him, his eyes are blazing red, his fangs bared as his lip curls in a snarl.

He looks at me and brings himself back under control. Barely.

"I will be back. I need to check on something." He turns to leave.

"Nicolas. The liqueur?" I didn't see the usual bottle and burgundy glass sitting on the bar.

"Ah. It won't be necessary." With a dark look at Dominic, he walks out the door.

Frowning, I shift my attention back to the man, who is still standing a few feet away, arms crossed as he blatantly appraises me. He's mid-thirties, quite handsome, and quite arrogant. His clothing is high quality, his attitude one that belongs only to the rich and powerful.

He reminds me of someone I know, and probably reminds Éva of him as well.

I also realize I've seen him before, out on the dance floor. He prowls through the dancers, collecting women, diverting their attention from The Chosen. He acts so much like a Chosen I wondered if he was in the midst of the Change, or perhaps being considered for it.

He would be perfect.

And he would be perfect to introduce to the Game. Ambition fairly radiates from him.

He could also be a threat.

As all this races through my brain, he clears his throat and reaches for my face.

I've leapt back nearly ten feet before he even registers that I moved.

He smiles, full of himself.

"Game player, huh?" He saunters over to the wet bar, rummages through the bottles, and pulls out a Chivas. Finding a glass, he fills it and recaps the bottle.

He takes a drink, looking at me over the rim of the glass, his expression smug.

Not so much like that other someone, I see now. Obviously lacking in basic manners. Too much into himself to consider the needs of another.

"So. I haven't seen *you* before. You must be . . . *new*." His eyes once again rake my body.

I remain silent as the beast crouches within.

"Éva's promised me whatever I want once I finish the Change. Perhaps I'll ask for you."

Oh really. Nicolas might have something to say about that.

"Would you like something to drink?" he asks after he takes another sip.

Fine. I'll play his game. The hunter steps forward, ready, anxious to hunt in this new way.

"Not anything out of a bottle." I give him a feral look.

His face lights up and he smiles.

"Oh. Do you like to play rough?" And his eyes narrow, his smile becoming suggestive.

Rougher than *you* can handle, you arrogant prick.

"Why don't you come over here and find out," I growl.

He smiles and takes another drink. Setting his glass down on the bar, he takes off his expensive-looking watch and sets it down as well.

He steps away from the bar, puts his hands in his pockets, and stands there.

Expecting *me* to come to him.

And I am there, and breathe into his ear, and am back across the room before he can even blink.

His cocky expression momentarily shifts to one of surprise, then to one of lust.

Gotcha.

He takes his hands out of his pockets and saunters across the room. I let him get within an arm's length, then step several feet to the side. I lean in, caress his throat with the back of my hand, and lean back, again before he even realizes I've moved.

He sharply inhales, his expression bright as he steps forward again. I step back and wait. We move toward the bedroom, the hunter eagerly enticing her prey. The hammer of his heart grows louder and faster as his excitement increases.

My skin ripples in savage anticipation. I've not had a donor like this before.

I allow him to back me toward the bed, his face twisting into a sneer as he strides forward. His confidence is exhilarating—I can almost taste it.

Stopping at the edge of the bed, I let him catch me. He reaches out and grabs me by the shoulders, hard, and leans in to kiss me.

But I avoid his lips and shift his focus when I reach down and tear his shirt open. His finely chiseled chest, honed in the gym no doubt, swells as he takes a breath.

He tries again to kiss me, and again I duck away. Frowning, his fingers slide up to clutch and tear at the straps of my dress. I reach up and knock his hands away as my excitement shifts to anger.

"You bitch," he says, his voice and his expression becoming ugly.

Oh, you have no idea.

Without warning, his hand swings up to slap my face. The beast roars and everything turns red as I catch his arm and hold it. He tries to wrest it free, but my grip is iron and I am so much stronger than he. And instead of this scaring him, his eyes fill with hate, and his fist swings up from the other side toward my face.

Woman-hitter, are you? The Chosen allow you to behave this way?

Not me. I don't care who you belong to.

I catch his other arm, and holding them both outstretched, press forward. His head whips from side to side as he struggles, cursing.

And his throat flashes, one side and then the other.

And both the hunter and the beast take over.

I jerk him to me and I sink my teeth into that flashing throat and I draw. Hard.

He screams and struggles vainly to pull away. I feel myself responding as any predator would.

I slam him backward against the wall and, releasing one arm, grab his hair to steady his head, and I draw again. He screams and shudders, knees buckling. We go down as the first of his blood rushes through my system. I pull again, and he groans as he beats me on the head and tries to push me away.

Loosening his hair, I grab him around his shoulders, pinning his arms, and rock back onto my heels, dragging him with me. I wrap myself tighter around him, savoring the domination of predator over prey.

And I pull, and pull again, and again, and give myself over to the sweet waves of a crimson sea.

He moans, and I feel him go slack, and I don't care, and I pull again.

And Nicolas is there, and he's kneeling down on the floor behind me, his hands on my shoulders.

And he is not stopping me.

The realization startles me back to myself and I freeze in horror.

I'm killing this man, and Nicolas is not stopping me.

He is not stopping me.

I release my hold and the man collapses onto the floor. I shove backward against Nicolas and lunge to my feet, turning toward him in fury.

"YOU PROMISED!"

He stands, the body of the man lying on the floor between us.

"It's supposed to be *my* Choice! *My* Choice!"

"Take him, Sunny. Finish it. Make the Change." He reaches out and grips my shoulders. "For us. For me. Please . . ."

I hear him, and I hesitate. He's right.

And then my daughter's face, and my granddaughter's sweet smile, blossom in my mind, and I realize that they have been absent from my thoughts for a long time now.

If I kill this man, I kill the last remaining shred of my humanity. And I will completely forget them, and those little black curls and bright blue eyes, and my existence in their lives. And I realize I can't bear the thought of that.

"I can't," I whisper as I stare down at the limp body.

"You must," he insists, his voice deepening in anger.

"I can't," I repeat. At least not yet.

Something in Nicolas snaps, and with a roar he reaches down, picks up the man, and sinks his fangs into the bloody wound I left. As he drains him, a rush of raw power screams deep within my core, a dim echo of the wild force racing through Nicolas.

Lifespark. I stagger with the impact of its energy, and I'm only feeling it secondhand as it explodes through every cell in Nicolas.

My vision turns momentarily white, and Nicolas throws his head back and inhales sharply, and a triumphant groan erupts from his chest.

As my vision clears, Nicolas lowers his head and stares at me. His eyes are completely white, and the expression on his face is the most inhuman thing I have ever seen.

He snarls and heaves the flaccid body across the room as though it were garbage. It crashes into the wall with a sickening thud and slides down, leaving a bloody smear.

I stare at him, reeling and shocked beyond words. I've not seen this Nicolas before, this alien cold-blooded murderer.

"He would have died regardless. He would not have recovered from the loss of blood *you* inflicted on him. So you see, you killed him anyway." His voice, along with his words, is cold and cruel and punishing.

I feel the horror flood through me again. I killed. A person. A human being.

Nicolas, glaring at me, wipes the blood from his face, his expression beastly and furious.

"And it was a waste, because *you* did not take his lifespark. You essentially killed for no reason. And now, you will have to do it again." His words are merciless, and I recoil in further revulsion.

And a new realization hits me.

The one I love *is* truly a monster, and he is making one of *me.*

Oh God.

Nicolas, I will do anything for you, anything to be with you.

Except this.

This . . . I . . . will . . . not . . . do.

CHAPTER 63

The black ribbon of asphalt stretches before me into the night. The BMW is heading north, the direction in which I pointed it several hours before. I gassed up in Denver, and then again in Wheatland, Wyoming. I bought a few maps and figure I can make to Casper before needing gas again. I'm hoping I can get there and into a hotel before dawn, before the sun takes me down.

Nicolas's rage followed me into the parking lot before I had the presence of mind to seek the stillness. It was difficult to find and hold on to as our emotional vortex spun wildly out of control. But I knew that shutting off the flow was the only way to keep him from finding me.

And search for me he will. I feel that through every vein in my body. I grip hard onto the stillness, using it to safeguard me from both him and the hurricane of emotion that threatens to pull me apart.

The empty black hole has returned, eating me from the inside out. But I learned to cope with it before, and can learn again. In the meantime, my quest for survival is enough to keep me somewhat distracted from its pain.

I just don't know what will distract me from craving the blood of human beings.

It's doubtful I can return to my old life of bartending. I can only envision a scene out of a horror movie, or the memory of a certain night in a club in the Springs, when a bar was bathed front to back in human blood.

So for now I'm heading back into the wilderness. There's lots of it in Canada, and it might be far enough away that Nicolas can't track me down.

They have grizzly bear up there, and the hunter thrills at the thought of the challenge they will bring.

EPILOGUE

It's been six months since I left the West Coast. A sick laugh escapes as I recall the events that triggered my flight to Colorado. They pale in comparison now and seem like something from a child's dream. Nothing like the nightmare I left in the shadow of Pikes Peak.

But part of me starts to argue that it wasn't all a nightmare, that I found something I thought to be impossible in this life. And I slap that part down and shove it back into the black box. My memories—the memories of what I lost—are too full of pain and regret to deal with right now. I grab the stillness, and relief flows through me as the gut-wrenching emotions smother under cold detachment.

I pull into the parking lot across the street from where she works, or at least where she did work. Hopefully she still does, because I don't have the patience to sit outside her house. Those days are over.

But I need to see her, need to reassure myself that my human life was not just another dream.

Tugging the brim of my baseball cap lower, I grimace at my reflection in the car window. My disguised self glares back in the form of a punk street kid—pierced and tattooed and wearing ragged clothes. The piercings will heal as soon as I take out the jewelry, and the tattoos will fade by evening. The tats aren't very good—I was never much of an artist. But they'll do the job. I put on my sunglasses and head to the building.

It's noon and the lobby is crowded. My jaw clenches as the fragrant chorus of human blood hits me. Even though I gorged on several deer last night, this may be harder than I thought.

Walking past the staircase to the far side of the elevators, I stop and casually lean against the wall as though waiting for the doors to open.

Andrea's always preferred stairs, and I'm hoping to catch sight of her as she comes down the wide stairway. I watch the other workers as they descend in twos and threes, deep in their conversations.

The elevator next to me opens, and people brush past me as they exit. I'm trapped between them and the wall at the end of this short hallway, and without warning, violence coils in my muscles.

I need to get out of here. Coming inside was not only risky, it was stupid.

Waiting until the last of the lunch goers leave the elevator, I start to follow them to the front door.

And then I look up, and she is standing at the bottom of the stairs, not twenty feet away, staring directly at me.

Oh shit.

I dart into the elevator, nowhere else to go. The doors begin to close, and I let out my breath. And then a slim hand shoots into the rapidly shrinking gap, followed by a slender arm, and her shoulder wedges into the opening. The doors rebound, and she steps inside.

She stands, facing me, and says, "Hello, Mom."

ACKNOWLEDGMENTS

First of all, I'd like to thank my initial beta readers: Lex, Janine, Lil, Dette, Will, and Vanessa. Without their enthusiastic responses and encouragement, I doubt I would have ever shown *Watcher* to another soul. My writers group, the Fresno Sci-Fi & Fantasy Writers, provided valuable feedback that helped me improve both my storytelling and my craft. Thanks especially to Toff, Mellie, Ed, Earl, and Chris, who suffered through my early drafts and provided me with tips and insights to make the story better.

I also received advice on a number of technical elements and would like to recognize those experts: Bill Moffatt, Park Ranger at the Tule Elk State Natural Reserve, California State Parks; Craig Stowers, Deer Program Coordinator, California Department of Fish and Game; Jeff Lawson, Physical Therapist, whose knowledge of hunting and physiology helped me with the hunting scenes; and the staff at Pikes Peak Ranger Station.

Thank you to my friends who put up with my obsession to write and publish this story: Jeanne, for traipsing through the Pikes Peak area with me during several monumental periods in my life (I still can't believe we found the castle!); Marcy, who endured endless phone calls while I prattled on about this book; Vicky, for giving her rapt attention to my oral versions of the story while we worked out in the gym; Cynthia, whose support and encouragement kept me moving forward; and of course, my TM friends Kim, Kirsten, Britten, Tierza, Dette, and Jess, who share my love for all things vampire and introduced me to sisterhood. I'll never forget our wild rides in Annabelle, Kim's silver convertible Mustang, and setting off car alarms in the Riverpark parking garage.

Many thanks to the editors whose suggestions not only improved this book, but contributed toward my ongoing development as a writer: Melanie Smith, Christopher Wood, Sharon Campbell, and Diana Cox.

This wouldn't have been possible without my family. Thank you to my parents, Bill and Joan, for your lifelong love and support; and to my son Nate and my daughter Alexis, for encouraging my writing and being such awesome kids, and for giving me the best job in the world—parenthood.

And finally, thank you to my husband, Bruce—my one love—for your patience and understanding, and for always being there for me.
I couldn't have made it without you.

SECOND EDITION NOTES

Many people have been on this journey with me since it began. Their continuing support and interest in my writing, and this story in particular, keep me moving forward through the gauntlet of publishing and the tribulations of life in general, and I thank them.

This edition is for them, and for all of the new readers who may follow in their footsteps.

The primary changes to *Watcher* are due to the meticulous efforts of professional editor Jodi Renée Lester. Her detailed comments on proper comma usage, sentence structure, and general grammatical rules not only improved this book, but my writing itself. My deepest gratitude goes to Jodi for her thoughtful instruction and patience, her willingness to spend hours talking on the phone with me, her dedication to Sunny's story, and most of all, the friendship that's evolved working on the Chosen project.

Previous readers will be surprised (pleasantly, I hope) with smoother dialogue, expanded scenes, and new scenes. And, most apparent, a new, professionally designed cover. My thanks to Milo, Kim, and Darja at Deranged Doctor Design for your work on the Chosen series covers. And a big thank you to Jodi Lester, Lex Feit, and Kirsten Starkweather for your valuable feedback on the series' new appearance.

And lastly, I'd like to thank my family once again for their unending belief in me and their support. None of this would be possible without you.

MUSIC PLAYLIST

Music plays an important part in my stories. From melancholic melodies to crashing crescendos, it enhances the mood and emotions in every scene. Many times I'll discover a song that belongs to a specific scene *after* the scene has been written, then I'll play the song over and over during subsequent editing sessions, using its energy to bring more life to the page.

One of the most influential music artists on the writing and editing of *Watcher* was Trent Reznor of Nine Inch Nails. Trent believes in artists sharing their talents and generously makes his tracks available for download on the NIN remix site. The resulting blend of Trent's music with that of various remix artists can be amazingly beautiful and moving. Along with Trent's instrumental originals and his own remixes, these songs created much of the background tone for *Watcher*.

Justin St. Charles is an artist I discovered on the remix site. His haunting version of NIN's "Leaving Hope" is the theme song for *Watcher*, and several of his own quiet instrumental compositions are featured on the playlist as well. He can be found at: http://soundcloud.com/justinstcharlesmusic/.

Enjoy.

* 04.04.10 Piano – Justin St. Charles
* The Red – Chevelle
* Corona Radiata – NIN
* 11 – Hyneria Moss Soundscape
* 04.08.09 Piano – Justin St. Charles
* Black Orchid – Blue October
* The Four of Us Are Dying – NIN
* Bosendorfer Morpher (Unheard) – NIN/As Serious As Your Life remix
* Leaving Hope, Still – NIN/Justin St. Charles remix
* Gone, Still – NIN
* Dracula's Return – Transylvania 1847
* The Frail – NIN
* Luna – Hyneria Moss Soundscape
* When He Thinks of Her – Justin St. Charles
* Black Heart Inertia – Incubus
* La Serenissima – Loreena McKennit
* Night Ride Across the Caucasus – Loreena McKennit

* Right Person, Right Place, Wrong Time – Justin St. Charles
* Quicksand – Incubus
* Every Right Things Fall – Hyneria Moss Soundscape
* I'm Looking Forward to Joining You Finally – NIN/Justin St. Charles remix
* 8 Ghosts – NIN
* Ripe (With Decay) – NIN
* Hurt, Slowly – NIN/Justin St. Charles remix
* Dig – Incubus
* Everything We Could Have – Hyneria Moss Soundscape
* Love Hurts – Incubus
* 34 Ghosts – NIN
* Soul Sleep – Justin St. Charles
* Shampoo – Elvis Perkins
* Another Version of the Truth – NIN/Enrique G. Müller & Kronos remix
* 23 Ghosts – NIN
* La Mer (Version) – NIN/Jerome Dillon & Keith Hillebrandt remix
* The Mark Has Been Made – NIN
* 24 Ghosts – NIN
* This Bleeding Heart – Justin St. Charles
* A Familiar Taste – The Social Network
* Penetration – The Social Network
* Eventually We Find Our Way – The Social Network
* Slipping Away – NIN/Trent Reznor & Alan Moulder remix
* Erased, Over, Out – NIN/Hyde, McDowall, Balance, Christopherson (Coil)
* Right Where It Belongs – NIN
* Hurt (Quiet) – NIN/Trent Reznor remix
* 26 Ghosts – NIN
* Early Exit – Justin St.Charles
* Adrift and At Peace – NIN/Vika Yermolyeva remix
* Zero-Sum – NIN/Stephen Morris & Gillian Gilbert remix
* In This Twilight: Fennesz – NIN/Fennesz remix
* In Motion – The Social Network
* 1 Ghosts – NIN
* Right Where It Belongs v.3 – NIN/Justin St. Charles remix
* Eraser – NIN
* A Warm Place Instrumental – NIN
* Nothing Else Matters – Metallica

ABOUT THE AUTHOR

Roh Morgon discovered the magic in stories at an early age, both in books and in those she made up in her head. As a child growing up in a remote Southern California canyon, she explored the wild hills barefoot with her brothers and rode her horse bareback at top speed. A wicked youth spent hitchhiking across the West and perched on the backs of Harleys eventually gave way to soccer mom duties and full-time college studies—at the same time. In her spare moments, she learned how to herd cattle, swordfight, and plant an arrow or a knife in a target—not necessarily at the same time.

Her years spent in the lofty mountains of Colorado and the stark plains of Wyoming, the red canyons of central Arizona and the rolling hills of California, provide some of the diverse stages upon which her characters re-enact their lives.

Roh currently shares her home in the Sierra Nevada foothills with three mustang horses, two crazy herding dogs, and a very patient husband who reminds her of the need to eat and sleep. She writes fantasy and urban fantasy for middle grade, young adult, and adult readers.

If you would like to read other works by this author or be kept up to date on new releases, please visit her website at www.rohmorgon.com.

And if you enjoyed *Watcher: Book I of The Chosen*, please feel free to leave a review on Amazon.

BOOKS BY ROH MORGON
THE CHOSEN SERIES

WATCHER
BOOK I OF THE CHOSEN

Sunny Martin's been a monster - or so she thinks - since the night she was drained of her blood and left for dead, but when she falls in love with Nicolas, the mysterious leader of The Chosen, she discovers a startling truth behind her savage nature which may force her to choose between her heart and the last remnant of her human soul.

RUNNER
BOOK II OF THE CHOSEN

(Fall 2017)

Sunny Martin is on the run from a monster—the monster within herself. When murder and betrayal end her affair with the mysterious leader of The Chosen, Sunny must face the death of someone she loves, and face the love of someone she fears—an outlaw Chosen even more dangerous than the one who broke her heart.

THE GAMES MONSTERS PLAY
A NOVELETTE OF THE CHOSEN

When corporate spy Colin O'Neill receives a personal invitation from Katarina Habsburg to join an elite high-stakes game, he fears his cover is blown. With his time running out, Colin must choose between finishing his mission and making his escape before the game's end in this chilling tale of industrial espionage.

THE LAST TRACE
A NOVELLA OF THE CHOSEN

Trace Pierre Tasman's simple life as a mountain man in 1842 Montana turns into a living nightmare when a beautiful but vicious she-demon begins stalking him. This is the beginning of Taz's story.

MONSTERS IN THE MACHINES
SHORT STORY COLLECTION

THE SEDUCTION

The first time Erica saw the black, low-slung sports car, she felt its sensual pull deep within her soul—but when she began succumbing to its whispered promises, she didn't suspect she might be losing much more than her mind.

THE MONSTER'S GROWL

The stakes of the game in the small-town bar are higher than Carly and her friends realize when a mysterious biker puts his quarter on their pool table.

HELLBOUND TRAIN

(coming soon)

A gambler's winning hand in a high-dollar poker game may cost him more than he's willing to pay.

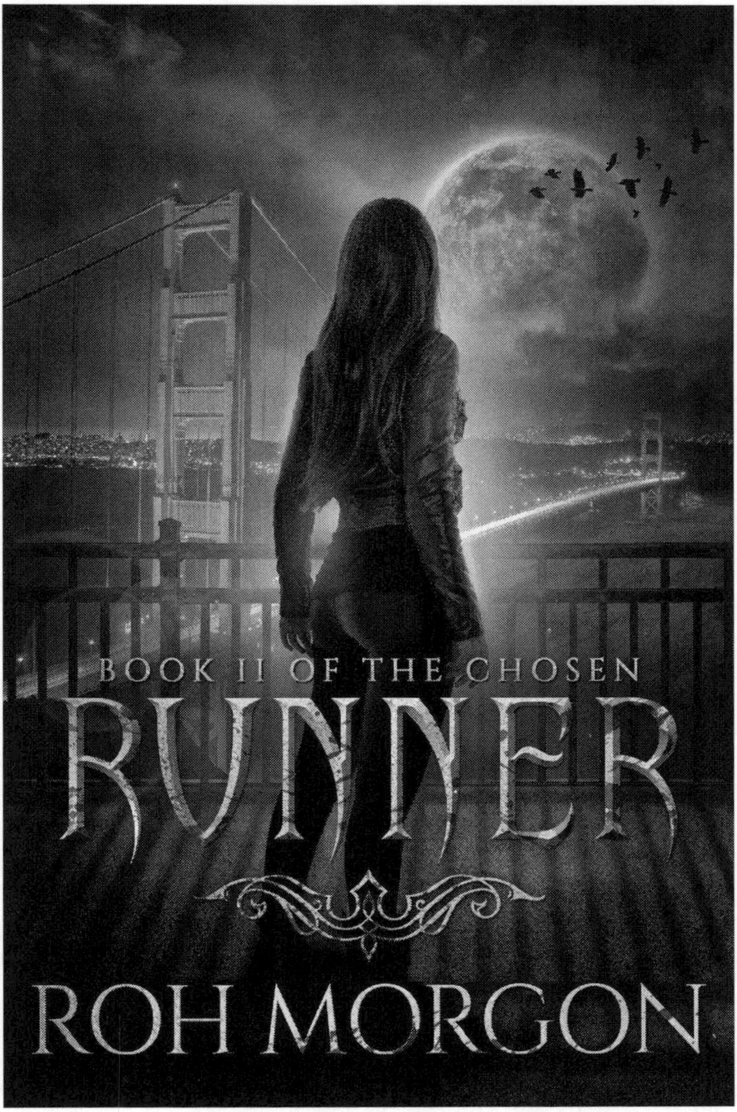

ddp

dark dreams publishing

www.darkdreamspublishing.com

Made in the USA
Columbia, SC
21 July 2024

39102774R00259